# STARFISH

## AND

# COFFEE

*Nipping at crime...*

*...one bust at a time.*

The SparkleTits Chronicles

# STARFISH

## AND

# COFFEE

Collen,

Cheers to you on
escaping the Contura Hell.

VERONICA R. CALISTO

Fickle Fox Books
Aurora, CO

Printed in the United States of America Published by Fickle Fox Books.

# DEDICATION

To the women who've come up against impossible odds
and blazed through.

# STARFISH & COFFEE

# 1 – CHAIN REACTION

THE SUITS STOOD in a ring around the hospital room when I walked in, sharks circling an ailing whale. At least these were Gabriel's sharks, for the moment. And paid well enough to carry out Gabe's wishes after his death released them.

Gabe looked worse for the wear. Too pale. Too many machines attached to his arm on the far side. But conscious. His steel-grey eyes dropped from the television above the wall behind me and locked on mine. Red-rimmed.

Probably the only color left in him.

"You look terrible." I frowned at him and at my own inability to shut my trap.

His eyes crinkled in the corners while the lips tried to replicate his signature smile. Tried and failed. The eyes still had the glimpse of his spark, for what it was worth. Which wasn't much and was everything.

"I feel better." He spoke too softly for me to tell if he lied or not. His eyes flicked past me. "They'll let you know."

Feet shuffled in the gloom around me as the suits left us alone. The door closed behind me, a lid on a coffin burying the both of us.

I heel-toed to the side of his bed. "How much better?"

"Numb in the places where I used to hurt." He lifted a shoulder. "No pain is better."

Balls. That wasn't the kind of better I wanted to hear.

"Greer," his fingers snaked over the sheet to grab hold of my limp ones. "Don't give me that sad face, girl."

I hooked my foot around the nearby chair to pull it close to the bed. The screech of the feet against the linoleum changed my mind halfway through. I sat on the bed beside him. "What? You expect me to smile?"

"It is the wish of a dying old man." He tipped his chin down and lifted his gaze to me.

The puppy-dog eyes might have worked if the skin around them hadn't gotten so translucent. I could trace the tiniest of his veins. The florescent light above his head leached more of his color away. Even the strands of black in his hair looked hollow. Husks. Just like the rest of his body.

He didn't fill out nearly enough space under the blankets.

"That's not funny, Gabe."

He squeezed my hand. Weakly. "It isn't funny, Greer. It's true. I want nothing more than for you to smile. Whether I see it or not."

I knew that. It had been the same since I first met him. Despite my initial distrust of his kindness. "Gabe."

"I know, Girly." He shook my hand back and forth. Even his voice had thinned, like it was wasting away to breath and light. "Nothing lasts forever."

The first thing he'd told me. Nearly twenty years ago. When Gabe had stumbled across a bloody, bruised, and weeping me. He'd reached across the years, so I responded in kind, with the first thing I'd said to him. "Forevers happen every day."

I smiled in spite of myself.

"That's my girl," came out on the breath of a whisper. His eyes eased closed, but he smiled wry like he used to.

His eyes didn't open again. The television mumbled low behind me; just enough noise to keep the machines from driving me batty. Something about a string of bank robberies with odd circumstances. None of the witnesses remembered anything and some had been disfigured. Dollar signs burned into their foreheads by some unidentified substance.

I made the mistake of glancing back and up to the screen at the wrong moment. The skin had melted away on the people. Clean muscle and sinew peeked through perfect, cookie-cutter holes.

Turning back to Gabe didn't wash the image from my mind, though it gave me something to focus on and to be grateful for. Pale and wasting away beat receiving that kind of facial.

Gabe, for his part, squeezed my fingers, grounding me like he always did. He just knew.

The machines marked the passing hours while his grip held steady in mine.

"I'm sorry," he whispered.

I leaned closer to him so he wouldn't strain to speak, or to listen. "For what?"

"I left you." He fought for another breath. His eyes rolled under paper-thin eyelids "In the…"

His grip slackened and his breath wheezed away. I kind of hated Gabe for that. Wanted to. But he'd already apologized.

Squeezing my eyes closed, I forced even breathing until the vice around my chest let it happen naturally. The hospital blanket scraped rough against my cheeks, but sopped up the moisture that had leaked out.

Face dry, eyes burning, I kissed Gabe's hand in my cold one. I pressed my lips to his warm forehead and left the room.

Just like he had.

I parked my car at my apartment without clear memory of driving there. Forcing my lead-heavy legs up the three flights of stairs nearly defeated me.

A skinny bar of moonlight sliced between the living room curtains. Twin blue lights glowed from the microwave and oven clocks, one a couple feet above the other. The only contrast to the blackness inside my home.

The darkness suited me, so I left the lights off and checked the time. 3:39am. Too late to sleep, too early to leave for work.

Sitting on the couch eased a familiar weight onto my chest. Pain. Anger. Guilt. Blame.

Stillness would not loosen the emotions constricting my chest. It wouldn't steady my hands. I needed to move, not collapse, but didn't want to wake Chad or any of my neighbors.

Didn't know what I wanted.

Yes, I did. I wanted my Gabe back. I wanted to never have needed Gabe. I wanted a life that wasn't my own. My hands burned to rip through the walls and bring the ceiling down on me. To destroy myself like Carrie White after she razed everyone else who hurt her. All fire and rubble.

Gabe's voice echoed in my head and turned me from destruction worthy of Kali Ma. I could use the restless energy in a positive manner. Gather some things and give them to charity. Rid myself of pieces of me and help others in the process. Charitable acts were the best way to carry my friend with me.

I padded my way past the bathroom and into the bedroom, doing my best to keep from disturbing Chad as he snored in our bed. Tearing my life apart didn't need to wake him. Not if I started in the closet and closed the door behind me. The door should muffle light and sound enough to let him sleep.

Pulling things from the shelf above the racks would be bad. My world would tumble down on top of me, burying me like a fabric Vesuvius. Something to do after the sun had woken, perhaps. I started with the taller rack of clothes in front of me.

The black dress in the corner stared back at me. I could get rid of it after the funeral on Monday. Burn it in Gabe's honor, maybe. For the rest, I went on instinct. Keeping things if I loved them or if they sparked a reaction. I tossed the rest over my shoulder.

The door opened behind me. My whole body jerked, clenching my hands around a red sequin shirt. The edges bit into my hands, giving me something outside myself to focus on.

"Greer?" Chad's voice split the difference between groggy and alarmed. "I didn't hear you get in. What are you doing?"

I didn't know if I could explain what I was doing.

Pretend to ignore him? Not possible. Not at this juncture. Not without sliding into full-on bitch, my safety zone.

My eyes dropped to the pile between us as I swiveled around.

"Greer." He sounded more awake this time. Less agitated. "Are you okay?"

Did I look okay? "No." I waited for the stupid question.

"Isn't it better that he isn't suffering anymore?" He used the soft voice.

Not the question I expected. Still. No, it wasn't better. Not for me. No matter how selfish that made me.

"Greer, why don't you come back to bed?"

*Back* to bed. Back.

Despite the lack of awareness that I'd never made it to bed, the question pulled my gaze up. Concern turned Chad's mouth down in the corners. His eyes burned a brighter red than Gabe's had.

I didn't want to think about the last image of Gabe.

Chad could hold me while I sobbed it all out. He would do it, if I let him. It would be so easy. Only a pile of clothes stood between us. "I can't." A pile of clothes and *me* between us, a six-foot-four island.

He nodded like he understood. The tightening of his lips said he didn't.

Damn everything. Damn me.

I gave Chad what I could. "I'll try to be quieter."

"The softer noise will just remind me you're upset." He scratched at his beard that was two weeks past a much-needed shave. "I can't sleep through that."

I wished he would. I needed this time to myself. I just couldn't think my way to a nice way to say it. My head pulsed, overstuffed and empty. Tired. But the kind of tired sleep wouldn't fix. Nonsense, comfort words wouldn't do much either.

"Can I help?"

I shrugged, shirt nearly dropping from my fingers in the process. I clutched it harder, just for the distraction of the sequins cutting into my palms again. "I don't know enough of what I'm doing to have anyone help me."

He did the nodding without understanding thing. Again. I kind of hated him for it, but it wasn't personal.

"Since it's—" Chad looked at his wrist, then at the alarm clock across the room once he realized he wasn't wearing his watch. "It's almost morning. How about I make you some breakfast?"

My face cracked into a smile. Pieces of me practically fell off in chunks. It hurt. I wasn't hungry, but it would get him away from me. "Breakfast would be great."

He smiled at me in a way much more convincing than the one bending my face. When he leaned toward me, I reciprocated. A quick kiss and he left me to my pathetic coping mechanism: purge so I wouldn't feel feelings. Better than alcohol and sex with anonymous strangers.

Four bags filled with clothes and the closet didn't even look half empty. Chad's things took up less than half. Even after I finished, I did not hurt for clothes. An indication that I owned too much in the first place. Perhaps this purge was for the best. Perhaps it was Gabe's way of helping me be a better person. Perhaps.

Somebody had to.

Breakfast was over and under-cooked at the same time. Soggy, burned eggs. Limp bacon with charred ends. Accidental molten-core pancakes with blackened sides. The perfect meal to go with the night-into-morning I'd had. I ate it without tasting it or remarking on the prep other than to give thanks. Chad apologized after he started in on his own plate.

I got up without waiting for him to finish, anything to get away from his in-my-face surveillance.

He caught up with me before I waddled out the door with my four bags. Worry bent his face all out of shape. "I can help you down the stairs with these."

Just let me leave. I gritted my teeth and shook my head.

My, "Thank you, though," nearly choked me as it came out. It was enough to get me out the door and on my way. Hours too early for going to work, but the timing would work out. I had a stop to make before I hit the office.

Too many cars with clueless drivers clogged the road, even this early in the morning. I wondered, not for the first time, if this was my superpower. Finding rush-hour traffic, no matter what time of day. Crappy power to have, but it was mine. All mine. Superheroes of the world beware.

Light haze had started to dust the sky as I finally pulled into the Hearts Open Wide donation center. Pulling trash bags out of my car bothered me; the people who bought from here deserved better than items out of a trash bag. I hoped the quality made up for it. I didn't shop designer by any means, but I refused to donate anything already losing itself to entropy.

More than one trip with the four bags would have been a better idea. This was not a day to make good decisions. This was a day to keep it together. Work. Dinner with Chad. Opening of my best friend's art show.

Keep it together so no one saw my cracks.

Bags twisted around and over top my hand so I could grip them, I huffed my way to the entrance.

A pile of clothes near the door moved and scared the bejeezus out of me. My stomach sank deep in my belly on a wave of panting breaths. I dropped a bag out of each hand then gripped the others tight, preparing to battle with squishy bags.

The pile coughed.

Clothes didn't hack away like a lung was mid-escape.

Clumps of naturally dreadlocked hair sifted out of the pile, hanging down from the source of the cough. A head atop a body.

I needed to get a grip.

The wet cough made me take a step back. Fatal diseases lived in those sounds. Still, I couldn't bring myself to walk around her without a saying something. Gabe would have flayed me with the slightest wrinkling around his eyes.

The woman spat out a wad of blood, mucus, things I would not identify. I averted my eyes before I started cataloguing. Blood was bad news, though. That, I couldn't ignore.

"Ma'am, are you okay?" Stupid question, Greer. Try better. "Is there anything I can do to help?" Better.

She hocked another piece of blood and offal as she raised her eyes to me. Cold eyes. Some light color. My brain said yellow but I knew the morning dusk played havoc with color recognition. Strange, though. Something off about the shape of them too.

Dropping my eyes to her bloodstained, too-wide lips didn't comfort me any.

"Oh, you want to help me?" Her voice could have cracked granite without the sarcasm sharpening its edges. "Pitiful me? Pathetic me? Pour unfortunate me?"

I hadn't said anything derogatory. Perhaps the tension on my body screamed my reaction. Couldn't fix that. Reflexes were reflexes. "I heard your coughing and wondered if there was anything I could do for you. No offense intended."

"No offense?" Her hair lifted away from her wrinkled face in a way no normal physics would allow for. Unless her hair wasn't hair. The locks undulated while tinier branches along the locks flared outward, made each piece almost fuzzy-looking.

Not hair.

Definitely not hair.

"Why would I need help from some stupid monkey?" It came out in razor-laced singsong.

Monkey?

Calling her a bitch wouldn't fit. Her not-hair meant she was...other. Some kind of not-human humanoid. Anyway, I liked dogs.

Rather than berate her, I lifted an eyebrow. "Because you're coughing blood and things?"

She rose from the huddled mass she'd slumped in. Her full height probably topped six-foot, which would have intimidated a shorter woman. Even standing, though, she curled over like someone let out half her air. She might have been my height in her heyday. Two-hundred years ago, when her face looked human, instead of resembling wizened, old, tree bark.

The stench that plumed out from her. Rotted, sour fish and long-dead things. It nearly knocked me over.

Milky eyes stared up at me. Milky with a horizontal squiggle of blackness in the center of them. The rest of her wrinkled facial features rippled as she studied me.

Rippled.

I let the last bag slip out of my right hand and held a little tighter to the one in the left. Free hand to attack; bag hand to shield.

Because that shit wasn't natural.

"You should not be speaking to me." Looking down her nose at me didn't work from her height, but she sure tried, bless her weird-creature heart.

I had neither the time nor the patience. "Listen. I'm having a shitty—."

"I do not care for—"

"Lady, the only reason I asked is I thought doing something good for you might cheer me up." Anger suited me so much better. I shouldn't like the heat of it. "If you do not want my help, just tell me."

She narrowed her eyes. "I don't want your help." The increased tension in her posture twisted her voice into a more grating tone.

My own throat hurt in sympathy. "Fine. Good luck."

Shoving a hand into a jaguar's mouth sounded safer than taking my eyes off her. I squatted to retrieve the bags I'd dropped.

She mirrored my steps as I moved around her on my way to the donation center, rotating to keep her eyes on me. She moved exactly with me. Step for tiny step. Almost like a dance, until I started backing my way toward the doors of the donation center.

The woman creature neither retreated nor advanced. She spoke instead.

"You cannot see me."

If she was trying to hypnotize me, her delivery needed a lot of work. "Yes. I still can."

"You misunderstand. For your safety and mine. You cannot see me. Cannot, did not, will not."

Ding. I got it. "See who?"

She nodded, sending another waft of impossible stench my way. Gods.

We stared at each other a few moments while I tried to choke rancid air down. Eventually, I realized she would not leave first.

Her warning meant that she didn't want to hurt me, probably. Here went nothing.

I hefted two of the bags over my left shoulder so they covered my back—just in case—then turned away from her and started toward the donations door. I centered my attention on listening to her, hoping against a sneak attack.

She moved in wet rustles and soft pops, like static on an old cathode ray tube or a steady rain. So long as she rustle-popped away from me, I could forget I'd ever encountered her.

Two people stood in line ahead of me when I walked in. I wondered what would have happened if either had come out while I talked to the woman. The one who didn't exist anymore. I fought to doublethink my way out of remembering her until it was my turn at the donation desk. Helping the man sift through my bags re-grounded me in my purpose for coming, rather than thinking about things I should forget and things I didn't want to.

Walking outside into the pre-morning of red-gilded clouds gave me something completely different to focus on. The parking lot had one car in it.

And it wasn't mine.

"Mother fu—" I held back the curse because I knew how much Gabe disapproved. I switched to what he did allow, even if it meant the same thing. "Oedipus Rex!"

Dialing the police, I ran through all the things I'd left in my car. Lunch. Breakfast. I thanked the god of unfortunate blessings I'd forgotten my dress for the evening at home. My registration was in the glove box, like they told people not to do anymore because the nogoodniks of the world could learn your address. Shit.

"911, this is May, what is your emergency?"

Emergency was a relative term, apparently. The sun rose in crimson and golden brilliance before an officer showed up. Brief talk, report filled out, and the man turned to leave. He frowned at me when I asked for a ride, but didn't refuse. I hoped he'd done so out of the goodness of his heart, but *my* heart said pity pushed him.

He pulled into my office parking lot fifteen minutes after my start time. I thanked him anyway. Taking the bus would have made me even later.

I sank into my desk chair, slouching like I'd eased into a hot tub.

"Greer, may I have a word?" My boss' voice cut into whatever level of relief I had.

Oedipus. Rex.

I followed my supervisor to my manager's office. Allison didn't smile. Neither did my supervisor. Not good.

Allison folded her hands on her desk, right behind one of two the small stacks of papers. "Please close the door."

Closed the door without an invitation to sit. I knew I was boned.

She took the reins, though they both said things in the nicest way. Their pleasant tones made getting fired worse. They asked for my opinion, input that could and would be used against me. I fully exploited my right to remain silent. Good fucking riddance anyway. I hated the guts out of this job and let my anger warm me for the second time this morning.

I only had one question. "Is someone going to pack up my desk and send it to me, or do I pack it up?"

"Andrew will watch you pack it up." Allison inclined her head toward my supervisor. "We can get you a cart if you need it."

I closed my eyes to sift through the things that were mine. "One box should be fine, but I'll need to have it stay here until I can come back with a car."

The two of them exchanged a look before my manager—former manager now—asked, "What happened to your car?"

"Stolen. This morning." I turned away from both and headed toward the door. Angry, but free of their power over me.

"I—" Allison stopped herself a moment to clear her throat. "Do you have a police report?"

Not quite certain why she wanted it. She just fired me. But I could adult with the best. I turned around and kept my voice pleasant. "Not yet. It takes a couple of days for it to be filed. I have the report number."

She pressed her lips together but did not follow with a single word of apology or empathy. Perfect. I strolled to my desk. My—former—supervisor set a box down for me. I ignored other voices and footsteps. They didn't exist. Only me and my work-appropriate baubles. Just me packing up another broken piece of my life.

Half hour's work got me out the door, basically empty handed. Part of me didn't even want to come back for the rest.

I should have headed straight home and updated my resume, but I couldn't. Not today. I let the heat of the morning sun pour down on me for a long moment, then I hopped a bus. Halfway to downtown, I realized my wanderlust drew me to the Denver Art Museum.

The scent of masterpieces and decades of fieldtrips surrounded me when I walked in. Same as it had always been. Same as it was each time I came with Gabe. I ducked into the bathroom.

"Row, row, row your boat gently down the stream," serenaded me as I splashed cool water on my face. Remembering how much Gabe delighted in the singing sinks broke the dam in me. Sobs shook me and tears ran while I fought to dampen the noise.

I splashed enough water on my face to shrink the puffiness, then took stock of myself in the mirror. A mess. The insides matched the outsides, then. I could handle that, so I left the relative safety of the bathroom.

Gabe's voice echoed in the corners of the museum. Discussion of what he liked and which pieces were made by talentless hacks. I saw the disgusted snarl of his lip when anyone mentioned Thomas Kinkade but far be it for me to criticize the stupid horse on big red chair outside. I wrapped the presence of him around my shoulders, a bittersweet warmth that kept me comfortable until it was time to meet Chad for dinner.

.

## 2 – BIG BADA BOOM

SIXTY-EIGHT MINUTES was enough time to accept the obvious. I'd been stood up. Perfect capper on a worthless, shitter of a day.

Oh well.

At least I could save the money I couldn't afford to spend any more. I waved the balding waiter over.

"Yes," he gave me the irritated smile.

I didn't care what he thought I'd done to deserve it. He, and all other worthless people, could go die on a spit. "It appears I've been stood up, so I'll pay for my drink and get out of your, um, scalp." If he could be rude, so could I.

Them's the rules.

He reached into his little apron with all the attitude of my five-year-old niece and slapped it down on my bread plate. I might have been angrier at him if he'd gone the other way. Piss and vinegar, I could handle. Pity, not so much.

Pity: the bitterest of fruits.

Gaze locked with his, I slapped a ten on top of the check folder because two could play that game.

Anyway, we both knew my soda was less than half of the tip I was giving him. I wouldn't play into the stereotype that black people didn't tip. From our hour-and-eight-minute-too-long interaction, I could tell he would be the kind to talk about it and play free with the details. Most of the other staff would know he was lying, but I didn't need that kind of energy directed toward me. No need to spread what had darkened my day.

The sun had well and fully set in the time I'd been in the restaurant. Only a rim of scarlet light gilded the mountains in the west and the air had slipped into more comfortable temperatures. Late summer in Colorado could not be beat. It almost made the idea of hoofing home a pleasant one. If I'd had a choice in the matter, I might have enjoyed it.

If I still had a job, I might have stayed to enjoy dinner. But, no. A penny saved sank ships, or whatever. Dwelling would get me nowhere. Neither would heading to the bar half a block down. Beginning the job search would have been the best use of my time. I headed to Rust anyway.

Before ducking in, I pulled my phone out in the off-chance Chad had called me in the last five minutes and I'd missed it.

I missed something, all right. A text from Chad. "I can't do this anymore. We're done."

Seven words.

They stopped me in my tracks. It wasn't enough to dump me, but to do it in text when he could have put on his big boy panties and told me face-to-worthless-face.

Perfect. A perfect end to a perfect fucking day. Jobless. Carless. Single. All within 24 hours. I must have kicked a lot of kittens in my former life.

A laugh choked out of me. It was laugh or cry and my body chose for me. Self-defense mechanism born in middle school.

People stop picking on you so much if you laughed in their faces. Eventually, people wanted to know why you laughed all the time, what was so funny. Then they were laughing with you, though the *with* me part had taken until high school. When my boobs finally grew in. Amazing how boobs changed so much in the world.

"Could you spare some change?" a rickety, old voice asked me.

Boobs didn't change everything.

The woman I turned toward had more wrinkles than I'd believed possible in someone who was not also a mummy. She shook as she stood there, waiting for my rejection without the courage to look up at my face. Old beyond her years and broken, not like the woman-thing this morning. That shriveled lady-ish had enough venom in her to kill half of Colorado.

Here I was complaining of the things I'd lost when this woman had nothing but her tattered clothes.

I handed the woman two twenties, what I'd planned to spend on dinner. One dinner. I hoped she got twelve meals out of the money, though I knew it wasn't probable.

She tried to pass one of the bills back, telling me it was too much. I folded her hand around it until she promised to keep it. She deserved the money even if all she did was remind me that things could get worse, most especially before they got better.

I headed to my favorite bar with a slightly lighter heart.

My boobs had won my way into Rust the first time I'd stumbled across it. It took three more visits for the bouncer to recognize my face.

"Hey, Greer," he nodded. To me and to each of my boobs individually. "How're the twins today?"

I'd given up being offended by him years ago. "Rough day for all of us, Brutus." Not his real name, but he resembled Popeye's nemesis more than a little.

"Sorry to hear that. Kai's pouring on the deck tonight."

Best news I'd heard all day. I gave him a hug for the info because I needed one. He didn't seem to mind it, even squeezed me back a little. The reciprocation made it easier to ignore his blatant stare as I pulled away.

The main room was practically deserted. Half owing to the early hour and half to the deck. One could only handle so much pounding, melody-lacking music before fresh air and starlit skies called. Or, at least, that had always been my experience. The other Rust patrons generally agreed, but the deck only had a ten more people than the inside.

Several stools had yet to be claimed at the gleaming wooden bar. I did my best not to flop down onto the one furthest from a filled seat. It placed me caddy-corner to the register. In an hour, it would be the most insufferable spot in the house. I would take my blessings where I could.

Lord and Lady knew I needed something to be grateful for.

Kai set down the glass he'd been cleaning and stepped in front of me. "What's up, Greer?"

"Nothing good, Barkeep. It's been a shitty day, Kai. A shitty, shitty day."

He frowned. So did I. I hadn't intended to let that slip out.

"Who do I need to beat up?"

"No one. Everyone. I don't know." I shook my head and it turned into a full body shiver. "Just give me something to drink."

A little cup or two of amnesia would shift the whole mood of the evening.

Or deepen it into a vortex of damnation that sucked the world in around me. But the odds of that were slim.

Mostly.

"What'll it be?" Kai held up a finger to forestall me before I'd even attempted to answer. "What darkened your day today? I'll choose based on that."

Hardship booze roulette. Why not? I gave him the lowdown.

His eyebrows climbed to attention on his forehead. "How did you manage that in one day?"

"One led right into the other like clockwork. Beautiful, ugly clockwork."

"I am sorry to hear that."

"Less sorry, more drinky." Because I would survive this night even if it killed me. The light of tomorrow always came with bright and shiny new problems. They could wait for me to get there.

"I have just the thing." Kai winked his golden eye at me, like we had something going on between us. He could give me any kind of look, so long as he poured like the wind. "Though what you really need is a nice, uncomplicated fuck."

I rolled my eyes and shrugged. "You offering?"

"Only for the last five years." He froze halfway through pulling out the big glass, and blinked at me hopefully. "Wait, was that a yes?"

"Depends."

Kai dropped the glass back in the crate and settled his elbows on the bar directly in front of me. "Tell me what I need to do to make it a yes, please." His golden gaze bore into mine as if willing me to succumb to his every whim.

"Kai, I'm not looking for forever and I'm damned sure not looking to be comforted. That leads to crying and no one wants that." I shook my head. I was an ugly crier and usually ended up with the headache to end all headaches for the three days afterward. "What I need is exactly what you said. Uncomplicated. And earth moving. Can you do that?"

Kai bowed, but kept his heated gaze on mine. "At your service, though my shift isn't over for a couple hours."

I shrugged. "No rush."

His eyes swept down me and back up. "Easy for you to say."

Heat washed over my skin at his attention. Maybe this wasn't the best idea, but it settled nicely in my chest. I couldn't have been happier for how it fell together.

Happy, that was, until someone grabbed my ass.

"Let go of my ass or I will hurt you." My calming breath didn't work. Eyes locked on my glass, I let the words in my head out. "Hurt you a lot and enjoy it."

"What's the deal baby?" His words slurred. "I got what you need. No waiting."

It took a special kind of someone to be this wasted at 7 p.m. for no reason. No holiday. It wasn't graduation season.

I shook my head but kept my gaze on the bar in front of me. If I didn't see him, I wouldn't do things that won me assault charges. Telling cops that the other person started it didn't work. "You do not want to play me today, Bucko."

He slapped my ass none-to-gently. I whipped around to the tiny man with the shit-brown eyes and kneed him in the balls with the same kind of gusto. Somehow, dude-bro didn't appreciate the returned physical attention. Funny how that worked sometimes. The man managed to not drop to the ground, but his voice shifted to soprano wheezes.

Music to my ears.

Kai, on the other hand, laughed. I'd anticipated him having the typical guy reaction, sympathetic cringing and clutching at his privates. The ringing of Kai's rich baritone rolled much nicer with my mood than Grabby Hands McHorndog.

Kai's enthusiastic, "That was hot," helped my mood immensely, as did the intensity in his gaze that said he meant it.

"What was hot?" It didn't matter. With his unblemished terracotta skin and shark-white smile, he could call me hot any day he wanted to. All day, every day.

All night too.

He tipped his chin toward the wheezing one. "Taking him down in one swift move."

"You like it rough, do you?"

"Depends." He winked at me and another wave of warmth rolled through my body.

This thing between us.

This would be good.

"You bitch!" The grabby guy's voice plucked me from moment Kai and I had been having.

That, more than anything else, pissed me off. He could call me whatever he wanted. He didn't matter so his words didn't matter. Interrupting the one good thing in my day *today*, on the other hand...

A spotlight lit up the whole place when I whipped around to face him. I didn't care the spectacle we made. I would lavish over whatever beef this asshole had the misfortune to serve. Kai said something from behind me and some kind of activity approached us from behind grabby dude's skinny shoulders.

Neither mattered as much as watching dude's body language. The way he balled his hands when he informed me all women needed to be taught "their place." The snarl in his lips before he narrowed his dirty-brown eyes and told me how grateful I should feel to have his attention. How I should bend to his every whim, because I was a woman and therefore beneath him.

Right.

His weight shifted. I caught his punch in the palm of my hand. Despite his inebriation, the punch was solid. My hand and arm stung from absorbing the force of it. But laughter wasn't the only thing middle school had taught me.

A moment passed before his eyes widened. His brain finally clued in to what the rest of his body had realized. I wasn't going down without a fight.

His anger overrode the surprise in him.

A growl came out.

I smiled.

And the world went white.

# 3 – NUDE AWAKENING

"GREER, WAKE UP, damn it."

Was I asleep? I didn't remember going to bed, but I did remember that voice.

Wait a second.

I pried my eyes open and had to slam them shut again. Too bright.

"Thank gods," Kai pulled me up against him in his awkward crouch. "I thought we'd lost you."

Lost me how? Clearly, I'd missed something. A lot of something.

Kai smelled nice. Woodsy.

"What happened?" I forced my eyes open again. Slowly this time, despite the lights scratching at my eyeballs.

"Well…"

Why was Kai shirtless? "Why are you shirtless?"

I hope I hadn't missed all the sex we'd planned to have.

Mind blowing was just an expression. I wanted to remember everything.

"My shirt was the largest thing I had on hand to cover you. Someone's grabbing a blanket."

His answer pulled my attention to the fact that I had on less than he did. Exactly nothing, to be exact. Kai's shirt draped artfully over my NSFW parts didn't count as much as I would have hoped. Regardless, I was beyond grateful for it. "Why am I naked?"

A crease in the middle of his forehead pulled his eyebrows together. "We're not sure. We're not sure why you're alive. Why any of us are alive. It probably has something to do with how you managed to find Rust in the first place."

That made no kind of sense. I needed to know what he meant with that, I really did, but getting un-naked took precedence. Thankfully, the fates took pity on me in that moment and dropped someone next to Kai with a taupe blanket. Old and ratty as it looked, cedar and flower aroma wafted from it.

Fantastic.

Kai shuffled me from arm to arm as he wrapped the blanket around the back of me and pulled me into a sitting position. He managed to tuck the blanket around me and retrieve his shirt without exposing the goods, suggestive looks, or unnecessary grazes. Impressive. And nice, since sitting up showed me the ring of people around us, all staring questions at me like I knew the answer.

My legs below the knees stuck out from the blanket, shimmering in the deck-and-star light, like a vampire in the sun. Now, I needed to know. "What happened?"

"As best I can tell, an asteroid, meteorite, or something, fell from the sky."

"Neet." I waited for him to giggle like a little boy and tell me what really happened. When the giggle was not forthcoming, I raised an eyebrow and waited a little longer. Nothing. "If that's true, then why isn't everyone dead?"

"We kind of hoped you might tell us that, Greer."

Good luck with that. How the fuck would I know? Anyone could have taken up the narrative while I'd been sleeping. A hopeful glance around won me hungry gazes. Yep. Nope. No one else seemed to know what was going on. Sweet.

Kai gave me an out. "Greer, can you stand?"

"We can find out."

He nodded and I returned it, but Kai didn't move until I did.

I shifted my weight to the side into a kind of side-saddle sit, to keep the flashing down to a minimum. Though, if Kai had to sacrifice his shirt for me, everyone had already seen everything. "Balls."

"What?" Kai tightened his grip on me like I might keel over at any moment.

Nothing to be done about it now. "Nothing, I just..." I shook my head. Voicing it would only call attention to it so I turned my focus to standing.

Which took no more effort than it usually did. No dizziness as I got my feet under me. I didn't hurt anywhere. "Where exactly did the piece of falling sky hit?" Several things sauntered through my head as possible answers. The severe lack of holes and flaming body parts around the club indicated the one that made the least sense.

Yep. Kai confirmed my suspicions. He went so far as to poke his index finger in the center of my chest. "Right about there, I'd say."

He was clearly mistaken. He had to be.

Still, I pulled the blanket far enough away from my skin to peek down at my cleavage. My breasts glimmered more than my legs did, and with less outside light to explain it. They practically glowed. Not practically. They did glow. Like twin moons behind inconstant cloud cover.

My boobs had become honest to goodness headlights. Great.

Kai might just have been right about where the piece of sky hit me.

What in the hell? My glowing skin didn't change the facts. None of this was possible. I wrapped the blanket more firmly around me. "I need a drink."

I needed more than a drink. I needed a grip on reality. And something to wear. The walk home, with only a blanket wrapped around me, would be a long one. When a cop inevitably stopped me, I would have the fabulous task of trying to explain exactly how I got in this position whilst still being sober. Yes, a drink would definitely help.

"Are you sure you wouldn't rather go home?"

"Can't go home. Car was stolen this morning." For a little while there, I hadn't planned on going home this evening at all. The escape would have been nice. The world could be cruel, sometimes.

"Right. I'll take you home. Someone will cover."

Hope mounted in me that the plans we'd made might be resurrected until I saw the complete lack of heat in his gaze. Denied without even asking. Depressing, really. I would try my utmost to convince myself that it was for the best. Rash decisions based on bad days were rarely good things.

Even if they were a blast in the moment.

Kai settled a hand on my lower back and pointed toward the deck bar. "My car's out back, but my keys and things are inside. You can either wait out here for me or..."

"Any chance I could get that drink if I waited out here?" I hoped. I hoped.

His lips twisted a little. I'd won. We both knew it

With a shake of his head, he turned to one of the people watching the spectacle that had been made of me. "Mike, would you mind?"

Mike broke away from the crowd enough for me to see him. His face looked familiar, though I couldn't place from where. I would have remembered seeing blue eyes that light and frosty. It contrasted well with the dark brown beard just past the point of scruffy.

He crooked an inviting elbow out to me. "I'll get you whatever you want. On the house."

I extricated myself from Kai and shook my finger at Mike. "See? I knew I liked you from the moment I saw you."

His smile pinged even stronger in my memory, but I still couldn't place him. It would bug me to no end. I wouldn't use the cliché line, though. The transparent, "Have we met before?" was old when movies were new. Instead, I asked a much more important question. "What happened to that guy? The one who was hassling me?"

The one I'd wanted to punch so badly. Whatever else had happened, my heart hadn't stopped wanting that.

"He didn't fare as well as you." Mike pointed to the other end of the yard, in the sand of the volleyball court.

I would take Mike's word that the lumpy and smoking pile of clothes was the asshole. One person stood over him, fanning their hand over top of him. I assumed there would have been more of a hubbub if he'd died. Everything seemed to be business as usual. Smoking man, glowing woman. Nothing to see here.

If they could roll with it, so could I. For the moment. "Yes, well, I wish him years of genital warts and diverticulitis."

"Wow. You don't pull any punches, do you?" Mike deposited me on the same stool I'd been on before all the unpleasantness and inexplicable things happened.

"Usually, I do," though not with asshats like that dude. Today had added special sauce to my wrathful little heart. He deserved what he got and so much more. So did every dude who thought they were entitled to a little action because they showed up.

Once Mike walked around to the business side of the bar he asked, "What'll you have?"

Some of the most beautiful words ever spoken.

"Why don't you give me your specialty."

He nodded. "You got it."

He pulled out a short glass and set it down. Then, his arms flew.

I lost count of how many bottles he grabbed, which shouldn't have been possible in the short glass. He moved without hesitation, a maestro playing his centuries old instrument. A sunrise of liquor flowed in the glass.

For the last step, he pulled out a lighter. Rather than set the liquid on fire the normal way, Mike pulled a slice of orange rind from wherever bartenders kept those things. He flicked the lighter to life in the same moment he pinched the rind, orange side out. The tiny spritz of orange oil passed through the flame, caught, and brought the fire to the surface of the liquor.

Super fancy. I'd been impressed halfway through the performance. The last blew me over the edge. Wherever I'd run into him, I would never forget him again. The man would be forever etched into my brain.

Firelight danced in the gradient of liquor from yellow to deepest red. The reflections mirrored the flicker of the flame on the surface. "It's beautiful."

A grin parted his lips, showing off all his white, perfect teeth. "Thank you. It's a double shot. You have to drink it before the flame goes out or it's ruined. All in one pour."

"I'm rather fond of my eyebrows," I lifted the glass to blow the flame out.

Mike inserted a hand between me and the rim. "It will recede as you tip it, from the lower proof alcohols."

Still skeptical, I narrowed my eyes. "You're not messing with me, are you?"

"I don't play around with Phoenix Breath." He pulled his hand away, pride and challenge playing at the corners of his mouth.

I guessed that was the name of the shot. Apt. My eyebrows might hate me when they grew back, but I figured, what the hell. I'd already bested a meteorite, or something. What was a bit of fire? "Bottoms up."

Tipping the rim of the glass toward my lips proved him correct. The flame did pull back from where my lips touched the glass. A different kind of fire erupted on my tongue. Sweetness to the point of being spicy, with the edge of a smoky salt to balance it out. As I got deeper into the shot, the smokier and hotter the drink got, completely leaving the sweet and salt behind. The last sip was all spice and smoke. Almost enough to make me cough, but I wanted to curl up around it more. Like huddling beside the fire pit on a camping trip.

Lovely.

Warming from the inside out, in a way that had nothing to do with the actual fire that rode the surface of the drink. My muscles loosened and my body sagged down on the stool. Almost like it detached from my head completely. Nice-y nice. I hadn't realized how high strung the day had made me. Who knew a drink could offer so much comfort? Mike did, clearly.

"What do you think?" He asked.

I had to force myself to look back up at him. It might have been the exhaustion playing havoc with me, but my head had tripled in mass.

Mike didn't look worried about how drunk I might get, though he did watch me with a good level of regard. He wanted to know what I thought about his creation. I could supply him with the truth without sugar coating. "I kind of want to hug you right now. Is that normal?"

His head tipped back and he let out a full, guffaw. Without answering my question. A little rude, but now was not the time to correct that.

"Why do you want to hug him?" Kai sidled up to me without my notice.

"He just gave me the best shot I've ever had."

Kai leaned back and his hand flew to his chest like an offended southern belle. "I'm usually the one who—" He narrowed his eyes and rocked his head toward Mike. "You didn't give her Phoenix Breath, did you?"

Mike tipped a smug nod in Kai's direction. "It seemed apropos. Considering."

"Like sugar coated smoke and fire in my belly." The smokiness still road my tongue. Licking my lips mixed the sweetness back in. Mmmm. Another wouldn't be the worst thing in the world.

Mike laughed at me. With bartending skills like that, he could do whatever he wanted.

"All right," Kai waved his hands in the air. "Let's get you home before he has you peeling your clothes off."

That couldn't have been an accident. I raised an eyebrow at him. "I don't exactly have any clothes." And everyone had already seen all of me. Complete buzzkill on the mood I'd been working toward.

"Then he's halfway there. Come on. I have heated seats." He held my purse out and wagged it at me.

I hadn't even thought about my purse. I kind of figured that it had gone when my clothes had. No one had taken anything from it either. Maybe my day was turning around.

# 4 – FLASHING LIGHTS

**H**ALFWAY TO MY apartment I let out an expletive. Or four. Kai flicked a cautious glance at me. "What is it?"

I'd had a plan for the day, one that kept my focus off me and on other people. Other people like my best friend and his big day. "I just remembered how much of a terrible friend I was."

"How's that?"

"After the dinner that never happened, I was supposed to go to the opening of my friend's art show." I'd allowed wallowing in self-pity take over the narrative in my brain. Selfish and not my style. I needed to grin and bear it. Repress, not express.

Repression, for women.

So. Lex's opening. No clue how I would get there. And home first, to change. Formal attire on the bus didn't sound good, but I couldn't afford a cab.

"Are you late?"

I checked my phone. "Not yet."

"Would you have enough time to change...errrr...dress and get there if I took you?"

I nodded. "Why would you do that? It's way out of your way."

Kai turned his eyes to me. The heat in his gaze warmed me more than his seats did and he didn't even dip his line of sight below my face. My brush with death or whatever happened hadn't erased what we'd started at the bar. When the light switched to green, he turned his focus back to driving and shrugged like he hadn't just stoked my fire.

"I like you, Greer. Always have."

His voice held no kind of expectation. He sounded the same way he always had with the bar between us. The flat, friendly tone hid a multitude of sins, apparently. I wanted to shake him out of it. Now was not the time, though. I couldn't let Lex down.

Unspoken words filled the rest of the drive to my apartment. When he parked the car, Kai poked his chin toward the building. "I'll wait."

"You can come up, if you want."

"Not if you want to make it to the opening."

Shit. Lex would understand, wouldn't he? If I told him about my day and sent him a picture of who kept me away?

No. No he wouldn't. "Damn it." I wouldn't forgive myself for it either.

I forced myself to get out of the car and trudge up to my apartment.

The couch was gone. TV too. The cabinets in the kitchen open and half as full as they had been this morning. A nightstand, gone. A chest of drawers was missing and my folded clothes sat—still folded—in the empty spot on the floor. My closet had a lot of holes, but only where Chad's clothes used to hang.

That rat bastard.

He'd waited until he knew I wouldn't be home to move out his things.

I would call to change the locks in the morning.

The bright purple dress I bought to wear to the opening now showcased my glittering chest. I didn't have anything else and no time to shop. I dug through the deeper recesses of my closet and came up with a shawl my sister bought me that I'd never used. A bird of some sort that my sister assured me was not a peacock with a long, fancy tail or reds and oranges embroidered on black velvet. A little heavy for the weather, but the fiery colors complemented the purple.

If no one looked too closely at my legs, they would think the shimmering was pantyhose. That, a swipe of bright red lipstick I'd also bought for the occasion, and I was out the door. I fought the lock until it succumbed, then bumped the door with my shoulder to be certain it was closed. Normal. Annoying as shit this evening.

Maybe I would call and have the whole door fixed while I was having the lock replaced.

"Shit." Kai gripped the wheel as I hopped back in his car.

"What?"

He knocked the car into reverse with a little more force than necessary. "You look good."

His voice sounded a little less steady. Win for me. I turned my smile toward the window. If I had any other plans, I would have canceled. I was tempted to anyway. Lex didn't need me the whole night. Probably. Maybe.

The ringing phone saved me from my self-centered thoughts. Kai answered it on speaker.

"This is Kai."

"You dropped her off yet."

"Nearly there."

There was a pause on the other line. "Boss man wants to talk to you when you get back. Like yesterday."

Kai cast another wanting look at me, this one laced with defeat. "Understood."

The other end clicked off without either of them saying goodbye. Men.

Kai turned on the radio and some terrible song serenaded the last few blocks to the Scientific Arts gallery. I wondered if he'd picked the song on purpose, to throw cold water on the both of us. It didn't quite work.

"I guess we're sunk," he said pulling up in front of the Science & Art Exploration building. He tilted his eyes half toward me, like he couldn't quite bear to look at me dead-on in that moment. "It would have been good."

I grabbed a tissue from the box in the middle compartment and swabbed at my lips for all they were worth. His eyes dipped down, glaring at either the tissue or my mouth. When I finished, he brought his gaze back up to mine. Curiosity twisted one of his eyebrows. I had all his focus now.

I tipped toward him. He met me halfway, pressing his lips against mine like I held his last breath. I licked his lips and he opened to me. Dark and rich and wild. His woodsy scent rolled over and through me, sparking fire where his hands graced the back of my head and side of my hip. Delicious.

We both panted when I pulled away. "Raincheck?"

He growled his affirmative. Good enough.

Before I could convince myself to stay, I grabbed his phone, programmed in my number and texted myself. "Call me."

He licked his lips. I took that as a yes as well and dashed out the door. His car stood at the curb a few moments as I climbed the steps, then he peeled out like a bat out of hell.

I completely agreed.

Multi-faceted frustration fueled my way up the steps, past the line of people. It was a good turnout already.

Lex would be proud.

The nerves that had been focused on other things spiked. I wasn't sure I wanted to be here, even if it meant disappointing Lex. Except, I had given him my word.

"You need to head to the end of the line," a mountain of a man informed me.

If we had been on the same stair, we probably would have stood eye to eye, but he had been to the gym a time or two more than I had. Self-preservation kept me from looking him up and down. My day hadn't gone so bad as to make me lose all use of my mental faculties. Instead, I adopted a polite tone. "I'm supposed to be in there. Actually, I'm about an hour later than I should be. You wouldn't belie—"

He held his hand up about an inch from my face. "I don't want to hear your sob story. It's not going to work. Back of the line."

Beef-brain didn't even pause to ask my name and see if there was anyone who needed to be in the gallery. I bit my lip on several ugly things I wanted to say and pulled out my phone. Speed dial number one. Perhaps it said a lot about my former relationship that I had never moved Chad into the first slot.

Lex picked up. "You're not coming."

Frazzled nerves and discontent trumpeted louder than his voice did. It made me glad I hadn't bailed for any of the reasons I almost let divert me. "Of course I'm here. Late. And the steroid-for-brains, asshole, bouncer guy won't let me in."

"Be right there."

He hung up before I could respond, which was just as well. Fifteen minutes to open meant he probably didn't have time to quibble over those kinds of details.

I tucked my phone in my left bra cup without flashing my glittering décolletage to the bouncer or the front of the line. Lex poked his head out the doors behind the bouncer as I made the last adjustment.

"Greer. Get your ass in here."

I didn't feel at all guilty about smirking at the bouncer and giving him a snide little, "See you in there," as I swept close enough for him to smell the burn.

Lex curled his arm around my lower back in an abbreviated and mobile version of his usual greeting. "I knew you had either bailed or something terrible happened." He ushered us through the doors into the main gallery.

Lex's work covered every wall, which I should have expected. Being surrounded by images of myself was just a little uncanny. No matter how Lex altered them to look anything but human. I knew the base for all the images and how long he'd had me stand for each. The bronze sculpture of me from the waist up made it all worse. It stripped away the façade of the others and just left me. Naked to the world. I wished he had agreed to my plea and cut my head off, from either the sculpture or my own shoulders.

"Greer?"

I turned from all of me to the one to blame for the room of me-art. If I didn't love him so much, I would strangle him. "Yes?"

"You didn't bail and you're never late. So, something terrible must have happened." He took the elbows of my tightly crossed arms into a soft grip.

"Several somethings, actually."

A frown turned his lips and the corners of his eyes down. "What happened, Honey."

This was why I came.

It didn't matter to him that this could be the night that launched his career into the ionosphere. He would drop the focus on everything of his because I'd had a bad day. The best kind of friend to have. Because I strove to be anywhere near as good a friend, I wouldn't let him shift his focus.

Also, the current alternative topic—me—sucked right now.

I shook my head. "Nope. I'm here. I'm not bleeding. No one's dead."

"Yet," Lex added.

Couldn't argue with that addition, so I moved on. "Tonight is about you. So, how are you feeling? Nerves kicking in?"

"Well," he gave me a grin that wasn't and pushed both of us back into motion. "I was feeling better when I thought you would give me something else to think about."

I knew the feeling. "At least your ass isn't on display ten feet high."

"I would switch places with you right now if I could."

Of course he would. The man only worked on two things: his art and his body. I loved to eat and was generally fine about how I looked, so long as hundreds of the most influential people in Denver weren't staring at my nakedness. Nudeness, Lex kept reminding me. There was a difference, so he said. He might not agree if we did switch places.

Lex smothered a laugh at whatever expression had seeped through my control. I couldn't hurt him now. Not with so many staff members finishing up the last-minute preparations. Too many witnesses. So, I scowled and let him give me the personal tour around the space.

Thankfully, Lex kept the bit in his showcase brief. The other rooms on the level had pieces from artist openings for the past year. A perpetual motion machine somehow inter-spliced with accelerated growth and decay of blooming flowers. Liquid magnet creatures I could have sworn were alive. A whole other world built of light and color that reacted to the mood of those within reading distance of the sensor.

Lex tried to shame himself because his art didn't show as much technological advancement as these did. I wasn't having that.

"The people from this institution reached out to you. Not the other way around, if you well remember." I poked him hard in the chest, lest he forget. "They know what they're looking for. They saw in your work everything that this institution stands for. The advancement of science and art and the interplay between them. Other than the statue of me, your work is beautiful."

He punched me in the arm with a rueful smile. Gratitude and annoyance all at once.

"Alex." The curator strode into the room effortlessly dodging clockwork ravens looping the ceiling. "We're ready to open the doors if you are."

Lex cast a quick, fearful glance in my direction. He only caught the first hint of my return smile before he turned back to the man. His hand tightened around my arm. "I guess it's time, then."

The curator's meaty hand patted Lex's other shoulder a couple of times. The force of it reverberated through Lex's grip on my arm. I didn't say a word about it. Tonight was not about me. So, I smiled for all I was worth.

"Relax, Alex." Somehow, the curator managed to sound like the antithesis of relaxation, despite the words. "Anticipation is always the worst of it. Come on."

Neither of them moved. My guess, the curator wanted Lex to move first.

My turn, then. "Do you want me to go with you?"

"No. No." He shook his head and waved his hands to emphasize. "If people see you with me at the start, they'll think we're together and use that to pump you for information. I might need you to be my safe haven. Like you're a client and we're talking business."

That plan only worked if people didn't recognize my face as belonging to the statue. Or any of my other parts. But, if that's how he needed me. "I can be a very important customer, provided no one sees me with you when you open the doors."

Hope lit up his face. "Would you?"

I jerked my thumb backward. "I'm going to go hide in the bathroom."

Lex leaned in to kiss my temple. "I love you."

"Love you, too." I cupped his cheek a moment. "Let's go get 'em."

He growled at me. I growled at him. We started off in different directions, the room echoing our footsteps.

Fifteen minutes was the longest I thought I could risk my bathroom vigil. I used the time wisely—freaking out about my sparkling skin and tucking my wrap around me securely enough for me to leave it for the rest of the night. I nearly bowled over a woman as I came out. Perfect timing. As usual.

People were still working their way in, which gladdened me while it set my heart aquiver.

Game face on, I meandered through the crowd. Snippets of overheard conversations set my mind at ease, some. Discussions of alien and spectacular landscapes, exotic frontiers, and haunting scenery. Nothing about the curve of my hip or my backlit nipple. I started to believe I might survive this event without blushing myself to death.

The curator called everyone to order after about an hour. Lex stood at his elbow, the two of them a few steps up the grand staircase so we could see them better. The smile on Lex's face didn't betray the level of nerves he'd had earlier. I couldn't tell if he had finally relaxed or if he deserved an Oscar. His smile brightened a bit as he caught sight of me, tucked under my statue's left armpit.

Oscar-worthy performance, all right. SAG award too.

I pulled out my phone as the curator introduced Lex. He would either want a record of this first step in his exploding career or beg me to delete it. Either way, I would hold on to this forever.

"Now without further ado," the curator continued. "The man himself. Alexander Lexington."

Lex's smile cranked up a couple notches at the applause. This might end up being one of the more blackmail worthy videos I grabbed. I hit record.

The lights dropped to a stadium-in-a-horror-movie flicker and the applause cut to nothing. No warning. No fade. No movement. People frozen mid-clap, mid-yawn, mid-everything. All around me was silence, stillness, and unsteady half-light.

Something funkadelic was afoot. The world's worst joke, or something. Head mostly still, I cast my eyes around with painful slowness. Hoping against everything that this was a prank Lex decided to pull on me for whatever reason

"Okay, people," a woman's raspy voice called out from behind me. "Get the masks on your comrades and get to work."

Work? Hmm. No one in my field of vision reacted to the voice cutting through the silence.

Not a prank.

Probably not a frozen-mime flash mob either, not with the raspy woman calling out orders.

I'd seen enough movies to know I needed to play mannequin with everyone else. Sticking out, showing myself as resistant to whatever was going on, would get me killed. Witnesses had short half-lives. I intended to have a full one.

More than anything, I wanted to flee. Just under that desire, I wanted to turn and see the person responsible for this. She didn't sound like anyone I recognized, and she should have. I should know anyone who hated Lex enough to ruin his moment like this.

I could have flipped the camera on my phone around to capture the faces of the people responsible. Too risky. Despite the funky flicker of the light, the steady light from my phone would draw attention. I nearly paused the filming when I heard the group of them circling from the back of the room.

They all had on the white top, black slacks uniform of the serving staff. Were they trying to blend in for later, because the ridiculous goggles they had on were a dead giveaway. One of them stopped near the closest still-frozen waitress and wriggled pair of goggles over her head. Not people trying to blend in with the wait staff. The wait people themselves. Though, as they made their way toward the grand staircase, they missed a few. So, not all of the wait staff. Good to know.

Seven of the mobile people congregated at the base of the stairs, passing something around. Something blue. Gloves. Nitrile gloves. That didn't bode well. But at least they wouldn't cause any latex allergies. Considerate criminals. Yay.

A few more of the staff came into the room pushing some plastic stackable carts.

"Make sure you get them all." The scrapy-voiced woman said as she climbed the stairs. Long, curly locks of white-blonde hair trailed down her otherwise black-clad back. No goggles on her.

So, the people with ridiculous goggles, Scrapy Voice, and me were the only people immune to the lightshow fantastic. The goggles had probably been designed for this purpose, so I could deal with that. Chickie and I had something else going on. Long lost doppelgängers?

# STARFISH & COFFEE

Sisters from another mother and mister?

Were we both robots?

The woman whipped around from the top of the flight of stairs. "I don't care how many of them there are. No slip ups. We can't afford it. Not when we're so close."

Shit. I needed to find a way to leave without them noticing it. But I couldn't leave Lex to their devices. I'd chosen a spot too far away to be any quick assistance. Calling attention to myself now would be less than useless. I needed a plan. Quick.

# 5 – IN PLAIN SIGHT

I USED THE ZOOM on my phone to figure out what the two-timing wait staff were up to. A lucky angle after much too long finally gave me the answer. They had brought in two groups of carts; one with empty glasses, the other empty and waiting to be filled with glasses. The staff with the blue nitrile gloves would pull the glass from the frozen fingers of one of the art lovers and set it in the empty carts.

As they moved to drop the glass, they would call out red or white and a number of fingers. The color of the wine in the glass they'd just stolen and how much. They were replacing the glasses of the people drinking wine.

As it had been free, most of the people had wine. Lex, thankfully, had no glass. They skipped him entirely. One less thing to worry about.

# STARFISH & COFFEE

I hadn't seen Lex with a glass the whole evening, which gladdened me further. I didn't know what they were doing, stealing the glasses of every person in this crowd, but I didn't want to drink anything these people touched. I wondered at their wearing nitrile gloves now when they had white-cloth gloves before. Something had changed in what they were doing. Something more than keeping their finger prints off the glasses.

I kept the video trained on their activities long enough to get a good survey of what they were doing and the faces of the people involved. When we made it out of whatever they had in store, I would make sure the police knew how to find those responsible.

Better than that, I could give the police physical evidence. They wanted the glasses for a reason. I shifted my gaze to the left as far as I could, hoping.

Some kind of luck was with me. Not the greatest, but some kind. The guy to the left of the woman next to me held a glass in his right hand, two fingers of white wine in it. Almost within arm's length.

Top of me perfectly still, I slid my left foot out. I eased my weight over, smooth and slow. Nothing to see here, criminals, just one frozen person sidling up to another. Easy peasy.

Tiny problem once I'd shifted, though. If the bad guys wore the nitrile gloves to collect the glasses, they had reason. The same reason they collected it in the first place. I needed a way to get a glass and keep it without touching it.

I didn't have a large enough purse to stash the glass in and this dress didn't leave much to the imagination. About the only place I would be able to get away with smuggling something without any second glances...

My eyes dropped to my own chest, reined in as it was by the shawl. The girls had held more for less. The shawl could be my answer to their gloves, provided I didn't expose enough of my glowing self to bring the attention to me. Flickering lights aside, my chest still shined a little too much to be disregarded as reflection.

Untucking the shawl took less effort than it should have. I could have come flying out for the world to see at any moment.

Not the time to freak out about that. Much more important things to do.

I snaked the shawl around the back of my neck just far enough to give me a nice reaching arm on the left and my chest remained obscured with the right side. Eyes darting around at all the moving parts in the room like a cocaine addict searching for his next fix, I trailed my shawl-draped hand out toward the man's glass.

A squeak nearly escaped me when my fingers made contact. Instead, I sucked my lips against my teeth and focused as much as I dared on wrapping the end of the shawl around the glass without my fingers making contact.

Time ticked in agonizing slowness. The world at the end of my fingertips refused to bend to my will.

In a Hail Mary, I took hold of one corners of the shawl and trailed it around the base of the glass bell. It worked. Thank everything good and holy. Pulling the corner wrapped enough of the material around the glass to hold the shawl in place when I let it go. I could change my grip. Actually take hold of the glass, with the buffer of fabric. Lift it out of the man's hand. Pull it closer to me and swaddle.

Mummy-wrapping the glass didn't take as much of the shawl as I expected, which was good. The extra slack gave me more freedom in how I settled the glass down in my cleavage, and how I arranged the rest once the important thing got squared away.

The whole thing looked like crap when I finished. But I'd well and fully concealed the glass and had no extra skin showing. Tipping too much in any direction would spill wine down the front of me. Hopefully, I could remain right where I was until the proper authorities relieved me of my burden.

For safety's sake, I pulled my phone back out from my left cup, pressed my forearms against me, and held my phone up where I had it before. They probably hadn't paid too much attention to me, but, better safe than sorry. Anyway, my phone was at the ready to catch any shenanigans.

When they got a couple of rows from me, I noticed something else they were doing. The people with the fresh glasses and wine also had stamp pads. Swap a glass, then a bright smack against the forehead of the frozen person. The smack came with much more force than necessary, accompanied by glee spilling through the odd goggles of the men and women. They were enjoying this, whatever it was.

Stamping the forehead tickled alarm bells of recognition in my gut. The news had a story. Dollar signs melted into foreheads. My shoulders tightened. I needed to do something to stop them, but I needed more people on my side. Otherwise, I didn't have a prayer of winning.

I took as long a video as I dared, then turned the screen off.

The speed of the team might have impressed me more if it had been for some positive endeavor. These people were a well-oiled machine, just like the Nazis.

I stared ahead at Lex when they came to my row. They passed me by with a dismissive once over. The guy next to me received the same. He should thank me for saving his forehead from some abuse. But I hadn't saved him from touching and drinking whatever was on the glasses. Also, he couldn't move.

Not moving while the goggled people worked through the rest of the room hurt more than it should. Something antsy-in-my-pantsy bit at me to do something, say anything. But what could I do? I wasn't a superhero and I didn't know any. The best thing for me to do was to wait and pass along my information to the authorities. I knew this. It didn't make things any easier.

"Are you finished?" Scrapy Voice asked before I caught sight of her.

I waited for her to appear on the stairs.

"Nearly there. Three more to go."

Silence buzzed through the room as deafening as it had been when the light's first dimmed. I hadn't realized just how much the banter and communication between the people had held the quiet at bay until it stopped. So many people in a room, standing without making noise, was unnatural. The eerie feeling of it crawled across the underside of my skin.

"Next time will need to be faster," she finally answered. "But they will be less densely packed. Have you seen to Silas?"

Someone to my right said, "We thought you might want to do the honors."

She made a noise like she'd just tasted the best taco ever. The pleasure moan sounded painful coming from her ruined voice. "Quite right."

The wave of her white-blonde hair finally swept into view from the right side of the gallery. There must have been another staircase somewhere.

My fingers itched to turn the screen on and hit record. But I couldn't give myself away.

The jingling and creaking of the carts signaled the wait staff crew moving toward the front of the room. When the last footsteps had passed from behind me, I turned my phone on.

Scrapy Voice stamped all over the curator's face before she pulled out a hypodermic needle. Her hands shook some as she tapped the barrel to clear the bubbles. Shit.

Crying out might make the woman pause, but wouldn't do much more. I had no power to do more than bear witness and collect evidence. And perhaps she wasn't trying to kill him. The quickest way would be to keep the bubbles in the needle when she shot him up.

Once she was satisfied, she scanned the room, gaze finally locking on me. I froze more surely than I had before. Her ice-blue eyes stabbed right through me. Shit. Shit. Shit. I was in big trouble.

"Hmm," she said. "It's a nice sculpture for the last show. Well. It's skillfully sculpted. Not a pretty subject."

Bitch. The trickle of relief that she was looking at the other me burned in the flames of my ire. I'd show her who was "not a pretty subject." With her too-wide, too-thin lips that nearly blended in with her too-pale skin. Eyes a little too narrow for her heart-shaped face and square jaw. Her dorsal fin of a nose was the only thing in the right proportion to the shape of her face, but her other features made it look like the odd man out.

And that was just the face. She didn't have an inviting curve on her body to speak of. All planes and sharp angles. And *I* wasn't a pretty subject.

"Nice rack, though," one of the waiters added as he came back from wherever they stashed the glasses they'd swapped out.

Despite everything, I kind of wanted to high five the man. He'd taken off the blue nitrile gloves, so it probably would be safe at this point.

Scrapy Voice scoffed. "Yes, if you like big breasts."

"Who doesn't like big boobs?" Another of the men shrugged like it was a given.

My thoughts exactly. I had suspicions the woman with the terrible voice felt a little lacking in the boob department.

Couldn't blame her.

Her lips thinned even more when frowned. "Are we finished?"

My first admirer nodded. "All loaded up on the truck, which is outbound as we speak."

"Good. Get everyone back where they were."

The mobile people spread back into the crowd in pairs, trays in hand. Decevious bitches. Once the conspirators moved into position and struck their servile pose, their partner would pull the goggles off for them. They froze in earnest, with whatever ridiculous expression pulling off the goggles left them with. Red indentations marred their skin where the eyewear had rested, all the way around.

The last person returned to Scrapy Voice and nodded. She stepped to the side a little without coming down a step, invading Lex's personal space more than a little. She jerked her chin toward the curator. "I need his buttock."

Something must have passed over the man's face. Hers twisted into a snarl. "Needles leave holes in clothing that don't disappear like the ones in skin do and the buttock is not the first place the EMT's will look when giving him the once over. I don't need you to strip him. Just expose the top of his left buttock."

Not good. Doctors also use glutes for shots with larger amounts of medicine in them. I'd been on the receiving a surprise shot in the butt for that very reason. Scrapy Voice didn't have the curator's good health in mind.

The man jerked the curator's pants back and a little down.

A scream bubbled in my chest. I clenched my throat around it, hard enough to hurt. If I gave up the goat now, my silence before now would be for naught. And I might win myself my very own shot in the butt.

Scrapy Voice jabbed the needle in with a tad more force than expressly necessary, thin-lipped smile plastered on her pale face. She seemed to take forever to depress the plunger. A relieved sigh nearly escaped me when she pulled the needle out.

It sank back into frustration when she tucked the sheathed needle in a bag she swept up off the floor. I had hopes she might slip up enough to leave that bit of evidence behind. But, then, she had organized the collection of all the glasses and had replacements, wine included. I needed to not underestimate her. But she would pay for all of this.

"The car's out back." The man replaced the curator's pants, disgust pinching his face. As if touching the upper buttock was the dirtiest thing he had done today.

I would make certain he got nearly as good as she did.

"Good." She swept her fingers out in an invitation.

The man started toward the right of the staircase. The same way the carts of pre-switch glasses had gone. She followed at the same pace, neither leisurely nor rushed. The click of her heels became the only noise in the room.

As her footsteps faded, I noticed a buzz. An inconsistent one.

Buzz grew loud buzzer. The light in the room dropped again. This time to only emergency lights and the flashing from the wall fire alarms.

A couple of beats after the fire alarm sounded, other noise erupted as well.

Cries and screams.

Feet across the floor.

Motion enveloped me. People turning to figure where the noise came from and which direction to go.

Out would probably be better than in, if there had been a fire. Leaving with the rest of the crowd would still be a good way to keep from looking suspicious to the dirty wait staff. First thing was first.

I looked to Lex, who was doing his best to bear the weight of the seizing curator. Everyone else was too focused on their own well-being to care about the drama on the stairs.

Shit.

I needed to get to him.

Chin tucked, I plunged into the writhing crowd.

# 6 — SECRETS MAKE FRIENDS

THE CURATOR WAS not the only person in the midst a seizure. I pressed the button to wake my phone up and got a big fat nothing. Dead. Of course. I only had a moment to hope I'd gotten all the footage I wanted before a man ran solidly into me. He didn't even stop, just adjusted his trajectory and kept going with a crying woman in his arms. Crying woman with hives climbing all over her forehead.

No texting and driving through the crowd.

I tuned in to the space between Lex and I.

Beyond the seizing and hives, bedlam reigned. A couple people had passed out, one had been left while two people dragged the other toward the door. Something more than hives bubbled on the forehead of a woman screaming as she ran past me. The news had shown me the picture of their future, called it a freak allergic reaction to unknown agents.

What else did I remember from the report?

A couple of banks had been robbed. No one remembered a thing. None of the cameras had shown time passing. Things had been normal, then they weren't. Without any warning. Only things inside the banks that showed the passage of time were the grandfather clock near the entrance and a couple of pocket watches. The completely mechanical watches. No one questioned had ever been able to explain what happened.

Except now someone could. I couldn't have been happier that I'd held my breath and my place.

Lex wrangled the curator to the ground by the time I made it to them. He had a firm hold of the man's head while the rest of his limbs trembled.

"I don't know what's wrong with him. We've got to get him out of here. Are you okay?" Lex didn't give me any room between sentences to answer.

When his wide eyes told me he'd finished, I spoke, "Just keep doing what you're doing. Keep him there. I'm fine. Where's your phone?"

"Left pocket. But, the fire alarm. We've gotta get outta here and we can't leave him."

I squatted down, carefully so I didn't spill wine inside my dress, and worked my fingers into Lex's pocket. His seated position didn't help, but he couldn't straighten without changing his grip on the curator to something less optimal. "There's no fire."

"What do you mean there's no fire?" He pointed at the wall alarms as best he could with sharp head turns.

How much to tell him? Despite the cacophony in the room behind me, too many people could overhear and that could lead to bad things.

Still, Lex deserved an explanation.

I managed to stall long enough to wriggle his phone out. "Someone pulled the alarm after they finished what they were doing. There's no fire."

Granted, Scrapy Voice had gone upstairs. I didn't know for a fact that she hadn't set things ablaze while she had been up there. But it didn't match up with the bank robberies, or at least the details that I remembered.

Of course, pulling a heist on an art and science institute didn't fall in line with the bank robberies either.

Motivation and connection were not my concern.

I had to make sure the authorities were on their way.

The dispatcher's greeting sounded put out when the line connected. Reacting to her tone would win me no battles. "I'm at The Science & Art Exploration building. Gallery opening. We need ambulances."

"I show that fire trucks are already on their way. What's your name?"

"Greer Ianto. There is no fire. We need ambulances and police to take statements. We have seizures, hives, blackouts. Dollar signs on people's foreheads." The last bit should get her moving.

Sirens bit into the air, on heels of the loudest voices I'd heard all night. Voices calling for order and giving direction. I looked up from the curator's sweaty face. Men clad in full fire gear. How long had it taken me to cross the room to Lex? Or was the fire station across the street and I simply hadn't noticed?

"A couple of officers were on their way at the fire call, but I have more coming." The woman's tone had switched to all business on the other end of the line. "Are you in any danger?"

Was I?

Nothing seemed to be leaning this direction in a threatening manner. On the base of the grand stair, no one would likely trample us.

"No, I think we're relatively safe." My gaze locked on Lex's worried one. "The firemen just arrived."

"Good. Just keep calm and follow their directions. I'm going to have you stay on the line with me until you see a policeman or a fireman gets to you."

Fine.

Whatever.

She kept asking me questions, simple things that I might know the answers to. How many people were effected? Did I see anything that might help?

Lying to the woman for half of her questions troubled me a bit, but the chaos around didn't guarantee my words would remain private. No one should hold it against me once I finally unburdened my chest.

I hoped.

Anyway, the woman probably wanted to keep me calm most of all. I could do calm. When I got home I might just scream my voice away at the day from hell. Right then, we were all in this thing together.

I lifted a hand in the air and started a slow wave to the firemen.

Not that they couldn't see us without the gesture. They needed to know we needed assistance and we weren't just sitting there for shits and giggles. Yelling didn't help anything. Too much hubbub to deal with on their way to us.

Eventually, one made it over. "You need to get out of here." He huffed with authority.

Not the time to tell him there was no fire. They had to check no matter what I said. With a polite, "Thanks," I hung up on the dispatch lady.

Lex replied to the fireman. "He had a seizure and kind of hit his head when I tried to lay him down."

The fireman took a quick survey around us, then called for a medic and a board. They ran over, around the thinning crowd. The two of them eased us out of the way with practiced smoothness. They checked vitals. Checked for blood pooling.

The shorter of the two medics slipped a mask over the curator's mouth and started slow steady pumps with the attached bag. "Anything else you can tell us about him?"

Now or never, but I kept my voice low anyway. "Someone shot him in his upper left butt cheek. Like with an injection, not a gun."

Lex raised an eyebrow.

I did my best to ignore his reaction. Trying to convince him would make me sound less credible to the paramedics.

The shorter medic's attention shifted to just me, though his hands kept pumping at the same even pace. "Any idea of what he was injected with?"

I wished I did. "No, but I'm sure it wasn't consensual. If there's any way to get the stuff out before it spreads though the rest of his body, though, it would be good."

He nodded with a slight frown.

Yeah, I didn't know enough about medicine to know if it was possible. Of course, freezing a whole room of people with flickering lights shouldn't have been possible either. What did humans really know about the world?

"If there's nothing more, please head outside. The police will direct you where to go."

I nodded to them though they'd already written us off. Lex gave me a significant look, but let me pull him toward the door without answering.

A symphony of flashing lights twinkled us a welcome to the outdoors. Firetrucks and cops galore. Good. They needed to check over everything more than once. Including my still hidden contribution.

The largest cop I'd ever seen in real life locked eyes with me. Just the sight of her made me believe the tales of giants living among us. She pointed a well-manicured finger across the street.

I hopped to it, Lex hot on my heels.

He grabbed hold of my shoulder before we'd made it halfway across. I opened my mouth to ask why. A fireball dropped onto the street in front of us, followed by a huge bolt of silent lightning.

Each man stepped out of his circle of seared asphalt, the golden masks of the local superhero union reflecting the emergency lights. The Phoenyx and The Bolt. I should have expected at least one of the Gold 4 to show up to this big of a show, but I'd been too concentrated on myself to watch for falling superheroes.

Being this close to their blazing arrivals made me pat down the front of me; my luck had already stripped me once that evening.

The dress was still there.

Glass hidden in the shawl in my cleavage, still tucked away.

Eyebrows present and accounted for.

Decent results, all things considered.

After I checked myself, I checked the men out. Who wouldn't? With all that tight-fitting, black leather on The Phoenyx. Denim and stretch cotton on The Bolt with the same kind of heart-stopping fit My own guilty conscience whipped my gaze up to their faces. Familiar faces, despite the masks. The Phoenyx looked familiar. From more than his image plastered all over the news for the past decade. The eyes clenched it, though.

Those eyes had gloated over my reaction to his specialty shot. Mike, from Rust.

Holy balls. I knew the secret identity of a superhero.

Right then, his eyes passed over me like he hadn't nearly seduced me with a shot of flaming liquor. Probably for the better. He didn't need his non-super identity broadcast all over.

I side-stepped to get out of his way, which meant running into Lex. He moved too, after nearly pitching over. I risked a glance at him. Yep, he had the same dumbstruck expression I'd felt on my own face. At least I wasn't the only one.

The superheroes walked past us without a second glance our way.

"Damn," Lex finally said, slightly breathless.

"What?"

"Look at that ass."

I was. "Which one?"

"Does it matter?"

It didn't.

A voice barked at us to get out of the middle of the street. We shuffled backward until the two heroes disappeared into the building. Then, we turned around.

The crush of people on the sidewalk was more than I wanted to deal with. Didn't matter. An officer ushered us that way. As some of the last to walk out of the building, Lex and I stood on the edge of the makeshift, human corral.

Small mercies.

Everything in me wanted to drop to the ground and cover my face until someone official acknowledged my existence. I couldn't. Not then. Too many important things could bowl me over. I had to stay up, stand firm. Later, I would collapse.

Alone in my bed. Alone, to deal with everything that happened.

Whatever. I was better without him.

Good riddance, or something.

I re-centered my head in the moment by turning to the wide-eyed people fidgeting in their formal wear. This time didn't need to be idle.

It was a long shot, but I asked the people nearest me anyway. "Does anyone have a piece of paper and a pen or pencil?"

A few of the people in earshot stared blankly at me, like I'd spoken Farsi at them. Thankfully, most of the people patted at their jackets or flicked open their purses.

An older gentleman produced a pen that looked like it was worth more than my car. The woman behind and to the left pulled out a crumpled receipt, with a, "This is all I have. Does this work?"

"Yes. Thank you. So long as you don't need it back." The last, I directed toward the woman. I didn't need to ask to know the man would like his fancy-schmancy pen back.

She nodded and waved to me, both a little distracted. Enough said.

What to put on a note to the police? How could I make them take me seriously enough to listen, without adding me to their suspect list or putting a target on my back? Also, short. I needed something concise.

Eventually, I settled for the most direct message: I saw everything and I don't want them to know.

Adding anything else might be too much, or make me sound paranoid. So, I thanked the older man profusely for the use of his pen. He nodded like it was nothing. Perhaps, for him, it was. No matter.

I waited for an officer to pass close enough to hear me when I called out to him. The bastard shifted his gaze to me, made definite eye contact, then continued on his way. In no kind of hurry. What the fuck? If I'd gotten a better look at the front of him, I might have used his badge number to report him.

Nothing to do but suck it up and wait for someone else. Because, it wasn't like we could leave at our leisure. The sectioned-off area had been arranged to keep us out of the way of the emergency personnel, but also to hold us until we could be questioned. And, yes, they would eventually question all of us, but I couldn't guarantee it would be done in the kind of privacy I needed.

To the next cop who passed, I waved and called out, "Excuse me, Officer, Miss."

The woman turned her head toward me. The hair on my chinnychin-chin told me I'd receive the same rejection from her as I had from the other officer. Her eyes narrowed, though, and she shifted her hips toward me. Wariness and weariness rode the line of her eyebrows and the curve of her lips.

"Yes?"

Her curt question didn't leave any room for joking around, so I held the note out toward her. Nothing I could do would make her take it.

She dropped her eyes to my hand a moment before coming back up to my face. A hard look tested me as she reached out slowly and plucked the receipt from my fingers. For the length of time it took her to return her gaze to me, she must have skimmed the note more than once, each reading thinning her lips more.

I couldn't blame her for the skepticism rolling off her. All I had was the truth and hope.

The woman turned on her heels and headed off without another word. I'd failed. At least she did me the courtesy of not crumpling up the note and stomping on it before she left.

Unmarked time passed.

The firemen stepped out of the building with jackets open and an easy swing in their stride. No fire. Just as I'd told dispatch lady. But I guess they had to check, regardless. The firemen conferred with the police a while before they collected their people to leave. I expected all the trucks to leave, but I'd forgotten about the paramedics.

Police officers finally started toward the group of us. Six of them. I had a moment of panic; too many ugly things on the news.

"Ladies and Gentlemen, we apologize for your wait and thank you for your patience." Of course the bastard who ignored me earlier would be the group's spokesperson. "I am Sergeant Lynn. We will begin collecting information and statements from everyone soon. Please be patient. We will cycle through all of you as quickly as possible."

I had a name for the bastard, at least.

Sergeant Lynn pointed at the front line of us witnesses and lifted an eyebrow.

The woman I'd given the note to, pointed at me. Hoping this meant good things, I threaded my fingers though Lex's and started toward her. She frowned some, but didn't forbid Lex tagging along.

He came without much resistance. I didn't want to hazard a glance at him to get the full reaction.

The police officers led whole pool of witnesses across the street again in a clump before they spread out. The woman took charge of Lex and I, leading us up the stairs of the Scientific Arts building. Farther from the rest of the people, but a little on display.

"What, exactly, did you see?" She didn't sound any kind of happy to be talking to me.

Okay. I could kind of understand some disbelief, but she had taken me at my word. "Is there any way we could do this in a place where the whole world can't see us?"

She frowned again, deepening the lines in her face. She must frown more than she smiles. Still, she surveyed the whole crowded scene outside, then pulled the door open for us. I would call it a win.

"Thank you, so much." I made sure to say it before I slinked through the door, dragging Lex in after me.

We waited to the side of the door for the officer to follow us. She moved farther into the room and to the side of the doors without further prompting. I might have thanked her again for her consideration, but her lips had twisted into a more unpleasant curl by the time she turned around to face us again. She raised an expectant eyebrow, like I should have kissed her toes for the privilege of telling her.

No thanks, then.

Just the facts.

"The lights dimmed into an odd flickering. Everyone in the room stopped, as in froze in whatever they were doing and stayed there. Or I thought it was everyone until I heard the people speaking behind me. The waiters—not all of them, but I'd guess most—were in on it. They had some kind of safety goggles they passed out amongst their people so the light wouldn't keep them frozen like the rest of the people. They moved through the room, switching out the wine glasses for new ones."

"And what were you doing while all of this was going on?" Cop lady didn't seem at all impressed with what I had to say, if the shift of her weight to one foot meant anything. No longer at attention, but also not considering me a threat.

I had to answer her like she cared, though, or I might never get it all out before she dismissed me entirely. "I was doing my best to not draw any attention, so I kept pretty still, like everyone else."

"And why do you think you weren't frozen with the rest of the people?"

Good question. What separated me from the rest of the people? "I think it has to do with what happened to me earlier this evening."

Another eyebrow raised in doubt, but not true curiosity. "Which was?"

"Hard to describe."

"Try me." Cold. Hard. Her patience was wearing thin.

"I was minding my own business," half-truth, but I would run with it. "Something weird happened. Bright light. Knocked me out. Not sure what happened in the in-between." She didn't need to know about me waking up without any clothes. Or the glowing skin. No one needed to know about that. Too many people already did.

"You expect me to believe that an unknown bright light knocking you out is the reason you were not affected by something no one else can verify happened." She smirked, in that superior, I can't wait to lock you up for perjury and worse, kind of way. Then, she turned toward Lex. "Did you see anything she's talking about, either here or earlier this evening?"

Lex lifted his hands in surrender. "I've been here since noon. And as far as what happened here is concerned..." he shrugged.

The officer rolled her eyes back toward me, smug satisfaction painted all over her face. "How do you expect me to believe you aren't just looking for attention?"

This is not the kind of attention I wanted to have. Of course, she didn't know me well enough to know that. I needed a sure-fire way to convince her I was not one of *those* people.

"I can vouch for what happened earlier this evening."

All three of us turned toward the voice. The Phoenyx.

Apparently, we would act like we'd met before. Good. It would save me from any slip-ups in that regard.

I nodded to him. "Thank you, Phoenyx." Phoenyx, not Mike, though they were the same person. This could get confusing.

He didn't acknowledge the thanks with more than the barest dip of his chin. "Lights flickering. People frozen except the ones with goggles.

Would you be able to point out who had the goggles and who didn't?"

I wanted to answer yes, but his heavy gaze made me hesitate. "Probably. I could finger most of them, but I got video of the ones who passed close enough in front of me. Before my phone died."

The barest hint of excitement lit a fire in his pale blue eyes. I'd done something right.

"Go on," he said.

"The ring leader was a blonde woman, who didn't wear the goggles. She went upstairs empty-handed and came back down with a black bag, like a cooler bag. Her face I remember, which is good because I don't know that the phone caught her before it died."

The Bolt joined our odd little band. "What did you say about wine glasses?"

He hadn't been close by when I'd mentioned the glasses. I hadn't even seen him in the room. He might have been hiding out in a nearby cubby or he had that kind of hearing. Which meant he heard Lex and I discussing their asses.

Embarrassment rolled across my skin until I realized that this could not possibly have been the first time people had discussed the assets of either of the men. Not with their fine, fine anatomy. They had to be somewhat accustomed to that kind of thing. Anyway, The Bolt looked at me with all seriousness. Even if he'd heard, he might not bring it up in that moment. So, I answered his question, and not the one in my own mind.

Both superheroes frowned as I mentioned the extra set of gloves that the wait staff used to trade out for their white cloth ones. They knew as well as I did that the neoprene gloves meant that something more serious had been on the glasses.

The Bolt half turned toward Phoenyx. "Anything on their fingers is sure to have been wiped off at this point."

"Probably. Nothing turned up on the witness fingers in the other incidents, but no one did a full screen." Phoenyx shrugged. "It's worth a shot."

"If it helps, I managed to snag a glass before they could switch it out." All eyes returned to me. I looked between the superheroes and the glaring cop. "What?"

"How did you do it without them seeing you?" The cop's voice practically dripped with disbelief.

"Very carefully, obviously." A little more heat slipped into my tone than I'd intended

"Ma'am—"

Before whatever else she might have said, The Bolt snapped his fingers and pointed at her like a little dog.

Condescending as shit, but it worked for me, so I kept my piece to myself. Even as he held the gesture and turned his head back to me. My restraint rewarded The Bolt with control of the conversation. Great.

"Greer, where did you stash the glass?"

"The only place I could think of in such a short time." I started to untuck my shawl, but a thought stopped me after I'd freed one corner. "Okay, I might have a problem. Small one."

"Which is?" The Bolt lifted his eyes from where I rested my hands.

"I used the shawl so I wouldn't touch the glass, just in case, but whatever it is might have wiped off onto the shawl and you probably need to take the whole thing."

The Bolt waited heartbeat before he said, "Yes?"

I shifted my eyes toward Phoenyx, down to my chest, then back up at him. "The...thing from earlier is still...with the brightness..."

"Ah," he said. "Officer Mowry, could you go get Greer an emergency blanket?"

Phoenyx got it. Not needing to explain things I didn't quite understand gave me a small bit of relief, as did the officer's departure.

"How big is the glass?" The Phoenyx pulled my attention back to him.

"Regular champagne glass-ish. Maybe a little wider."

His eyebrows dropped. "Stemless?"

I shook my head.

"How do you have a whole champagne flute tucked into your chest without anyone noticing?"

Mentioning the obvious, that I had big boobs, wasn't going to help any of us. Pretty certain we all knew it. So, I went with the less obvious answer. "There was a lot of hubbub going on. And no one really stares at my chest when it's covered up."

"I'm sure that's a lie." Phoenyx managed to answer without dropping his gaze or sounding like a college frat boy on a bender. He sounded reassuring, like he was giving me a boob pep-talk.

Weird.

The Bolt, on the other hand, stared. He didn't quite drool.

With a sigh, I glanced at Lex, whose face battled between outrage at the audacity and bursting out in laughter. I wanted to hate him a lot, but his premier show had been ruined by some hooligans. He might deserve a laugh. Even if it was at my expense. I deserved one too.

"Well," I shrugged and returned my gaze to Phoenyx, catching The

Bolt still staring as my eyes flitted past. "Most of the time, people don't stare when I'm covered. They usually stop when I've made it clear I see them and don't appreciate it."

Nope. That didn't clue him in. It clued Phoenyx in. His face fell into an expressionless mask before I could figure how he felt about it.

"Bolt, why don't you see if you can figure out what might have been stolen from upstairs." His voice had also dropped most of the personality that had animated it before. Interesting.

Bolt blinked. "Hmm?"

"He said stop staring at my chest and go make yourself useful."

He jolted like we'd caught him with his hand in the candy jar.

"You can't order him around like that," my favorite cop lady said as she stalked her way back toward us.

"She can if he's rude," Phoenyx answered for me. "Seriously, Bolt. Go."

He did. No apologies or slinking away. No lingering looks either. Just a quick about-face and a pointed step toward the main stairs. Whatever. So long as he left.

Officer Mowry handed the emergency blanket over to me with all the truculence of a sleepy two-year old. Phoenyx took it from her, almost like he knew what I might say to her if we interacted any more. I didn't need a trip to jail to cap off my day.

My hero. I would need to thank him later.

"I'll take custody of the evidence as well, Officer," Phoenyx said in the professional voice.

A dismissal if I ever did hear one. She jerked her head back like she'd been slapped, but did not argue. She removed herself as quickly as Bolt had. Good riddance.

"Would you rather extract the glass here or in a more private venue."

I took a quick look over his shoulder, to the white jump-suited men and women flashing pictures and carefully cataloguing everything in sight. "The bathroom, if you wouldn't mind." I'd spent some good bonding time in that bathroom with my shawl and sparkling skin.

"Bathroom's full of the crime scene people too, I'm afraid, but follow me."

Phoenyx started past the doors. I nearly balked until I realized he didn't intend to head back outside.

He led us to the room Lex and I had conferred in right before the doors opened. The lights shifted when we walked in, to a soupy blue-green, but little else had changed.

The room loomed too large for me to be digging into the front of my dress. But there were less people. Things wouldn't get any better than this.

# 7 – UNBURDENED CHEST

I'D REALLY WEDGED the glass in there. The shawl didn't help. Too slippery. I nearly choked myself with the thing until Lex jumped in to help. His fingers moved with the all the skills of an artist.

"Um, Greer, I don't mean to alarm you." His hand trailed to my shoulder after freeing my neck from the traitorous piece of fabric. "You've got a real...glittery boob situation going on there, Greer."

"I know, Lex."

"What the fuck happened to you tonight that turned you into a Sparkle Vampire?"

He had to compare me to that. Of course. Because he secretly loved the series but continually slammed it to hide his guilty pleasure. I wanted to expose him, but enough of that was going on in this room already. "I already told you I will explain. Right now is not the time. Okay?"

Lex, frowned but nodded. Good enough.

Getting a good grip on the shawl meant tipping the glass one way or the other, potentially spilling the wine and nearly exposing my boob to the glass itself. After a few tries, I accepted the inevitable. "Alright, Lex. You grab the glass and I'll spread 'em."

He laughed. I glared. Phoenyx piped up with, "I can help you. Either of you."

Did he forget he was still in his superhero get-up?

I shifted my glare to him. "Not gonna happen."

"I am at your service." He tipped his head like a courtly gentleman. His good sense to keep his eyes on mine was the only thing that saved him from winning a nice, new black eye.

I lifted an eyebrow. "Remember what happened to the last guy who tried to grope me without permission."

"The chances of that happening again are astronomically low."

His answer made my eyes narrow. "I'd say the chances of a knee-ball interaction are increasing by the second."

"Oh, that." He laughed and waved it off like it wasn't a big thing.

If he kept on like this I would make it one.

Clearly, the only way to win this exchange was to end it. Which meant extracting the glass and parting ways as quickly as possible.

"Okay, Lex. You want to grab a good hold of it?"

He did so with no hesitation. He was a good friend. Even if he laughed at me when he shouldn't. This wouldn't even things out between us, as far as the evening went, but it helped.

Lex nodded to me when he was ready.

"Okay, we're going to go slow. Just let me part the red seas and, as much as you can manage, don't let it tip."

He nodded again.

I settled my fingers on my chest with the nails just touching the wrapped glass. Then I spider-walked my fingertips down into my cleavage, peeling back my boobs as I did. The biggest problem was the base of the glass. Nice and wide and tucked neatly below the crest of my chest. Lex pulled it out, smooth, like Arthur and his sword.

For all his banter, Phoenyx shook the emergency blanket out and handed it to me without the hint of a joke or unwanted glance. Either he remembered he was supposed to be the good guy or the rest had been more for fun, rather than actual assholery.

Lex handed over the glass carefully, the same way Phoenyx accepted, though his eyebrows dropped and his cheek twitched as he adjusted his grip.

I had to ask. "What, Phoenyx?"

"It's warm."

What did he expect? "I'm not a zombie."

His lips twitched. "Moving on. Your phone is dead. Do you have a mobile charger?"

"In my car." Not what I wanted to think about right then. With luck, this would be the last reminder of my fucker of a day until I relayed it all to Lex.

"Right," Phoenyx said.

I wracked my brain. "Lex, do you have yours?"

He was giving me a look. Probably because he couldn't figure why the charger in my car was a problem. "At home."

My back up charger was also at home, farther away than Lex's. Naturally.

"Well, if you have a charger that will fit it," I turned the butt end of the phone toward him, so he could see what kind he would need. "You can just take the phone, download the video, and return the phone to me when you're done. If you forward any calls from the police about my car or this to Lex's phone."

"That could work." He sounded surprised at the simple solution.

"Good." I offered my phone to him.

He had both hands securely around the glass. It seemed like overkill to me, but what did I know? This was not the first incident of this kind in the past few months, though it was certainly the largest I'd heard about. From what I knew, no one else had provided much helpful information. The wine glass might have been the only major piece of physical evidence anyone had come across. If it was, I could understand his caution.

Tight as his pants were, my phone wouldn't fit in his pocket. I tucked it in his waistband. Amusement danced all over his face. This time, I let it go.

He asked, "Is there a lock code?" without a hint of the smile in his voice.

"The Rust logo. From the bottom."

He nodded, then smirked. "From the bottom?"

Gods. "Can we go now?"

"Honey, I thought you liked it from the bottom." Lex, this time, with a grand old smile.

"Like you would know." Rolling my eyes only brought my gaze to Phoenyx. Not exactly a vast improvement. "Seriously, though. Can we go? I need to go lick my wounds. Probably with some whiskey."

All levity left Phoenyx's expression. "Can you go through everything that happened with me one more time? I want to make sure I didn't miss anything, and that *they* don't miss anything we might otherwise overlook." He pointed over my shoulder with a pinky.

I figured he meant the police collecting evidence, without the gesture. Whatever. If it made him happy.

Going through the night, from the lights through the action, took more time than I would have liked. Which didn't say much, because I wanted my time to be my own in that moment. Phoenyx turned on his superhero persona again and zoned in to everything I said. He asked all the right questions, possibly a few bad questions as well. And then some.

Whatever energy that had fueled me through the rest of the evening waned. Too much for one day. I'd pushed myself to my limits without trying to. Now, the shadows closed in on the three of us. It might have been the reactive-light exhibit reflecting my deteriorating mood, compounding what was going on inside my head.

"You look pretty wasted," Phoenyx finally said. "Maybe we should call it a night. Anything more and we can contact you."

"Since you have my phone, you can just call Lex if you need me." A repeat of what I'd said earlier. Sign two-hundred seventeen that I'd used all my spoons for the day.

Phoenyx nodded. Enough of a dismissal for me. I turned to Lex. "I know it isn't too far of a walk to your place, but is there any way we can call for a ride to your place and then you take me home?" Puppy-dog eyes might have accompanied my query.

"No need." Phoenyx answered before Lex could. "An officer can drive you both home."

There had to be a catch. Always was one. Tired brain couldn't noodle my way to it. Lex shrugged. He didn't care either way.

Worked for me. "Fine, but if you bring officer stick-up-her-butt back to give us a ride, I will hurt both of you and win myself a ride to anywhere else with anyone else."

Phoenyx chuckled at that, but got a move on. We followed him, back through the main gallery and to the far side of the stairs where several officers conferred. He asked the group for someone to take us home in a way that left no wiggle room. Someone would take us. The first man who balked was informed that I had brought them the first eye-witness report and the only piece of strong physical evidence in this case. Gratitude and surprise sprung up amongst the men. Everyone volunteered to take me home.

I picked the least excited. I couldn't deal with the energy of the rest of them, positive or negative.

We left via the back door, for which I was grateful. I didn't know how many of the attendees were still waiting outside. Didn't care. I'd done about as much as I would to help them that evening.

I expected a dimply lit, seedy parking lot behind the Scientific Arts building, for whatever reason.

The whole thing was lit nearly as bright as the day, and full to the gills with cars. Nice cars too. Perhaps they had some sort of surveillance in the back here. Of course, if blonde woman didn't care about video catching her inside, she probably had taken care of the cameras in the back as well. Maybe even with the same kind of program she used to deal with the surveillance inside.

Sitting down. What an amazing feeling. Even if it was in the back of a cop car. I couldn't imagine how many of the unwashed masses had been shoved back there. I ignored the possibilities, and the sour smell I really didn't want to think about. The trip was mercifully short, though. I waved at the officer as he drove away. I appreciated him going out of his way like he had.

"Are you going to come in and tell me what happened to you today?" Lex asked with more attitude than he should have.

"If I go in right now, I'll get comfortable and crash. Take me home and I give you everything you want."

That drew a deep belly laugh from Lex, as I'd hoped it might. I didn't have it in me to join in. Not right then.

"All right, lady." Lex slipped his keys out of his pocket. "Stay right here. I'll be back."

I saluted him and shooed him up the stairs.

Cool night air curled around my ankles and knees. The moon glowed warmly down on me. The stars winked. I wanted to hurt it all. How dare things be pleasant while my life had slipped in to the first ring of hell? Whatever. It wasn't the sky's fault. This time.

# 8 – THIRD TIME'S A CHARM

LEX STARED AT me like I'd lost my mind. I wished I had. Perhaps I could indulge in a little insanity once I was curled up in a blanket nest. The light shining into the car switched from red to green and still he stared. I understood the reaction and all, but, "The light's green."

He twisted toward the road and eased into the intersection in a smooth motion. "You don't think you're going to change the subject so quickly, do you?"

"Who's changing the subject? I just want to get home and hermit for a little while. You can talk and drive."

The steering wheel creaked at his tightened grip a couple of times. He released the wheel completely with one hand to shake a finger near my face. "That sounds completely crazy. The light-splosion thing and everything."

I agreed. "And yet you saw how glittery my chest is."

"That, I did."

I crinkled the emergency blanket closer to me. "Best I can tell, all of me is covered in the sparkling whatever. My chest is just the most densely covered."

"Or your skin has been changed *into* sparkling whatever."

That was just the kind of negative thinking I didn't need in my life. I couldn't live the rest of my days as a glittering freak. "Let's hope not."

"Come on, Greer. It could be a good thing. All will envy your mighty sparkling tits."

Killing Lex while he was driving would kill me too. More than likely. Also, since he drove me home, it was rude. I would need to wait until he pulled up to my place.

He laughed, though, without seeing my reaction in more than the periodic orange glow of the passing lights. I reconsidered my idea to wait until he stopped the car. Dying wouldn't make my day much worse than it already was.

If I didn't look at him, I could spring a surprise attack he couldn't prepare for.

"I can hear your murderous thoughts from here."

Maybe averting my eyes had given more away than I'd hoped. "If you can hear them, perhaps you could try something that would make me less stabby."

"Are you hungry?"

Damn. He knew my weakness.

Because I was. Adrenaline and anger had subdued my hunger, but the slight acknowledgement was enough to free the beast. My stomach growled. On cue, the traitorous bastress.

"I can take you wherever you like. Wherever that's still open."

"I don't really want to deal with any more people tonight. I've got leftovers. Raincheck." Leftover cookies and milk. I deserved that kind of dinner tonight.

"How about fast food now and tomorrow a place we won't hate ourselves for afterward?"

I leaned my head against the window, already hating myself more than I should. My body trembled like I'd climbed a mountain or twelve. "I guess."

"Some place with crème brulee."

"Deal."

A glance his way showed a satisfied smile in the passing orange glow. Yeah, he'd won this round. But I won crème brulee. My kind of exchange.

By the time Lex pulled up in front of my building, I managed to pull my head out of my own ass enough to think of someone other than me. "I'm really sorry, Lex."

"For what?"

What did he mean? "I'm having a pity party for twelve over here while your big night got ruined and you're still acting like a person."

He turned off the engine and flipped on the overhead light. The better to see me with. "My night wasn't ruined."

The light-flickering must have lasting effects no one had mentioned on the news. I wouldn't have thought it would carve out such a large window of memory. Rather than lead the witness, which might cause bigger problems with his psyche when his two realities collided, I went with something open ended. "Why do you think it wasn't ruined?"

"The people who came to the opening seemed to enjoy the work before the night careened off the tracks."

Oh, he was in silver-linings-coping-mechanism mode. I could roll with that for a little while. "That's good. I certainly didn't hear anything negative."

"And even if they have some post-traumatic stress reaction to my work, my name will be—has already been—bandied about on the news. Connected to the latest of these encounters, granted, but people who know nothing about art will hear my name."

Perhaps he wasn't just licking his wounds. "I hadn't really thought about that."

"And," he shrugged with an expression too innocent to be real. "If people feel the way that you do, that my big break-out gallery was ruined, they might seek me out and buy things out of pity. It's a win-win for me, as far as I see it."

Couldn't fault the logic on that one.

"And your nude image can grace rooms across the country."

That's what his faux innocence was all about. Rather than dignify it with a response—a violent, violent response—I took hold of the bags of still-hot food and stepped out of the car.

His laughter trailed me up the stairs. Perhaps, I would shut him out of my apartment and eat all his fries. That would show him and warm my belly at the same time. Yes. I liked the plan. I liked it right up until the point that I turned the corner on my floor and saw my door hanging wide open.

The bags of food started to slip from my slackened grip. I clenched my fingers into a fist with a heartfelt, "Fuck!"

"What? What is it?" he settled a steadying hand in the center of my back.

"Call the police."

"Why—" he cut himself off, probably after registering what had set me off. "Let's go back down stairs. I'll call while we head down and we can sit in the car while we wait for the cops."

He steered me around and I let him. If I fought back in that moment I might end up hurting him, me, and the whole world.

Tears spilled out of me before we made it to the car. I let them happen too, around a growing stream of cursing, because what the fuck had I done in a past life to deserve all this shit happening to me in one day. Seriously. What the fuck?

In the nicest, and smartest, thing Lex could have done, he didn't begrudge me setting my butt on the hood of his car and eating all the fries. Somehow, though, neither the heat of the hood under me nor the food I ate warmed the stone sitting deep in my belly. Lex stood near, arm slung around my back. It should have warmed me as well. Too many things at once. My own tears stole the heat from me.

The third set of cops I'd seen today rolled into the parking lot at a slow crawl. They'd probably driven the whole way at the snail's pace. Whatever. It wasn't like speeding would save my apartment from being broken into.

Lex waved them over and gave them all the pertinent information, floor and apartment number. Two of the uniformed men set off for another piece of my ruined day, while the third stayed with us and tried to leech more information out of me.

"Are you certain you locked your apartment before you left?"

I tried not to glare at him. Cops didn't like that. Not even from the victims. I worked out my frustration on the burger. Meat. Flesh to rend.

One of the men came back before my self-pity boiled back into anger.

"No one is inside, but the place has been tossed," he told the officer prodding me. "Door was forced open, not pried."

At least that meant they would stop asking if I was a ditz who just left my shit open for burglary. I focused on him rather than the man who thought me an idiot.

He turned to me as well. "We have CBI coming to collect evidence. We'll have you start a written report, but it may be easier to do once you've done a walk though and assessed the damage."

Easier. Ha. More thorough, perhaps.

I shoved the last of the burger in my mouth and swallowed it down before I scooted off Lex's hood. My feet fell a little more solid on the ground than they had before. Perhaps the food had done me some good. Still, I shook my head as I started toward the door to the stairs. "This has got to be a fucking record."

"How's that?" The officer managed to keep his voice in the softer, talking down a crazy person, tone while also sounding suspicious. The look over his shoulder he gave me matched his tone. All mixed up in emotion.

"Three separate incidents. Three separate police reports in the same day."

Lex squeezed my shoulder.

The officer gave me another one of those looks, slightly colder this time. "What do you mean by that?"

"Car stolen. This. And the thing at Scientific Arts."

He didn't answer that right away, so we made it up to my apartment in silence. I stopped dead in front of the doorway.

Lex rubbed the back of my neck. "Are you okay?"

"No, I'm not, but I've gotta do this anyway, right?"

He swiped my cheeks to dry them. "And when you've finished, you're going to pack a bag and stay with me until we can get everything cleaned up here." No question in his voice or on his face. He was just telling me what would happen.

I dropped my forehead on his shoulder. If I hugged him, I'd fall into the slobbering mess the food had half-saved me from becoming. "I love you, you know that?"

"I know." He patted my cheek. "Now get a move on."

My nod might have been an excuse to nuzzle him a few seconds more before pushing away.

The first cop who came down had not been wrong. The place *was* tossed. More than the missing pieces and holes Chad had left.

The overstuffed chair had been knocked over and slashed. Every cabinet hung open, insides rifled through and shuffled about. Fridge open. Freezer too. The contents of both knocked out onto the floor and nearby counter, melting. All of the books—all six bookshelves-worth— littered the floor, some ripped, some with obvious footprints. A boot print also graced the TV in the bedroom, broken on the floor.

My bed had been flipped off the frame and also slashed. Springs sneered at me from the shredded fabric. My stacks of folded clothes, kicked over and stepped on. Like a man-sized toddler had thrown a tantrum at that little bit of order, right before he punched a fist into my wall mirror.

My broken expression mocked me from every shard of the shattered surface. It pissed me off. I would not cry. Not for this.

I expected the clothes in my closet to litter the floor. Not so.

The closet remained as I left it. Everything on the shelves above and the shoes in the cubbies, untouched. My purchased-last-month-with-all-the-bells-and-whistles laptop sat on its own shelf, still plugged in. Like the searchers had run out of steam, or something spooked them into leaving before they could finish destroying my home. Or, they'd found what they were looking for and left.

With all the disorder, I couldn't tell if anything was missing. None of the big items were gone. The important ones weren't either.

I turned around and found one of the police officers studying me.

"So?" he asked.

"Hard to be sure, but I don't know that anything is missing. Broken and ruined? Sure." Not going to cry from anger either. Hold it. Hold it back.

He jerked his chin to the closet behind me. "Closet's not ruined and a there's a whole bar and a half empty."

"Yeah, well, my asshole ex moved out while I was gone today."

His eyes narrowed, like he didn't believe me. Whatever. I'd give them Chad's number and they could get it from the horse's mouth.

"Do you think he might have done this?" he asked.

"Doubt it. He had a key and..." How did I explain this without sounding petty? Fuck it. I had no obligations to anyone to remain mature. Not today. Not on Rex Manning Day. "If he was too much of a pencil dick to face me to break up, he wouldn't have to balls to come back when he thought I might be home."

The cop's lips twitched, either in a smirk or a frown. "Okay. We'll have you exit the apartment while we collect information. While they're working, you can fill out your report."

"Right-o." More paperwork that would probably lead to nothing.

"Be sure to include your ex's information as well."

I couldn't even get excited at the idea of blaming Chad for this. If he was capable of this, it meant I had grossly, grossly, underestimated him and didn't know him from a pine tree. Anyway, there was no reason to drag him into the shithole of a day I was having. That he'd helped worsen. The chicken-shit way.

Hmm. Maybe it would be good to inject a little fear or guilt into him.

Still, I made clear in my report that I didn't believe he had anything to do with the desecration of my home. If it turned out he did, however, I would decimate him. In private, so the cops couldn't save him.

Their investigation took less time than I preferred. Some photos. Dusting for fingerprints on choice surfaces. Reports filled out by Lex and I. An officer gave me the number for the case file and the men left me with the disarray. All but Lex.

"Gather what you need for the next few days or a week or two," Lex said. Simple as that. I loved that man.

I had to go with the clothes in the closet, because I couldn't trust the rest to be clean and un-ripped. It didn't leave me with any safe underwear. Bastards. I grabbed a handful of underwear, one of socks, and shoved the lot into a separate bag. Separate, just in case the bastards who broke in had showered something foul on them.

The clothes I tossed in the other bag happened in a blur. Since everything was in the air for the moment, I grabbed my simple black dress. I might not still be at Lex's by then, but I didn't want to be late to the Gabe's funeral because I had to find a way back here first.

The funeral reminded me. I grabbed the photo of Gabe and I, still unbroken in its frame on my nightstand. It slipped nicely into the second pocket of my laptop bag.

Someone, in a hastily thrown on suit, stood in my front doorway as Lex followed me from my bedroom. My hands clenched around my bags reflexively. I would bash whoever it was in the head.

Granted, bad news rarely knocked, but I still stomped my way up to him. "What do you want?"

"I'm Ricardo, from the leasing office." He didn't cross over the threshold as he spoke, probably owing to my blatant aggression. "Someone called about a disturbance and some repairs that need to be made."

About damned time someone from the complex showed up. I had to remind myself that Ricardo had no part in this. His wide eyes taking in the damage only verified that. "If you can find a way to secure the door closed, that would be all I need tonight."

His eyes flicked to the door itself, finally noticing the state of the doorframe. "I'll need to call maintenance."

"Good. You do that. I'm leaving."

He blinked. "Don't you want to make sure no one steals..."

"The cops have photos of how everything looks right now. If anything, aside from the door, changes, we will all know who's at fault." I didn't want to threaten him, but even my reserve nerve had burned away. "If I stand in the ruins of my life any longer, I'll hurt everything and everyone. Do you have any real reason to keep me here?"

His Adam's apple bobbed. "No ma'am"

I nodded and started toward him. He nearly tripped over himself to get out of my way. More people needed to treat me with that kind of respect. At least until I'd recovered from my lovely day.

# 9 – LIGHT-SKINNED

I ANALYZED MY REFLECTION in Lex's mirror as the fog from my shower cleared. My gross structure hadn't changed. Same nose and cheekbones. Perhaps a little more sadness in my eyes. The skin, though.

If I stared long enough, the light shining from my face dappled and changed. Not as bright as my décolletage above my towel, or even my thighs below, but my face glowed and shimmered. Barely, just barely, but it did.

"How are you holding up?" Lex leaned up against the doorframe, arms crossed like he was posing for a GQ cover.

"I don't even know. If all of..." I flailed my hands a little at the world, "that wasn't enough, now I'm some sort of Christmas decoration."

His lips thinned. "I hoped the shower would wash off the glitter you got stuck with."

"No dice. It's not glitter and I don't think it's stuck to me. I think it *is* me now. Like, my new normal." As if shimmering skin could ever be normal.

"Well," he lifted the shoulder not resting against the wood. "It could be worse."

"It could be worse?"

"Yeah. It's not that bad."

Not that bad? He must be crazy. Or he didn't know the extent of what I was dealing with. "You're telling me that this is not that bad."

I hooked the top edge of the towel and inched it down far enough for him to see the worst of it, without fully exposing my nipples. Not that he hadn't seen them on quite a few occasions. Exposing myself didn't translate well outside of his art studio.

Nothing but silence from the man. I looked up.

Lex stared at my chest with an intensely blank expression. Akin to the rapt air he sank into during a photo session, but without the driving intelligence. Zombie-esque even, minus the side of hunger. Creepy as shit.

"Lex."

"Hmm." The dull sound that came out of him barely registered as a response.

"Lex!" I barked it this time.

"Yeeee..."

Better, but not intelligible. I grabbed hold of his shoulder and shook him lightly. "Alexander Lexington."

He blinked and raised his gaze to meet mine again. "Whoa, easy on the full name."

"Easy on the staring at my chest and not answering me."

His eyebrows pulled together in his confusion. "What do you mean by that?"

"I mean—" I stopped myself. Something really weird was going on here. Per usual, the bizarre thing revolved around my chest.

"Greer?"

I released my grip on him to shake my finger in his face, asking with the gesture for a few moments to think it through. His eyes dropped and his expression dulled again. Balls.

But, wait. I had an idea of what was going on. I had to test it.

A finger to Lex's nose brought the light of his personality back. He gave me an annoyed snarl and pulled his head back. Back out of my reach. And he disappeared from his own expression again.

Yep.

Readjusting the towel brought him back out of the staring stupor a little more gradually. He blinked at me sleepily, like he was Alice and my chest was the rabbit hole she dreamed about.

Okay. The boobs enthralled people. Covering them up broke the spell but not nearly so fast as touching the person. At least, it worked that way with Lex. Fantastic.

Lex lifted an expectant eyebrow at me. "Well?"

For the life of me, I couldn't remember our conversation before I figured out something about the new me. "Well, what?"

"I asked you a question, didn't I?"

He sounded a little less certain. I nodded anyway.

"What did I ask you?"

Hell if I knew. "It doesn't matter. I just found out another fun fact about the glitter-skin that won't wash off."

"Which is?"

"When you stare at the boobs you can't do much of anything else unless I'm touching you."

Lex dropped his chin and smirked. "Prove it."

He asked for it.

I pulled the towel down again. He lost himself again. I wondered just how far gone he was.

"Why don't you come in here and sit next to the sink, but make sure you don't touch me."

He moved. Smooth motion. No sign of him struggling against my suggestion. My own Lex-sized automaton courtesy of my new hypnoboobs. I might have been more excited about it if I controlled someone else. Or if I could hypnotize people with something conventional, like a charming smile.

We shuffled around each other in the bathroom. Once he'd hopped onto the sink, I resettled the towel.

A few groggy blinks and Lex stared at me with a mix of horror and surprise. I shrugged. What else could I do?

"Okay..."

At least he sounded calm-ish. I didn't know if I could handle scaring Lex away, so I waited for him to speak.

"You said mind control was *another* thing you found out about your skin?"

I nodded.

"What was the first?"

Provided that the first hadn't changed. If it had, perhaps it meant the hypnoboob thing would go away too. I hoped, I hoped. Before I got ahead of myself, I tipped my chin toward him, "Turn off the light."

It said a lot of our friendship that, after I showed my power over him, he didn't hesitate in flicking the light switch.

My eyes took no time at all to adjust to the dimmer light. The dimmer light coming from me wherever the towel didn't cover. I waited for Lex's reaction, practically willing his pupils to expand and for him to decide I'd become too weird for him.

When he finally spoke, it was in a low intense whisper. "You're a fucking nightlight, Greer."

"Yep." Rudolph had nothing on me.

He hopped off the counter and came toward me, eyes flitting over my exposed skin. "Is that everywhere?"

Rather than risk entrancing him again, I lifted the towel to expose quite a bit more thigh. The light from me brightened the higher up I raised it.

His eyes widened. "I need you to get—"

"Out? I got it, but can I wait until my underwear is dry?" It hurt a lot, but if he needed his space I would give it to him. Perhaps it would give him enough time to salvage our friendship.

He jerked his head back up to mine. "What? No. Get into the studio. Right now. Before you fade any."

Oh.

I probably should have expected that. Whatever else he was, Lex was an artist.

My own skin gave off enough light to lead me to the studio. Lex trailed me the whole way back, only veering away to flip off the lights in the kitchen.

I turned back toward him as his weight squeaked on the floorboards right outside the studio. "Where do you want me?"

"On the stool, for starters." He had that faraway intensity painted all over his face, the kind that usually took an hour or so to fully set in.

He'd either burn out quickly or smolder all night. There was no telling, though his remembering to turn the space heater on gave me an indication. He had sunk deep into his art-head and would ride it out as long as possible.

I sunk down onto the stool, hooked a heel on the highest rung, and left the toe of my left foot on the floor. I couldn't figure what to do with my arms, so I crossed them and let my head hang all the way back. Lex would prompt me to move when he saw fit.

"Beautiful," fell out of him in a whispered breath.

Good enough.

Modeling time warped around me as it always seemed to. The praises or directions came at unpredictable intervals buffeted by near silence. The murmur of the space heater wasn't enough to distract me from my thoughts. Without the flashbangs of emotion spiking at every turn of the clock, I had to come to terms with everything that had happened to me today.

Not the outlandish things. The sparkling and the robbery situation at Lex's gallery opening didn't matter. Not in the long run. The other things, though.

I hadn't loved my job. The five years of cubical farm filing-and-retrieval held no kind of challenge any more. No joy. I would miss a lot of the people, and kick my heels up at never seeing the others again. I only had enough saved to scrimp by for three months. Not having a car would put a crimp in the job hunt. And Chad...

The cowardly way he ended it made me glad he left. I should have seen it coming. I might have. Might have sensed the hard conversations coming. Perhaps he had too and couldn't handle it. I still loved him, but I couldn't cry for him. Somehow, I'd already mourned the loss. Or maybe that was me trying to convince myself I was already over the death of our relationship.

Gabe's death hurt. He would have been the person to get me through the worst of everything today. The one to slap some sense into me. The one to keep me from sinking into the darker places in my head.

I would need to find a way to keep my own head above water.

My stomach growled loud enough to break Lex's concentration. His lips curved, but he clicked a few more pictures before he straightened and handed my towel back to me.

The warmth of the towel surprised me as I wrapped it around me. Lex, apparently also had the foresight to set it next to the space heater. Consummate professional when he slipped into his art-head, Lex was.

Soft light joined my glow when he opened the door. Adrenaline spiked through me, pulling my head from the calm attention needed to pose for Lex. I stood to my full six-foot-four and searched for a weapon. Burglars always chose the worst time to spring.

Every inch of my body protested and my eyes tried to droop against my speeding heartrate. The war in my body clued me in to what the other light might be. Aside from an intruder.

"Lex?"

He still had the manic look in his eyes when he turned back around. "Yeah."

"Did you keep me up all night in here?"

A giggle slipped out of him. It resonated with his charged expression. "I guess so."

"No. That's not a reason to giggle. That is the reason to feed me. Like now. Like hours ago."

"Yes, yes." He wiggled his fingers at me, but started for the kitchen without more prompting. "What did you want to eat?"

Everything, really. So, I told him, "It doesn't matter."

He cast a doubtful look my way over his shoulder. "You and I both know that's a lie."

It was and it wasn't. I tried again as he flicked on the kitchen light. "Food."

"Specifically?"

I should say something nutritious, rather than things I needed to justify into being healthy. It was breakfast time, but staying up all night left everything on the table. The joyous day yesterday granted me a little leeway. "Do you have ice cream?" I hoped.

He nodded. "Breakfast sundaes. Coming up."

I didn't know what breakfast sundaes entailed, but it didn't matter. Lex started pulling things out of cabinets, the freezer and the refrigerator. I sat down to wait.

Breakfast sundaes apparently meant the most beautiful meal-sized sundae I'd ever seen in my life. One all to myself and one for him. With a brownie and a blondie, each he'd baked from scratch. He made the ice cream too. And the whipped cream.

He spun the thing in front of me with panache and a, "Since it's mostly from scratch, and has a piece of fruit, it's completely healthy for you."

Exactly what I needed to hear. "Bless you, Lex."

I would have thanked him more, but it was hard to do with a mouth full of bliss.

Halfway through my sundae someone knocked at the front door. Because I couldn't have a whole meal to rest. It was much too early for visitors. The darker shade of blue over the mountains I could see from my seat at the kitchen bar confirmed it.

Lex and I exchanged a look. The manic charge in his face had faded some. The food in his belly had grounded some of that feral energy. Once he came down completely, he would crash hard for half the day. I would be right after him. A nice rest before I began measures to rebuild my life.

From the pitch of his eyebrows, Lex didn't know who might be at the door either, but this was his house. He needed to get the door.

Also, I had the whole still-wearing-a-towel thing going on. Not exactly door-answering attire.

Lex heaved himself from his stool beside me with a big, heavy sigh. Like he suffered so much for me.

"I'd be dressed and tucked in bed for hours if it wasn't for you." I shrugged

"You liked it."

I rolled my eyes at the doorway he'd already passed through. Wasted effort. I would need to be sure I aimed the next one better.

"Um," Lex called from the front of his house. "There's someone here to see you."

To see me? Who could possibly have known where I was? The cops—the last set of them—might know. We gave them his phone number. Lex would have given his address on the statement he turned over to the police.

No one else would come for me here. Except, maybe Chad. He would know this was my refuge. The bastard.

Without turning my head much, I yelled back. "Is it alright with you that they come in?" If Lex objected, it would tell me a little about the kind of people who decided to show up so damned early.

"Too late." Lex's voice came in a tad higher register than usual.

It sounded ominous. I rotated my whole body toward the doorway to face off with whoever it was. Face off with them without climbing out of my chair.

Phoenyx walked into Lex's kitchen. My surprise would have slipped right into a pleasant one if not for the scowl on the superhero's face. Lex trailed him, stumbling at the speed Phoenyx dragged him. Phoenyx had the front of Lex's shirt in a grip death couldn't break.

I raised my gaze up to Phoenyx's anger. Not quite bubbling over, but heading there if anyone invited that kind of ugly to the party.

"I need you to come with me."

He glowered at me from two feet away.

Asking "why?" would probably be the thing to set him off. To keep the damage to a minimum, I went with another question. One that would not poke the sleeping dragon.

"I'll go with you willingly, but is this a dire, life and death kind of thing?"

The edge in him smoothened at my first words. My question whetted the blade.

"Not yet."

Ice cold frost in the two words. But the answer I had been looking for, so I didn't complain. I moved the conversation forward with as much aplomb as I could manage. "Like I said, I'll go with you, but I'm going to finish this sundae first."

"You will come now."

Ordering me.

Who in the hell did he think he was?

I mean, yes. He was a superhero; it came with some benefits the rest of us would never, in our lives, see. Still. He needed to not be rude to the bystanders and people who wanted to help. Not if he wanted this bystander to keep helping him.

"Listen. I had a shitty day that finished with someone breaking into my apartment. This fool," I jerked a thumb Lex's way, "kept me up all night. Hungry, only clad in a towel, and swinging is not the way you want to take me in. It really isn't."

Not a threat. I didn't want it to sound like a threat to him. Not that Phoenyx could be scared away with smoke and mirrors.

"That is what you're eating for breakfast?" The barest hint of his non-superhero personality pierced through. The Mike guy who poured drinks to die for.

"That, or dinner, or dessert, or I can eat whatever I want when I want. Because I'm an adult."

He glared at me, gaze practically burning a hole in my face. "You will dress when you're finished eating?"

"Absolutely." I nodded as well, in case he doubted me.

He sighed and took Lex's seat.

Lex didn't seem to mind. His eyes flitted all over Phoenyx, half artist-brain and half lusting over the hero in our midst. I left him to it. He deserved a cheap thrill as much as I did.

Phoenyx's shoulders sank, sloughing off another layer of superhero persona. "Someone broke into your apartment?"

"Yep. Lex said I could stay here a few days."

Phoenyx nodded. "You should probably focus more on eating than talking to me."

Rude.

He'd asked. Whatever. Focusing on the bowl of ice cream was not a hardship. I didn't let the presence of either of the two men distract me further. The murmur of their conversation rolled in and out, waves on an ocean shore. I could practically feel the sun beaming down on me while I laid on a warm patch of sand. My spoon scrapped the bottom of the bowl.

Time to move, again.

# 10 – JUST PUSH PLAY

I SHOULD HAVE PAID more attention to what I tossed in the bag. I'd known it at the time, but my brain had been too fried to care. A lesson for next time, because I'd given up the idea that this kind of emergency-all-the-damned-time life wasn't mine for good.

A leather pencil skirt and a red, zippered vest-shirt might not be the best thing to respond to a (not-quite) request from a superhero. My other shirts left me more exposed than was safe for the world. I zipped the vest all the way up to my chin. As far as wearing the leather skirt, I needed the power it sank into my step, however mental the power might be.

Lex whistled as I walked back into the kitchen, which prompted

Phoenyx to swivel my direction. His eyes widened and his lips parted slightly.

"Damn, girl," Lex said from behind Phoenyx. "You look like you're about to storm the castle."

His praise warmed me more than the barely reined in wanton looks Phoenyx was giving me.

"The rest of my shirts are too low for current situation." I gestured at my chest, in the event Lex didn't know what I was talking about.

"SparkleTits."

I narrowed my eyes at him. "And I went with the leather in case I need to cut a bitch. It wipes clean easier."

He threw his head back in a full chest laugh. So glad he was enjoying himself. Just like that, I couldn't have been more thrilled at Phoenyx whisking me away. I didn't even care why. Funny how that happened.

My, "Can we go?" only fueled Lex further. Rather than try to talk him down, I pivoted on the balls of my feet and started toward the front door.

"Is there a back door?" Phoenyx asked, setting Lex off again.

He even snorted.

The snort tugged at my lips as I swung back around to the two of them. "You just want to leave your car in the front?"

"My car's at home."

Oh, right. Superheroes didn't always need cars to get around. Still, "I can't fly and I don't want to be fried in your fireball."

He shook his head and stood up. "Fireball's simply the fastest. And it clears a landing zone."

"Yes, it does." If he wasn't worried about baking me, I would just have to trust him. He was one of the good guys, after all.

I slid open the back door and stepped to the left to let him outside first.

He paused—one foot on the deck, one still inside—and cast a spirited side glance at me. "Though I wonder if you really would fry."

"What?" My voice dropped low.

If I pushed him when he wasn't expecting it, I might be able to close the door before he could force himself back inside. Of course, he could create fire.

Phoenyx lifted his hands in surrender. "Something fell from the sky, smacked into you, and didn't burn you. There's bound to be other effects."

"SparkleTits," Lex piped up from behind us.

I caught the barest twitch of a smile on Phoenyx's lips.

Ohhh, he would suffer before I killed him. Suffer and writhe. Both hims.

"Just saying. I'm curious." Phoenyx continued the conversation we'd been having as if the peanut gallery hadn't added to it.

That saved Phoenyx from my wrath, which meant double the helping for Lex. But later. When I was well rested and had time to plot out a flowchart of pain. "I'm curious too. Just not enough to put myself in danger to test."

He lifted a shoulder, cartoonish arrogance tilting his eyebrows and pursing his lips. "What's the point if there's no danger?"

Adrenaline junkies. There was no talking to them about things like *safety* and *serenity*. Even if Phoenyx didn't completely believe in his statement, something made him a superhero. Some drive beyond simply (simply?) having superpowers.

All in jest; half in seriousness.

Rather than allow myself to be dragged into that conversation, I closed the door behind us. "You're going to fly us to the place?"

He crooked a finger at me. We weren't exactly worlds away from each other, though we needed to be closer for me to fly with him. Still, the impish curve of his lips raised my shenanigan hackles.

I stepped toward him like a half-feral kitten.

"You need to hold on around my neck, but don't choke me." He lifted an eyebrow.

It was a challenge, then. Men.

I slipped my arms up around him. He waited for me to secure my place before pulling me in closer to him with an arm around me. I had to turn and tilt my head to the side so my nose didn't bump into his chin. While I was there, I figured I'd rest my head on his shoulder.

"Are you ready?" he asked.

We could have been at prom at the end of a teen romance. Or a horror movie, right before the shit hit the fan. "Engage."

Phoenyx scoffed a little. "We'll need a little hop on three, Captain."

He counted. We jumped. I braced for the deck to smack my feet again for fifteen seconds longer than necessary. If it didn't happen in the first two, it probably wasn't going to in the next thirteen. Still, when I opened my eyes, I expected to see Lex's house. Not sky on either side of us and rooftops below.

"Whoa."

"If you feel nausea coming on, please close your eyes until it passes. If vomit is imminent, let me know so I can whip you around."

Vomit was the last thing bubbling in me. The speech told me he'd been burned before. Probably more than once. Since a girl didn't get this kind of opportunity every day, I had to poke at him a little. He had laughed at Lex's SparkleTits comment, after all.

"I figured that's why you wear all the leather," I said with the most innocence I could muster. Which wasn't much. "You know, for easy clean up."

"Actually, I wear it so people tell me my ass looks good."

I twisted my head around and up to look at him. His face was too close. From this angle, I could only see the big smile stretching his jaw.

Yep. He'd heard us discussing him. No use denying that we looked. That we judged. That we approved. That we discussed it in no uncertain terms. Or that he had one mighty fine backside.

Still, there was fun to be had. "Does it work?"

"It has lately."

"Well, let me know if you need an expert opinion."

"And I will do the same for you, sunshine." He tilted his head just enough to wink at me before turning it back to the business of flying us in the right direction. "The next time you turn around."

I had no doubts that he would. "My butt is not my best asset."

"I am well aware." His chest shook a little, almost enough to make me ask what was so funny. He cleared up my confusion without me needing to. "SparkleTits."

Death to all. Starting with him. And Lex. "Drop me now. I don't care." I could die of embarrassment and come back to haunt them. I would rock the shit out of being a poltergeist. I already had the glowing thing down.

His, "Watch your feet," came out with more than a little suspicious tremble. A little too bright.

My anger distracted me from what he said and why he might have said it. It clicked, though, when land smacked the bottom of my feet.

We stood on solid ground again. Good. I could catch a cab from wherever this was. Or walk.

Just so Phoenyx wouldn't think he'd gotten away with calling me that, I punched him. Right in the sternum, so the bruise wouldn't show without him taking the effort to explain who punched him and why.

He clutched a hand over his chest. "Ow."

I believed the ow, mostly because of the shocked look on his face. He probably hadn't expected a girl to throw such a solid punch. And I hadn't given my all to it. I just wanted to hurt him a little. And I succeeded. That would learn him. Perhaps. But it *did* stop him from laughing at me.

Momentary win secured, I turned my attention to our surroundings. Our oddly familiar surroundings. If I wasn't mistaken...

I turned around in a circle. Full daylight painted with different shades than twilight and the darker hours did, but I'd know that bar in any colors. "We're at Rust?"

Still rubbing his chest, Phoenyx nodded then started toward the bar. I hadn't come this far to defect now. I followed.

He pulled the door to the storage room open and held it for me. I liked Phoenyx, as much as I knew him. Correction. I liked Mike, the man I'd met a couple of times with a bar between us. I loved the shot Mike could make. Though Mike and Phoenyx were the same person, they were *not* the same person. I wondered how much Kai knew. It wasn't the kind of thing I could bring up to him and I couldn't figure how to ask Phoenyx.

The storage room opened to a refrigerated room for the chilled bottles and foods. Phoenyx pulled open the heavy, industrial freezer door and gestured for me to precede him. Not even the hint of mischief tickled his face.

Daddy didn't raise no fool. I motioned to the door with my chin. "You first."

He swung into the freezer, like it was the most natural thing in the world. He didn't even seem to catch why I offered him the lead.

It didn't occur to me until after the door closed behind me that Phoenyx would survive much longer in the freezer than I ever could. He could create his own personal circle of heat while I froze to death. "Crap on a cracker."

The crack of the door closing behind us rocked loud in the too tiny room.

Phoenyx asked, "What's wrong?" Like nothing could possibly be wrong with us being locked in the freezer.

How did I begin to explain everything wrong with this?

I opened my mouth to start on the diatribe when he stepped to the side, holding another door open. A door to what looked like an elevator.

A lot of odd things had happened and I hadn't slept in more than twenty-four hours, as far as I knew. Everything after Rust might be a coma dream. Before I convinced myself of it, I asked. "Is that an elevator in the freezer?"

Phoenyx gave me a self-satisfied smile. "This isn't where you keep yours?"

That bit of smugness and the bad, almost put-down, convinced me that I was awake. I wouldn't be quite so ridiculous in my own mind.

"Just like Queen Elizabeth, eh?" My dream dialogue would be much better than this drivel.

We stepped in and swiveled around to face the front.

Like you do.

Once Phoenyx closed the door, warm air wrapped around us. A note of optimism rang in the back of my head. Maybe Phoenyx was *not* trying to hustle me off to a quiet place to dispose of my corpse.

He pressed the button, the only button on the panel in the elevator. Nothing happened. Doubt slipped back into the soles of my feet. The quiet and inactivity shook my patience in ten seconds flat.

I turned an expectant gaze over to Phoenyx. "Is this elevator supposed to do anything?"

Before he could answer, a bell dinged like something had happened. Perhaps the bell was to warn of things about to happen.

Phoenyx gave me nothing but a flat smile.

The door opened to a much brighter and much larger room than it had closed on. Three-story ceilings at least, barely visible through tree branches and palm fronds. Vines twined over most everything. Bright white light that had to originate somewhere lower to the ground, but hidden. The canopy would have filtered out all but the smallest beams from the top. Flowering bushes and fern finials filled in the ground beneath the taller plants. Warmth and rich, loamy soil permeated the air.

Amid the jungle-forest, a carpeted path lead to a desk that looked the love child of carved marble and the stump of a redwood. I could imagine an elvish gnome sitting behind the empty desk.

Weird.

We'd ridden the elevator. It had to have gone down, because Rust only had the two stories and the trees in this reception room, or whatever, were taller than that. Underground, I guessed, though how people grew such healthy trees underground, I would never know.

Phoenyx didn't give me much time to take it all in before he started forward. I followed him around the desk and into the cove made by the trees behind it. Bamboo walls buffeted us on both sides, too thick to see anything past them.

We walked through a curtain of hanging vines and into a plain office building. Glass walls around sizable offices on the right. Some occupied, some dark. All well-appointed. Solid wooden tables. Stone desks. Computers. Telephones. Shelves filled with books or papers. The whole nine yards.

The couple of well-stocked laboratories on the left were walled off with more than the one layer of glass. The layering made the room behind each squiggle like an image in a funhouse mirror. I trained my eyes on Phoenyx's back.

I wasn't supposed to be here. I recognized the faces in the occupied offices, even if they took a couple of heartbeats to place them without the masks. Faraday. The Menace. The Miasma. All superheroes who graced the papers and the skies in this region of the country. And I was in their secret hideaway.

Balls.

Phoenyx walked into the office at the end of the hallway.

"I expected you back much sooner, Phoenyx."

The announcer rhythm and tone of the man who spoke sounded familiar. I stepped out from behind Phoenyx. Yep. The Magus, animalist extraordinaire.

"She was eating," Phoenyx answered, without much annoyance or amusement riding his words.

Did that mean Phoenyx respected The Magus or he disliked him?

"Then you interrupt her breakfast and take her."

I was going with dislike.

"And she was naked."

Both of us stared at Phoenyx in silence a moment. The Magus recovered before I did.

"You eat breakfast naked?"

I whipped my head toward the frowning Magus. It wasn't his fault, really, so I punched the responsible party in his shoulder and explained. "I had a towel on and, since I haven't been to sleep since five a.m. yesterday, I don't know that I would call it breakfast."

"Huh," Phoenyx said. "That does explain the sundae."

I gave him a sidelong glance, wondering if he'd listened to anything I said earlier. "That and the shit-tasm of a day. Now, can we tell me why I'm here so I can sink into a nice, day-long coma?"

"Follow me." The Magus stepped around us to exit the office.

Good. More delays. I hoped this was the last one. Through the left-hand hall and down some stairs we went. The downstairs hall wasn't so brightly lit and there were opaque walls. Given the choice, I would have set up shop down here. Or in the jungle-y reception room.

The Magus knocked once on a door halfway down this hall and opened it without waiting for the response. "She's here."

"About damned time," a higher baritone voice said from inside.

My skin crawled before I walked into the room filled with black tables. Like my subconscious recognized the feel of Bolt before the rest of me did. Pieces of electronics in different levels of disrepair littered the tables. The computer nearest Bolt looked to be the only functional thing in the room.

I had the gag-worthy privilege of dealing with this fool again.

Great.

He took a good look at me when I walked in. Down and up and down and up again. Oedipus Rex. I couldn't knock him out until we'd solved the problem that brought me here. Maybe not even then.

But, his rudeness opened the door for me. "Could you stop fucking looking at me like a bodybuilder staring at a Baby Ruth and tell me why the fuck I'm here?"

His head jerked back like I'd slapped him.

Good.

He lifted something up for me to see. My phone. "We can't get your phone to play the video you supposedly took of the events last night."

Supposedly. And that tone. He must have been pissed that I called him out but he couldn't justify staring at me like that. Forcing us to focus on his disrespect would be petty. Not to mention the crimes that had brought this happy family together.

He continued, slight snarl to his lip. "Do you have some sort of password to play videos?"

"Is that even a thing?" He probably wouldn't be asking me the question if it wasn't. "Never mind. Can I see my phone?"

Bolt made sure to give me the full-on superior huff and eye roll before he passed the phone back. Petty. Childish. But we had crime to solve. He would not drag me into the mud with him. This time.

Unlocking the phone? No problem. None with opening the camera app either.

Huh.

Here went nothing.

I pressed play.

And the video played like it was supposed to. Was this a joke? An excuse to get me here? If so, why?

I looked up at the three of them, opened my mouth to ask the question, and said nothing. It wouldn't have mattered. They were all frozen in place. Like everyone had been in Lex's opening. I stopped the video. "Idiot."

"Who are you calling an idiot?" Bolt sounded ready to jump at me.

I forced a breath out. No waving the red cape at the bull. "Myself, mostly. The phone's fine. So is the video."

"No," Bolt said. "It isn't."

No need to rise to the bait. I would simply explain. "Listen. I took the video because people were frozen by the odd flickering of the light, which the video captured perfectly."

Understanding dawned on Phoenyx's face first. "So, the video froze us too."

"Bingo," I gave him finger guns and even added, "pew pew pew."

He smirked.

Bolt frowned. "That's not good."

"Not really, but I can get you some screenshots of the people involved." I couldn't imagine why Bolt was being such a drama queen about this.

"That won't solve the problem of us being frozen when we swoop on Anterograde."

Okay. He had a point there. One that I couldn't think my way out of at the moment. I went with what I could do. "Do you still want the screen shots of people?"

The Magus answered for the group. "Yes."

I swung around toward him. "Do you want to shut me in here and you go out in the hall, or y'all stay in here while I go out in the hall?"

"Why is someone going in the hall?" Bolt, again. Smugness nipping at the edges of his tone.

I would have thought it was obvious. Silly me. "So I don't freeze you people when I play the video."

"You people?" Phoenyx said in mock offense.

I shrugged. You people was apt.

"Yes," The Magus said. "You should go out into the hall."

I saluted and exited the room. Just to be safe, I closed the door behind me.

Finding the faces was not a problem. Finding the clearest frame to screenshot and stopping there, became my goal. The goggles the people wore didn't help. They never seemed to sit well in the light. Not well enough to take a clear picture. Frustrating.

Scrapy Voice turned out to be the largest issue. When she was near enough, I only caught her uber-blonde hair trailing down to her butt. A fuzzy profile was the best I could get. After she climbed the steps and started to turn toward me, the video ended.

"Damn it!" I wished my luck didn't shit all over the investigation. The universe could take my tendency for misfortune out of rotation for this. Just for long enough to capture the evil doers. Couldn't it?

"How is it you look better in that than in what you wore last night?"

My head whipped toward Kai's voice. "Well, sir, this has less fabric."

His lips curled and his eyes danced all over me. "That must be it."

He was a feast for famished eyes, but I had to ask. "Is everybody a superhero and I'm just that oblivious?"

"No, but most of the people at Rust are."

If that didn't just get all. That meant the ass who tried to grab mine was a superhero. Kai stopped with respectful distance between us. I wished he'd invade my space a little more.

He jerked his chin toward my phone. "Did you get it working?"

No secrets among heroes, I guessed. "It was working. The lightshow I captured froze them when they pressed play."

Kai frowned a little as the door beside us opened. "Not good."

"Neither is the computer she killed." Bolt.

Every party needed a pooper.

This one, at least, I could address. "Not sure what you mean. I haven't touched anything but my phone." I could go for touching Kai a bit.

"When your phone didn't work—"

"Froze y'all and you didn't realize it." I interjected because he couldn't seem to get that bit straight.

He harrumphed, and rolled his eyes as he headed back toward his table in the room. "Whatever. We tried downloading it to a computer to play."

I already suspected the punchline, but I followed him back in the room and asked anyway. "How did that go?"

"Downloaded just fine. Opened in the player just fine. Pressed play and nothing. Just like your phone." He lifted an eyebrow. "And now it won't do anything. Won't close the program. Won't shut down. At least your phone had the decency to work, apart from not playing the video."

"My phone played the video." I sighed. Not a hard concept.

"Apparently." A fourteen-year-old cheerleader would have killed to fit so much attitude into one word.

Impressive.

I'd had about enough of it. I pressed play and turned the phone toward him. The last bit wasn't necessary, apparently. He'd stilled before I aimed it at him, which made me wonder how little light was required for this signal to function. Something for someone else to investigate. Right then, I had things to do.

# 11 – BOOB IS MIGHTIER

P HONE SAFELY ON the table, I knocked some electronics out of my way and climbed up on top of it. My first impulse, to yell about my captain, I squashed. None of these men were superior to me and this wasn't that kind of book.

When the video finished, Bolt blinked once at where I'd been, then started at my "sudden" appearance above him. Tiny fringes of electricity spiked out of him, a few quick pulses before dying down.

I only waited for the arcs to subside before I spoke. "The video played and froze you. Get it?"

He narrowed his eyes at me, a little more caution shaking in the base of the gaze. Good. Perhaps he could stop douching it up around me.

"Why is it that your phone played it but the computer cannot?" The Magus didn't seem surprised at me. Just running things through in his head. "It may be that the computer is having the same reaction as we do, but has no way to pull out."

A larger problem occurred to me. "This computer isn't connected to all of the ones upstairs, is it?"

The Magus shook his head. "We have isolated systems to test foreign tech on." He pointed at the only whole computer in the room.

Part of me wanted to poke around on the computer, but I didn't have the knowledge to do more than what had already been tried. Except maybe trying to play it with my phone attached, which wouldn't help anyone in this room see it better.

"Was your phone on you yesterday?" Kai stepped around The Magus and Phoenyx, closer to me but a length of table remained between us.

"It's always on me."

"As in, was it *on you* on you when all the lights turned on and knocked you down yesterday?"

Huh. Good question.

So many specifics were too fuzzy before the sky fell on me. I remembered having the phone when I left the restaurant. Because, break-up text. I did often tuck it into my bra. It could have been there when the thing hit me.

"Maybe. I tuck it sometimes." I tapped my left boob.

"I know." He let out a flash of smile that let me know he hadn't given up on us coming together.

My mouth went wet and dry at the same time.

"What exactly happened yesterday?" The Magus broke into our moment with practical and pertinent questions. The bastard.

Hard to be mad at the boss trying to get work done. I managed, despite the crimes I'd been pulled in to help solve. Still, I didn't take my eyes from the feast of Kai quite so easily. "Would you like to explain, Kai? I didn't see much but white light and then you woke me."

"Hard to say exactly what happened." He pulled his gaze from me with a promise to devour me later. The Magus received a much less interested regard. "Fairly certain something fell from the sky and right into her. Comet. Asteroid. Satellite. Whatever it was, it was bright. And silent. But it only knocked down the closest person to her. Nothing else. No glass breaking. Nothing even tipped over. All of the force of it sank into her."

That wasn't possible.

"She glowed as bright as the thing for a few moments, before she dimmed to a more mellow glow."

The last wasn't possible either. But I knew it to be true.

"Glowing and naked," Phoenyx added.

Revenge for that, and the rest, would be sweet.

The Magus waved Phoenyx's comment away and turned a much more focused study on me. Narrow-eyed and curious. He reached a hand out to me after a few silent moments, palm up and inviting. Without a polite reason to refuse, I set my hand in his.

He poked at my hand, flipping it back and forth to find...something. I couldn't tell if he saw anything, but his hands crept up my forearm in almost clinical palpation.

"Magus?" Kai asked.

The Magus blinked, looked up at Kai, then at me. "Apologies. Now really isn't the time to dive into that mystery. Another time?"

Knowing what happened to me would be good, but I wasn't certain I wanted to submit to a bunch of testing. It sounded a lot like going to the hospital. Hospitals weren't my best thing. Bad memories. Bad dreams. Bad—

"You have the pictures, yes?"

I blinked, thanking the gods of small mercies and interruptions. "From the video? Yes."

He nodded. "Send them to Bolt and I'll try and figure a way to get something other than your phone to play the video. And a way for us to view it." He frowned at the last.

I wondered if he frowned because no one knew how to play the video or if he worried more about the superheroes' susceptibility to the light show. Could have been both, frankly. Not my monkeys.

"What's your email address, Bolt?"

"Actually," he held his hand out for my phone. "There are some apps that slow video down. I can download one of them and work it that way."

"Cheap apps?" I tried my best to keep my voice from lifting a few octaves.

He lifted an eyebrow without looking at the rest of us. "Does it matter?"

Asshole. I wouldn't have asked if it didn't. "Lost my job and car was stolen yesterday before all this went down."

"Hmm."

No inflection. Possibly a note of sympathy, but it was not an answer. I kind of needed one. Just before I opened my mouth to make that point and ask again, The Magus spoke.

"We will reimburse you for any charges garnered in our pursuit of this matter. Naturally." He nodded, then shifted attention to Kai. "What results do you have?"

"Very little." He started ticking things off on his fingers. "Chromatography confirms the stamps on the foreheads came from the same ink source. Either the same batch, well mixed and sealed each time, or someone with laboratorial levels of precise mixing. Caffeine. Small hydrocarbons. Molecules in small enough amounts that I still can't identify. Amphiphilic, though. And something else too. In smaller amounts. Small enough that they shouldn't be the active ingredients, but I've yet to identify them too, so they might be."

My face had fallen completely slack-jawed by the time he'd half finished. He caught it out of the side of his gaze, or he wouldn't have mounted such a confused expression before he turned to me. "What?"

"You're a nerd."

His confusion melted away, half-lidded interest replacing it. "You have a problem with nerds?"

I folded my arms. "Just the ones who look like you and keep their clothes on."

The Magus coughed and looked away.

Kai let out a low, rumbling laugh. His eyes never strayed from mine. The combination made me drool again.

Bolt just scoffed. "Get a room."

I intended to.

Now, if possible.

A body blew into the space between Kai and I. "Kai, the hospital just sent this over."

The breeze that carried the dirty-blond man in, swirled around the rest of us a couple times before it dissipated. That and the squirrel wingsuit didn't leave a question as to who he was. Gale Force.

I recognized his voice from somewhere else as well.

"What is it?" Kai took the specimen from him and held it up to the light.

"Not sure, but they pulled it outta some guy's ass." He let out a cartoon-character worthy laugh. "You think it would be brown."

Some guy's ass. Wait. "They got something useful from the injection into the curator?" I hoped.

Gale Force turned around to look at me and I recognized him. The douche who wouldn't take no for an answer at Rust the evening before.

At least all my friends were here.

"What the fuck is this bitch doing here?" Gale Force so lovingly intoned.

If he kept his hands to himself, I could ignore him. In that spirit, I leaned around him to regain eye contact with Kai. "I told one of the paramedics that I'd seen chickie inject something into the curator's left buttock, but I wasn't sure it would help."

Kai's eyes widened and shifted to Gale Force. "Is that what this is?"

"I'm not sure which side of his ass they suctioned this out of, but it was from the Scientific Arts head curator— "

Kai pushed Gale Force out of the way, pulled my head toward his, and kissed me hard enough to bruise my lips. When he pulled back, his eyes danced with excitement. "You are a wonder."

I opened my mouth but had no breath to respond. I wished I could have said something to keep him from swinging around and speeding out the door. He called back to me, "You're the gift that keeps on giving."

Okay. I'd take that. I would have taken a little more.

"What was that all about?" Gale Force asked the room, except for me. His eyes skipped over me because I could not possibly know anything about what was going on.

"By the time anyone swabs them, the forehead stamps have absorbed most of whatever was stamped there, save the color. The people who don't have dollar signs burned into them," The Magus tipped his head a bit to the left. "If the curator was injected with the same substance, we might have just gotten a large enough sample for him to figure out what they're using."

That was good. Not necessarily worth Kai taking all his excitement away with him, but good. If his lab wasn't too far down the hall, I could avail him of some of it.

"You need to let him work." Phoenyx said it low, but the room had been too quiet for the words to go unnoticed by the other men. His direct stare at me left no question as to who he was talking to.

A frown pulled the corners of my mouth down before I could stop it. Presumptuous ass, even if he was right.

He smiled. "I know, but you're a distraction."

"I'll take that as a complement."

"Do." He nodded. "And a deterrent. We might have enough to figure out the identity of the woman causing all of this."

"Thanks to me." Lest he, or anyone else in the room forget.

He nodded again. "Yes. Thanks, in large part, to you."

"How do we know the person responsible is a woman?" Gale Force asked around me again.

"Woman or a very convincing transvestite." I shrugged. "Her voice was really painful. Like she spent seven-hundred years smoking unfiltered cigarettes. Seriously scrapy."

Gale Force finally deigned to center his gaze on me. "Wait, you're the new source of information?"

Every response to his dismissive tone that popped in my head had too many expletives to come right out and say. Too many for people who didn't know the reason for my aversion to him. Counting to ten didn't sift anything more helpful out of my brain. I had to move on.

I turned to Phoenyx. "Has the glass helped any?"

"Cinnabar hasn't said."

I blinked at him. "Cinnabar?"

Phoenyx jerked a thumb in the direction Kai had gone. "Kai."

Ah. I shouldn't have been surprised he had a superhero name too.

"Why are you telling her that? Why is she even down here?" Gale Force sputtered. "I don't trust her one bit and— "

"You didn't trust that I didn't want your greasy hands on me either, and you see where that got you." He could be angry all he wanted, but I wouldn't let him tarnish my name.

His eyes widened, his face reddened, and he held there. Just like he was. Not moving a muscle. Like he couldn't quite let out everything in his head in front of his superior (in every way) superhero.

I flicked my eyes at The Magus, who also wasn't moving. Perhaps Gale Force stopped for an entirely different reason.

Bolt's finger rested on the play icon of my phone screen, and the video was a-playing. Slower than real time, but, apparently, not slowly enough. I lifted his finger from my phone screen and pressed stop. His thumb pulsed against my fingers, then he lavished a glare at me.

"That one didn't work, Bolt. Try something slower." I released his thumb.

His glare turned contemplative. I waited for him to ask me something or for something brilliant to flash in my head.

After the fifteen seconds or so of quiet, Bolt nodded to me and shifted his focus back to my phone. Not a bridge mending, but lack of hostility. Best I could ask for.

Gale Force sputtered something during the exchange between Bolt and I, but I only caught Magus's shushing response. Not entirely a suggestion to mind his business, but certainly a shut your mouth until something useful came out. Nice

"Greer."

The Magus's soft voice straightened my spine and shifted my shoulders back. "Yes?" How did he do that?

"Considering your immunity, will you work with Bolt to find a solution for the light effects?"

I nodded. "Sure thing."

He dipped his chin. "Bolt, contact me when you have it. The rest of you have other things to do."

The odd impromptu meeting broke up.

Being left alone in the room with Bolt was not my favorite idea. But, there was work to be done. If we could focus, we wouldn't blow up on each other.

"I hate that guy," Bolt mumbled.

Bolt and I weren't on that level. I decided to ask him anyway. "Which guy?"

He brought his fingers up to make air quotes. "Gale Force. More like Weak Breeze."

Commiserating over mutual hate was not the best way to bring people together, but it did bring people together. "Yeah. Kind of surprised to find out I kneed a superhero in the crotch."

A real smile bloomed on Bolt's face, the first since I arrived. "You did that?"

"He got grabby. He got kneed." I shrugged.

"Remind me not to get on your bad side."

Like he couldn't shock me senseless for anything that I did to him. "I gave warning. Not that I should have needed to. If you don't know a person, and they haven't invited you to touch them, keep your hands off. Simple."

"Not usually that simple, for whatever reason."

Depressing. True, which the interwebs made clear every day, but depressing. Now was not the time to focus there. "How did you want me to help you?"

"I just need you to do what I can't." He shook my phone at me. "When I freeze, stop the video."

I could do that.

It should have been simple. Several increasingly-priced apps gave us nothing useful. Either the app degraded the video quality too much or didn't slow things enough to keep Bolt in motion.

Nearly two hours later, Bolt dropped my phone with more force than necessary. Disgusted. Lamenting that his computer could do what he needed if it wasn't frozen by this damned video. Turning his stink-eye my direction broke my resolve to keep quiet.

"Why don't we just use the computer, then."

Eyebrow raise.

Not the same level of sass as before we bonded a bit, but he'd give Spock a run for his money. "Frozen."

Rather than respond, I pushed away from him and headed toward the black-screened computer.

"What makes you think you can make it work when I couldn't?"

"Because I fucking sparkle." I plopped down in the chair.

He lifted his hands in mocking surrender. "Well, hell's bells, let's all bend—"

His expression dimmed when I pulled the zipper of my top down and the collar open. Hypnoboob worked on superheroes too, apparently. I'd needed him to shut up right then, so the effect relieved me. The guilt would certainly sink in later.

For the extra few moments of quiet, I directed Bolt to stand near the computer. The video played with me turned halfway toward the screen, which was good. I didn't know how I would justify freezing him if it hadn't. It would be hard enough anyway.

The video played through, pulling me back into the helpless moments in the dimmed gallery. I hated that, knowing people got hurt while I stood and watched.

When the video finished, I gladly zipped back up.

Bolt blinked a couple times.

"What was I..." He looked between me and table he'd been working near. "Wait a minute. What just happened?"

"Hypnoboob happened. The computer's working."

I pointed next to him, in case he didn't catch where it was.

He whipped around toward the screen and started clicking around. Everything seemed to be functioning.

"Yee haw!" He glanced at me out of the corner of his eyes. "Score one for your boobs."

# 12 – EYE OF THE BEHOLDER

BOLT ALMOST MANAGED to look me in the eye when he complemented me on my chest's victory. Almost, but not quite.

Just a foot or so lower.

Best cure was to give him something else to focus on. "Do you want to set up whatever needs to happen with the video? I can start and run it if you walk me through everything first."

"Right." He nodded with a tiny wave of his hand. "If it pauses me, just roll me out of the way and stop it. Work for you?"

It didn't matter either way for me. As long as he fixed the problem and let me get on with my miserable, crumbling life.

Why did I want to go back home again?

Bolt had a program that could pull a video apart frame by frame. It took a while, he warned me, and the only way to load it in was to play the thing. Rather than leave the room as I suggested, Bolt guided me into the computer chair.

I sat and craned my head all the way back to look up at him. "You really think I'm going to give you a view from the top?"

"Wishful thinking," he smirked, then leaned past my right side to click around on the computer.

After a dry run with a safe video, Bolt gave me the helm and turned away without a backward glance. He didn't even twitch at the sound of my zipper coming down. Couldn't figure how to feel about that, so I set to work.

Nothing exploded when I clicked play. Bolt froze. Same ol', same ol'.

Watching the thing for the umpteenth time, at half the speed, didn't make me feel any better about what I'd witnessed. No one had died. I tried to console myself with that thought. Time dragging on made feeling better more difficult.

People's wills, their ability to think and move, taken by a trick of the light. A complicated one, but still, light. Just like I could do. Like I had done. Accidentally, the first time. I had the power, though. Over men, even super men, and computers too, it seemed. So much power and responsibility rested on my chest. Because I didn't already have enough weighing on me.

When the video finally finished, I'd never been more grateful to cover myself up.

"Is it good? Are we done?" I hopped out of the chair like he'd already confirmed it.

Bolt slid into the chair I'd abandoned. "Let's see."

My impatience bubbled as he clicked through a few things, typing intermittently. I willed him to speed up, but I had to turn away. If we'd finished I could go home and finally sleep. If we hadn't, I might just need to kill Bolt.

An eternity later, he finally said, "Yes, I think we're good."

"Saints be praised."

"Now, we can analyze the magic pattern."

Fuck. I'd spoken to soon. I had to pinch my fingers together to keep from an epic tantrum. "Do I need to be here for that part?"

"I don't know that you do," Bolt answered as if he could feel my stabby mood. "Magus, I think we have what we need."

I swiveled back around in time to catch Bolt's finger pulling away from a panel of buttons next to the computer. That bit of gesture relaxed me a bit. I'd not heard The Magus could hear people outside of a normal human's range. Knowing people had limits comforted me. Even if they were super people. Especially if they were. Hopefully, I had limits too.

"Report." Magus' voice came from the doorway behind me.

Since I didn't report to him, I let Bolt handle the information transfer. Instead, I stared at the doorway while my heart longed for a bed or halfway comfortable couch. A cot. A warm enough slab of sidewalk.

"That is fine, Bolt. Greer, if you will come with me?" The Magus' words came out more like an order.

Going with him meant leaving this room and possibly heading home.

I followed.

Back down the hall and up the stairs to the brightly lit glass kennel for all the super hero dogs. I wished Kai could come out to play with me.

The Magus hooked a right in the middle of the bamboo-lined hallway, at a point that looked as impassable as the rest. Apparently not. Still, I reached a hand in to the midst of the skinny trees. Eventually, my hand found clear air.

Into an office that looked nothing like any of the others I'd seen. Gravel pits. Perches. Rocks with heat lamps aimed. A thick patch of grass. Animals occupying every fit surface. The rest— huge mahogany table with electronics and papers galore, plush fainting couch, shelves of books—had no errant scratch or bit of bird poop.

None of the animals reacted to my entrance. Not a screech or growl. All of them, even the ones who appeared to be asleep, oriented themselves toward him. Eerie as fuck, though I was more than happy to relinquish my fair share of attention from the jaguar curled on the branch hanging over his desk.

"Please take a seat." The Magus gestured toward the couch.

The nervous part of me wanted to ask him if I should take a seat next to the bunnies munching on grass or next to the vicious-looking, plumed eagle. The survivalist in me sat me down on the couch without any of my usual lip.

The Magus set his butt against the corner of his desk and crossed his ankles, a purposefully casual pose. "I would first like to thank you for your assistance in this incident. It is a rare thing when a civilian aids us so greatly."

Not sure why he needed to bring me into his office to tell me this.

Thanks were nice, though. "Anytime," I shrugged.

"I hope for everyone involved that such an occasion never arises again."

"Magus," Kai's voice entered the room before he rushed in. "Bolt said they'd finished. You haven't yet, have you."

Kai pointedly kept his eyes off me. At least, the focus on the other man *felt* forced, since he was asking about me.

"Not yet." The Magus, also not looking my direction.

Conspiracy. I didn't like it.

"Good. Don't, Magus." Kai's words came out in a plea rather than an order. "She's helped a lot and there's no telling what other information she might be able to give us, piggy backing on what she's seen here."

"The rules are clear, Kai." The Magus didn't sound remorseful or angry. Just matter of fact.

The tone dripped ice water down my back. Awareness of how many creatures could attack me at the slightest aggressive move kept me from standing. I took a calming breath so my tone didn't offend any of the animals either. "I would very much appreciate you telling me exactly what you're going to do to me."

Both sets of eyes shifted to me, Kai's guilt and fear-riddled, The Magus's even. Kai's chest moved in an inhalation, but a raised finger from The Magus made him press his lips together.

The Magus answered. "It is not the practice for civilians to be brought here, though there are protocols when it is deemed necessary. The memory of the experience needs to be wiped from the mind of the civilian to keep the secrets of our base."

"Oh." I let out a breath that had lodged in my chest.

"Oh?" Confusion and guilt still battled for supremacy on Kai face.

"I had images of being chopped up and fed to the pretty kitty up there." I pointed to the jaguar in case either of them didn't get it.

The Magus's eyes widened in offense. "We wouldn't do that. We're heroes."

"No one is the villain in their own mind." I answered without thinking. The impact of the words shocked across their faces. I had to fix the mood quickly, so I tried my best to wave it away. "Verbal diarrhea. If you need to take the memory of this place, go ahead."

"Really?" Kai looked doubtful. An almost relieved doubtful.

I couldn't blame him. "Yeah. Just don't take too much."

"Very good," The Magus nodded before squatting down in front of me. "Keep your eyes on mine."

I leaned forward to set my forearms on my thighs and gave him good eye contact. He had pretty eyes. I hadn't noticed until then, but they were more than simple brown. Honey and gold hid in the depths of the darker brown, setting them on fire. Lex would love to get a picture of them and turn them into a sunset.

"You have really pretty eyes."

He blinked at me, then narrowed his eyes. "What do you remember?"

"Everything since I got here." I gasped a little. "Does it kibosh your mojo if I talk?"

"Huh?" Even in his confusion, he appeared unruffled.

What part didn't he understand? I tried again with a little plainer English. "Should I zip my lip for you to work your magic?"

He searched my face for something. "You shouldn't be able to speak at all. Not while I'm working."

Except that his working wasn't working. The look he exchanged with Kai said this was abnormal. I hoped they didn't get any drastic ideas of how to explain things or overcome them. Evasive maneuvers needed, but subtle ones. "Would it work better if I was more relaxed?"

His lips pinched some. "Perhaps."

That, I could work with.

I swung my feet around and leaned back against the curved side of the couch. I held my feet above the leather a few moments, asking him with raised eyebrows if he minded my shoes on the furniture.

He nodded, either agreeing with my general posture or to okay the shoes on leather. Without the specificity, it was open to interpretation. I set my feet down and rolled each of my joints to loosen things up a bit. Once my body moved a little better, I turned my head to The Magus. "Alrighty. Shoot."

We locked eyes again.

His eyes didn't start out as beautiful. The nearly black-dark brown lightened to show the honey and gold. Probably when he started manipulating people's memories. And because I could see the change, his powers probably weren't working. I tried. Forcing myself to relax more, ease my heavy limbs deeper into the couch, only see the dark brown.

No dice. I didn't even know what his power felt like to let it bend me. Laying there, all relaxed, made it harder and harder to keep my own eyes open. I didn't want to be the one to pull out first, but he of all people should have known my memory hadn't been touched.

The Magus finally straightened. "I don't understand it."

Neither did I.

"What are the rules for this?" Kai sounded smug. Smugger than I would have risked when speaking to my boss.

Of course, I wasn't certain how the superhero union worked. How people got in or left a chapter. Could people leave? Could they strike? Being intermixed with the military somehow, their union held more complications than normal. I needed someone to ask. Someone who might answer, when we had a moment alone.

The Magus didn't answer Kai's question. The silence screamed that he didn't have one. Or that there wasn't one. I guessed the latter. Too many wordless glances told a girl a lot about the uniqueness of her situation.

"I will need to consult my books." The Magus spoke to Kai, but his answer was as much for me.

But I was right. He didn't know. Or no one in the union had imagined little old me coming about. Fancy that.

Fancy me.

"Until then?" Kai asked before I did.

"She will need to remain here until I sort this out."

Kai frowned. I didn't have the energy to argue much about it. Sitting up took more effort than it should have. "In that case, point me to a place I can lay down."

"Greer..." Kai asked, but stopped before finishing his question.

Too many options and not enough energy to care. "I don't have anywhere to go until Monday morning. It's fine."

The Magus stretched his fingers outward. "I want you to have very real expectations of what's going on. I've had maybe five people in my life not susceptible to me. All of them for unrelated reasons. As so, I cannot guarantee that I will have solved the mystery by then."

Red flag. Anger danger. My lack of control over it might have scared me on another day.

"Listen, Magus." I forced myself to stand in a slow, single motion. Nothing jerking so as not to set off the watching animals. "I think I've been fairly accommodating, helping you guys and all, but I've had a shitty-ass, mother fucker of a day or two. Enough is enough. I don't care if one of you takes me the funeral, sticks to my ass throughout, and brings me right back here. But, gods witness me, I will not miss Gabe's funeral. I will not."

Magus and Kai exchanged yet another of their epic looks, this one longer with shifting expressions. One eyebrow up on Magus. Kai's lips flattened. Magus flared his nostrils. A tip of a chin by Kai.

Eventually and without looking at me, Kai answered. "I will take you there."

I eyed him a long while. He turned to me and held my gaze long enough to convince me he wasn't just placating me, so I nodded to him. "Very good. Thank you."

The warmth of the adrenaline flowing through me cooled. I would crash soon. Hard. It would be beautiful and ugly.

"And you will come back afterward if it is required," Magus' voices lilted at the end. Almost like a question.

I said it, didn't I? "I don't have anywhere else to be. Now, about a place to lay down, or is this a curl up in any corner kind of joint?"

"I have a free bed down—"

Magus cut Kai off with the tiniest shake of his head. "There is space across the hall."

Kai frowned a touch, but said nothing.

Magus started for the exit without further ado and I could have kissed him. Kai's feet fell in behind me.

I *would* kiss him.

The bamboo closed around us again. It took longer to push through than it had before. I started to wonder if we had taken the wrong turn at Albuquerque when Magus stepped into some clear space. Darker than I remembered the hall being. Smaller too, and with furniture. I spun around as I came out of the bamboo.

We were in a room. Low light from wall sconces. Barely large enough to stave off being claustrophobic. Black leather couch. Chairs on either side of it, dark wood and crushed red velvet. Shelves filled with books covering the wall to the right. Big-ass fireplace to the left, hulking and unlit.

"I regret that we have nothing more comfortable available to you," Magus said.

Something in his words rang like a lie, but it didn't matter anymore. "More than twenty-four hours up makes even your kitten's branch look comfortable. I'm guessing I'm to stay put here until someone comes to get me."

He nodded.

This room was most certainly a trap. My give a fuck didn't give a fuck anymore. I saluted. "Will do, Mein Fuhrer. I'll take an order of French toast, bacon, and fruit cup for my breakfast."

He stared at me, nonplussed. If he didn't care enough to ask me, I wouldn't explain.

I sauntered over to the couch and tested it with body weight and a bent knee. Cushy, but not so soft it might swallow me whole. The seat was deeper than it should have been, almost like it had been built with Andre the Giant in mind. I could work with this.

"Are you sure you'll be okay in here?"

Magus had left the room and Kai stood a mere two feet from me. I hadn't noticed either. I didn't know which was a bigger indication of just how tired I was.

"I've been up for..." I didn't know. I took hold of Kai's wrist to bring it toward my face.

He didn't fight it.

A few minutes past eleven. Shit. Too long. "Thirty hours. At this point, a soft enough pile of trash sounds appealing."

I didn't like seeing the frown on his face, but he stepped a little closer to me. That made it better.

"Why haven't you slept?"

"Someone broke into my apartment at some point between you taking me there to redress and getting back home after Lex's gallery opening fiasco."

Kai slid a warm palm against the side of my face, which brought him a little closer to me.

I kind of melted into it.

"Greer," his voice came in low, intimate tones that had little to do with sex. "I'm sorry to hear that."

Somehow, his voice managed to curl its way down my spine anyway. "It's fine. I mean, it's not fine, but it fits with the disaster day I was having. Bad week. Disaster day, and Monday will start itself off with a bang too."

Kai leaned down and pressed his lips to mine in a chaste kiss. Despite the restraint, fire rode his eyes when he pulled back. "I can make you forget for an hour or two."

Two hours. Goose pimples rolled pleasantly over me, but that was it. I just didn't have it in me. "I'm going to need some sleep to make it through two hours." And a stretch. Probably some oxygen too.

"Maybe I'll take you home when Magus gives the green light."

"Maybe before."

His eyelids dropped halfway closed and a wicked little curve twisted his mouth. Parts of me woke up, pulling the blood and energy from others. More important ones, like the brain.

"I could take you now." Kai pulled me against him, stealing more blood from the reasoning centers of my brain. "Fifteen good minutes, to make sure you get to sleep?"

My mouth went dry again.

He needed to stop doing that.

Or keep doing that.

"Kai," Magus' voice thundered into the room. "Hands off the doxy. You have work to do."

Mood killer. Right there. And after all the civil words that had passed between Magus and I.

I would be certain to grant him the same kind of respect.

Kai narrowed his eyes and cast a glance to the side, though I couldn't even see Magus from my vantage point. His nostrils flared as he brought his gaze back to mine.

He breathed, "Fuck it," and kissed me anyway.

This kiss held all the promise our first had held. The one that nearly made me abandon the art opening. All warmth and woodsy darkness.

If he kept this up, I might just muster.

I bit his lip. He pulled back with a hiss that made me grin in the worst kind of way.

He growled at me before heading for the door. "Later."

Now would be better.

Magus stood just inside the room, in front of the last bit of bamboo, with arms crossed and disapproval bending his face unpleasantly. "If I need to rip you away from her, I will do so."

Kai's, "Worth it," came out with more rumble than not, making me smile more.

As Kai passed him, Magus turned his disapproving expression to me. Like he could intimidate me. He could not, at the moment, manipulate my memories and he was not my boss. I crossed my own arms and shifted my weight to my right leg.

"Do you have something to say to me, or are you just going to call me another name like a child."

He blinked at me, probably surprised that someone called him on his shit. "I need my men focused on the task at hand, not chasing some floosy."

"Ah. Name calling again. Mature. But let's remember who is helping who out."

He opened his mouth to speak.

"No, no, Magus." I waved a finger at him. "You lost control of this conversation when you stooped to kindergarten name calling. What is your problem with me? The real one."

Magus straightened his arms, tension vibrating off him in almost visible waves. "I don't like things I don't understand. You are an X factor and I don't trust you because— "

"Because you cannot control me."

His eyes burned into mine, but he spoke not a word. The silence sounded like a big fat yes to me.

I nodded, trying to not be smug when I did. "I don't understand what's going on with me either. At another time, I might volunteer for some testing to figure it out. But your need to control everything makes me distrust the information you would give me. You might want to look to that. It's the song of a baby despot. I thought despots with mind control was the kind of thing you fought against."

He narrowed his eyes to slits, lips thinning into non-existence. Ooooo, he didn't like that one. Something stayed his hand from putting me into my place when I'd given him every reason to. I'd overstepped some bounds most definitely. I needed to watch my smart mouth before I bulldozed over him with my view.

That way, too, led to depots and villainry.

I took a breath and exhaled some of my piss and vinegar before re-starting. "Listen, I'm not here to be anyone's enemy or distraction. We all have the same goal. Stop bad guy. Girl. Whatever. I can kind of see why you suspect someone with evidence that only she can help decipher. But, I've done no harm to you people. You have no right to call me anything derogatory."

Magus obviously still didn't like me, but his posture relaxed and lips loosened. The narrowed-eyed gaze didn't change much. "I have the right to call you whatever crosses my mind."

Truth. Technically. I nodded, conceding the point. "I have the same. But, I'm a tad more inventive and have no reputation to uphold. I'm inconsequential. You have a whole group of men who look to you."

That implication widened his eyes right up. "You wouldn't."

"No, I wouldn't. Not unless pushed." I sighed. I was done with this whole thing. Threatening people wasn't my bag. It pulled me back to the blubbering mess I'd been in middle school before I found myself.

Magus wouldn't let this end until he had the upper hand. I didn't have it in me to wait for that to happen. I had to make the decision.

I dropped my butt on the couch. "Look, since your mind mojo isn't working on me at present, probably your best guarantee to keep my lips sealed would be some sort of contract." My fingers fumbled their way through untying my shoelaces.

"What do you mean by that?"

Quick glance up at him.

He'd managed to put on his pleasant mask.

Good. We were all friends again. Right.

Our relationship didn't matter right then. Big picture. Needed to focus on the big picture.

I kicked my feet up onto the couch and scooched all the way against the back of it. I didn't relish sticking to the leather. "Advisor. Resource. Consultant. Whatever term suits you better. You write it up and I'll look it over. Though, you should probably work on the 'give respect to earn respect' thing."

Sticking to the couch didn't matter when I finally lay horizontal. Bliss.

"What do you think you're doing?" His voice sounded closer.

I peeled an eye open. Yep. He stood right next to the couch. Looming over me.

Neet.

As he already knew the answer to his question, I considered ignoring him and letting go of consciousness. Sleep was only a matter of time anyway. "Pretty sure we discussed this."

"We're not finished."

I was. I rolled to my side, back to Magus. "We'll talk later."

"I could molest your sleep."

Didn't care anymore. "I trust you not to."

# 13 – CALL AND ANSWER

I NTERMITTENT BUT PERSISTENT ringing pulled me out of a dream I couldn't quite remember by the time I fully woke. Something about climbing stairs forever. The large, fuzzy, breathing warmth I was curled up against took most of my waking attention. That and the ringing. I patted around for my phone.

Hot, musty breath blew in my face. My eyes shot open.

Gorgeous jade-green eyes stared back at me a moment before the jaguar's mouth opened wide. Rows of teeth yawned threateningly at me, the tongue curling lazily.

I froze.

Must not freak out the jaguar.

Ringing continued in the background while I tried to figure a way out of this. One without my death.

The cat's mouth closed and he stared at me from inches away.

What did a person do in this situation? Soothing tones, certainly. "Uh, hello."

The tongue slipped out and swept me from chin to forehead. Great. Kitten slobber. Big kitten slobber. I couldn't wipe it away. Being rude to something with that many teeth was a no-no in my book.

So was letting a phone ring for that long. Didn't anyone work around here?

"No one's going to answer that phone, are they?"

The jaguar slipped out from under my arm by standing up on the couch before stepping off. It padded halfway to the entrance, stopped, and looked back toward me.

Invitation heard, loud and clear.

I nearly tripped over my own feet climbing off the couch after the cat. He waited until I'd come even with him to start walking again. We pushed through the bamboo forest wall, ringing gaining volume with each step through. I wanted to stab my ears with sporks by the time we made it into the hall. It might hurt more, but it would be quieter.

The cat loped down the bamboo lined hallway to the left. I charged after him, away from the glass lined offices and toward the front desk. The desk where the infernal ringing emanated from.

Coming into the office, I hadn't noticed the big red phone sitting on the smoothened wood. Cliché to the max, but the second light down on the phone flashed at me. This had to be a test of some sort, jaguar leading me to the phone and all.

Probably.

I cradled the phone to my ear before I figured what to say. I didn't know where I was but I knew the name of the organization. "Gold 4, How can I help?"

Good. Neutral. Open.

"Who is this?"

If this was such an emergency, perhaps asking who I was took more time than prudent. Arguing with him would take even more. "Greer Ianto at the front desk. What's the problem?"

"Oh, um." The man on the other end huffed twice. "We have zombies."

Not what I expected. Kind of wanted to scoff it off, but I doubted anyone who had this number would prank it.

I sat down on the counter next to the phone. The jaguar settled its chin on my knee. I scratched him behind his ear. Definitely a test. Definite maybe. Regardless, it was time to get my game face on. Rise to the occasion, and all that.

"How many zombies?"

"Two."

Not bad. Not as good as no zombies in existence anywhere in the world, but two could be contained. Shit. What a way to wake up. "Whereabouts?"

"Cherry Creek area. Came from the east, headed down Alameda but turned from the main road after the mall and heading North."

Not as good. Better than zombies roaming downtown, but the Cherry Creek shopping district had enough foot traffic for the situation to pull a Hindenburg in a relatively short time. I hated myself for answering the phone. This kind of thing was none of my business. Too late. "Okay. Are the zombies hurting anyone? Biting people?"

"Not yet." The man sounded hesitant. "They're just kind of shuffling along the sidewalk, bumping into each other and anything else that pops up in their way. People are too freaked out by them to let them close enough for a nibble."

Also good. "Follow them. Keep them from hurting anyone, however you need to, but follow them."

"Why?" He sounded so young when he asked. Maybe he was. If he was a little older, it might have been obvious to him.

I cast a guilty look down the hallway. Someone with the right answer should be coming along at some point. I couldn't have been the only person who heard the phone ringing. For the moment, though, I was all this guy had. "You can either figure out who is calling zombies to them or what their target is. Either way, it's more than you had before."

The jaguar purred against my knee.

"Where did they come from?" His voice crept a little up the scale.

Wow. This one must have been an intern or something. "That is something for you to find out too. Get the police on it if you need to while I pass the information up the ladder here. Then, send the info in."

"Where should I send it?"

Good question. "The same place you send everything else. Probably best to gather all the info into one bulk packet with as detailed and brief an explanation you can manage. Unless that's not the policy."

"You don't know the policy?"

"No."

Neither did he, from what I gathered in his tone. Of course, I had to find an excuse because I was the ringer here. "I'm new, so I haven't had the time to read over too much of anything."

"Don't let the man get you down," was his response.

The phrase seemed out of place for the moment. Flat. Almost as dead as bodies doing the curly shuffle down the street. I nodded to give myself more time to answer and still had nothing.

He saved me without knowing he did. "I'll keep collecting the intel and send it in."

"Fantastic." I nodded again, like he could see it. I needed to stop doing that. "Call back if anything else happens."

Gods. I was bad at this.

He answered, "Will do," in a voice that could have announced on the old superman cartoons.

I almost let him hang up before I realized I'd forgotten the most important thing. "I'm sorry, just so I can log it, what was your name?"

"Jas—I mean The Hound."

He had to be really new to make that kind of slip. If he was in the midst of zombie-ville, too many people could overhear him. Secret identities saved lives. And I knew too many of them. Probably part of the reason why Magus had turned sour on me after he couldn't wipe my mind.

"Excellent, Hound. Well, call back when you need more."

"Bye, Greer."

He hung up before I could return the goodbye, which was fine. I'd already repeated myself a bit.

"What in the hell do you think you're doing?" Magus stormed down the hall toward me, Kai, Phoenyx, and another man behind him.

My whole body jerked like I'd been caught with my hand in the cookie jar. I had to force myself to set the phone back in its cradle.

I didn't waste the breath asking what he meant.

Excuses would win me nothing. I chose to go on the offensive in the best possible way. "Hound called. Two zombies are shambling in Cherry Creek, heading north. No bites yet, nor attempts to bite."

Eyes dancing in anger, nostrils flaring in fury, Magus stepped to me. The impulse to shrink from him lessened when the cat press himself closer to me. My own wrath, I would take, but I would not allow the cat to get thrown into the mix. Hand planted firmly on his head, I do-si-doed around him so Magus would deal with me first.

"You'll be okay, bub," I murmured to the jaguar. "Let him deal with me."

Magus halted two feet from me. Not quite encroaching on my space, but looming within easy reach distance. "Who are you talking to?"

"Your guard kitten."

Magus' eyes dropped, and narrowed at the jaguar huddled behind me. He didn't say anything before his eyes came back up to mine. Anger hidden behind a calculating mask. "What did you think you were doing answering the phone?"

Telling him I answered it because it woke me would win me no love or favors. Different tactic was needed. "It rang for longer than it should have for an emergency."

"Doesn't matter. Everything here is classified, need-to-know kind of information and you don't need to know."

My mouth parted to call out his cliché, but I shut my trap before I dug myself further in a hole. "I just got enough of the basics to pass along, which I already told you. The rest, he's going to send."

Magus crossed his arms. "To you?"

I pulled my eyebrows down. "All I want to know about a zombie situation is where they are so I can be elsewhere. I'm assuming he's sending it here. I didn't ask for specifics. Just told him to send things where he usually does. Though I think you heard that part of the conversation, so you already knew that before you asked me." As much as that kind of thing pissed me off, saying any more would spark a louder conversation.

My phone rang. I jumped and hated myself for it. I'd had enough embarrassment for at least the next month.

As my fingers closed around my phone to pick it up, Magus barked an order at me. "Speaker phone."

I considered ignoring the order. He wasn't my boss or anything like it. But the refusal was a dick move. This conversation already had too many of those. My own included. I accepted the call and switched the sound to the speaker.

"This is Greer."

"Hello, Ms. Ianto. This is Officer Parker with the Denver Police Department. Did you report your car as stolen?"

"Yes, sir. I did. Yesterday morning around sunrise." A little relief oozed out of me when I realized it wasn't one of my friends on the phone. They had no kind of maturity and could tell when I'd chosen the speaker option.

"Good. Well, we found your car."

Finally. Something good in this gods-forsaken, shitter. "You did?" I asked because I had to, to believe it.

"Silver Volvo Station wagon with wood paneling, license SIN-667."

Yep. "That's me."

I looked up from the phone to see Kai lifting his eyebrow at me.

Phoenyx grinned a little. I shrugged. "It's not a vanity plate. Luck of the draw."

"I'm sorry?" the officer on the phone asked me.

"Nothing. What do I need to do? What is my next step?"

Garbled police radio noise came through the line. I waited, knowing that my car situation was not the most important thing going on in the world. It wasn't even the most important thing going on in the room.

"Two options. We're about to collect evidence from the exterior, fingerprints and whatnot. Afterward, we will tow it to the secured section of impound to open and test the inside before releasing it to you. If you get here soon enough, you can come open the car and let us collect the interior evidence without the tow."

It was more than I thought they would do. Of course, collecting evidence didn't mean it would be analyzed. Thousands of untested rape kits in the country spoke to this. "Where is the car?"

"Third and Detroit, in front of Creme n' Crepes in Cherry Creek North."

I looked to the men watching me and listening to my conversation. I bit my lip and shrugged.

Phoenyx rolled his eyes skyward and shook his head. "Ten minutes."

I touched the tips of my fingers to my chin then tipped them toward him, what little sign language I understood. "I can be there in ten minutes, if that's soon enough."

"That should be fine. I will see you when you get here."

The officer hung up before I could thank him or bid him goodbye.

"She cannot leave." Magus. Raining on my one-person parade before it even set out.

Gods. I pinched my lips against my knee-jerk, mouthy reaction. Saying much of anything would let loose the secret of Magus not being able to hypnotize me. Spreading that bit of knowledge sounded like a bad plan.

"I can bring her back after she's handled what the cops need," Phoenyx said, without questioning why I needed to come back.

It should have occurred to any one of them that I had already been there way too long. But no. And I wouldn't be the one to blow that whistle. Until I needed to.

Magus nodded. "Very well."

Balls. He accepted that a little quicker than I thought he would. I should have asked for more.

It would have been nice to get out of here for the reals. A little time out would have to do, apparently. I gave the jaguar a worthy parting scratch as I slid out from under him. I took the sandpaper tongue up my arm as a complement.

"Allll right." I clapped my hands and squeezed away from the desk, which meant wriggling through the wall of men who had boxed me in. Half way through, my butt got grabbed. I returned the favor, with a slap for good measure. Kai grinned.

I felt Phoenyx reach out to do the same. I swiveled my butt out of range and raised a threatening finger. "Don't test me."

He laughed, but didn't push that button when I started moving again. I appreciated it. I probably couldn't do much of anything to hurt him. Maybe throw cold water in his face. He had to have a weakness. Other than my boobs.

A mirrored door in an alcove between two trees split to reveal a regular-looking elevator. It didn't give me pause this time. We walked into the elevator shoulder to shoulder. The doors closed with Kai, Magus, and the other men watching us go. I wondered how many times heroes left this place to fight the bad people in the world. My chest warmed for just a moment's thought of what it might be like to be able to help people with such light hearts.

# 14 – THRILLER

THE ELEVATOR OPENED to a room filled with gunmetal grey lockers, echoes of men, and humidity. Grateful as I was to not walk through artificial winter, I was mighty confused. Phoenyx exited the not-so-normal elevator before I could ask him about it. I plunged into the locker room behind him.

At the first sight of a naked back, I dropped my eyes somewhere around Phoenyx's leather-clad derrière.

"Hey, Phoenyx, what's the deal?" A voice called out from somewhere to the right. "You can't bring your girlfriend through here."

"She's not my girlfriend." He said it in a tired enough tone that I couldn't even take offense.

It made me wonder how many times this kind of thing happened.

"She's prettier than the last couple you brought through." The same voice replied to Phoenyx. "You even have matching outfits."

Never had I lamented my choice of leather more. More than the matchy-matchy problem. Leather clad women in the locker room with men in all states of dress. Bad plan. Unless the woman wished to involve herself in an impromptu porno. Which I did not. Not today. Not with cameras. And not without hand-picking the men.

Hmm.

"Yeah," a lower voice added, pulling me out of my reverie. "If she's not yours, can I get a crack at her?"

"Try me and I'll snap your dick off." It was all well and good to have a superhero defend your honor, but it didn't matter much after the hero left. Establishing lines in the first impression was a must.

"Oh ho ho," the first voice replied. "Did you hear that? She threatened an officer of the law."

This was a police locker room? What the fuck with the crazy elevator connecting a bar, a hero hideout, and a police office. Not that I would have changed my response if I'd known, but the whole thing was weird.

"If it's out and I don't want it, you pull it out of cop vs. citizen and into man vs. woman."

A hand closed around my right arm and turned me around. Yep, cop. Mostly dressed, without the accessories. Soot-black hair, sea-blue eyes, and a smile a teen girl would swoon over. He would have been more attractive without the narcissism dripping down is blade of a nose.

"And what if I whipped out my gun first?"

"Then you'd be fucking a corpse, you sicko." I looked him down, then up. "Gross."

He fell into a belly laugh, echoed by the men near enough to hear my comment. Good. Belly laughter meant friends and not pieces of meat to be picked over.

"Let her go, Marco. We've got places to be."

Marco released my arm with a couple of harder than necessary pats to my shoulder. "You're okay, miss."

"No miss. Greer. Greer Ianto." I took hold of his hand and shook it to stop him from touching me all willy-nilly.

He shook vigorously, squeezing like my hand held the last of the toothpaste. "Travis Marco. Greer isn't a name you hear every day."

I did, but I didn't feel like sharing that punny laugh with him.

"If you can't remember that," Phoenyx started, "she also goes by—"

My free hand snapped over his mouth. I slipped Marco's grip and doubled my hands on Phoenyx's mouth. "Don't you fucking dare. We're leaving now. Go." I pushed him in the face, slow enough that he could move with it. His eyes danced at me over my impromptu muzzle.

"What was that?" Marco trailed behind us.

Phoenyx turned for the exit without answering him. Which was good. As he pulled the door open, he flashed me a smile that said one of two things. Either, he started to throw me under the bus to get me moving, or he planned to tell Marco later. The way cops gossiped, once one knew, the whole precinct would. It would only be a matter of time before the whole front range of precincts heard of SparkleTits the Great and Powerful.

Balls.

I might enjoy a giggle or two if the joke hadn't been on me. If I could find a way to rise above, the thing might simmer down enough to be old hat. If.

Phoenyx waved to several people as we passed from the locker room to the grand entry way. We weren't in just any police office. We'd popped into the Aurora City Municipal building with the courtrooms, bursar, and DMV. Upstairs held mysteries I didn't want to know about.

My stride widened as we crossed the stone mosaic of the Aurora City seal in the floor of the building's grand vestibule. Phoenyx fell in beside me with a curl to his lips.

I frowned. "What?"

"Now that Officer Fabulous isn't all over you, you want to move fast."

My eyes wanted to roll. I held them steady. "Groups of men are wily beasts. Especially cops. Come across as weak the first time, and they'll eat you alive every time thereafter. I'm guessing it's the same with you people." I pushed through the first set of doors and held it for him.

"I am not a wily beast." He pulled out the finger quotes on the last two words, before opening the second door for me.

"Tell me you don't poke and prod at a new guy to see if he can take it." I took the stairs down in twos.

He caught up to me with little effort. "That's different."

I didn't know where we were going, but I figured someplace away from the building would be a better launch site. Something in the parking lot perhaps, but not super close to people's cars. "How is that different?"

Phoenyx stopped. I turned around to face him. He curled a finger at me. Since he had no mischief in his expression, I came back over and assumed the prom-dance position.

"That kind of prodding has a purpose. On three."

He counted. We jumped. My feet still expected to land again even if my brain knew the drill.

"We work in high stress situations and you need to know how the people around you will react to things. Where their strengths and weaknesses are."

"Huh." That made more sense than I expected.

"It's not as if there's a training program to be a superhero."

There wasn't. Huh. "Shouldn't there be?"

He shrugged, which adjusted my grip on him a bit. He still held me solidly, but I reset my hands.

"When powers spring up, the guys are tested. Their powers are. Those with low level abilities or knacks, like heat resistance without being fireproof or super-fast nail growth, are monitored. Some are even helped with scholarships so they can get jobs suited to their knack."

Money would be nice, but something not so good hung in the air with that one. "What if they don't want to have their biology dictate their life like that?"

"If they only have a knack, they're free to do what they please, though, as I said, they are monitored by the local union for the rest of their lives."

Biggest Brother watching. "And if they have more than a knack?"

"They join the union."

"What if they don't want to?"

"They join the union. They don't have to assume the mantle and fight crime, but the guys join. No choice, really."

Yep. That was the ugly worm in the super-power apple. Forced enrollment into a club. Like the Jews with their arm bands. Different colors depending on the type of prisoner, but all had to be identified. Separated. Isolated.

"That sucks."

Phoenyx tipped his head left and right. "Yes and no. We have a more than generous—seriously large—salary. Benefits, legal and medical. You have someone you are accountable to when situations fall sideways, so the public doesn't vilify you as a lone unit. The union will protect your anonymity from the public if a guy chooses to live the quiet life, though he still pays dues. Brothers in arms, if you wish."

Something about what he said irked me.

"And what about the women with knacks or powers?"

He didn't answer for long enough that I switched my head around and leaned it back enough to see his face. A whimsical kind of smile tugged at his lips. A smile I didn't trust.

"What?"

"Watch your feet."

I did this time, bending my knees slightly to lift them while buildings rose in a haze around us at an alarming rate. Despite the initial speed, we landed with a soft touch. Years of practice. I straightened my legs and we let go of each other.

Phoenyx pointed behind me. "I believe that is your car." He started off in that direction.

"No, no, no." I hustled to catch up before he made it too far across the empty street. I didn't even check for cars. If they saw him, they saw me. "Not so fast. Answer my question."

"There are no women with super powers. Of any kind."

Huh.

I kind of begged to differ, but we'd reached my car. A couple of police officers stood on alert by it, while two other people put things away in to multi-compartmentalized carriers. The other two must have been the crime-scene people.

Phoenyx and I would continue the conversation later. Because I couldn't be the only one. True, I'd not heard of anyone else being struck by a fallen piece of sky. We didn't exactly broadcast that it happened to me, though. More had to be going on than what the general population was made aware of.

Since this was my car, I stepped ahead of Phoenyx with a hand out. "Officer Parker, was it?"

"Greer." He met my hand with his and gave it a decent shake. "We were about to give you up for dead and have it towed later."

I checked my watch. Nope. Only eight minutes had passed. Ten minutes wasn't even a time frame he'd given me. He'd only said soon. This was not the kind of argument one started with police. So, I let it pass.

He did not. "It's not that. We've been told to evacuate the area, so if you would just unlock it and go, I can call you when they've finished with it." Parker gestured to the people wearing something close to low-grade hazmat suits.

The two person CBI unit packed up the last of their things without acknowledging us. They stood and headed across the street.

After they rounded the corner, I had to ask. "Are they coming back?"

Officer Parker nodded, "When we get the all clear."

"What's going on?"

"I'm not at liberty to say."

Standard cop talk for, "Butt out, nosy."

Several things clicked in my head. I turned toward Phoenyx. "It's probably the zombie thing." I half mumbled.

"You did tell Hound to clear the area."

I did. I hadn't expected him to follow my direction, but I had been on the other end of what was probably a secret-ish phone number. He had no reason to think anything untoward was stirring. Having someone listen to me with something like that made me smile. In another life, I could be one of the cool kids. The behind the scenes, not forcing people to do my bidding, cool kids.

Officer Parker cleared his throat, bringing our attention back to him. "The CBI's are heading to a safe zone until the danger has passed. I cannot force you to leave, Phoenyx, but the civilian will need to clear out once the car is unlocked."

I couldn't argue that I wasn't a civilian, even if I knew about the zombie situation. I wasn't supposed to.

Phoenyx kind of fanned himself out, wider stance and arms folded loosely enough to make the top of him wider too. "If that is your concern, she is under my charge."

He was a rather big man. I wondered how often he used his size to intimidate the world away. Certainly less flashy than sparking flames everywhere. It probably reminded people that he had more than one way to fend them off.

"I was really hoping to get my car back today." I might not be able to drive it anywhere but Lex's, not before Phoenyx whisked me back to the superhero bunker. It would be worth it. One less thing to worry about. "If we waited for them to pass and the all clear, can I take it after the CBI get done with it?"

The cop's eyes widened at something behind me. "Times up. Unlock it and clear out. Or clear out and come back after."

I turned to see what had spooked him. There they were. Two honest to goodness zombies. Their pale skin had puckered around the edges. Eyeballs sunken in. The bloated bodies moved in uncoordinated fits and shuffles, like the puppet master had just learned to walk their new toys. The animated dead bodies could not be mistaken for anything else. No one could do make up that well.

A breeze ticked through the otherwise still air. A breath of formaldehyde wafted over us, chased by a wave of rotten stink. Dead meat stench clung to my nose and rolled around in my mouth. I'd never be able to eat again. I almost didn't care about the car at all, but I didn't want to have smelled this for no reason.

I coughed. "I'll unlock and we can go."

Phoenyx nodded. His flared nostrils said we were in the same boat.

Flapping my mouth made it worse. I slapped my lips shut, though the damage had been done. I would taste it forever. We needed to go.

The cops had started backing away to the other side of the street. Phoenyx's ownership of my well-being must have been enough for the two. Or they were chicken shits. Hard to say.

The key fob didn't unlock it. The battery must be completely dead. I flipped through my keys twice before I found the right one. Knowing how my luck was running the past day or so, I inserted the key gently and turned it with the same care. That's all I really needed to do, but I checked the handle to make sure anyway.

A wall of heat and flame slammed into me, picked me up, and smacked me against something hard.

Seconds passed while I self-assessed.

Back, hurt.

Front, hurt.

Delicate tickles of bleeding in my skin in more places than I wished to count. Later.

I moved my face around. Sore, but not crackly or bubbly. Just to make sure, I touched the front of me.

Face, passed fingertip inspection. No scrapes, gouges, or pebbles stuck in me. Grimy. Warmer than normal. I still had eyebrows.

I sat up and found my clothes aflame. Great.

My soon-to-be-bruised body protested an attempt to roll. I patted the front of me ineffectually.

Hands settled an inch above me and sucked the flames away. Phoenyx's eyes rolled over me. "Tell me where it hurts."

Kind of everywhere, but I didn't want to tell him that. Windows had shattered in the buildings across the street. I tipped my head back and found the same true on this side of the street. Pieces of car, my car, lay everywhere. Not just my car. Mine was the most completely splintered.

Someone yelled out in pain. Maybe they had been the entire time or they had passed out a moment before coming to. There hadn't been too many people here to get hurt. Not outside on the street. Except the two cops.

Balls.

My feet had some issue with finding flat pavement. Too many car pieces and broken bricks around me. "Help me up."

"You need to stay. Lie back down, actually." Phoenyx slid a hand behind my back and set one lightly on my shoulder.

"Phoenyx. I think I'm good."

Ish.

He shook his head. "You got hit face at point blank range with some sort of explosion. Just lay down and someone will come help you."

"Phoenyx. Mike. Do I look burned?"

He blinked a couple of times. "No." He sounded shocked. Like it hadn't occurred to him before I said it. Perhaps it hadn't.

"Except for my clothes. Score another one for mystery from the sky." I lifted my hand for a high five.

Phoenyx gave me a pathetic excuse for one. I grabbed a hold of his hand anyway. "Pull me up. I think the cops need more help than I do right now."

The last got through to him. He lifted me up without any more fuss. The world only wobbled a bit. Much less than my knees did.

Couldn't let either stop me.

Walking to the nearest cop, my legs wiggled like the first few steps on a tiny boat. I managed it and shooed Phoenyx toward the further cop.

Officer Parker's face hadn't fared as well as mine. Pebbles and glass stuck out of the skin. His uniform smoked a little, but nothing appeared to be on fire or smoldering. The shallow moan coming out of him didn't bode well.

I took his radio off his shoulder as I tucked my fingers under different parts of him to check for blood. "Hello, this is Greer Ianto using Officer Parker's radio. There was an explosion at 3rd and Clayton, where the missing car belonging to me, Greer Ianto, was found. Also, where the zombies were. Officer is down. The other one is too. Please send help."

Mumble-y bits sounded before someone addressed me directly. "Greer Ianto, are there any other casualties?"

"None that I can see." I gave another cursory glance around. "They'd cleared the street for the zombies to pass."

"What is Officer Parker's condition?"

"Shallow breaths. No bleeding around the abdomen." A gash on the inside of his left pant leg gave me worry. I moved cloth out of the way to find a shard of glass and blood oozing out in a frightful rhythm. "Shit. Artery. Not quite squirting out, but pulsing. I've got to take care of this, so I'm gonna put you down. Tell the emergency team we're right in front of the crepes restaurant and there are only four people out here right now. Should be easy to find."

"Hold on." The woman spoke some more, but I tuned her out. Bigger fish to fry, and all that.

I needed something I could turn into a tourniquet. His belt would be perfect. Taking it off would require jostling him more than I would like. It would probably take more time than I wanted to as well. Nothing nearby was strappy enough.

I patted myself. The charred skirt didn't have enough straps and wasn't long enough if I unzipped it. My shirt was more charred than the skirt. Holes had burned clear through to my skin below. The bottom of my bra even peaked through one of the holes. Bra. That could work. If it didn't, I would resort to direct pressure.

My phone looked no worse for the wear when I pulled out from where it had been tucked in my bra. Something to think on later. I set the phone on Officer Parker's chest with a, "Hold that for me."

"Sure," hissed out of him.

Not much. But it showed me he was still with it. He didn't reach for the phone, though. Probably, he recognized that moving needed to be kept at a minimum.

Reaching the hooks in the back proved easier than I expected. The hole in the back of my shirt helped. Maneuvering my arms out the straps took more time. Practice made perfect, though. The girls were free under my charred shirt and I was wriggling the strap under Parker's leg in no time.

"No, nonono." He tried to pull away from me.

I set my knee on his right hip bone and kept my fingers moving. "Officer, you're bleeding. People are coming. I'm going to stop the bleeding the best I can until they get here. You with me?" I raised myself up far enough so he could see me without lifting his head.

He tried to train his wide eyes on me. They swung around a bit more than I liked. He nodded at me, though. A clear, if shaky, gesture.

"Fantastic." I removed my knee to get a better angle.

My fingers met under his leg. I hooked my right pointer around my bra strap and pulled it just far enough to see on the right side of his leg. Looping the rest of the bra through the bit of strap moved smoothly. His blood all over my hands lubricated the motion.

I pulled my bra tight and it cinched around his leg like I wanted. Until my hand slipped. I threaded my hand through the free bra strap, and curled my wrist around. At the same time, I grabbed a hold of the radio I'd abandoned.

When I leaned back, Parker let out a guttural moan. Ugly, ugly sound, but it took more breath than he had when I first came over. Tiny wins would get us through this.

The radio barely stretched across his body to my half-reclined position. But it reached.

"Hello. Is someone still there? This is Greer Ianto back on the line."

"Greer. What is Officer Parker's condition?"

Pale and critical, I'd say. "I've stemmed the bleeding but it'd be good if the emergency crew brought some blood. Hey, Parker what's your blood type." I reached the radio toward his mouth as much as I could without releasing tension on his leg.

"AB. Positive." It took two breaths for him to get it out, but he managed and his eyes remained mostly on me when he did. Another tiny win.

Radio back against my mouth. "Did you get that? Officer Lucky here takes anything you'll give him."

"AB. Pos. Copy. Crew is a less than a minute out."

I wondered that I didn't hear sirens, but when I pulled my head out of the special moment Officer Parker and I were sharing, the noise pierced our happy little cloud. "You hear that, Parker. Rescue is nearly here."

His eyes slipped to half-mast.

"No, you don't." I couldn't reach his face to smack his cheek. Pulling in the bra to help me sit up bulged his eyes open again, which was good. Someone would ask apt questions about the nut shot I intended to give a man spilling his life's blood all over the pavement.

In a breath, our moat of isolation filled with people peppering questions. With other people there, I let someone else handle keeping Parker conscious. I gave the paramedics the quick rundown. A man with gorgeous golden hair pulled back in a ponytail took it in with a calm nod.

"You just keep holding on until we tell you," he told me, green eyes drawing me into his placid pool. "We're getting the IV in first, then we'll check on the wound. Okay?"

My hand had to be losing the same amount of blood flow that I was preventing in Parker's leg. But whatever. It wasn't my life and Captain Green Eyes could probably bring my limb back if I asked nicely enough.

They worked fast. I could give them that. Cut away the pant leg below my bra, flushed the wound out with a squeezy bottle, and came to the same conclusion I had. I let out an internal sigh of relief. Tourniquet was the Hail Mary of first aid, usually resulting in loss of limb. Femoral artery puncture meant loss of life, though. A limb wasn't worth a life.

"Okay, Ma'am," the woman told me without looking my way. "We're going to trade places. You release the tension and Miles here will keep the pressure, okay?"

The dark-haired man I'd mentally passed off the responsibility of keeping Parker conscious had switched places. He crouched above Parker, fist poised upstream to my blood-soaked bra. He looked ready. I needed to get there.

I turned back to Green Eyes and nodded.

He returned my nod with, "Ease it up slowly."

I straightened from my recline at his leg's expense.

"Good. Keep it coming."

I did, as much as I could from this angle. The woman snipped the bra between the cups. Maybe I wouldn't want to wear this bra again as remembrance of this day, but she could have asked me. Bras were too expensive to just be sacrificing them for someone else's leg that was obviously going to be fine.

Blood rushing back into my hand hurt. I pumped several fists while Green Eyes turned his attention to me for some reason. If more people hadn't come over to swarm the officer, I would have protested.

He lifted one of my eyelids to flash a light in. "How are you doing?"

"Fine." I leaned around him to see the paramedics shifting Parker to a stretcher. "Hey. That's my phone. He was just holding it for me."

Parker must have heard me over the commotion going on around him. He wrapped his hand around the phone and tried to hand it to me. He flashed me a smile as he did so. It gave me faith that he might make it out of this okay.

The distance between us was too great. One of his paramedics passed the phone off to me. I took it with a salute. Parker tried the same, but they shuffled him into the back of one of the trucks. I puffed out a breath of air.

Green Eyes flashed the same light into my other eye. "How are you? Where do you hurt?" He wasn't going to give up on this for some reason.

Okay, yeah. Explosion. I should be in pain. Sharp, burn-y pain. Not the achy, turn into bruise-y variety pulsing in me. Admitting that would get me the next express ride to the hospital. I couldn't shake the feeling that someone else might need the ride more than I did. Still, lying to the paramedics would win me nothing.

"I feel like I've been hit by a Mack truck, but not full on."

"Uh huh." He touched my throat just below my ear. "What hurts?"

Not enough for what happened. "Can you help me stand?"

"I think it's best you stay down."

I pinched my lips. He was trying to help. How to get him on board? "Listen, what was your name?"

"Tom Greenly."

That figured. "Greenly. I need to get up and move around so things don't stiffen from the aftermath of adrenaline dump and I don't go stir crazy from the same. I won't run away. I just need to stand and walk in tiny circles."

A line formed between his eyebrows. He didn't like it. But I spoke reasonably. I think he only relented and gave me his hand because we both knew I would get up without his say so.

Standing might have been a mistake. The air near the ground only held the aroma of concrete, burned things, and blood. Nice, clean, normal things.

The air at my head height walloped my nose with powerful funk. The rotting-meat stink that had breezed my way before my car exploded permeated the air, but now with a couple of stinky new friends. Cooked, rotten flesh and old, fishy goodness joined the fray. Fun. Except, not.

I coughed at the nasal violation, nearly doubled over to lose the lunch I hadn't eaten. Thankfully.

"What is it?" Greenly bent over to meet me at my level.

"Exactly. What is that smell?"

His lips turned down a bit, like he had only just noticed it. "I don't know."

Not good.

Medical people got to smell most of the bad things in this world. If they didn't know, it meant unknown things were afoot.

Again.

Wheee.

# 15 – FOOD FOR THOUGHT

AS MUCH AS I wanted—and didn't—to figure out the source of the smell, I'd promised Greenly to stay still-ish for his examination.

He palpated. I turned my head to the side and did my best to not grit my teeth.

"Well." He straightened to meet my eye, though his hands still tapped around my shoulders and neck. "You're not bleeding that I can tell, but you're warmer than I'd like. And there's this."

Greenly dropped his hand to my abdomen and pressed like a drill digging for oil. Breath hissed out of me while I tried to remember important things. He was a good guy. One did not kill the good guys.

He kept pushing until I stepped away from him, testing my conviction.

"Near as I can tell, you're a walking bruise. There may also be some internal bleeding."

Internal bleeding would have showed itself by now, between the time passed and the adrenaline.

He should know that.

A fireball dropped from the sky, saving us from me reminding him in the most direct terms. Phoenyx looked to the paramedics with only the slightest glance my way. "How's she doing?"

"She needs to go to the hospital."

Of course I did. So they could poke and prod at my sparkling skin. I needed a new subject. "Did you find anything, Phoenyx?"

He paused just long enough for me to sweat. If he didn't come on board with my topic change, I'd be in if for the long haul.

"A few more people with cuts from glass or shrapnel," he finally said. "Nothing more serious than the two we found. They did a good job of clearing the area."

I tried to not sigh my relief too loudly. "That's good. Serendipitous, actually."

The intensity of Phoenyx's gaze tripled. "It certainly was serendipitous."

Too much weight to those words. I didn't like the sound of it. A soft-shoe exit was probably out of the question.

My stomach growled. Loud enough for Phoenyx to pinch his lips at the sound. "How far is the Cherry Cricket from here?" A good burger would hit the spot and they were the best in Denver. Crepes would be good too, but the windows had the boxer-teeth thing going on. Nowhere near a full set. They probably wouldn't be serving for the near future.

Phoenyx narrowed his eyes at me, but only slightly. I suspected the mixed company for the lack of deeper expression. "I don't think many of the things around are open. Explosion and all."

I nodded. I got it. But. "I need something or I'm not going to make it much further."

The paramedic pulled out a packaged protein bar of some sort. I usually steered clear of the things. My stomach growled again to tell me who was in charge. I snatched the thing from him with the barest of thanks.

Whole thing shoved in my mouth, I closed my eyes. Bliss before I even tasted it. When it hit my stomach a few minutes later, my eyes rolled back in happiness again.

That was the good stuff.

"Greer?" Phoenyx asked.

I blinked my way back to the moment. "Yes."

He eyed me a few more seconds before a hesitant shift to the paramedic. "As no one else is in immediate danger, why don't we pull out of this crime scene so the cops can do their jobs."

That, I could get with. Especially if it meant eating a little more. Funk in the air notwithstanding, I was starving. Right then, I could have picked up one of the pieces of rotten-and-fish smelling zombies and started chowing down.

Phoenyx seemed to understand the black hole in my stomach. He air-lifted us to a restaurant right outside the evacuation zone.

The host at Elway's sniffed some at my smoking and holey outfit, but did not refuse Phoenyx. Benefit of being a superhero, I guessed. No burgers on the menu, but steaky-steak-steak with no wait.

Finishing my sixteen ounces and the sides only took the edge off. Phoenyx eyed me something fierce, but he ordered me another. When his intense eye contact didn't dim, I asked, "What?"

He shook his head. "Just trying to figure you out."

That made the both of us. But I had no reason to voice it.

"You aren't feeling weak in anyway?" He leaned forward on elbows planted on the table. "Ill, dizzy, anything?"

"Bruised and hungry."

He frowned, for whatever reason. What else did he want from me?

"Remarkable." He shook his head as he spoke.

That was more like it. Still. "What, exactly, is remarkable?"

"No one got hit more with the blast than you. You should be ripped apart."

While I agreed, I thanked everything holy and unholy that I hadn't been.

A phone rang nearby and it was not mine. Phoenyx answer his. I let him see to whatever he needed while I saw to steak number two.

He clicked off with a weary sigh. "Cops want to talk to you."

Naturally. Why wouldn't they? "Can I finish first?"

"Probably better if you do. I don't want you passing out while they talk to you."

A nap might have been nice, but not an impromptu nap in front of police I didn't know. Fainting woman at a crime scene. A cliché I did not wish to become.

"You should have desert too."

I could have kissed the man. I nearly did when I took the first bite of crème brulee. My stupid smile must have been on full blast by the time we made it back to the cops. Their frowns said they could use a steak or two. And a brulee.

"Greer Ianto?" the taller brunette cop asked.

As if there would be another person tooling around with Phoenyx right then. I nodded.

He lifted a disapproving eyebrow. "You want to tell me what happened?"

The informal question and anger bubbling just below the surface told me I needed to tread only with truth statements. "My car was stolen this morning. Officer Parker called a while ago, let me know they'd found it. It exploded when I opened the door. Not sure if it was rigged or if someone shot at it."

"No heat signatures flew at it before it exploded," Phoenyx offered. He would know.

I wished he would stop eyeing me that way, though. It might make the cop think there was more to this situation than there was.

"Do you have any enemies that you know of?"

That I knew of, not really. But there had to be something. This much bad shit didn't just happen to a person. Not in this short of a time span. "I don't know. I don't think so."

"No people at work who have a grudge against you?" He barely looked at me when he asked.

"Got fired, so I can't imagine anyone would seek me out. Anyway, the car was gone before I got to work to get fired."

"Family members?"

He had me there. "I'm fine with my brother. The relationship with the sister is a little rocky at times but she lives in Miami. Dad's dead."

"And your mother?" He looked up at me when he asked this one.

My omission must have sparked his interest. I couldn't weasel out of this answer. "Maybe. She's..." I hissed, trying to not to erupt in expletives. "We don't get along. She's in town."

"Address?"

"I've got name and number. You'll have to look the address up." I pressed my lips together a moment before adding. "Don't tell me the address when you find it unless it breaks the stipulations of the restraining order."

He lifted his eyebrow like he'd just found the thing to crack the case. I didn't think he had. Sure, my mother was a piece of shit, but I doubted very seriously she had this in her. If she could figure out how to rig a bomb, she probably would. And claim to be in fear for her life as she did so. But she lacked the kind of intelligence to learn bomb-making and she didn't have the money to hire someone.

Last I knew, anyway.

Also, she wouldn't do something like this out of the blue. Years and opportunities abounded for her to push the limits of the law. She had done nothing of the sort.

At this point, she wouldn't know what my car looked like. It had to be something else. Something recent that was out of the ordinary enough to have sparked this kind of retaliation. The only extraordinary thing that had happened recently, outside the cloud of bad luck misting around me, was meeting up with that odd, spiky woman the morning before.

The odd spiky woman who smelled like rotting and fishy things, just like the zombies had. The woman who had warned against revealing to people that I'd seen her.

Shit.

I'd kept my bargain. Either someone didn't believe I had or wanted to make certain I didn't lose my resolve.

Bomb more-than-threat meant I needed allies on my side who knew what I did.

Officer Parker's pained face trying to smile flashed in my head. Perhaps, the police were not the people to tell. I'd only end up putting them in danger they couldn't handle.

Lifting my eyes from this officer to Phoenyx found him still studying me. Phoenyx. Unscathed from the explosion, though his shirt looked a little worse for the wear. He'd be safe from whatever the chance meet-up with the spiky woman wrought. Probably.

# 16 – CONNECTING DOTS

I COULD TELL WHICH way the wind blew when we left the crime scene, so I called Lex mid-flight back to the police station.

"Hey, SparkleTits, what's the sitch?"

I would kill him whenever I got a free moment. Phoenyx laughed in chorus with Lex, but hurting him while he flew me through the air struck me as suicidal. His grip around me hurt enough with my undiagnosed bruising.

The best way to get Lex to stop, though was to distract him. "So, my car exploded and Phoenyx is— "

"Hold it. Your car expl—that was yours? The one on the news?"

Of course it was on the news. His question gave me a little hope, though. "Do they have footage of me at the scene?"

"Shit, Greer. Whose cornflakes did you piss in, or did you kill someone's child in a past life?"

"All good questions." Which I had no answer to. "But not right now. I just wanted to check in to tell you I'm fine, but things got a bit complicated."

"Your car exploding is just a bit complicated?"

Less so than most of the other things going on. "And I'm heading back with Phoenyx...to a place...to exchange information." There. That was sufficiently vague enough to keep all parties safe.

The other end of the line was silent long enough for me to prompt him. "Lex, you still there?"

"Yes. Too many things buzzing in my head all at once. Just. Hmm. Be careful. With the break in, the car exploding is...not a good sign. Like things are getting worse."

Maybe.

The car had been gone long enough that the thief might have booby-trapped it before the break-in happened. Lex's caution was well founded, though. Too much bad. "I got ya. But I am in excellent company, as far as safety goes."

"Their safety perhaps. Despite their best efforts, the lives of superheroes are riddled with casualties."

I cast a careful glance up to Phoenyx to see if he'd taken offense. He didn't look affected one way or another, which meant he'd hidden his reaction well. Could be good or bad for me. But he hadn't dropped me, so I'd take it as a positive sign.

The silence on the other end had a waiting quality to it this time. Lex wanted a response and would prod until he won the appropriate one.

"Warning heard loud and clear."

"Good. See you when I see you. Check in again when you can. And one last thing."

"Okay?"

"Get me a nice picture of the ass on one of those men."

I nearly choked on a laugh trying to swallow it. "I'll do what I can."

"See that you do, Babe."

He hung up the phone before I could respond. Not that I could think of anything to say while one of the nice-assed men in question had me pressed against him.

"Land." Phoenyx said it with no inflection.

We climbed up the stairs in silence and I had hopes that Phoenyx wasn't privy to at least the last bit of conversation. Then he pulled the door open for me with, "Does he want me to pose or would he rather a candid shot?"

No sense in being embarrassed for the good taste of my friend. "He'd take a calendar of different ones if he could get them. You offering?" I passed by him with solid side-eye.

"Are you the photographer?"

"That sounds like a trap I don't want to trip." I'd go for the candid shots.

Walking through the locker room from this direction was much more awkward than the other. This screamed intention. Intrusion. No cure for it but to keep lowered eyes to Phoenyx's heels and follow.

The playful mood in the locker room earlier had evaporated.

One man stopped Phoenyx in front of the door to the secret-ish fake elevator. "How bad is it?"

"I got hit with the brunt of the blast on the driver's side. Parker and

Thomas got some action, but the area had been well evacuated before so there aren't many other casualties."

Phoenyx completely glazed over my getting most of the blast. There weren't many people to refute him, two of them in the hospital being treated as we stood there.

"How are Parker and Thomas?"

The officer asked Phoenyx and I knew the question was for him, but I answered my part anyway. "They sewed Parker up. I think it was soon enough that he should keep the leg." I stretched my hands open. My blood-stained and blood-caked hands. The sight of them gave me the strength to look up at the officer asking the questions.

He had a hard look about him, all planes and angles, but his frown at me softened his expression. "Are you okay?"

We both knew he had seen more in his time. It was nice of him to ask.

"He was conscious when they took him. I had a hand in that." I shrugged like it didn't hurt and dropped my hands to my side. "I can't really ask for more at this point. How was the other guy?"

"A little rough for the wear," Phoenyx said, "but better off than Parker."

Good. They would both survive. Now, we needed to ensure no one else got caught in the crosshair of whatever I'd attached myself to.

"That's good to hear." The cop patted Phoenyx's shoulder a couple times and moved on to mine. "Thanks for the help out there today."

His pat had a little more force than was necessary. I clenched my jaw so a pitiful moan didn't escape in its wake. It would only lead to questions I didn't him to know the answers to. Right then, I could use a little less attention, not more.

"We should get going." Phoenyx finally said with a nod.

I gave the officer the same kind of nod and trailed Phoenyx to the elevator. My stomach waited for the doors to close behind us to make its will known. Or it had been yelling for a while without surpassing the ambient volume. Either way, I needed to feed the beast. Soon. The protein bar only calmed the hunger for the barest time.

Phoenyx chuckled next to me like this wasn't a serious situation.

"I'm going to warn you. I need food. Or it's going to get ugly. Soon."

"The protein bar? And the steaks?"

"Gone. And my will power to not hop on you and start chowing down is nearly gone too." I clenched my fists, mostly because I'd forgotten about the steaks that quickly. Something not right about that, but I'd consider over a meal. "Do you people have food in your hideout?"

He nodded. "Well stocked."

The doors opened to the now familiar forest-ringed reception room and we debarked. I took a couple of shorter steps so Phoenyx could lead the way around the reception desk. Magus stepped into our way at the head of the bamboo hallway, jaguar at his side.

"Report." He addressed both of us at the same time, treating me like a person and everything.

I appreciated it.

My stomach growled again, louder than any other emotion in my head. I pinched my fingers together to rein in the hanger.

"Sir." I gave him all the respect he'd just shown me and then some. "I will tell you everything you want to know about what just happened but I need to eat something substantial before I eat you."

Phoenyx let out a low, disapproving, "Greer."

Magus held his hand up to him. "I have more than enough experience with hungry animals to recognize that look in her eye. I will question you while you eat."

"Works for me. Phoenyx?"

He didn't take any further prompting to head down the hall, bless the man. "You need some medical attention too."

I waved that concern away. My tender midsection would need to be seen to. I didn't worry so much about a person they trusted to check me out. Not with my hunger blinders on.

We came nearly to the end of the bamboo before we turned left, plunged through the skinny trees again, and came out in a large dining hall. Larger than it should have been.

From what I remembered of Magus' office, this room could not have been bigger than a janitorial closet. Not with it sharing the space on this side of the bamboo-lined hall. This expansive room, with beautiful wooden tables spread throughout and television screens for walls, was not possible. Should not have been possible.

Said the girl with glowing skin.

Touché, Universe. Message received.

Currently, most of the wall panels showed a tropical beach somewhere. The news lit up the last, breaking reports about the scene we'd just left. Whatever. I had food to find.

Phoenyx hadn't lied about how well-stocked the kitchen was. Industrial fridges, several ovens and ranges. All stainless steel and dark granite, with a couple marble slabs dotting the surfaces. Beautiful. Gorgeous. Overflowing with food and dishes waiting to be cleaned.

# STARFISH & COFFEE

Men.

I nibbled my way through a couple of slices of fantastic sourdough while I made three sandwiches out of a slab of roasted beef. For good measure, I piled some roasted potatoes on a second plate.

The other three—jaguar included—did not partake. They sat near and under a table along the far wall. I grabbed a jug of juice and joined them.

No one said anything as I inhaled the first sandwich. The jaguar laid its head in my lap, but that was it. I drank half the juice and tipped my head back to enjoy the loss of the gnawing pain in my belly. One deep breath, and I opened my eyes to look at Magus.

He didn't look annoyed at any delay I'd given him, perhaps because the sandwich had practically disappeared. But, it was time to pay the piper.

"Friday morning, I dropped off clothes at the Hearts Open Wide near Colorado and I-25."

Magus' patient expression fizzled a little around the edges. I held up a staying hand. "I swear this relates. At least I think it does."

After a pause to study me, he nodded.

His placid welcome of me was much more superficial than I'd hoped. This needed to be fast. "I saw a woman outside the HOW, but she wasn't exactly a woman. Or at least, not human. She seemed to be a she-whatever. Hunched over, with hair that moved like tentacles. And the smell. Awful. Death and rotten fish. She warned me not to let on that I'd seen her. To anyone. Which I didn't. Even when my car got stolen, probably by her, and they asked if I had ideas of who might have done so."

Magus leaned a little toward me and narrowed his eyes. Not aggressive, that I could tell. I seemed to have piqued his interest.

I pushed on. "So, my car went missing, other things happened, and I smelled the same kind of thing coming off the zombies today."

His eyes shifted toward Phoenyx. "You were supposed to take her to her car, not to these supposed zombies."

"Same place, same time." He shrugged. "Which was probably a good thing. It'd already been evacuated by and large. Fewer casualties. Fewer witnesses as well, though the two witnesses we do have are cops."

I shook my sandwich at him. "Injured cops who will be on all the drugs for a while."

"Hmm." Magus brought his attention back to me. "Are you certain the smell coming from the zombies was the same as the woman?"

"Kind of hard to mistake it."

Magus touched his fingers to the wall-screen flashing the news at us. "Call Hound."

The news minimized upward, mostly replaced by a cell phone-like call screen. Three rings and the other end was picked up with a, "Yes, sir."

"Are you still on the scene?" Magus watched me as he spoke.

Not sure what that was all about.

"A little upwind, but nearby."

"Good. There are pieces of the bodies you tracked. Scent them then go to the Colorado Boulevard Hearts Open Wide and see if you can find a similar scent there."

"Any place in particular at the HOW?"

Magus raised an eyebrow at me. My cue, I guessed.

~ 191 ~

"In front of the donation doors." No one protested me speaking. So, I continued. "There should be some coughed up bloody mucus near the curb."

"Got it."

"Hey, Hound?"

The surface of approval dissolved from Magus' face once again. I would probably need to get used to that. At least until they wrapped this whole thing up. But I had to say this before either of the men cut me off.

"Be careful. That explosion wasn't an accident and I'm 97% sure its related to the zombies."

"Will do. I'll call back with any updates." He paused a moment. "If that's all, Magus?"

"Yes, Hound." Magus took back control of the conversation. "Turn your tracker on as well."

"Will do."

The screen went black for a moment before returning the news to its former glory. Magus still had his eyes on me. I let him work through whatever he needed to by shoving more food in my face.

A conclusion must have been reached. Resolve settled over his face and shoulders as he touched his finger to the wall again. It pulsed a little, something I must have missed the first time he did it. "Cinnabar, report to the kitchen. Bring your kit."

Ominous. I redoubled my efforts to fill my stomach without looking like I was doing so. He could throw me in the gulag if he wanted to, but not on an empty stomach.

# 17 – Hot Bod

"**D**ID YOU CUT yourself on the ceramic knives again?" Kai's voice preceded him into the kitchen. "I've told you—"

The sight of us at the other end of the room shut him up and made him move double time to us. The white bag over his shoulder looked large enough to hide half of me inside comfortably. All of me, if I didn't care too much about comfort or breathing.

"Where are you hurt?" he asked me and only me.

I could get angry about Kai zeroing in on the only woman in the room or I could be practical. Magus hadn't left the building. Phoenyx was a certified, unionized superhero. As nothing about him looked distressed, other than his clothes, I was the best candidate for needing medical attention.

Lying would win me nothing. Honesty it was. "Kind of everywhere and nowhere at the same time."

He frowned a little. "Let's try it like this. What happened?"

"My car exploded when I opened the door."

Kai blinked at me a couple of times. Then he looked to Phoenyx, Magus, and circled back to me. "Run that by me again."

"She doesn't have a scratch on her that I could tell," Phoenyx offered with a quick survey of my face. "She even has unsinged eyebrows."

He noticed that too. I'd thought it was just me. "So do you."

He shrugged. "Fire is kind of my thing."

It was.

"You're serious?" Kai's voice deepened in concern.

Why would I make this up, like this was a funny, ha-ha kind of joke? I swiveled away from the table and toward him, sandwich in the right hand, pointing at the front of me with the left. "Do my clothes look like I'm joking?"

"Greer." He took another step toward me, like he wanted to hug me but wasn't sure it wouldn't hurt me if he did.

Magus lifted a finger. "Samples first. Checkup second. The rest later."

Most of Kai's distress faded into a more business-like shade. "Right."

He set the medical bag on the edge of the table gently before pushing it more solidly into the center. The bag shoved my plate in its wake. I rescued the last sandwich before it got too far. He unzipped the bag, pulling out swabs and tubes. "Can we do this without the hunks of meat and bread?" He lifted a wry eyebrow and flashed me a saucy glance.

I had lettuce and cheese too. But that wasn't his point. "I kind of feel like I can't right now."

The flirt frowned out of him. "Keep it out of my way, then, okay?"

"Roger."

Kai sped through a dozen swabs in different locations. The ones on my face surprised me, but I hadn't seen what I looked like. Retaining my eyebrows didn't mean that I wasn't covered in soot and debris. At least I got Parker's blood off my wrists. Watching Kai work, I realized that my hands hadn't been the only recipients of it.

"Pretty sure that blood belongs to Officer Parker."

Kai's, "Uh-huh," sounded more professional than truly tuned in. He'd figure it out soon enough.

I grabbed his wrist when he gripped the bottom edge of my shirt. He looked up at me, question all over his face.

"Um." There wasn't another way to say it but to say it. "I kind of have a hypnoboob thing going on since the incident at Rust. Not sure how my belly effects people, or how close to the boobs it works from the underside."

His lips quivered a bit. I could understand the amusement. It would be funnier if it wasn't me. At least he didn't ask me if I was serious this time. I appreciated it more than I cared to show in front of the other men.

Instead, I continued my warning. "Best I can tell you right now is keep in contact with my skin and you won't be snared."

The smile won out on his face, triggering my own mouth to purse in annoyance. His, "I'll be careful," didn't do much to cool my reaction. The flirtatious curl to his lips as he turned back to his work helped. A little. Damned if the man didn't have lips that called out to be nibbled.

His feather-light touch sent shivers down my spine and erected goose pimples everywhere else. The deeper probing thereafter killed the butterflies. I hissed to keep from cursing, then cursed for good measure.

He frowned a little. "This hurts?" He did it again.

Oedipus Rex. "Yes. As much as it did the first time."

"Hmmm." He set his hands against my midsection with just enough pressure to stave off the shivers without hurting. His eyes slipped closed as he did so, then he shifted his palms outward from where he'd set them. "You're a little warm here."

"I don't feel warm."

He set a hand on my cheek and let the other settle on my knee. "You are everywhere, actually." He pulled out a thermometer and paused a moment before switching it out for one that read from the ear.

I waited. We all waited for the indicative beep.

"113."

That wasn't possible.

"That's not possible." Magus echoed my thoughts.

Kai turned the thermometer on himself and Magus, who both got normal readings. He tried me again, same thing.

"What about him?" I jerked a thumb at Phoenyx.

"He always runs hot." Lines sunk into the space between his eyebrows. Kai checked Phoenyx anyway. "108.4. Normal."

Normal for him. Perhaps this temp was the new normal for me.

"Damn, girl." The three of us turned to Phoenyx. He waited for it before he followed up with. "You're hot. Hotter than me."

"Shut up, Babe. I know it."

Stupid joke. But I laughed. Probably harder than I needed to. Much harder than I should with the soreness in my torso. Phoenyx joined me. The jaguar just licked my knee. Not the worst reaction. The other two just brooded for one reason or another.

Kai refocused his brooding into an intensified palpation of me, this time making sure to hurt me as little as possible. After he verified where I hurt he asked to take a blood sample. Usually, I was a big no-needle kind of girl, unless absolutely, absolutely, necessary.

Or for a tattoo.

This situation qualified as a necessary. I gritted my teeth, nodded, and turned away to brace for the prick.

Which wasn't that bad. The pressure of it didn't even make me flinch.

Kai's, "Huh," swung my head back around.

He held the syringe, what was left of it after the needle broke off.

"Tell me that didn't snap when you tried to poke me."

Kai looked up at me. "What do you want me to say instead?"

A pretty lie that didn't make me any more of a freak. I sighed, "Though that kind of thing *would* explain why an explosion didn't hurt me as much as it should have."

"Let me try this again."

I shrugged. The first could have been defective. The second was a pattern. I started to protest at the third. Anticipation a third time in less than three minutes had me sweating. This time Kai went slow instead of the typical quick jab.

The needle bent. He held still a moment then, gently, stretched the skin around the needle point with the other hand. The needle straightened. It hurt like a bitch. I kept my mouth shut about it as the little vial filled.

"I'll grab a few vials so we don't have to do this again."

Might as well.

"And I can grab a pint or two while we're here."

My forehead hurt at the force of my confused frown. "Why in the hell would you do that?"

He switched out the first full vial for a second without jiggling the needle in my arm at all. "Sometimes when things happen, the safest and best transfusion is one of your own blood."

His answer made more sense than most of the things that had fallen out of the woodwork today. And, while I didn't see the occasion arising for me to need a transfusion, my world was becoming a much odder place. "Better safe than sorry, I guess."

"That's my girl."

A new voice coming into the kitchen saved me from overanalyzing Kai's statement of ownership. Bolt's heavy-footed tromp pulled the attention of the other two from me. Kai kept his focus on my arm and stealing blood from me.

"We just received the latest message from Anterograde." Bolt didn't even blink an eye at me or at Kai sucking me dry. Nope. Normality had not been shaken in this house.

I mumbled to Kai, "Did you chose that name, or did she?"

"She did," Bolt swung his hips around the table to get to the wall near us.

"Lucky bitch."

"SparkleTits is a fine name," Bolt answered in such a dismissive tone, he might not have realized what he had done.

It didn't matter if he realized the misspeak or not. "Urge to kill, rising."

Bolt touched two of the panels and did some computer magick with the mini tablet he'd tucked under his armpit. Pictures filled the two nearest panels. From the corner of my eye, I could only tell that one was mostly blue and the other green with a little red.

"Along with typical threats of annihilation and mayhem, she sent these." Bolt scowled at the wall as if it had offended him. "She loves her stupid games."

"Games?" I asked Kai, because if he was going to take from me, he could give me a little in return.

He set the fifth and final vial aside to grab the collection bag. "She likes to send in images of the places she is about to strike, but the images don't make sense until the police are sorting through the crime scene photos. She uses a particular detail on something insignificant that you don't notice until you're analyzing everything."

Not information the public knew. Come to think of it, the public didn't know that chickie had a name. I knew too much for a civilian. I didn't dare look to see how Magus reacted to Kai spilling so many beans.

"I've run every image recognition I could. It's like the others." Bolt continued reporting to Magus rather than the rest of us. His words flowed in a way that told me he didn't remark on my presence much, if at all.

To avoid Magus's disapproval, I turned toward the wall panels with the pictures still up. The mostly blue one sparked a ping of recognition, but I knew the red and green.

"Horse on Chair?" I asked.

The three men stopped mid-conversation and stared at me. Kai's hands stilled on my arm.

"You know these?" Bolt asked. Not incredulous, as he might have been earlier. More baby-bird hungry.

"That one." I shook my finger at the blue-dominant photo, that had vertical slits with brown and black cylinders peeking through. "I know I know but I don't *know*-know. The other is Horse on Chair."

"What's Horse on Chair?" Magus asked, calm but commanding.

I looked from face to confused face. How did they not know? "You know. Downtown-ish, Capitol Hill-ish? The sculpture of the brown and white horse on top of the huge red chair? I don't know it's actual name, but that's one of the legs where it's bolted down."

"Are you sure?" Kai, this time.

I nodded. "My friend took me to a lot of the festivals in Civic Center Park when I was growing up, after my Dad died. That was a nice place to escape the sun for a few breaths." The friend who just died took me. But they didn't need to know that. "The red steel beam on a concrete block in the patch of grass is a dead giveaway."

Bolt's neck practically squeaked as it rotated back to the wall displaying the photo. "I'll be damned."

"What about the other one?" Calm and commanding tone from Magus again. Probably a good one for him to take when shit started hitting fans.

I squinted at the thing, as if that would help. That only sharpened how one saw. It didn't help if the available image was taken to confuse people. I chose a different tactic.

After cleaning the hand not in Kai's clutches, I pulled up the internet on my phone. Denver Civic Center Art. Image search. And I scrolled. Through several pages. A picture of the newer, crumpled-paper-design Denver Art Museum building struck me. If Ol' Scrapy Voice wanted to do a thing, and her first photo featured an outdoor sculpture, perhaps the other was too. Or had something to do with art.

Scrolling through a couple pages of Denver Art Museum results brought me something. Almost a side note to the angular mangle of a new art building. A sculpture that had never been my favorite. Anger fueled my recognition and I searched for the giant dust pan in Denver. There it was. Blue pan a story high with a broom to match, brown and black bristles.

"Ha!" I spun the phone around so Magus could see.

"What is this?"

"Giant Dust Pan. Not sure of the name of this one either."

"And, where is it?"

I quirked an eyebrow at him. None of the other men answered, so I assumed they were equally clueless. "You men need to get out more. This is right in the shadow of the crumpled-paper art museum building."

"The what?"

They seriously needed to get out more, but I needed to learn proper names of things. "The newer art building they built across 13th from the old art building with the singing sinks."

Magus blinked at me. Perhaps the singing sinks had been too much information. I continued, without prompting this time. "Anyway, both are down in the same area. Giant Dust Pan is not even a five-minute walk from Civic Center and the other is along the street surrounding it."

He nodded, almost like he didn't know how to take me, but he appreciated the help. "Bolt, run up a list of potential targets, both people and business. Split between more and less likely to be hit based on the pattern, but don't leave off anything."

A memory jumped into the forefront of my head. I clamped my hand over Magus' closer one. His lips pinched some. I didn't care. Not completely.

"The Taste of Colorado is this weekend, isn't it?"

His eyes shifted to Phoenyx, who confirmed. "Yes, it is." He sounded as excited about it as I was: not at all.

The potential damage that could be done. If the drinks were contaminated, if the lights on the stage were bright enough, if her injectable could be pumped into the air. All this assuming a bomb wouldn't be set off, or zombies reanimated to run amok into the crowd. I pulled my hand back so I wouldn't squeeze Magus' to death.

"Bolt?" Magus said.

"On it." Bolt pressed a few things on his mini tablet and the walls flicked back to a continuation of the beach and the news. He left the room with the same kind of determination he'd entered it with. Of course, since he could move in a bolt of lightning, perhaps this was his easy, cruise speed.

The persistent burn in the crook of my elbow spiked then dropped to nothing but the pressure of Kai holding a cotton ball to my skin. "Hold that, will you?"

I did, marveling at how much better the world could get by simply removing a needle. The initial poke was supposed to be the hardest part. Something else to analyze once I had my wits about me.

Kai wrapped me in purple tape before he stood over me and told me, "Don't move."

The order coming from him made me want to defy him just to see the reaction. I could totally get with an angry Kai. Now wasn't the time. Not with this audience and not with everything on me tenderized. He came back to the table with a glass of juice and two pints of ice cream.

I took a sip of the bitter salty nothing beverage and held it back out to him. "No, thank you."

He shook his head and pushed the glass back to me. "You've already gone for the meat. Good protein. Good iron. You need to replenish the salts and fats as well. The powder in the water will help with that and reduce the soreness you'll feel tomorrow."

"Chocolate milk helps with that."

He nodded. "True. This is better and helps stimulate your blood production, since I took some. But if you finish the water and a pint, I'll get you the milk. Choose your poison."

One of the pints of ice cream had banana in it, so I took the other, still uncertain how to deal with being drained and slipped supplements. But I trusted them, even Magus. Under Kai's watchful eye, I downed the bitter, salty water. It just got worse the deeper in I got. I chugged it all and handed the glass back to him.

"Ugh," I shivered. "The tears of my enemies should taste better."

Kai quirked his mouth to the side and handed me a spoon he Houdini-ed from somewhere. "Eat your damned ice cream."

It was hard to be angry at him with that kind of order coming out of that kind of mouth. Glaring at him for all I was worth, I flipped the lid off. The heaping spoonful I shoveled in my mouth drew a different kind of smile from Kai. I nearly choked.

"When you're finished treating her, and she's finished eating, take her home."

That was enough to draw my attention from Kai to Magus. Home. That easily. With no fuss from him. This was a trap. There was no other explanation.

He shook his head. "For the moment, it is more beneficial for you to retain your knowledge. We'll be keeping a close eye on you, but it's getting late and you have somewhere to be in the morning."

Shit. I did.

As hard as I would fight anyone who wanted to bar me from the funeral, the little girl in me wanted the excuse to not face the music.

Kai passed his healing hands and attention all over me a little more thoroughly than necessary. Perhaps my distaste was more a function of the focus lacking the barest of flirtation. I should have been happier he didn't take advantage.

The other men trickled out of the room as Kai worked. Only he, the jaguar, and I remained when he professed me healthy enough to be discharged. I just needed to not leave town all willy-nilly. Worked for me.

"You sure won Magus over." Kai zipped the last of his pack away. "How'd you manage that?"

I shook my head. "I'm useful right now. It's a big difference."

# 18 – BETTER NEVER THAN LATE

THE SHARP NEW keys to my apartment from the leasing office disturbed the calm I'd held tight to for the last day. In a world of zombies and exploding cars, the violation of my apartment was a pittance. Almost unreal. Insignificant. Stepping out of Kai's car in the parking lot swiped away the lies I'd been telling myself.

It did matter. Even if it only mattered to me.

I shouldn't have insisted Kai stop off here before taking me back over Lex's. What had I been thinking? This was too much on top of everything else.

"You vindictive bitch," a voice yelled from the left of me.

Familiar voice.

Turning toward it confirmed. My ex. Charging toward me like I stole something. Neet. I did not need this. Not now. Not ever again.

Too late. "What's that supposed to mean?"

Kai came to stand at my shoulder. Solidarity without pushing me behind him. I appreciated it. Chad slowed to a stop a few feet in front of us, face red and muscles noticeably tight all over his body.

"You change the lock a blink after I move? Like I wouldn't have forgotten something and need to come back."

That was his beef? I cast a glance sideways to Kai. He had his eyes on me, but he looked relaxed and ready for whatever came. He lifted a questioning eyebrow. Whatever his question, I shook my head. "The only thing you forgot was how to end things like an adult rather than a scared little baby."

"And I should really care about your judgement of right and wrong?" He waved his hand in Kai's direction. "You've already shacked up with this meathead, you whore."

I gave Kai the down and up survey. He didn't look like a meathead to me. Trim. Nerdy without the glasses. Beautiful ebony braid hanging down his back that I wanted to wrap my fist in.

Kai smiled like he knew what was on my mind, but he turned his attention to Chad. "I've not had the privilege. Yet."

"Like I'd believe a word from either of your whore mouths."

"Believe that I will enjoy her fucking me, when she so chooses." Kai kept his voice low, riding the line between intimate and menacing.

I'd enjoy that too.

Later.

Chad sputtered, trying to come up with a response.

"No. Aside from the fact that you slipped out of the apartment when you knew I'd be gone and broke up with me via text and therefore have no right to be jealous or even curious about what—or who—I choose to do." I took a breath and shrugged. "I'm tired and he has to get back to work, so let's just cut to the quick. What did you leave in the apartment that you think is yours?"

He glared at me like it might pop my head off, then answered. "Some things in drawers, in the laundry and bath room. The television."

Naturally. I wanted to be angry, but I was tired. I just wanted this done. This whole conversation would help ease me over the loss of our relationship even more than his chicken shit exit from my life.

"Come on up, then."

He blinked, surprise slacking his face. It kind of made me happy. I could be the bigger person and make him feel that much more of a twat.

"Are you certain?" Kai asked lightly.

This did put him in an awkward situation, the encounter with the recently broken-off ex. The hesitation was understandable. "Yeah. He can salvage whatever he wants."

I started toward the stairs and Kai took hold of my hand. I needed it so much right then, a frog caught in my throat and I couldn't look at him until we were at my front door with Chad standing behind us. I beamed a smile Kai's way as I released his hand to open the door. "Thank you."

"Anytime."

"Oh, get a fucking room, you disgusting, two-timing—" Chad's roll of fowl speech cut off in a guttural gulp.

I didn't look back to see what happened. If I looked, I knew and if I knew, I was liable for the situation. The low, muttered threats that followed were also none of my business. No matter that they warmed the cockles of my heart. Blinders on, I stepped inside my still ruined apartment. Would that the rest of my things could be replaced as easily as my keys.

Inside smelled of stale piss. Shit. I should have cleaned things up better the last time I was here. My brain couldn't at that point. Now, my nose didn't want to.

"What the hell did you do, you vindictive—"

Both Kai and I whipped around to face Chad, who looked like he might pee his pants. He snapped his mouth clothed, but his eyes burned in fury.

"What I did is get burglarized." I rubbed the bridge of my nose. "Salvage anything you can, but run it by me first. I didn't exactly get to see what you took with you the first time and now there's no telling what's actually missing and what isn't."

"Greer, I— "

"Save it. It's done. I'm done. We're done. More important things to tend to." I swiveled toward Kai so Chad wouldn't see my lips quiver at the edges. "Watch him for me."

Kai nodded and, over Chad's protesting, said, "As you wish."

I blinked and turned away from him because I was a coward. But beating myself up would need to wait. I didn't want to let the sadness that had seeped into my apartment do the same to me. I needed to grab more clothes and leave as soon as possible.

The garbage bags hadn't been touched, as far as I could tell. My piles of clothes in the bedroom hadn't been touched since I'd last seen them. They also reeked. They were the source of the stink of the house, that and the mattress. I would make the bastards who did this pay.

If I'd had the money to replace everything, I would have chucked it all and started new. For the moment, Lex had a washer. I would reclaim, wash, and rewash. Later. The closet looked undisturbed, so I bagged up the lot of those to take. I planned to wash them again too.

"Holy shit, Greer," Chad said as I came out of the closet.

I hadn't noticed him on my tail, but Kai was close enough behind him that I didn't worry.

"They really did a number on this place, didn't they?" Chad said it like we were in the same place we had been a week ago.

What tied me to this man for so long? I stared at him, disgusted at the whole affair. So much potential. And we threw it out the window. "You did to."

He frowned. "That's cutting below the belt."

"You already ripped me to ribbons." I shrugged like it didn't matter to me anymore. The motion hurt more than it should have. "Kai, I think I'm done for today. I have pictures to send to insurance and I'm hoping to get some decent sleep tonight."

"Yeah, right." Chad, the peanut gallery, sneered at Kai and I. "Sleep."

I could have been the bigger woman and let it go, but I'd already done so in letting him in. "Get the fuck out my apartment."

"I'm still on the lease." He smiled, wide and proud.

Kai took a step. I lifted a hand to stay him. I had this. Things didn't need to get violent. If and when they did, I would be the one to shoot first. "You are, but you sent a text ending it and moved your things out conveniently before the apartment was broken into."

Why hadn't I made those connections before? I crossed my arms and glared at Chad, daring him to lie.

His eyes widened, mouth hanging ajar a moment or two. "How could you think I would do something so...so..."

"You have no idea of what I'm capable of. Right now, neither do I." I took three steps toward him, only leaving a foot between us. "Now, move."

He flinched, though he tried to hide it and stand firm. I didn't even care. It brought me neither joy nor sorrow. Just another thing in my way today.

Violence boiled in my belly, but I forced myself to pull my phone out and dial emergency.

Apparently, Chad believed I was bluffing. Right until the cops showed up.

Chad exploded, yelling and arms waving. Kai clamped a hand on my shoulder to keep me grounded or hold me back from crushing Chad in the palm of my hand. Both were necessary. I filled the paperwork out for yet another police report. At this point I was a pro. Still, I decided against pressing charges. Doing so would only lock me into a legal relationship with Chad. Neither of us needed to linger over the dying embers of us.

A couple of officers escorted Chad while another held me back, eyeing me for all I was worth. I waited. He would come at me when he needed to.

"Do you work at Shepard Insurance?" He asked it with his eyes still narrowed, like he expected to catch me in a lie.

"Not any more. Got fired Friday morning."

His lips pursed. "Mmm-hmm." The warmth in his expression dropped to winter tundra levels.

"If you don't believe me, you can ask them. They have the paperwork there. And a box of my stuff I couldn't cart away right then." Yet another thing I needed to do. Perhaps tomorrow after the funeral someone could take me there to pick it up.

The officer pulled out his note pad. "And when did you leave there?"

I didn't like his tone. Something was up. "Not sure exactly. Cop drove me there. Left fairly soon after. Went to the Denver Art Museum after that. The regular building, not the crumpled paper one."

"And then?"

He wanted a recount of my day off the record. I'd given him about as much as I was willing to.

"What is the purpose of this inquiry?" Kai asked before I made it there.

Something told me the officer wouldn't have reacted to my question with the same respect he seemed to give Kai.

Rather than deflect, he answered. "A little after two on Friday, someone shot up the place."

My hand leapt up to cover my mouth from the gasp. It wasn't possible. But neither was anything else this weekend. "Did anyone d— How many people got hurt?"

"There were no survivors. An incendiary device was also used. Possibly more than one."

I dropped into a crouch and covered my face with crossed arms. "Shit. Shit. Shit. Why? Why the fuck is this circling around me? Is it my fault? Did they die because of me? Am I the reason they're all dead?" I lifted a pleading gaze to Kai.

I wanted him to lie. I wanted him to tell me that I had no part in it. I wanted him to tell me no one had been killed.

He crouched down next to me, golden eyes drawing me in, but held back from touching me. "The only people responsible are the ones who committed these murders. And we will find them. And we will bring them to justice. Okay?"

"What does it matter if justice is served?" I covered my face back up. "They'll still be dead. And it would still be my fault. Not directly, but they died because they knew me."

A hand settled on my back between my shoulder blades. It rubbed tiny circles into me. I willed it to be comforting with middling results. Too many faces of people who did not go home to their families.

"We're going to need you to come down to the station and give a statement."

Yup. That sounded about right. And he couldn't wait for my breakdown to pass before he dug into me. Best time to strike, really. You could find out all kinds of things. I wasn't prepared for an onslaught from them as well.

"We'll get that bit." Kai's hand paused on me a moment before resuming the circles. "We can pass the interview on to you. The information we have clearance to pass to you."

Footsteps left my epicenter of freak out. The door closed to the right of me. I peeked below the wall of my arms to check. No feet but mine and Kai's.

One less thing to worry about.

"Listen, Greer." He set his hand on my shoulder for long enough for me to look up at him. "That kind of thinking, the taking blame for everything that goes wrong in the world, it will be the death of you. It's dangerous and not true. Not until you pull the trigger yourself, or construct the bomb with your own fingers."

I heard what he said, "But—"

"But nothing. Come on." He hoisted me back up to vertical. "Let's grab what you need and keep moving."

What I needed was people to stop dying, stop getting hurt around me. Anything else paled.

My feet stuck in place and I couldn't find a reason to get me moving again.

His hand slipped under my elbow, voice soft at my ear. "Come on, Greer. I got the bag you stuffed. Let me take you away from here."

The gentility pulled me out of my blank stare to look at him. Kai's lips stretched into the approximation of a smile. The eyes watched me, sad and careful, like the wrong move might shatter me. I didn't know what to do with a look like that, but I did know one thing. If someone could show me that much care, I might have done something in my life to deserve it. Not recently, but some time. And if I could do so once, I could again.

Such a tiny ember of hope deep in the pit of me, but it set me in motion again.

# 19 – GREEN EYED DEVIL

L EX'S DOOR OPENED as I raised my key to unlock it. He had me in a bear hug before I could caution him against it. My breath wheezed out with the force. My poor, sore torso.

It took several tries to make my, "Lex. Please," audible enough for him to release me. Perhaps he heard and hadn't cared. I had to hold my sides a bit once he let go.

"I know you were fine, but I was worried sick with the explosion and Phoenyx was sighted and who is this?" Lex's tone slipped out of panic into the warm bath of interested inquiry. Funny how quickly the switch flipped.

"Can we come in first?"

He practically jumped out of the way, eyes wide to take it all in. I didn't swing back around to check, but I knew him well enough. He held the door for us so he could get a nice long look at Kai's backside. Rather than begrudge Lex the fine view, I led the way toward the heavenly scent billowing out of the kitchen. Onion and garlic and tomato-meat goodness curled around my head.

The timer on the oven ruined my dreams of diving into something magickal. "How long have we got, Lex?" I asked him despite the timer that had just ticked under ten-minute mark.

"Fifteen. Meat's gotta rest, you know." He stared at Kai. Almost to the point of glaring, except for the drool trying to escape the corners of his mouth.

Arms crossed, I leaned against the counter next to Kai. Lex would never forgive me if I ruined his line of sight. "Lex, you're breaking my heart."

"Waited as long as I could while I hoped you would come home." He crossed his arms, either to mirror mine or to keep his hands from wandering embarrassingly. "And you didn't tell me you were bringing *that* home. I would have made more."

I bet he would. "Lex, this is Kai. Kai, this is Alexander Lexington."

Hands were shaken. Lex certainly let the shake last longer than standard. I pinched my lips to keep from smiling.

"I can't really stay." Kai's gaze slipped from Lex to me with a little more intensity than I expected. "Just here to drop her off. I am still taking you tomorrow, though, correct?"

I nodded mutely with the shift in subjects.

"What time should I pick you up?"

"Service starts at noon. Fairmount. Viewing at ten. I kind of wanted to get there a little beforehand." I'd had the time in the hospital to myself. I just wanted a little more.

"If I'm here at nine, we can be there around 9:30."

"Sounds..." Good didn't feel right. I couldn't think of a word to fit.

Lex cleared his throat to pull my attention to him. "I thought I was taking you to the funeral."

He was, or he had been.

"Because of recent events we thought it better that she has an escort from the local Gold 4." Kai's gaze captured mine again. "I should get back."

That was a damned shame. But he had bad people to catch.

I, on the other hand, needed a shower. Alone, unfortunately. The front of me still stunk of char and explosion. "Let me walk you to the door."

He didn't protest.

I wished he had.

But he didn't let me move too far from him. He matched my pace toward the kitchen door. "Chad was your only boyfriend, right?"

I furrowed my brow without turning his way. "Yes. Why?"

"Your friend has been glaring at me since I first walked in with you."

A giggle escaped me. I couldn't help it. When I covered my mouth and turned back toward the kitchen, Lex had moved to continue his vigil. He had the decency, at least, to grip the doorway rather than follow us and get grabby.

"Lex?"

He took a long blink before he shifted his attention to me. "Yes, m'dear?" His voice had dropped into full-on charming devil.

This had to be nipped in the bud.

Eyes locked with Lex, I pointed to Kai. "Mine."

Lex's eyebrow quivered. "What?"

"You heard me."

He moved to the center of the doorway, hands on hips. "That is not fair. He is gorgeous."

"I know that." I wanted to peek at Kai to see how he was handling this conversation, but I thought it better to finish first. "Come on now. You remember Elissandro and Marcus and Derek."

His gaze dropped a moment and a smile crept over him. Cat with cream.

I nodded. "Exactly. My turn."

"But he's better looking than the rest of them."

I lifted a shoulder. "I agree, but the only reason I haven't had him already is bad timing. The worst timing."

"Are you willing to share?" Lex leaned to the side like I blocked too much of his view of Kai.

"That is entirely up to him."

An arm curved around me. Firm grip, but not enough to agitate my bruised body. Lips pressed against my neck and curved. "No sharing."

The hot breath along my clavicle sent assassins to take out my knees. Holding me against him, he laughed, the wicked man. I would make him pay for that. And a lot of other things. Until he had credit and I owed him.

"I am so pissed at you right now." Lex licked his lips, catching well-warranted drool.

I had to be the one to put on the breaks. Lex wouldn't look away and Kai seemed hell-bent on keeping me up half the night with thoughts of him. The kiss he left me with would certainly haunt me.

Lex stood with me at the front door to watch him walk away. "That is a definite upgrade."

I hated to say it, so I didn't. Though I agreed. "He was part of why I almost didn't make your show."

Lex hugged me tight before pulling me back inside with him.

He left me trailing after him back to the kitchen. "What was that for?"

"For loving me enough to give up *that* to come support me."

I kissed his cheek. "Postponed. I'm not crazy."

"That's my Greer."

Despite the fabulous meal Lex had prepared for me, I had a hard time getting through it. My eyes drooped before I'd half finished. By the time I finished my third helping of the peach cobbler I had slipped well into the slow-motion head banging of an exhausted baby. When Lex shooed me away from the dishes, I didn't protest.

The alarm woke me almost before I remembered laying down. My awkward sprawl in the charred leather told me I might not have chosen to sleep when I did. Sat down to take a load off and that was all she wrote.

I moved a little easier getting to the shower than I had to the bed the night before. The shower massaged out the rest of the kinks. I felt almost like a person as I slipped my dress over my hips. Bacon and eggs tickled my nose as I came out the bathroom, holding the dress to my shoulders. Lex didn't miss a beat with breakfast while he zipped me up. I had a plate piled high in front of me as I sat down.

"I didn't know if this was a too-upset to-eat-much kind of day or a need-to-eat-my-feelings-and-fuel-up-for-the-day kind of day." He poured me a glass of juice. "I erred on the side of too much."

It smelled divine. "Option 2. You keep doing this kind of thing and I may never leave."

He chuckled over his coffee cup while he watched me moan over the first forkful. "You can stay as long as you like."

If he kept feeding me like this neither of us would have a choice. I'd grow too large to fit through the door.

The doorbell rang with me halfway through my plate.

Lex straightened like something electrocuted him. "I'll get it."

This was his house, so it really was up to him to answer the door, but we both knew who rang the bell. Which is why I kept to my plate while Lex bounded toward the door like a gazelle.

"We're just having breakfast," Lex said as he led Kai into the kitchen. "I can fix you a plate."

Kai managed to sound gracious with his, "No, thank you."

I smirked at the two of them. "You're early." By five minutes, but early was early.

He nodded.

"I like that in a man." I couldn't quite bring the right flirtatious tone to it this morning. No matter how good he looked in his suit. Long hair pulled back in its usual braid. Charcoal suit. Light gray shirt. Tie a stark black contrast to the rest. Not flashy, just cleaned and polished.

His smile came warm, not heated. "Yes, you will." Not over heated, anyway.

My head tilted too out of sync to give him the correct response. I nodded to him then applied myself to the last of my plate.

"I like a woman with an appetite."

I smiled at my plate rather than at Kai. It widened more at Lex's muttered, "Bitch."

"Hey. You watch it."

Lifting my gaze, I caught the last of Kai wagging a finger at Lex.

"He made me bacon." I slipped off the stool and walked around the two of them get to the sink. "Bacon wins a lot of leeway."

This time, Kai muttered. "Note to self."

Much more of this kind of thing, and the two of them would join forces. I couldn't decide if it would be a good or bad thing. Then I remembered Lex's new favorite nickname for me. I plucked a couple more slices of bacon from the pile near the stove and planted a kiss on his cheek on my way past.

"There's a pint of your favorite ice cream in the freezer for when you get back home."

How could a person not love this man? I came back to give Lex another peck on the cheek before I started crying all over everything. That would be for later. "You're amazing."

"So are you, SparkleTits."

And just like that, all the warm fuzzies exploded.

Like my car.

I snarled at him, snatched all but two of the remaining bacon, and stomped my way out the room. All to the soundtrack of his raucous laughter. With all that had happened to me, no one would question me snapping and killing the world. Except that I had bacon. Hard to snap with bacon.

# 20 – Uninvited Guest

I HATED FUNERALS. MY stomach dropped to my soles at the sight of the same mausoleum looming over me. Gabe knew this would be hard on me. He also knew I wouldn't let anything stop me from being here.

The viewing and service were to be held outside, thankfully. Gabe and the podium under a beautiful oak tree with the chairs set out in a wide swath in front of it. The sunshine greeted us, breaking up the chill from the night, promising brighter tomorrows than this one.

A man in a dove gray suit with a tie and pocket kerchief in matching dusty rose came toward me. He reached a hand out to me and I took it.

"You must be Miss Greer Ianto." Despite his age—he looked barely old enough to vote—he had the soothing tones of a seasoned funeral director.

Must I? "Yes."

"Excellent. Everything is set up and ready for you." He released my hand to twist and settle his fingers near the base of my spine. Forward, perhaps, but his fingers didn't wander from the gentle pressure to escort me toward the casket. "The lawyers wanted me to inform you that they will be holding the reading of the will in the office shortly after the service, but not to rush. They will not start without you."

I wanted to stop and break away, but the steady pressure at the base of my spine pushed me inexorably forward. The shade of the oak sent chills down my back.

The casket seemed to suck in all the light. I forced myself to look away, to the display of pictures. A ring of Gabe shaking hands with the local movers and shakers. The center and largest by four-fold, one he'd taken of the two of us before the decline in his health. The same one I'd kept on my nightstand. That man loved his surprises. He chose the center photo himself. I knew it.

I couldn't bring myself to walk all the way to the casket. My knees failed me right at the front row of chairs. The funeral director didn't force me any closer. Kai sat beside me in silence. From this vantage, I could see the tip of his nose. I watched the tiny bit of him and let the waterworks come.

After a time, people came. I felt them. Shivered at their combined heat reaching out to me. Heard their steps in the close-cropped grass and their subdued voices as they came from behind. They passed between us, flies at a barbecue. I wanted to swat them away, but I knew how selfish it was. I was not the only one Gabe touched.

I barely heard the preacher. When he caught my eyes in a prolonged gaze and beckoned with an upturned hand, I knew it was time for the eulogy. Kai gave my thigh a squeeze the same moment I took a steadying breath. I could do this.

The walk up to the podium was shorter than I thought. Shorter and longer. Gabe's face haunted my peripheral vision.

I focused my attention on the crowd.

The large crowd. Larger than I thought. All the seats had butts filling them and a throng of people stood behind. Many more than had come to look into the casket. More surprising than the size of the crowd, were the faces. Faces I recognized from very recent adventures. Why hadn't Gabe told me he knew so much of Colorado's superhero population?

Magus, sitting on the other side of Kai, looked more surprised to see me than I was to see him. Superheroes I'd met and glimpsed in passing populated the first few rows of chairs. Those I'd interacted with had the same kind of confusion on their faces Magus did. I could take comfort in that, at least. Gabe hadn't blabbed about me to other people either.

Now was not the time to ask the questions. I shifted my gaze to encompass the whole crowd.

"Wow," I breathed the word into the mic and heard it amplified. "They say you never truly know the measure of a man's life until he's gone. Seeing you, from so many walks of life, I am humbled to have been able to call Gabe my friend. He meant a lot to so many people. I'm sure he'd hate me for this, but let me tell you why he meant the world to me."

The familiar stench of rotting fish breezed past my nose, almost too fast to notice. If I hadn't smelled it twice attached to such strong memories, I might have ignored it as a normal odor of a cemetery. I dropped my head to get a better idea of where the scent came from because wherever it came from, it needed to be handled without ruining the service.

I lifted my gaze back up to the people. "Gabriel Maxwell was annoyingly persistent at the worst times."

Several people laughed, confirming I hadn't been his only target.

"In my darkest times, in my blackest moments, the man would not let me drown in my own sorrow. Always found a way to make me smile. Even on his own death bed, the bastard."

The edges of my vision warped with yet-unshed tears. It drew my attention to movement happening far from the outskirts of the mourners. The same kind of herky-jerky movement I'd seen just before my car exploded the day before.

"That was how we met. Me in the middle of a sea of despair and him throwing me something to float on. 'Nothing lasts forever,' he told me. He was right, of course, but he was also wrong. Even in my teenage doldrums, I knew how wrong." I locked eyes with Magus on the last word. Made sure he knew I glared at him purposely before shifting my eyes to my left, his right, and back to him. "I told Gabe, forevers happen every day, which he threw in my face at every opportunity thereafter."

Another chuckle struck a few people. Magus, for his part, shifted his gaze from me to his right, my left. He stilled a moment when he saw the reanimated bodies heading toward us.

Good. Not great, though.

Great would be no zombies. I could deal with zombies showing up so long as the superheroes dealt with the zombies themselves.

"We were both right, of course. We can make anything live forever in our own hearts. The bad and the good, and we cannot separate the two. No light without shadow. No joy without sorrow. No loving someone without the pain when they're gone."

I tried my best not to watch Magus slip from his chair along with several of the other men in the first few rows. They dodged to the right and left. Looking to the right would only bring me a visual of things I didn't want to know and turn everyone else's attention to the things going on. I needed to keep the collective attention on me.

"And so, we cannot separate Gabe's generosity from his relentless drive to force a person to right the wrongs they had done. Not just to apologize but to make amends, to brighten the world more than you darken it."

A scream rang out from Magus' direction. It took everything in me to not no join in the gawking. "So, in his spirit. I challenge you, all of you, to inconvenience yourself for the sake of someone else. Someone you don't know, perhaps. Someone you dislike." No one had their attention on me anymore. Zombies were hard to compete with. Even, or especially, ones whose rot smelled more of fish than the others had.

On the plus side, the presence and action of the superheroes kept the crowd from panic. People stood. Some stood on their chairs. They didn't merge into a screaming school of fish. Also, no one had their attention on me, save Kai. Half the time.

So, I spoke to Gabe almost unobserved. I thanked him for forcing me to see the light hidden in the darkness, the shadow in the light. I thanked him for his warm heart and hearth. I thanked him for the hole he left in my heart. The rest of us could only hope to shake someone's world that way.

From this vantage, I finally turned to look at him in his satin-lined box. Black on black so his whole suit gleamed even more brightly. Just as he wished.

But he wasn't his body anymore. Like the baby entombed in the nearby mausoleum. Just matter. Dust once more.

"Enough," someone from the back of the crowd said. I shouldn't have been able to hear it over the fighting commotion. The woman hadn't even raised her voice to yell, but I heard it. So did the rest of the crowd. Everyone stilled, even the one's fighting.

No, not quite. Something more nuanced than the superheroes stopping. The zombies did. They still stood erect-ish, but didn't come any closer.

A stout woman pushed through the standing-room-only people. She had the same kind of hair the woman outside the donation center had. Bright, shiny black and moving of its own accord. The same kind of eyes too, yellow with horizontal squiggles for pupils. This woman had smooth, shiny-looking skin, not dried out like the other.

Four men followed the stout woman, flanking her as she made her way up the center aisle. All with short spiky hair that also moved. The people in the aisle seats leaned away and pinched their noses.

She couldn't have come for anyone else but me. I knew this. I told my legs to move, fast. My feet rooted my parts in place and my hands clung to the sides of the podium. We weren't going anywhere.

"Where is she?" the same strong voice asked me from a pasty face.

Feigning ignorance would get me nowhere. Even if I didn't know much. I maintained eye contact when I answered, "I don't know."

The woman sneered, revealing needle-sharp, black teeth. "You let her borrow your car and you expect me to believe you don't know?"

"Borrow? She stole my car, stranding me, and when I finally found it again, it exploded. I wouldn't mind speaking to her again myself."

The woman's brow line lifted some at my car being stolen, but not at the explosion part.

Not a normal reaction.

I shook my head, but it wasn't as if she betrayed me. "*You* blew up my car."

"You prematurely sprung a perfectly good trap, mouse." She sucked in some air through her teeth.

Cold-hearted bitch. "You owe me a new car, whatever you are."

She only gave me a lift of one eyebrow and twitch of her mouth in response. She would not be recompensing me for her sabotage. Now was as good a time as any to try and pepper her with questions we all wanted to know. "What's with the zombies?"

"Zombies." She scoffed. "The Bearer would never allow..."

I waited for her to finish her sentence. She narrowed her eyes and craned her neck toward me. My eyes widened in response to the heightened scrutiny. I risked a glance or two at my friendly superheroes. Those facing me all wore wariness like a cape. I couldn't tell if they knew this woman and had reason to fear what she may do or if she was an unknown quantity.

The woman shook her head. "That infuriating man."

I knew that reaction. I'd been the victim many times when dealing with Gabe or him dealing with me. That he had the same effect on this woman gave me faith that she wasn't completely unreasonable. It didn't make me feel better when she started toward me again, without the men on her heels.

She moved slower this time, not so much the march to war. I had to take it as a sign that she wouldn't kill me if I moved to meet her. If I let her come the whole way, Gabe and the podium blocked too many routes of escape.

The stench from two feet away nearly knocked me off mine. I stood strong. Plugging my nose would be the worst kind of rude.

"My daughter overheard a conversation she should not have and ran off to take care of things herself. She has neither the tools nor the skills to do so."

Daughter. Yep, that I believed. There couldn't be too many people who wreaked so strongly of fish in the city. That kind of thing couldn't go unnoticed in New York City, let alone Denver. I needed to move this along, if for no other reason than my nose demanded it. "What conversation made your daughter come here?"

The woman blinked clear eyelids sideways. Nictitating membranes, if I remembered my biology correctly. Like something a shark would have. "That you are not in cahoots is enough for the moment. The rest necessitates a different time and place."

I wanted to ask why she could turn the burner down now. Instead, "Are those your doing?" This time I pointed to the zombies, since she didn't appreciate the name earlier.

The black squiggle in her right eye rotated to the side without the other joining in the movement. That kind of thing never looked so creepy on chameleons. Perhaps the size difference saved me.

"The drones," she finally answered as she brought her wandering eye back to focus on me. "That is part of what I am here to handle."

Drones.

Not zombies.

Got it. "That was not a yes or no."

"Either answer would be a half lie." Her hair shuffled itself around her shoulders while she took a moment to consider me. "When you have finished with the memorial, come to the mausoleum."

Delivered like a writ to be carried out. Still, she held my eyes and waited for response. "Do I need to come alone?"

"As you prefer."

I nodded to her and received one in return. En masse, the group of them turned toward the mausoleum. As they passed the drones, the decaying bodies turned toward the woman and her group.

The superheroes, for their part, noticed this shift as well. They let the drones go and the lot of them followed in the wake of the fish-smelling woman.

All of us watched the woman and her train of drones make their way across the grass. The murmurs started once she's moved far enough away. Kai, Magus, and the rest had their eyes on me, at least the ones not guarding us from the zombies. No one could blame the crowd for staring. I would have. But right then, I had something to do.

I cast a quick look at Gabe as I made my way back to the podium. Without moving, his lips practically curled up in the corners.

The bastard.

It took the people in the crowd less time than I would have thought to turn their attention to me. Perhaps they needed an explanation. I certainly did. Mine would come later and with less people in attendance.

For the moment, the explaining fell to me.

"Gabe left us with one last surprise, naturally." I hoped it was just the one.

Knowing him, this was the first of many.

A few people smirked at my quip. The rest stared at me hard, willing me to give them more information on the interruption. Not my department. I needed to work my way back into the eulogy I'd written. Connecting the dots. I could do this.

"That kind of irreverence, not knowing what to expect from him but knowing he would stand with you, shoulder-to-shoulder, through the thick of it. That is what I will miss the most of him. And, while I will forever be sad for my loss, I will ever feel privileged that our lives intersected.

"So, I will smile in my sadness and cry through my brighter memories. As he would want. And the next time I see him, I will sock him in the gut for putting me through this. Thank you."

Some people laughed at my closing, a sign that I'd managed to regain some of the focus the drones stole. Still, after I abandoned the podium, it took the pastor a couple beats to replace me.

"Thank you, Greer, for the kind words." He nodded toward me in the magnanimous way people of the cloth did. "Does anyone else want to come up here and say a few words of their own?"

Stillness and mutters met the pastor's invitation. Eventually, someone stood and shuffled their way toward the front.

Things went smoothly after that. I knew people didn't forget what they'd seen. Or at least, they didn't until Magus stepped up to the podium. He dipped his voice into a low, rhythmic purr and flashed his eyes that particular way. Mass hypnosis, simply done.

I didn't dare turn my head and break his spell on the rest of the people, but I strained my eyes looking to the side. Kai had his head down and eyes closed as if deep in prayer. That explained it. I waited for Magus to finish so we could all jump into the next fire.

# 21 – STILL WATERS

AFTER THE PROCESSION of people paying their final respects dwindled, six of the superheroes in the front row shouldered Gabe's casket. Feeling like little more than a drone myself, I fell in step behind them, clutching my bouquet of stargazer lilies for all I was worth. The mausoleum's chill wrapped around us, a pacific wave drawing us further in.

The interior wasn't as dark as in past visits, either owing to the sconces blazing away along the walls or the faint glow coming off my exposed arms. At least no one here would need an explanation about the latter.

"I must say," Magus murmured to me after we had crossed the

threshold of the white granite and black marble building. "You kept a cool head out there when things turned a little off kilter."

"I've found that panic rarely solves..." As the men lowered the casket into the stone base I caught sight of where the fishy woman had gotten to. Back of the mausoleum, on top of a three-step dais, and under a stained-glass window that bathed the dais in rich violet and rose, she sat.

Fire exploded in my belly. "Get the fuck off of there. How dare you?"

Magus snatched a hold of me before I could break away. Everyone seemed to stare at me all at once. My own voice echoed harshly in my ears. Fishy woman looked like she might just squash me like a bug after all.

It didn't matter. As long as she stood up.

She sniffed and snarled her top lip like she smelled something half as disgusting as her own stench. "Apparently Gabriel took no time to teach you respect of your betters."

"Respect?" I stomped on Magus' foot and elbowed him in his side in the same moment, in case he had a counter for either. Most of the other heroes in the mausoleum had their hands full with the casket. That just left me, the woman, and her guards.

Not to mention the shambling corpses lined up along the right wall.

I didn't let them stop me. "You want to talk about respect? To me? Get the fuck off of her!"

Magus grabbed a hold of me again before I made it halfway to the woman and her entourage. "Control yourself."

Later.

I pulled against his hold though he had my arms pinned painfully.

"Get that woman off her."

"Her?" Fishy woman blinked at me. "What her?"

I growled my answer, struggling against Magus. There had to be a way to break free. The woman dropped her gaze down to where she had plopped her fat butt and stilled a moment. Finally, agonizingly slow, she lifted herself to standing. I sagged and panted in Magus' grip. The rest I could deal with.

"My apologies," the woman said as she came toward me. "It was such a beautiful place, I thought I might rest there while I waited."

My anger didn't want to give up on me so soon. "There is a reason it is beautiful. And some one is already resting there."

"And waiting for you too, I imagine." She nodded to me.

I nodded back.

"What just happened?" Magus asked. He didn't let me go when he asked.

"Not very perceptive, is he?" Fishy woman asked me, then sniffed again in that disgusted way. "Do let her go."

His hold on me relaxed in fits and starts, like I might launch myself forward again and he needed to catch me. I wished he had let me go in the first place. Releasing me then didn't quite make up for it.

The woman opened her hands. "It appears we have a common problem."

I shook my head. "I need a few moments."

"Of course." She nodded and stepped out of my path.

"Lana, we don't have time— "

Fishy woman whipped around to the man who dared speak up to her. If his reaction was any indication, I did not want to see the expression she had levered on him. "If we do not take the time to honor those we've lost, then what do we have time for?"

Whatever else passed between them, I didn't care to listen to. I pulled one of the hand brooms from the wall beneath the stained glass, the multi-hued broom to match the harvest season of fall. No spiders had taken up residence around the tiny sarcophagus, but I brushed the whole thing clean anyway. The practiced motion of light brushing and whispered prayers to her calmed away any of the anger that had taken me.

She was fine. I was fine.

We were fine.

The stems of the lilies had more bruises than I would have liked, but I knew she understood. I unwrapped the bouquet. Laying twenty-three of the two dozen on the stone, covering the whole surface. The last, I held onto for the moment.

I had the attention of the whole room of people on me when I turned around. No matter. I walked back to the freshly-laid casket and set the last lily on top before the men could close the stone lid over him. Just as I had done for her. "You know I don't have the money to cover yours as I do hers, Gabe, but consider this a start."

My game face had all but dissolved by the time I made it back to the fishy woman, Lana. Too bad I didn't have the luxury of ten minutes to pull myself together. I tried my best.

"My name is Greer Ianto." I held my hand into the space between us.

She took my hand without hesitation and shook it. "You may call me Lana."

Telling her it was nice to meet her would be a lie and I'd had enough of that kind of negativity today. "So, you say we have a common problem. I would just like to clarify what you think the problem is."

She released my hand. "Someone found a clutch of our children and they are experimenting on them."

I knew it would connect to us somehow. "Okay." I nodded to encourage her to continue.

"Our larval form, our babies for lack of a better word, look little different from some of your sea stars. Spiny. Poisonous. Venomous. One of you removed our whole nest and is extracting samples from them to inject into you humans."

"Why would someone do that?" I asked, then thought through what it might have sounded like. "Not that I disbelieve you, I'm just trying to figure out why so we could figure out who."

She shook her head. "In my experience, humans do some things for the sheer fact that they can, and to find out what will happen when they do. No matter the impact to the world at large."

I could not deny that. Human nature was oftentimes the least humane of man's creations.

"But the evidence is there." Lana pointed to the wall of drones standing against the other wall. "Serum from our children pervaded their bodies before they died. The bodies, without will of their own to control them, now react to the field any Crowne beyond larval stage emits. Taxis animation. Simple moth to flame reaction when low levels are introduced."

That did explain why she called them drones, though it didn't mean they weren't also zombies. "What happens when high levels of whatever is introduced?"

"More useful drones." She shrugged in a way I did not appreciate, though I couldn't put my finger on why until she continued. "A high enough concentration of venom does not require the body to be dead to react to our field. Most of the personality of the drone is subsumed by that of the Crowne in control."

Yep. My instincts had been on point.

Couldn't really get excited about it in the moment, with everything else racing through my head. "So, you came here..."

She nodded like I knew how the sentence I hadn't thought through would end. Then, she finished it for me. "To find my daughter and the children stolen from their homes. They will be together, no doubt."

"If you emit a field, would you not be able to sense the whereabouts of your daughter with the same field." Magus joined our conversation.

"Quiet, peon." Lana hissed the words while her hair undulated violently in his direction.

Much to his credit, Magus neither stepped back nor reacted. He didn't speak again though, which was also a smart move. I chose a less prudent course of action.

"He makes a good point. Why aren't you able to sense your daughter? Your field seems plenty strong enough." I glanced toward the drones, if she had any question as to my meaning.

Her hair dropped all at once, like someone pulled the plug on a lightning machine. Violent thrashing, to dull floppiness in less than a second.

"I tracked her to this place, to where she crossed over. Then her presence disappeared all-together from my detection." Lines formed between where her eyebrows would be if she had any. "I cannot find her."

I recognized that worried-mother look. We needed to help her. Beyond it being the right thing, I got the impression she didn't care how many of our people died in her pursuit. I almost couldn't blame her.

Almost.

"Could you give me a more detailed description of what your larval stage looks like?" Kai had his phone out, but his eyes were all on Lana.

"I could, but I won't." Dismissive snarl again.

I was beginning to get the impression that she disliked men. Or, at least, she did not hold them in as high esteem as she did women. Why else would she be talking to the clueless one in the middle of a room full of super-capable men? She needed convincing to speak to Kai and my nose said he knew something the rest of us didn't.

"Chances are good, Lana, that if he is asking, he has good reason."

Her eyes flicked to him, then back to me. "You trust him?"

"Yes." No hesitation in my answer, though I wondered why she would trust my judgement.

She did, though. With my assurance, she reached a hand out for Kai's phone.

Pulling up the answer didn't take much time, which told me a couple of things. She was familiar enough with our technology to manipulate it to the correct information with ease. She also knew what to search for to find the information Kai wanted. Their larval form must have a scientific or layman's name to look for. Hidden in plain sight. I wondered where the adults lived.

Kai's eyes widened when Lana passed the phone back to him, excitement prickling off him in palpable waves. "You said they're poisonous. Are the poisons saponins? Asterosaponins?"

"Yes." Lana didn't sound as dismissive this time. I would have said she sounded impressed, but it was more the way a dancing dog impressed a person. A step in the right direction, if only a small one.

"That's very good news." The excitement in his tone made me want to be excited with him.

I shared a confused look with Magus. He was the one who asked, "Why is that good?"

"Most of the samples from the other Anterograde scenes were too small to verify much more than a soapy, or soap-like residue left behind. The art gallery gave me more of the same, but in a large enough quantity to verify that it was the substance, the x-factor I'd been trying to isolate and test. We might already be on a case leading us to your daughter. The woman responsible for the crimes we're investigating might also be the one syphoning off substances from your children."

"You know where my daughter is?" Lana's words came out more as statement than question.

He shook his head. "Not yet, not right now. We may know where the woman responsible will be later this week. But this is only educated conjecture. I would need a sample to compare it to."

She narrowed her eyes a bit, though the pupil squiggle widened some. The combination left me at a loss of where her head was at or what she might do. If Kai offended her, there was no telling.

She reached across her body to take hold of her left shirt cuff and peel it back, slow. After about an inch of clear skin, tiny filaments peeked out. Larger ones followed. Tiny, then larger needles with dew drops glistening near the ends. Poison leaking out all over her, or venom. The shirt should have been soaked with it.

A wave of fresh funk rolled off from her exposed arm. A couple of the super men coughed. I took a short breath and prayed I could maintain.

Kai patted his suit, searching for something in one of his pockets. His frown told me he didn't find what he hoped. "I don't have a vial to collect it in, but if you wouldn't mind." He reached a hand out to hover above Lana's exposed arm.

She lifted an eye ridge, her hair undulating in an almost seductive wave. With a nod that was every bit as much approval as challenge, she said, "If it is your desire."

It was poison. Kai had to know it was poison. He suggested it might be the same poison. I opened my mouth to protest.

Too late.

Kai wrapped his hand around Lana's spiny arm, closer to her elbow than the wrist. He made a face somewhat like a disgruntled ox. Snorted the same way too. He pulled a hand away that looked like a pixie-sword pincushion without any more reaction.

Tips of smoky-quartz needles no longer than a centimeter stuck out of his palm and fingers. Tiny beads of red started to form at the base of them. He'd closed his eyes. Stillness rolled over him as he lifted his hand toward his face. He inhaled deep and I didn't envy him the breath full of fishiness.

We needed to get him to a hospital before he started reacting, or dying. Maybe this stillness was a sign the poison had already started its work in him. Why was no one doing anything to stop him, or help him, or something?

He stuck his tongue out, delicately working the thinned tip of it around several of the spines piercing his palm.

What the ever-living fuck?

Nostrils flaring, Kai opened his eyes and looked to his boss. "It's the same thing. This solution is being mixed in with some coffee extracts and another substance."

Okay.

We needed to discuss better methods to get that information later. For the moment, other things pressed. "So, same substance means we've been searching for the person behind the theft of your children."

"Lead us to her." Cold anger boiled out in Lana's tone.

I could understand, but I couldn't bow to it. "We know where she will be this weekend, but we have no specific time."

"Then we will take her now."

"We don't know who she is, nor do we know a motive behind what she is doing to track her. We would need either."

"What do you know?" Her anger turned to me, this time.

That, I could not let stand. "We all know more than we did ten minutes ago and we have more assets than we did before. Now, can you put those people back in their graves." One of those sentences you never thought you'd say.

She lifted an eye ridge. "I can."

Not that she would, but she could. "Fabulous. If you could do so and take down the names, death dates, and birth dates for them it will help narrow our search and we will work things from our side."

"And you will keep me apprised." Order to be followed. Not a question.

Not doing so might kill me, so I nodded. "If you give me your contact info."

Lana held a hand out for my phone. I passed to her. It had survived far worse than her in the past few days.

I didn't appreciate the sly expression she levered on me when she passed my phone back. For a fleeting moment, I wondered if she knew a code to make my phone explode the next time I pulled it out. She probably wouldn't care about my face full of fire. She hadn't cared about the first one.

"If no one has a claim on him, I would love to add him to my harem." Lana cast a mildly covetous look at Kai. One having little to do with sexual desire. "He has many uses."

I just wanted him for the one. Multiple times. "He is spoken for."

Kai said not a word.

Smart man.

"Do you know who he kneels to?" She rolled her lips in, "Perhaps his Mistress would consider a trade?"

"He's mine, and I am not willing to trade."

She lifted an eyebrow ridge, then a shoulder in defeat. "I see. It was worth a try. Come." She jerked a chin toward the door and headed that direction.

Her men followed close behind. The dead people followed behind at a slower shamble. The living and non-fish among us watched the odd parade in silence.

"Zombies," Bolt finally broke the quiet. "Honest to goodness zombies. I have seen everything."

My eyes narrowed in confusion. "Don't you travel by lightning?"

"Yeah, but...hmm. Fair point."

I knew it was. I saw no need to rub that in, until he followed up with an overloud, "SparkleTits."

"Listen here— "

Kai stepped out of my way. Three people grabbed me before I made it four steps in Bolt's direction. He threw his head back in a raucous hyena laugh, the bastard, while I struggled.

"This is beginning to be a habit with you." Magus didn't even sound winded.

I went full limp baby then tried to launch myself out of the altered grips. Still no dice.

How did toddlers wriggle away so easily?

"Can someone at least punch him in the stomach for me?" I panted. This wrestling without a hope of winning tired a girl out.

My pal Phoenyx stepped over to Bolt and bowed to me. "As SparkleTits commands." He balled his fist and swung something a toddler could avoid. When he made contact, Bolt slow-motion curled over then backed away on his tippy toes. The two men spit laughter without the courtesy of trying to hide it.

I could get them all. If I didn't care about pulling the hem of my dress all the way up to my clavicles, I could force the two to cluck like chickens for as long as my influence lasted. Or make out with each other. They wouldn't even need to remember that I'd pulled my dress up. Or something devious. Permanent drag queen makeup. Penis tattoos on their faces. Piercings through their penises.

Bolt stopped laughing first. "I don't like that look on your face. Hold her tighter!"

"It doesn't have to be today, Bolt." I smiled.

He smacked Phoenyx in the chest. "Hey, dude. Stop. She's plotting to kill us."

"Death is a breath in the wind." The hands that had been loosening on me, tightened once more.

Phoenyx only looked somewhat alarmed. Anxiety zinged up and down Bolt's body. "Uh, Magus, you want to put the whammy on her so she doesn't maim your employees?"

He wished. I had enough discretion to not blab that Magus could not affect my mind like he could everyone else. Not my secret to tell.

"Shouldn't we be figuring out what to do next on this case?" Phoenyx chose a different tactic. Diverting the conversation with the weight of responsibility. He knew me well enough to know it might work. Did he know me well enough to know it would only delay the inevitable?

"I don't know about the rest of you," I'd regained enough control for my voice to come out easy and light. Like the crisis had been averted. "But I have a meeting with some lawyers then a reception to go to."

"Lawyers?" Kai asked, still staring at his palm. He might have missed the whole episode, except for the pointed side-step earlier.

"Gabe said he would leave me something." I hoped it was the massive pot he taught me to cook in. Thanks to the pot and him, I couldn't get the proportions right unless I made enough food to feed an army.

"Good." Magus let me go, which signaled the rest of them to release me. "Go to the will reading. Kai needs to catalogue the specimen he collected."

"About that, shouldn't he be dying?"

Kai barely looked up at me when he answered. "I am immune to poison and the like."

Ho-hum. Like that wasn't something fantastical.

It did explain the lack of reaction from the others. "Second question. Kai is my ride for the day. How will I get to the reading?"

"I can still—" he stopped at Magus' raised hand.

"Catalogue first. I will take her to the reading and reception after. If you have not finished by the time she is ready to leave, I will take her home." He turned his head to me. "It will allow me to gain the names of the...drones...in the quickest fashion."

I wished Lana hadn't left. She wouldn't take that kind of crap from him. Even if it solved the surface problem. Arguing the points would have been selfish.

Still, when Kai nodded to me with a, "I will take you home," my shoulders settled.

Business tended to, the mood inside the mausoleum shifted back to a more somber one. The pall bearers and the other superheroes who followed the casket each said their last goodbye to Gabe. I nodded to him and to the much smaller tomb in the back. The sound of stone scraping against stone chased me back out into the light of day.

# 22 – MS. GARSON, IF YOU'RE NASTY

I STARED AT THE lawyer reading the will, dumbfounded. He didn't laugh. He just rolled on, reading through the end of the paragraph like what he said wasn't a joke. "Wait a second. Wait." I shook my hands as I spoke.

He looked up at me over-top his glasses. "Yes, Ms. Ianto?"

"Can you read that part back to me again?"

"Which part?"

He had to be kidding, right? "I think you know which part. The part about me."

"The remaining assets, including all moneys, residences, and artifacts, shall be passed to Ms. Greer Ianto, daughter of my heart if not my own making." The lawyer murmured on detailing amounts and holdings that made my head spin.

It didn't matter. The details were ancillary to the central point. The part where Gabe made me the primary beneficiary to an estate much larger than I'd realized.

What had he been thinking?

"This is absolutely preposterous." One of the men half-yelled once the lawyer set down the will. "All of his money to a fat young thing who hopped into his pants at the last minute to get to his money? No one knows who she is and suddenly she's giving the eulogy and raking in all of the dough?"

The reading hadn't shocked me enough to keep red from bleeding into my vision at the gray-haired, jowly asshole. Magus' fingers on my shoulder kept me in my chair, mostly by reminding me a fight in the lawyer's office would be in bad form. They might be my lawyers now. I needed to research. Later.

The lawyer pulled his glasses from their perch on the tip of his nose with great aplomb. "Ms. Ianto's name has been included in Mr. Jones' will for nearly two decades."

My head snapped back to the lawyer. "What?"

The angry man echoed my reaction with a growlier version.

The lawyer nodded with a particularly pleased curve to his lips. He kept his focus on me when he answered. "The original amendment included provisions for...before the funeral."

My chest screeched to a halt for what should have been several heartbeats. But the lawyer didn't say it. No one in this room needed to know that information. So, I settled back against the seat and stared at the bookshelf behind him with an, "I see."

I'd known Gabe didn't have any family, but he wanted to make certain I wouldn't need to worry about mine. When I had the beginnings of one.

"Well, I don't." My new biggest fan threw his hands up in growing frustration. "This is...I'm going to appeal."

"Perhaps the fact that you're arguing over money and property instead of mourning his loss is part of the reason he chose to exclude you." I shrugged, Gabe's reason for adding me dampened most of my anger. Enough that I could speak through it, at least.

The man stomped to my chair and leaned over me. His shit-brown eyes practically glowed. "Exclusion would have been better than the paltry five-thousand-dollar token he left me."

Mentioning the saliva he sprayed me with as he spit his words in my face would have been petty. Instead, I stood, enjoying the sliver of uncertainty that leaked into his anger when he realized I stood taller than him by five inches or so.

"Five thousand could change so many people's lives. You should be glad he thought to give you anything and stop dishonoring his memory by throwing a hissy fit worthy of a spoiled two-year-old."

He opened his mouth.

"Hmm-mmm." I shook my head before he could start. Before I yelled at him, I took a breath. "Sir. I don't know who you are. Don't really care to, after all that. Let me just warn you before you say anything to really set me off. You're on my reserve nerve. Now is not the time to try my patience."

He puffed his chest up, trying to make himself bigger to scare off the better predator. "I don't care."

Like he could scare me away. I didn't need to make myself bigger.

My left tit was bigger than his head. "Push me and you will."

His eyes twitched around shrinking pupils. Something in him wanted to fight me despite his body understanding what a bad idea it was. He stepped back. His body won. Good for him, but it left me with nothing to punch.

As he sulked his way out the room, his sexist and racist muttering made me want to reconsider my decision to warn him and let him go. The two people nearest the door looked scandalized. Magus had on one of his well-practiced frowns of disappointment, but he hadn't turned it on me. Winning. For the moment.

The lawyer had a sly twist to his mouth.

"What?" I waved my finger at him. "What's that look for?"

"Mr. Jones had a few paragraphs at the end of his will that were not to be read aloud." He probably tried his best to hide his enjoyment. He failed miserably. "One detailing what to do with the allocations if anyone balked at their portions. The other, for you. Specifically, this."

He picked up an envelope I'd been too distracted to notice and reached it out to me. Most of me didn't want to take it. I took it anyway.

Gabe had gone all out with the heavy, thick paper and finished it off with a wax seal. There couldn't have been more than a couple of pieces of paper folded up inside.

"You're to read it later. When you have a moment alone."

Moment alone. If this weekend were any indication of my new life, that would never happen again. I would need to find a jiffy a little sooner.

I nodded to the lawyer anyway. "Thank you."

"Excellent." He shifted his focus from only me to the rest of the room. "If there are no further questions, we can break. If you give my assistant your name, he has envelopes with information and checks for the rest of you. You'll need to sign for them. Ms. Ianto, I have a few papers for you to sign before you leave."

Since I wasn't going anywhere soon, I dropped back into my seat.

The lawyer undersold how many papers I had to sign. He explained them all to me when my skimming didn't give me any usable information. Contract and law language was for the birds, but all the things Gabe left me required signatures and initialing aplenty. My hand hurt by the time I made it back outside.

Magus kept mercifully quiet through the whole thing. Soothing, while I blazed through contracts and other legal papers. Annoying, as we walked to his car.

"How did you know Gabe?" I blurted as he opened the door for me.

"I can't tell you that." He smirked at me and waited for me to climb into his SUV before closing me in.

Of course, he couldn't. I should have known, but I wished his answer hadn't killed the conversation I'd been trying to open.

As he started the car, though, he gave me something to go on.

"He was the only other person whose memories I could never adjust. Outside union members." He narrowed his eyes at me, curiosity rather than outright suspicion. "Was he your father?"

I almost wished he had been, but I loved my dad too much to wish him away. My mother, on the other hand. "Nope."

"Are you certain?"

Laughter bubbled in my chest. "Well, my mother is white and so was Gabe, so..."

"Ah."

"Yes."

"There has to be some other connection between you, though." He gave me a quick glance. "Two people that I cannot affect know each other. Well. It's is too much of a coincidence."

He was probably right about that, but I couldn't think of anything that might clear it up. That would require understanding how his mind thing worked. Which would probably get me in more hot water than I'd already jumped into. No one needed that. Least of all, me.

"But I am going to stop searching for a way to wipe your memories."

Good news. "Finally trust me?"

"I wasted a lot of time trying to figure out Gabriel's immunity." Magus kept his eyes on the road.

Naturally. Why would he trust me? I hadn't helped enormously this weekend without spilling any of the beans to the world, or anything.

Oh wait. I had.

He lifted a shoulder, almost a shrug. "And Gabriel didn't give his friendship out haphazardly."

"He certainly did not." He also didn't tell secrets. Not mine to other people nor theirs to me. Admirable. But I could have used a bit of a heads up. Like maybe on his death bed. Most everyone forgave deathbed confessions. Gabe wouldn't have, though. Especially not from himself. "I'm going to miss him."

Magus nodded. "Yes. We all will. But I think you had a part of him that no one else did."

"How do you figure?" I didn't disagree with him. I just wanted to know why he thought that way.

"Simple." He shrugged. "He didn't let anyone else call him Gabe. Kind of jarred me when you said it the first time. Gabriel Jones, philanthropist, cutthroat business man, island unto himself. No family to speak of. And someone calling him by a nickname."

"Everyone goes by many names. Even you." I tilted my head to emphasize. "Magus."

The last won a chuckle out of him. "Gabriel only went by those he was born to, as far as I knew, and only a few people were close enough to use his first name."

As nice as it was to know Gabe held a special place for me, it didn't make the loss of him any easier. I tried to not dwell on that by focusing on other things. Magus, in particular. I stared at him, waiting for an answer to the question I'd implied.

After several beats of silence, and a couple of side-eyes my way, he sighed. "Karloff."

"Wow."

"My mother was a fan of classic horror."

My nose turned up like it wanted to at the zomb—drones. "Clearly."

"I'll thank you not to spread that one."

I lifted my hands in surrender. "I understand. It isn't easy being named after an actress no one my age has ever heard of."

"Who's that?"

Proved my point. "Greer Garson."

"Huh."

No fires of recognition flashed on his face. Of course.

Magus (Karloff) pulled to a stop in front of the kind of reception hall wealthier high schools rented out for prom. I expected nothing less from Gabe. Everything taken care of with style and in a way that no one close to him needed to lift a finger.

"Do you wish for me to walk you in and wait for Kai's arrival, or would you rather walk in alone."

I knew the answer I should have given. Instead, "If you don't need to leave right away, I would appreciate the company."

Magus eased the car forward. "There are plenty people inside who would love to make your acquaintance. At least they will, once Senator Marcus makes it known who the primary beneficiary to Gabriel's will was."

"That douche nozzle is a senator?"

"State senator."

Balls. "He's either the best actor in the world or people weren't paying attention when they went to the voting booths."

Magus laughed.

I wished I could. That kind of man shouldn't be making decisions about which gerbil food to buy, let alone voting on state law.

Putting on my game face took the whole time from Magus' search for a parking spot through our walk to the door. Magus didn't poke or prod me while I built my public mask. Tiny blessings, probably born of his keen animal sense.

Few people looked our way when we walked in. The benefits of being more than fashionably late and not familiar to the movers and shakers in Colorado. Or outside Colorado.

Garlic and onion overrode the expensive perfumes in the air. Food. I couldn't be out of place so long as I could muster up a nice plate of food.

I slipped past several people in black, a few who thanked me for giving such a lovely eulogy. It hadn't been perfect, but who knew what they remembered around the missing parts about the drones.

Regardless, I thanked and side-stepped them on my way to the line of entrees.

All my favorites, of course.

Bless that man.

Magus grabbed a plate as well. I couldn't tell if he did so to blend in to the other people laughing and crying and eating, or if he was hungry. So long as he ate instead of wasting it, his reasoning didn't matter.

He'd only made it halfway through his food when Kai walked in. I'd finished mine, so I went with Kai so we could both fill our plates.

The conversations I overheard as we passed made me smile. Tales of stubbornness and generosity.

Gabe, in a nutshell.

The three of us enjoyed peaceful minutes of relative anonymity in the middle of the buzzing people. Until someone broke into our companionable silence.

"And here is the lovely lady who gave us such a moving eulogy."

The voice grated my peace of mind before I looked up to see the face behind it. Senator Tantrum Because He Only Got Five Thousand Dollars. I wondered at the kind of scene he might make once he learned that his lack of grace took even that from him. If there was good in this world, a large crowd of his constituents would witness him finding out.

Despite what happened between us, he smiled at me like I was his long lost...money ticket. All empty hunger and covetous charm. He needed to leave.

Hadn't I suffered enough this weekend?

I put on a brave face. If there was to be a scene, he needed to be the one to initiate it, just as he had behind closed doors. I would need to start all peaches and cream. "I don't believe we've been introduced." There. He could stick that in his craw.

His smile sharpened like he could slice through me with it alone. "Perhaps not. I am Senator Nathaniel Marcus." He reached a hand toward me, which put his forearm right in front of Kai's face. The senator didn't seem to notice Kai dip into the colder spectrum of annoyance. Or he noticed and didn't care.

"I wouldn't want you do dirty your hands." I turned my palms toward him, displaying the barbecue covered glory.

Sharpening the smile again. The force of it should have broken his perfectly-straight, painfully-white teeth. "Of course." Oh, he knew what I really meant, regardless of the plausible excuse.

Common sense told me to make a token effort to clean my hands off.

"Gabriel was truly blessed to have such a good friend in his life." His eyes dropped to my hands too frequently, monitoring my progress. He wanted me to hurry up while I hoped he would hurry off.

I tipped a little water onto my napkin to give my actions any level of credence.

If he would not back down, neither would I. Two opponents entered. Only one could win.

My phone buzzed on the table next to my plate. Three vibrations back to back, then a pause before more. A phone call. Saints be praised. I would take a telemarketer right then.

Lana's name lit up the screen. I cast a pointed look to Magus as I wiped the moisture from my fingertips. "I need to take this call."

Magus lifted an eyebrow until he peeked at the lit-up screen. "You do."

It didn't dawn on me until then that he had only remained at our table to get the information from Lana as soon as he possibly could. Whatever the reason, we hadn't come to any fighting words.

I stood from my seat and answered at the same time. "Hello, Lana."

"Greer. I apologize for the length of time it took to get back to you."

Hearing her as I darted through the room of half-filled tables took quite a bit of effort. "That is perfectly fine. Legalities around Gabe's death took longer for me to finish than I thought." The atrium was blessedly free of people, but it echoed more than I liked.

"We found a few more drones fighting to break free from their graves, so I took care of those as well."

"That is greatly appreciated." I needed another place to be, quiet and not echoed.

Magus passed by my slowed pace and tipped his head toward the outer door in invitation. Good idea.

"It was nothing more than the completion of what I committed to." Her voice came through crystal clear when I stepped outside. "I sent the names to you before I called. The interesting thing is the dates. One woman died four full years, almost to the day, before the rest of the people started cropping up. Then they come in pulses. Several people die in the span of a few days, then a break. In waves."

Four years, a break, then a pulsing pattern. She was right. Interesting. "What's the name of the first woman? And the date, if you please."

"Margaret Corliss. She was the weakest of all the drones I encountered. Perhaps it is only bias from the isolated sample of this one cemetery, but she had the lowest concentration of poison in her. She died five years ago this coming Saturday."

Balls. I knew a well-scheduled portent of doom when I heard one. "Did you get a birth date for her?"

"I took the liberty of snapping photos of every memorial stone. I can send them all to you, if you wish."

"Maybe a little later, Lana." The other people would probably only lead me to the incidents that killed them, which Magus knew all about already. This was new. Important. A break. "Just send Margaret's for right now."

"You believe there is significance in the timing?"

"Yes, I do."

She chuckled in a way that reminded me of mud pots in Yellowstone. "Excellent. Happy hunting and remember your promise to me."

That I would include her in the final take down. "I won't forget."

The other line went dead. Apparently, she had the technology thing down, but not the courtesies of signing off.

Whatever.

She had given us excellent information.

Magus' attention rested on me without any anticipatory fidgeting. Quite a feat.

"What about someone named Margaret?" He asked without breaking the outward calm.

"Margaret Corliss. Died four years, to the day, before the first of the other drones did. The fifth anniversary of her death is Saturday."

His pupils widened, though the rest of him gave nothing away. "And Lana is sending something to you about her."

"Picture of her grave stone." I smiled.

He smiled right on back. "Be certain to send that to me as soon as you get them."

My phone vibrated as I finished saving Magus' cell number. I flicked to my texts and found the list of names of everyone recently undead. Lana was as good as her word. I forwarded the list to Magus. A gesture of good faith.

"Brilliant." He actually appeared delighted to the news. Without his usual masked expression. Happiness looked good on the man. Someone should give him a bouquet of flowers or something else he liked, just because.

"Greer," he cut off my mental train wreck.

Probably for the best. That kind of thought train got my mouth in trouble. "Yes, Magus?"

"I have several things I need to pin down, and others to set on the straight and narrow." His lips retained his smile while the eyes settled into their more familiar planning and calculating odds.

"Go, do your thing, Magus. I'll send you the rest when I get it."

"Thank you." He blinked a couple of times, almost looking confused. Like the thanks surprised him as much as it did me.

Poking at it would sour the moment, so I replied as Gabe always taught me. "You are most certainly welcome, and the same to you." I heard the rhythm of his speech in my recitation of the phrase.

Another piece of him to hold onto.

"Are you going to be okay?" The smile had slipped from Magus' face, replaced by a more serious, but no less open, expression.

Because he didn't appear to be asking for effect or social niceties, I didn't give him the standard answer. The real answer, I didn't know. I knew what I should say, that I would be okay eventually. Honesty came out instead, "Are any of us ever really okay?"

He pressed his lips together a moment, nodding a bit in contemplation. "We all have our moments."

Not enough of them. Despite what I'd said in the eulogy, it didn't feel like there were near enough rays of light to make the shadows worth it. "I wish there were more."

"Sometimes you have to fight tooth and nail to make your own." He tipped his head toward me like he meant to tell me a secret. "And sometimes the fight itself is our ray of light."

With that, Magus saluted me with his phone, as much an exit as a reminder to send him the drone information. Then he spun on his heel and headed for his car. I stared after him, half awe-struck. His overseeing this branch of the union made sense, finally. Useful as his power was, power did not a leader make. The last bit, though. The unhurried wisdom. That was a man a person could get behind.

Even me.

# 23 – THE WORLD'S A STAGE

THE EXACT OPPOSITE kind of leader still lingered near my table. Senator Marcus smiled a joyless smile at me from across the room. I could make him go away. Maneuver my top down far enough to force him to do as I said. The thought of him seeing any of my cleavage sent dirty-water chills down my back.

He wouldn't remember, but I would.

I gritted my teeth and sucked it up, weaving across the room like nothing could bother me more than the reason we'd all come here.

Kai lifted his eyebrows as I sat back down next to him.

"Later," I answered.

He nodded.

The senator didn't take subtleties, apparently. "What was all the hubbub about, my dear?"

His dear?

Gross.

But not the thing to correct him on. Not with such a mixed audience around us. Instead, I cast a questioning glance of my own to Kai. "I'm fairly certain I'm not allowed to share that information with a civilian."

Senator Marcus' lips flattened a moment. A fleeting sign of disapproval I might have missed if I hadn't been watching for it. "Ah, well..." He shrugged like it didn't matter to him. If it really hadn't mattered, the shrug would have been a smooth, easy one.

If he lied this poorly to me, how had he won any election. A high school freshman could sell it better. I needed to pay more attention to politics. Right then, "If you don't mind, it's been a rough weekend, so I'd really like to just finish my meal and fade from view."

"Of course, m'dear." He dipped his chin. "Speaking of plates, I have a campaign fundraiser dinner in a couple of weeks that I would love to see you at."

I'm sure he would, the money-grubbing, sleaze thing he was. In asking, however, he finally gave me something I so desperately needed. An excuse.

"How dare you bring up money, campaign fundraising of all things, right now?" I raised my voice just enough to be heard over the din by the nearest tables. I hoped, hoped, hoped, people farther away picked up on the tiny scene I was making and hushed up so they could hear it too. "A man has died. He's not even been interred for half a day and you're here, right now, asking for money?"

Panic flared his eyes wide. He lifted his hand in classic surrender-because-I-caught-him, position. "I apologize. I simply didn't know when I would see you again to invite you to the dinner."

"Because you don't know me. Because we aren't even close to colleagues. Because you decided that hours after I had to speak over my friend's body would be the perfect time to pounce and ask me—again someone you don't know—to give you money." Everything in me wanted to stand and physically intimidate him again. But, no.

The visual was just as important as the words I said in this play. With me seated, he stood over me and I had to defend myself. Because I was a woman. And he was a big, strong man.

Sometimes a girl had to work with the stereotypes she was given.

Especially when the whole room was watching. Time to bring it home.

"What kind of man are you, Senator Marcus? If you don't have the decency to respect the man who just died and the reception held in his honor, at least have the decency to respect the people who do."

Several possible responses flickered through his expression, half of them probably ways to apologize that would not make him look like a bigger putz. I waited. It was his turn to speak, after all.

"Perhaps my desire to befriend the person who spoke so eloquently about our mutual friend got the better of me." He finally said, probably more to play to the witnesses than for any feelings of indebtedness toward me.

I held back harping on the "eloquent" comment. And the "mutual friend" comment too. I highly doubted Gabe kept this man in his sphere for happy reasons. Enemies ever closer, as they said.

Instead, I lifted both eyebrows and pressed my lips together. The only civil, non-escalating thing I could manage. Because I would not accept his apology. He did not deserve my forgiveness. Or anyone's, for that matter.

He tipped his chin to me again. "If you will excuse me."

Again, I said nothing to him. Just let him stew in his public ridicule and watched his whole retreat.

Mmm, tasty.

The hardest part of the episode was turning back to my plate without grinning like an alligator. I could control it, though, so long as I didn't look at anyone else for the next few minutes.

Conversation picked back up in the room, slowly but surely. After a sound threshold of some sort had been reached, Kai leaned toward me.

"Smack me if the timing is off, Greer." He moved in a little closer, nearly pressing his lips against my ear. "But that was hot."

My eyes closed in a long blink. I reared my head back and turned toward him at quarter speed. There it was again, that intense heat in his gaze swallowing me down. Unabashed, yet not levered with the weight of expectation.

I nearly dropped my fork. Had to lock it in a death grip to keep hold of it.

His lips curled a little in the corners. He clearly enjoyed the effect his words had on me. "I wonder what that tongue could do against a worthier foe."

My breathing deepened. Shit. "I need to fuel up, first."

"Then, finish your plate, woman."

# 24 – FIVE THOUSAND REASONS

K AI KEPT HIS hands completely to himself as he followed me out of the reception hall. I kind of wished he would set his fingers in the small of my back, if nothing else, but I knew why he didn't. It wouldn't stop there. The slightest touch would spark us. Not something I wanted to happen in front of a reception full of mourners.

"Hey, Greer!" Chad.

What the fuck was he doing here? Did he sense I might get a brief respite from the perpetual shit-fest my life had become? I stopped in the middle of the parking lot to turn toward him. "What the fuck are you doing here?"

"I thought I might find you here."

Easy breaths. To push the sexual-frustration anger back. "You dumped me. You even came back for the second round of scooping your shit up. We're done. *Done* done. Why the fuck did you come looking for me?" If he said something about us reconciling, I would punch him in the face.

He shuffled a bit. Grabbed the back of his neck and pulled at the skin there. He looked uneasy, at least. That was a step in the right direction. Eventually, he dropped his shoulders down, like he'd come to some sort of a conclusion.

"I know I didn't end things the right way."

And Titanic sprung a leak. I kept my expression to the professional coolness. It was the only way I could stop him from seeing how he affected me.

"I have to live with that." He poked his finger into the center of his chest. "But I did it for the right reasons."

I wasn't sure I wanted to hear this. I wasn't sure I didn't, either. "Which would be?"

Chad's mouth twisted in several interesting ways before he straightened. "Do I have to do this in front of your new fuckboy?"

Looking at Kai or defending our interaction would be a sign of weakness. Instead, I shifted my weight to one hip and raised the opposite eyebrow. "Do or don't. You're the one who sought me out."

Chad blinked at me, like he couldn't quite figure out how to play off my reaction. I'd had too much thrown at me the past few days for his antics to throw me into hysterics. The last time he popped back into my sphere should have let him know that much.

"Fine." He glared at me as if I caused the situation we were in. "I got a little underwater with someone. I thought I would be able to stall him a little, at least until I got paid and give him another five hundred to give me some breathing room. He gave me until midnight Friday."

He threw the last at me with all the frustrated anger he could confine in his inside voice.

Regardless of his anger, nothing he said put me at fault.

Things started to come together, though. The picture forming rubbed me the wrong way. I kept my mouth closed.

"I moved out to protect you," he yelled. The yell shattered whatever control he had on his anger. He took a step toward me.

I balled my hands into fists and lifted them like I'd seen every boxer ever do. Loose, mobile elbows. Hands protecting the face. I couldn't manage the butterfly-like floating, but I set myself in a more stable stance.

Chad narrowed his eyes. "You think I'm going to hurt you? Jesus, Greer. I love you. Despite the way you always pull back from me. You never want to have the hard conversations. Not even when you're hurting. You pull back. You avoid. Never ask for help or reach out. I love you but you're cold."

He was right. I hated needing people. It only led to loss and pain. Especially when you let them know you needed them. Asking for help, that's when they bent you out of shape. I refused to let Chad twist me anymore. "What's your point?"

"I was trying to do the right thing." Despite his words, he didn't back down. Didn't step back. Didn't stop projecting he yearned for a fight.

"The right thing was lying for however long about gambling—"

"I was not gambling." He spat the words at me, daring me to refute him.

"I don't care what you were doing. You dealt with some shady people, got in trouble, and instead of explaining things, you decided breaking up was the best idea." I started shifting weight from foot to foot. I needed to keep my feet out of complacency. Just in case.

He frowned. "I think that's oversimplifying things a little."

I didn't. This all coming to light made me want to thank him for ending things. More than enough had piled itself onto my shoulders. Thanks would have been petty, though. And probably draw this whole conversation out longer. It was already too long. "Let's just cut through the bullshit, shall we? And this time, I want answers, not excuses. Why, the fuck, did you come looking for me today."

His cheeks pulled in, like he needed to chew his cheeks a moment or two before he calmed enough to answer. "I thought Gabriel might have left you some money and I hoped you would give me five thousand."

He had the decency to drop his eyes from mine as he finished. Down and away, the shame-filled way.

The downward cast of his eyes gave me the freedom to spare a glance toward Kai. He kept his vigil on Chad. Trusted him less than I did, I guessed. I asked him anyway, "Why does everyone want money from me today?"

"I don't know." Kai shook his head without looking my way.

"And did I miss that five thousand was the magick number today?"

"Did the senator ask a specific number?" Despite his attention on Chad, Kai spoke free and easy. We could have been talking about a particularly nice selection of cheeses.

I wondered how much it would take to get me to that level. My voice gave my emotion away more often than not, even if the face hid it all. "That's what Gabe gave him. Not sure if he knows it yet, but he bitched, moaned, and racist-ranted himself out of it."

"Greer?" Chad asked, almost sheepishly. More like starving-wolf-in-sheepskin-ly.

I rolled my full attention back to him. "What?"

"Are you going—I mean, would you consider helping me out?" He tried puppy-dog eyes on me. Not completely. Just the slightest dipping down of his chin to look up at me with a little more of the white in his eyes showing. Blood-shot white. Practically screaming at me to ignore all the wolf parts. Pet the pretty, pretty sheep.

Right.

"No."

"Greer, I—"

"No."

"Greer, just listen—"

"What could you possibly say that would make me want to give you anything other than a nice, satisfying punch in the face?" I almost wanted to hear whatever sob story he would concoct.

He heaved a couple of breaths, eyes searching my face with wild desperation. "Didn't Gabe always teach you to be generous with those less fortunate than yourself?"

I slapped him. Stepped and turned my hips with it. Got my whole palm against the side of his face. Rocked his head to the side far enough he had to stumble quite a few steps to the side to keep from falling.

My heart thumped against my sternum, blood thrumming through me and ready for more. I could have beat him to a pulp. I really could have. But witnesses then cops then handcuffs then everything would spiral. A downward spiral from the bottom of the well would be quite the shit storm.

One, two, three, shit-nado coming for me.

Three, two, one, this could be a lot of fun.

Feet wide and stable under me, my left hand stung like the dickens from the impact with Chad's obnoxious face. My right wanted to try it with a fist. I reined my violent tendencies into a sharply pointed index finger in his face. "Don't you ever speak his name. Not my name for him. He deserves more than to be remembered on your lying lips. Why don't forget you ever knew my name while you're at it?"

He held his cheek with wide hurt eyes. My resolve to stay out of jail kept me from smacking the look off his face. Just barely

"I can't believe you just did that." The words came out all breathy.

I needed to go. "Kai, where's your car?" I asked without taking my eyes off wounded-animal Chad.

"In the furthest corner possible," Kai said, "but close to the exit."

Music to my ears. I needed the solid exit strategy.

Kai interposed himself between Chad and I, then tipped his chin in the direction we'd been headed before the interruption.

Leaving first stank of retreat, but I didn't want to deal with Chad any more. Convincing him to walk away would be another fruitless waste of my energy.

I swiveled a hard turn and power-strutted toward Kai's car. After I'd made it a couple car lengths away, Kai's footsteps crunched behind me.

"That's assault," Chad yelled after us. "I'll sue."

He didn't sound any closer than where we left him, so I let it be. I laughed, because the only other option was to cry.

"How're you going to sue me, Chad?" I yelled back toward him. "Lawyers cost money, and you don't have any."

Almost let it be.

# 25 – WOOD

I LET MY HEAD drop against the seat, doing my best to will the last ten minutes out of existence. Kai's car purred to life around me. Just a short ride and I could shut the world away from me.

Several minutes of sitting there without moving made me open my eyes and turn my head slightly to Kai.

He watched, unreadable expression painted on his face.

When he didn't say anything to me looking at him, I had to ask. "What?"

"Seatbelt?"

My face twisted in confusion. "I survived a bomb exploding in my face, and you're worried about me putting on my seatbelt?" Despite my question, I pulled the belt around me and clicked the thing in.

"It's the law."

I shook my head at the absurdity. "Happy?"

"Not quite."

I blinked at him a couple of beats, hoping he would fill the silence with explanation. He didn't, naturally.

"Okay?" I prompted, even added in a rolling wrist gesture for good measure.

"After all the extra things today, I should probably take you home, or wherever you're staying." He spoke in a cautious manner, analyzing me for a reaction.

If I hadn't publicly shamed a state senator and smacked the daylights out of my ex in the last hour, I might have been more offended at his vigilance. Before that... My mood *had* been a little unpredictable today. Even to me.

Since he waited, apparently, for me to give him leave to speak again, I did. "And what is the problem?"

"I want to take you home and fuck you senseless."

A heatwave thrummed across the surface of my body. Much nicer than anything else in my head. "Let's do that." I practically panted the words.

With the tiniest upturn on the edges of his mouth, he shifted the car out of park. His pupils widened until only the barest ring of gold remained. "Good."

He nearly stalled the car pulling out.

It sparked a bubbling laugh out of me. Come hell or the ten plagues of Egypt, this would happen.

Kai cast a look at me from the corner of his eye, burning with the same heat of his full-on stare. "This is not a laughing matter."

"Right now, I can laugh at everything else." Lana and Anterograde could rip the world into shreds for all I cared. So long as they left Kai and I an undisturbed corner in the world for an hour.

Tracing the line of his suit with just my eyes made me re-evaluate. I needed half a day with him alone. At the very least. "Do you have condoms? I don't have any on me."

He shook his head. "I don't get sick."

"Right."

"It's the same thing as poison to my body, as far as I can tell." He shrugged. "I can't catch anything so I can't pass it on, outside of an orgy."

He levered a warm look at me, like nothing would please him more than to involve the two of us in one.

I narrowed my eyes at him. "Not today. You're all mine today."

Kai nearly stalled the car again, over-revving like he did.

Shit. I hoped he didn't live far.

After a few swallows and a little white-knuckling the steering wheel he asked, "What about you? Are you on the pill?"

"Nope."

Some of the single-minded heat in his expression dimmed. "We can stop for condoms."

I shook my head. "No need. I can't get pregnant."

He gave me the same kind of wry look I'd given him. "Right."

Getting into this would pull me right out of the mood, but he needed assurances. "Seriously. There's too much scar tissue."

I willed him not to ask the next logical question. Asking would break me and this shiny thing we never got to play with might break too.

Don't ask. Please don't ask.

"You want to talk about it?"

He danced around the anti-arousal zone, inviting me to dive in.

"Nope." I danced with him.

"You're sure?"

"Yep."

"So, we're good?"

"Go for launch."

Kai nodded.

Saints be praised, he took me at my word and didn't push. I would reward him handsomely for it.

The tires screeched a bit as Kai turned into the Rust's rear parking lot. I started to ask, then stopped myself. He knew where he was driving. The smaller garage door next to the delivery entrance opened at the press of a button on his sun visor.

I'd climbed halfway out of the car before he came to a full stop.

A door in the back of the garage opened. Rust's bouncer, Brutus. "Hey, Kai. I'm glad I caught you."

"Not now." Kai stalked around the car, a hungry tiger just taken off leash.

"No, I just had a quick—"

"If no one is dying, it can wait." I glared, pointing at Brutus from half a car's length away. "If someone's dead, it can fucking wait."

His eyes widened, deer in headlights, from my aggression.

I didn't care.

Kai snagged an arm around my waist and tugged me toward the

door on the passenger's side of the car. "Be kind to the locals." He smiled as he said it. Half tease, half enjoying the hell out of my impatience.

I slipped a finger under the knot in his tie, pulled him toward me, and bit his chin. His irises shrunk into his pupils once again. Just how I wanted. Now that I had his full attention, I repeated myself. "It can fucking wait."

"Well shit," Brutus said. "Get him."

I planned to.

Kai dropped his eyes from me long enough to fumble, one-handed, with his keys and open the door. He used the arm around me to press us together as he pushed me inside.

The door closed with a solid kick, neither of us stopping to make sure it stayed closed. My hands were too busy pulling his tie off. He leaned down to claim my mouth. I had to speak up before I lost my head.

"Ground rules first." The words came out on breaths almost rapid enough to be pants.

He raised an eyebrow while a wicked smile curled his lips. "Really? Rules." His hands massaged their way down my backside, pressing my pelvis against his.

I nearly forgot what I meant to say. But I needed to. Fast. "Since the thing at Rust my skin has been a little odd, especially at the chest, so you have to keep touching me once my top's off."

"I intend to." He came at me before I could protest any more. All hard lips and soft, teasing teeth.

The cushioned wall hit my back and my hands danced over his shirt buttons. His pulled my skirt up past my waist. It gave me the surge to push him back. "I mean it. My skin glows all over, but my chest hypnotizes people."

"I agree."

His hands slipped upward. I abandoned my grip on his shirt to hold his hands still. Kai stopped where he was, hands halfway up my torso and lips a breath away from mine.

I swallowed to give me a moment of clear thought. "I'm serious, Kai. Like what Magus does to people. Complete loss of control. Not in a sexy way."

He nodded to me, grazing his lips against mine, nearly stealing my control. "Hands on at all times. I think I can manage that. Anything else?"

He seemed to get it. I hoped he did. I didn't know how else to explain without showing him and I refused to ruin this moment any more than I had already. So, I answered his question. "Yes. You get naked first."

Kai smiled. Kissed me again. Slipped his tongue in my mouth. His hands didn't move again until I let them go. Then they rolled over my skin, massaging and pinching.

I ripped the last two buttons pulling Kai's shirt open. He laughed at me, low and easy, as he pulled away. Not far. With the hand still hiking my skirt above my waist, he pulled me deeper into his home. Through a circle of mature trees and into a sunlit patch of grass ringed in flowers.

The change from modern building to fairy wonderland broke into the spell of lust between us with magick of its own. Fat bumblebees buzzed in the flowers. Butterflies fluttered. Growing and blooming things perfumed the air like the first breath of spring, despite the fruit hanging from many of the trees. Bright sunlight bathed the whole scene; I couldn't see the hint of a modern ceiling above us.

"Wow." I took a deep breath.

"Greer."

I turned my gaze back to Kai and nearly choked on the air in my lungs. In the time I'd taken to look over his indoor grove, he'd lost his shirt and jacket all together. All that red-brown skin, scars painting a map over him, and it was mine. I wanted to meet his bare chest with my own, mold our skin together, but I had to wait. I had to make sure there was enough of the rest of us touching first.

He watched me as I undid his belt. Stole kisses as I unzipped his pants. Stared into my eyes as I slid his pants—he had no underwear—down, sinking to my knees as I did so. Kneeling brought me face to face with his welcome erection, and his prosthetic right leg.

# 26 – BRIGHT LITTLE DEATH

LOOKING UP AT Kai's face from this angle took most of my self-control.

Gods.

Everything looked good from this angle. His expression set my chest aflutter. Wide eyed, dilated lust waltzing with vulnerable need. I let my fingers trace along one of the carvings in the wood of his leg.

His whole body shivered.

"You can feel that?"

"Yes."

The huskiness of his voice pulled a smile out of me. "You didn't tell me you had this much wood."

He pulled me up from kneeling, hands on either side of my head. He kissed me hard and fast, only pausing to pull my dress up and over me. Shoes were kicked off. One twist of Kai's fingers unfastened my bra. He trailed his nails down my arms as he pulled my bra from me. I pinched his nipple. He groaned and cradled my chest in both his hands.

"What are your thoughts..." Kai leaned down to press a chaste kiss on my left nipple. "On foreplay?" He touched his lips to the other.

My knees trembled. I pulled him closer to keep me vertical. "I don't have the patience for it right now."

"Good."

Kai picked me up long enough to lay me down on the grass beneath him. I rolled us over so I ended on top and grabbed a hold of his penis.

"Shit," he whispered into my neck. "Shit. Shit. Shit."

I rocked my hips and guided him into me. "Shit," I agreed. Relief surged through me in the same breath as an arc of pleasure.

"Move for me, Greer."

I did. And he did. It took a few thrusts to synchronize. We found our rhythm. Heat and sweat poured out of us. The sweat mixed with the crushed grass and soil in the air. Kai pulled me down to kiss me, mouth mirroring the rhythm of his hips. He tasted of wild oak and darker forest, sharp and fragrant.

Perfect. Raw. Beautiful. A sharp pain in my right buttock forced me out of my absorption in the moment.

"Ass cramp. Ass cramp."

Kai sat the two of us up. "Better?"

I twisted my legs around so they circled around him, but I still had to rub it out. Kai helped, more of a distraction than effective. But it worked. And we moved again. With his face an inch from mine. Teeth bared and lips pulling back with each rock. Eyes locked on mine.

This angle struck me deeper. It didn't take long. A few thrusts and he pushed me over the edge.

My head tipped back. My blood pulsed. The room brightened. Kai rolled me back onto the grass. "Not yet."

He pushed into me again, forcing a scream out of me and another pulse of light. And another. Another. Again and again until a guttural moan shook out of him and he finally collapsed on top of me. His panting rolled over the skin of my collarbone pleasantly, but he'd rung me out too much to react to it.

Kai rolled partially off me. I snagged a leg around him before he moved too far. The dichotomy between the cool grass against my back and the heat of his damp skin along the front of me. Magick. Perfection. Too divine to give up just yet. Kai didn't make much effort to get away from me.

His eyes were on my face when I rolled my head toward him. Mischief shined in their depths. I narrowed my gaze. "What?"

"Was it good for you, LightBright?"

I laughed, letting the shake of it reveal all my lovely sore spots. It felt good. I felt good. I planted a sloppy kiss on his cheek. "We'll do better next time."

"I hate to break it to you, Greer, but I need a couple hours to recharge." His hand slid down the side of me, despite his words. "I'm about a minute from passing out."

I didn't even have the energy to hide my relief. "I'm with you, I just need to use the restroom first."

"Me too."

Neither of us moved.

My eyes threatened to close so I raised up on one elbow. "If you point me to the restroom I can hobble my way there. I think."

"I could carry you there."

Not on his life. I shook my head and pushed myself to sitting. Kai untangled his legs from mine, but I set a hand on his abdomen before he completely disengaged. He lifted an eyebrow. I Vanna White-ed my still glowing and shimmering chest. The brightness had dropped from supernova pulses but I still shone enough to see in the sunlight.

Kai leaned forward to kiss each nipple reverently. "Yes, I see."

My legs revolted at standing, but they held me steady. Kai waited for me to nod before leading me with a hand at the base of my spine toward the far edge of the tree circle.

The light dimmed as we stepped through the trees. Grass gave way to moss beneath my feet. A huge bed sat low against the wall to the left. The wood of the nightstands on either side looked gnarled enough to have grown in that shape. A low dresser on the close wall appeared just as natural. Ferns lined the walls bare of furniture and vines climbed behind them. Even with the unbroken trough of windows trailing around the room just below the ceiling, the light from my skin cast everything in moving shadows.

"Bedroom like this and you had me on the grassy knoll?" My attempt to chide him rang hollow.

"Between the light bathing you and the joy on your face when you looked at my unconventional living room." His fingers circled around my hip, pressing our sides together. "My patience ended. We can christen the bed."

Mmm, yes. "We will."

"Later." He nodded, without slowing to toss me on the bed.

Later indeed.

A partially overgrown door on the opposite side of the room opened to the largest residential bathroom I'd ever seen. Marble and wood and tile all mixed, beautifully. Tub large enough to fit a party. One of those showers with heads spraying from 9 different angles. Plants held court on almost every horizontal surface.

I pulled my eyes from the room and back to him. Smug satisfaction curved his lips.

"I think I might need to take a shower before I pass out." I coughed in what I hoped was an unassuming kind of way. "To keep me from stiffening before morning."

He smiled at my choice of word, but swept his hand around to the room. "Towels in the walk-in. Use anything in the shower. Keep away from the bath; all the plants around it are poisonous. I would join you, but I'm too close to passing out. Wake me when you come back to bed, by any means necessary."

Gods, I wished I had enough in me. A morning pursuit, or rather whenever we woke up. Mouth clamped shut, I nodded. He returned the gesture, detached from me, and froze mid step. From the direction of his feet, I gathered he was headed to the tiny closed off room hiding the toilet. Rather than touch him, I grabbed a towel off the nearest rack. Second nearest. The hand towel didn't cut it for coverage.

Kai's head followed my progress across the room, completely absent of his personality. When I covered my chest, he blinked out of his stupor, then narrowed his eyes in confusion. I wasn't where I had been.

I opened my mouth to explain. He stopped me with a raised hand. "No. You already told me. I just didn't expect..."

The thought trailed off. I wanted desperately for him to finish it, but he didn't owe me any explanation. He shook his head at me and continued to the toilet closet.

Standing there, listening to him pee. A little awkward. I didn't dare start my shower. The idea of stepping out to see him staring at me like that creeped me out. So, I leaned my butt against the sink counter and waited.

He flushed and washed his hands. He dried them on the towel I'd draped across the front of me, eyes locked on mine. Drying them shouldn't have taken as long as it did. It didn't matter. Small smile turning his mouth, he kissed me again. Soft at first, but I pulled him deeper with teeth, dragged my nails down the back of him. When I finally let him go, his breaths heaved as much as mine did.

"Shit, woman," he breathed before breaking away and stiff-legging to the door. The door closed behind him with another, "Shit."

A cold shower might have been a better choice, but I cranked the temp up as high as I could stand. Searing hot water pulsed at me from nine different directions and rained down in a steady flow from the top. I could marry the shower, but I was too tired to consummate right then. I made a promise to it before I washed myself in something woodsy and musky.

Kai had sprawled out on the bed in the too-short time I'd been in the bathroom. The not-wooden leg had the corner of a sheet over it. The rest of him lay bare, on display for me whilst tiny snores bubbled out of him. Kind of adorable.

I traded towel for sheet as I sank down on the bed. The towel went on the night stand as I lay down next to him. He wanted me to wake him, but I didn't have it in me. We both needed the sleep. Kai rolled toward me as I sidled up to him, wrapping the wooden leg around mine until I couldn't escape if I wanted to.

The heat and weight of him stripped away the last of my resistance.

I didn't remember where I was when I woke. The sheets were too smooth to be mine. The room too cool for this time of year. Too humid. The scent of rich soil and growing things broke into the fog in my head. Trees and moss meant I hadn't left Kai's, though the weight of him was gone. Patting the cold linens around clued me in. He hadn't been in the bed with me for a while.

I risked slitting my eyes open, but needn't have worried. The bedroom maintained its cave-like atmosphere. More strongly, now that the sun had set. I stretched everything. My body sang back at me.

My phone held a piece of paper on top of a folded pile of fabric where I'd left the towel. Kai had handwriting as clear as typeset. Odd for a man.

*Didn't want to wake you. There's food in the kitchen, if you wish. I'm at the bar.*

No sign off, but who else would have written it? The same person who thought to plug my phone in before setting it onto a pile of my folded clothes.

Three missed calls and thirteen missed texts. Most of them from the same person. I hit dial. Lex picked up the other end in half of a ring.

"Where have you been? Are you okay? Whose knees do I need to snap?"

I snuggled deeper into the pillow. "Hello, to you, too."

"Hello? I've been out of my head worried about you and all you give me is hello?"

"It's only been…" I didn't know what time it was. My brain hadn't registered it when I looked the first time. I pulled the phone from my ear to check. "It's almost nine."

"Exactly."

If I didn't feel so good, I might have been annoyed. "Do I have a curfew I don't know about?"

"Curfew? I'd just appreciate you letting me know when you're going to drop off the radar for a day. Especially with what happened to your apartment and your car. You can't blame me for worrying." He clipped each word. He'd switched from worry to angry in a hurry.

"Calm down, Lex. Twelve hours since I've seen you is hardly a day."

"Twelve hours? Dollface, I haven't seen you since that beefcake picked you up for the funeral yesterday."

Yester—I pulled the phone from my ear to get a better look at the time. Still just after nine. The date, though. The date said Tuesday. Well shit. "No wonder I feel so good."

"What?" So much heat in the one word.

Damage control time. "Kai took me to his place after the funeral."

"You will give me details when I'm not pissed at you."

"I will, but don't be pissed. I just woke up and calling you was the first thing I did."

There was a pregnant pause on the other side. I waited for Lex to work through whatever he needed to.

"What, did you have a tantric extravaganza and forget the rest of the world?" The harsh tone in his voice had given way, for the most part. "Because I could forgive you for that kind of thing. After a thorough cross-examination."

Crisis averted. "It was more like one good shot knocked me out. For more than a day, apparently."

"Girl."

I agreed.

"Now, I'm a different kind of angry."

He should be. "Is there a reason you called, beyond my Rip Van Winkle?"

"Yes, actually. Some cops came by looking for you about the shooting in your old workplace. They need your statement."

Right. They did.

It had kind of slipped through the cracks of everything else exploding around me. "Did they leave a number?"

"They said you should have it, but gave me a card for you anyway. I sent you a picture, but I guess you hadn't checked your texts yet."

"Nope."

Lex cleared his throat. "You should probably ignore the death threats."

That pulled a laugh out of me. "Now, I'm excited." For the leverage he had probably given me.

"And I'm sorry, Greer."

He would be. "Anything else?"

"God, I can hear you plotting against me. No. That's it. I'm going to go prep tasty foods for you. When might you be home to eat them?"

Bribery. He knew many recipes to win me over. He would win this round and both of us knew it. So, I moved the conversation along.

"Tonight, sometime. I can't hazard a guess of when right now."

"Gonna hop on your beefcake again?"

"Not sure I can risk losing another day right now." It might not be just the day. I needed to be ready for Saturday and whatever crime the chickie tried to pull at the fair. "But there's always booze and friends."

He grunted in his disappointed, disbelieving way. I could see the attitude through the phone.

"Well." In the pause, I knew he shifted his weight from one foot to the other. "Call me if you're not coming."

"Will do, Lex."

"Details." Lex hung up on me before I could respond.

There wasn't much to say to that.

I slipped my clothes on before I ventured out from the bedroom. If Kai popped back in, he didn't need the boobs to put the whammy on him again.

Gods.

This thing could get complicated. Half of my wardrobe needed to be replaced. And I couldn't wear short items in the summer if I planned to be in mixed company after the sun set. Huzzah, that my exploding car didn't kill me, but the rest of this was hard to swallow.

Rather than crossing through the grassy knoll, I skirted around the trees in search of the kitchen. Several of the trees bore fruit—apples, pears, peaches and the like—but I didn't risk picking from them. Kai hadn't mentioned the trees in the note, so I didn't want to cross that line if there was one. But really, I feared that the trees might pelt me with fruit without Kai there to soothe the exchange.

Instead, I trailed my fingers along the trunks of a few as I passed an entertainment room complete with a koi pond and woven-wood furniture still rooted in the ground and growing. A library hid around the next curve of the room, a few glassed curios on display here and there. Only a rumble of my belly kept me moving past and into the kitchen.

A vat of beef stew, half eaten, and a whole loaf of French bread.

Bless that man.

With no one to witness, I razed the vat and stuffed myself. The thing was more empty than full by the time my stomach stopped yelling at me. The loaf of bread, completely gone. Kai sure knew how to work up a woman's appetite.

Sate it too.

# 27 – ABNORMAL NORMAL

WHEN I FINALLY wound myself through the storage room and out onto the patio, the bar had the *between* feel. After happy hour and before the committed drinkers and booty-call seekers trickled their way in. The uncrowded, night air caressed my skin and eased in my lungs. I took a deep breath before seeking out a familiar face.

Though, familiar faces abounded in the sparse patio. Most of them, superheroes. The three women were all attached to one of the ten men in some way. I wondered if they knew the company they were keeping, but I had bigger fish to fry.

My favorite stool at the bar was free. Right next to a backside I recognized as Phoenyx's and in front of my favorite bartender. Kai's eyes bore into me. He must have been watching me since I stepped out the door. The rest of his face held little emotion. I didn't know how to take that. I sauntered over anyway.

"What's up, barkeep?"

Kai's lips softened some. "Hello, Greer. How're you doing?"

"Great." I toyed with the idea of ordering a beer. Did I want to stay long enough to enjoy it? Should I even risk alcohol after my long winter's nap. "I think I got the best sleep I've ever had."

"Bored her to sleep, did you?" Phoenyx smirked at his own cleverness.

Kai frowned.

I replied, "Knocked me out, more like."

"But you're okay?" A little of Kai's happy mask slipped. Worry lines formed between his eyebrows and pinched the corners of his eyes. His body practically pulsed with tension.

Huh.

"I am faaaantastic." I held a hand up, though neither man made a motion to speak. "Scratch that. I am peachy, *you* were fantastic."

The vibration in him eased with the very masculine ego boost. That smile, off center with eyes diving south from my face, made me want to get a little boost of my own.

"Shit," Phoenyx mumbled into his glass.

If he had said more, I might have pushed him to explain just what he meant.

Kai finally asked, "Are you hungry?"

For so many things. Few for public consumption. I finally told him the only thing vanilla enough. "I could eat." Again.

Despite the stew, I was running on a half-empty tank. The day of sleeping and the weekend before must have taken more out of me than I'd realized. I would need to take better care of myself. At least until this weekend.

"Mike?" Kai nodded to Phoenyx.

The two-names thing again. And Phoenyx was not in his superhero guise so he was Mike. I considered whether I should choose another name for myself. Of course, that would mean I planned on taking up the saving-the-world mantel.

"What do you want?" Mike asked, then grinned. "Aside from Kai, of course. He's a little busy at the moment."

If he wanted to embarrass me, he would need to try a lot harder. "Burger or wings without the sauce. Something with meat and not a lot of middle men."

"Coming right up." He stretched himself as he stood.

I took no shame in watching him walk away in his snug little jeans. When I tore my gaze away, Kai had a terrible glare fixed on me. I narrowed my eyes. Then, I shrugged. "I am an admirer of fine behinds. Tell me he doesn't have a nice one."

Kai opened his mouth, but nothing came out. Conflict marched across his eyes, though, so I added. "Not the finest I've seen recently, but nice."

My attempt to bridge the gap only did so much to ease his reaction, so I let it drop. "Can I get a soda while I wait?"

"That's all you have to say?"

I rubbed the sides of my hair down in a petting motion. The better to soothe me with. "Admiring does not mean desiring. Other than that, what did you want me to say?"

"Perhaps something about why I couldn't wake you for more than a day then you plop down here like nothing's amiss. And the blinding glow that happened when we..." He trailed off with a surreptitious glance to the side.

My brain kind of exploded. I mean, huzzah, he wasn't stuck on me staring at someone's ass, but what the fuck with the rest? "So, you're questioning involuntary reactions that happened to me the first time they happened to me and trying to blame me for them?"

He dropped his gaze from mine. Oh, he chopped limes, but we both knew the real reason. "I'm not blaming you. I just wanted to know why you didn't warn me beforehand."

"I warned you about what I knew about. Repeatedly."

"I'm getting that." Chop chop chop. "It's just. I was scared."

The last killed the swell of anger in me. Admitting fear took a lot of strength. "I've had so much happen the past few days that I might be beyond fear."

He looked me in the eyes, gold of the irises chilling toward amber-brown. "No one is beyond fear."

Interesting sentiment, but absolutes were a slippery wicket.

Shut up, Greer.

Kai set a soda in front of me with the softness of an apology. Phoenyx—Mike. Mike came to the rescue not too much later, burger and fries in hand.

I hadn't wanted more than the meat when he left, but I devoured the fries with the burger. Background music volume rose with the influx of people. The night owls were gaining ground. I didn't feel much like playing this evening.

Kai waved off my wallet when I pulled it out. I thanked him with a quick kiss that fired heat straight down my spine. He swore as I pulled away. Mutual fire, then. Good. It would have been better if he had offered to take me home. He voluntold Mike to be my chauffer, which was probably better.

I really didn't want to lose another day.

"I'll meet you in front in five," Mike said sweeping my plate up. "I have a couple things to do, then I'll pick you up."

"Like, in your car?"

"Well, certainly not on my bicycle." He walked away without giving me the time to throw something back at him. Mike in his tight jeans wouldn't be able to fly where I needed to go.

My spine popped as I stood. Relief.

"Greer."

My name on Kai's lips swung me back around toward him. He had that heat in his gaze, though his hands worked their way through a small bounty of lemons.

"Yeah, Kai?"

"I'll call you."

"Yes, you will."

He'd better

I waved and dodged my way through the loose crowd of people inside. Walking through grounded me a bit, even if I missed the night air. I gulped it down when I pushed far enough outside the front door to appreciate it.

"Rough night?" a brusque voice asked me. Me and only me. Despite the line of women along the side of the building. Brutus the bouncer had something up his sleeve. If he mentioned what he witnessed the night before I'd maul him.

How to answer his question, without throwing my marbles at him. "Tonight wasn't as bad as the past few, but the competition is fierce."

"I hear letting someone touch your boobs is the cure for whatever ails you."

So many ways to respond. I chose the higher ground.

I set a hand on each of his pecs and squeezed. "Wow. I do feel better."

A few people in the front of the line giggled. Brutus waggled his eyebrows at me in a comic, come-hither way. "Can this be mutual?" He grinned, wide and proud.

"Not on your life."

The rumble of a car that had seen better days drew our attentions to the street. Truck that had seen better days, not a car. It eased to a stop in the no parking zone in front of the doors. The window rolled down and the light came on. Mike. "You molesting the staff again, Greer? Because we charge extra for that."

I gave Brutus one more good squeeze before I let go with a wink. "Put it on my tab."

"I only trade in kind." His laughter chased me all the way to Mike's car.

Glaring at Brutus with all the seriousness of a French clown, I hiked my way up into Mike's truck. The soft leather inside belied the dented exterior, but the thing had been jacked up higher than was absolutely necessary.

"That'll do," Brutus said.

His eyes locked on the bits of thigh I'd exposed while getting in the truck. A panicked assessment of my skirt reassured me that my underwear remained hidden. I could deal with that much. I waited until I'd situated myself and closed the door behind me to yell, "Lecher," at him.

"At your service." He took a bow. The man certainly made it hard to stay mad at him. Or at anything else, for that matter.

The wind coming in the window as Mike drove blew colder than comfortable. The temperature had been fine at a standstill. The briskness suited the moment, so I left the window down. I knew Mike wouldn't mind.

"Are you okay?"

I whipped my head around to look at Mike. He risked a couple glances my way, assessing in the few seconds before he turned his attention back to not killing us.

Rather than answer, I asked a question. Because I was a chicken. "Why do you ask?"

"Kai said you passed out after you two..."

He could have said it. I let the sentence trail off without me filling in the blanks. His prudishness was his business.

"Not right after. Took a shower first."

Mike nodded. "Then slept for more than twenty-four hours."

What was he getting at? "After the weekend from hell and back again, in which I got maybe twelve hours of sleep over four grueling days. Physically and emotionally grueling."

His lips pressed together like a carp and he tilted his head side to side. "When you put it like that..."

"Not to mention the glowing thing."

He took a longer look at me after he stopped at a red light. "I see what you mean."

I dropped my gaze to see my legs shimmering faintly. "Well, yeah, this, but I kind of went supernova when I came."

Mike whipped his head forward and did not look at me. Deer in headlights expression stretching his face into a tight, almost-smile. Men with their prudishness.

Eyes rolling, I saved him. "Anyway, to answer your question, I don't know. I don't know if I'm okay or even if I should be. And I also feel numb, like the next thing that happens couldn't possibly phase me at this point. It's just too much, too much."

None of that killed the paralyzed deer in him. I tried again. "Physically, I'm fine. No injuries or bruises."

Which was odd. Phoenyx and I had been in an explosion and I'd been bruised all to hell. Now that I thought about it, I didn't have any of that kind of sensitivity or tightness. I pulled my top far enough away to see down my belly.

In the glow from myself, I didn't see any bruises on the skin.

"Huh."

"You need me to check something out for you?" Mike cast a sidelong glance at me. Nowhere near innocent. Especially not with the sly curve to his lips.

Men. One minute too prude to discuss a woman's supernova-laced orgasm, the next, asking for a taste. "No, I just realized that all the bruises from my car's untimely death are gone."

He didn't say anything, didn't even react except to nod.

"What?"

"Well, Greer. Odd things are to be expected when someone first comes into their powers."

Apparently, it didn't matter if the person's powers came from their blood or outside forces. My powers *were*. Tougher, glowing skin, hypnoboob and all. No way to go back to normal. And if I managed to revert, somehow, what kind of life would I have to go back to? My life had disintegrated, like porcelain ground beneath a mammoth foot.

Walking toward Lex's door, I was fairly certain I didn't want to live the pretty-doll life anymore.

# 28 – THE REAL MONSTER

CHEATING ON YOUR favorite bar wasn't cheating when you didn't want to see any of the people there. The darker, moldy atmosphere reminded me of why usually avoided this one, despite the walking distance from my apartment. Lack of transportation and need for booze won right around happy hour the next day.

The people trickling in mirrored the dank feel of the bar, though they smiled more than suited my mood. They made me glad I'd snagged a seat on the corner of the bar before the bulk of the crowd flooded in. The corner right under a couple burned-out lights. The relative darkness granted me some measure of protection from people cramming in next to me.

I let the darkness and noise of the bar sink into me while I downed the last of my second drink. Wishing the other people would tone down their cheer until I got a good buzz on, I waved the nearest bartender over.

The woman narrowed her eyes at me. "If you keep drinking at this rate, I'm going to have to take your car keys."

Really.

I leaned toward her, prompting her to tilt toward me. "You know that car that went boom in Cherry Creek."

She frowned. "Yours?"

I shrugged and smiled a bitter smile.

"I'll get your next round."

She started mixing without another word.

I hadn't expected that much. "You're my hero."

Without looking up, the woman nodded. Like she'd heard that kind of thing before. It was probably true every time. Hero didn't have to mean a man with superpowers. Anyone with the right kind of heart going slightly out of their way for another person was a hero.

I could do that. Help people on the small scale. Maybe more than a little after I got my feet back under me.

The world had a way of testing resolve, or at least mine did.

A waif-ish blonde woman plopped a pinch of pills in the glass of the man between us. She covered the move with a flirtatious smile of cherry-red lips and a caress along the man's chin. Enough to put the whammy on any unwary man and quite a few women. No less than five minutes after the quiet altruism passed through my head.

I hadn't meant I wanted to help people in the next breath.

Too late.

Things were in motion.

A minute or two passed and I wavered. Should I? Was it my place or should I shove my nose into my own glass? Perhaps he'd asked for the pills, but then, why the distraction?

The man slipped his hand around his rum and coke.

I cupped my hand over the top, banging it back down on the bar. "Nope, nope, nope."

They both turned to me. Simple confusion glowed from his muddy-blue eyes. Annoyance and the cool edge of anger from her aqua. Enough to convince me I'd been right.

"What the hell?" The man kind of puffed up.

I tipped my chin toward the woman. "She put some pills in your drink."

His head jerked back, eyebrows pulled down and toward the center. Surprise or disbelief. Combination of the two. Didn't really matter.

The woman tried for shock. "Why would I even—"

"Not sure. Why *did* you?"

"I didn't." This time she sounded convincing, at least.

The man pulled at his drink. I curled my fingers around it.

His lips thinned. "Look, ma'am, maybe you should butt out."

"Yeah." She echoed him like of those tiny puppies in cartoons. The ones doing all the yapping for the much larger dog. Her slipping off the stool, nearly a head shorter standing than she had been seated, increased the resemblance to the yippy sidekick.

"If she proves me wrong, I'll leave the two of you alone." I shrugged, but clenched my hand tighter around the glass. "She can drink your drink."

He rolled his eyes. "You want to just shut this bitch up." He jerked his thumb at me and stepped out of the way.

The woman stepped and punched me in the cheek.

I dropped off the stool. Backward. Onto my ass. Breath knocked out of me. I heaved in breaths, fighting against the pain in my chest and in my face. By the time I climbed back to a vertical-ish crouch, the woman was long gone.

A hand reached down to help me. The man. He believed me now, apparently.

I swatted his hand away and pulled myself to standing.

Quite a few people had their eyes on me.

Naturally.

Center of attention in a bar again. This time, at least, I hadn't passed out. And I hadn't started glowing enough to light up the night. Just the low-level glittering on my hands I had when I came in.

"Do you want me to call the cops?" The bartender asked me once I'd settled back down in front of my glass.

Being knocked on my ass hadn't spilled my drink. I'd take it as a win.

To the bartender, I shook my head. I'd stuck my nose in someone else's business. The consequences were mine and well-deserved. "No, thanks." I downed the rest of my drink.

"Are you sure?" She didn't look concerned for me, exactly. More like she hoped I didn't cause anymore ruckus.

"Yep."

"Can I buy you a drink?" The man reclaimed his spot by me, facing my way this time.

Great. Now I had *this* to deal with.

If I'd wanted to talk to him, I would have sparked up a conversation in the first place. Before the woman sidled up. "No."

He stretched his fingers out. "You saved me from...something. I can't just leave it at that."

Yes, he could. He wouldn't, because that would allow me to fade into the background again. The world wouldn't let me do that.

None of which was this guy's fault. I forced a breath out. "Fine. A thank you drink, then. That's it." Not even a name exchange, if I could manage it.

He set his elbow on the bar near me and leaned against it. Had he touched me, I might have snapped, but he kept an inch or two between us. Not much, but enough. "Are you sure that's it? Are you meeting someone here or..."

Gods.

He thought he could turn this into a pick up. My face hurt too much to deal with this.

I turned toward the bartender, who hadn't wandered too far while she filled another order. Something going my way, at least. "How much do I owe you?"

She shook her head and flapped a free hand at me. "I've got it. Why don't you go and have a better day?"

Couldn't get worse.

"Come on, girl. Don't be like that." He stood with me, though some of his confidence dropped when he realized how much shorter he was.

I could work with that, in a roundabout way. Without looking away from him, I told the bartender, "If he follows me out, could you call the cops for me?"

Lips flat, she nodded. "Will do."

Hoping the threat was enough, I dodged around him. He didn't grab at me. No one did. Despite the evident absorption in whatever they were doing, the people along my way to the door parted in a smooth-zipper motion. All the world was a stage and I, apparently, had been cast as the fool.

The shock of cooler air outside strengthened my light buzz into full-on tipsiness. The wavering in my head felt nice. Nicer than focusing on the pain around my nose and eyes. I would have some shiners. Later. After the nice inebriation left me. I hoped it would last me the two blocks to my apartment.

An arm circled around my waist as I passed the alleyway adjacent to the bar.

"Wha—"

"You don't like when I flip the switch and drug a guy." She wrangled me downward and backward. Off the main street, so the alley could hide her actions from the rest of the world. Small as she was, she knew how to use her body to the best advantage. Struggling didn't loosen her grip.

Something pressed against my neck. Too wide to be a knife or a gun.

"If you keep fighting like that, she'll stun the hell out of you," a voice from deeper in the alley informed me.

This new woman stepped out from behind the nearest dumpster. Her hair, silver as the moon and twirled into a bun, practically hovered above her worn leather jacket. A wet dream of a tough grandmother. She cut at me with her sharp gaze.

"Brittany tells me you narc-ed on her hustle."

Hustle.

Like drugging a person to take advantage of them wasn't one of the most pathetic things one person could do to another. What the fuck? It was time to go. I bucked like a rodeo bull in her grip.

The thing against my neck spiked warm. Heat flashed across my skin and light pulsed out of me. Once.

The woman's hold around me clenched with the pulse of light, then slackened all at once. She collapsed to the ground behind me. The older one smacked against the wall, pushed by an unseen force. Or by the light that came out of me.

What the hell?

I stepped away from the younger woman, kicking something plastic as I moved. A stun gun that looked a little burned. I smelled something burned too, not so much the plastic. Something much meatier.

I didn't want to look. I had to look anyway.

The front of the woman who grabbed me looked like I should have after my car exploded. Blisters and charring and weeping wounds. She smelled of barbeque. The breathy whimpers coming out of her turned my stomach. Cooked as she was, she was still alive. I covered my mouth at the horror. Despite what the woman had done and tried to do to me, I couldn't be glad.

Because this was me. My fault. She tried to stun me and the shit going on with my skin made it backfire. Stronger than the stun had been in the first place.

"What have you done?" The silver-haired woman had levered herself back to her feet. "What the hell are you?"

Ten-million-dollar question. I didn't have an answer before. Now, I knew.

I was a monster.

"I'm calling the 911," Silver Hair informed me in the same tone she'd threatened me earlier.

Good. The cops needed to come. Come take me and lock me away for the rest of my life. I would never use my power again, purposefully or not. Except, Lana and Anterograde and all of that. I'd sunk too far in the mud for Atreyu to pull me out now.

Silver Hair's "Get out of here," shocked me enough to make me look at her.

"What?"

"I'll have a hard enough time explaining this to the cops as is." She pressed three buttons on her phone and raised it to her ear with a trembling hand. "Get the fuck out of here."

Leaving the scene was the worst thing I could do right then. They had laws against it and everything.

I rotated on the balls of my feet and ran, as much as I could run. The wheeze in my chest reminded me of the burbling breaths from the woman who attacked me. The sound implanted itself on my brain, reminding me of my baby's last noises. Reminding me of the cost of getting involved with other people and things.

After we took care of Anterograde, I would hermit myself back into my safe, boring life. This weekend would be my last foray with the world and all the trouble therein.

# 29 – UNEXPECTED VISIT

TWO AND A half days of cleaning and the apartment finally measured up to my standards. Clean. Orderly. Livable, even. But not for me. Not anymore. The destruction and mayhem still lingered, angry ghosts resistant to bleach and elbow grease.

Happy memories lingered too.

How the excitement of moving in with Chad had overrun the frustrations of moving. Moments where he tickled me into submission or we curled up on the couch with junk food and fell asleep. Talking of our future together and how panic fluttered in my belly at the thought. I didn't tell him that. Couldn't find a way to tell him it wasn't him, that it was me, without sounding like a cliché woman in a two-bit RomCom.

The conversations cooled to nothing at some point. Three months ago. Six months ago. I couldn't remember. A symptom of my problems. It was no wonder Chad had sunk himself into a crippling, dangerous debt without my notice. I'd been too focused on our still waters to explore the depths.

I watched my own hazel eyes in the mirror above the bathroom sink as I washed the last of the cleaning grime from my fingers. Flat, guarded, and wary. The lines between my eyebrows and pinched bottom lip only supported my waiting expression, waiting for the shoes to trickle down like rain. I didn't look like someone who was easy to love.

I wasn't easy to love.

Escaping my own judgement as quickly as possible, I took the hand towel into the hall with me. That much introspection called for lunch.

Pizza sounded lovely. Too bad I could only afford the frozen, already in my freezer, kind. At least, until all of Gabe's assets transferred. I didn't know what I would do once it all got squared away. Probably cry more.

Stepping between hall and kitchen, I froze.

Two men stood in my entryway. Hard, thick, and wearing menace like capes.

Neet. I'd locked the front door. Hadn't I?

Both men stood shorter than me, but either looked strong enough to snap my spine at the waist without much forethought. The gun in the hand of the brunette rendered all the muscly bulk unnecessary. Their eyes widened a bit when they saw me. Either I was the person they were looking for, or they liked what they saw.

"Greer Ianto," the gun-toting man spoke first.

Yep. They were here for me.

At this point, I couldn't muster up too much surprise, so I nodded.

"You need to come with us."

Of course I did.

I folded the hand towel and set it nicely on the kitchen counter to dry. Leaving the apartment in good repair before a grey wizard whisked me away on an adventure. What could be better?

I reached for my purse where I'd tucked it on the kitchen barstool.

"No, you don't," the gun-toting man shook the gun like it also disagreed with my action. "Let's go."

"I'm coming. I just want to grab my bag."

"Leave it."

Making certain my hands were up and in full non-threatening mode, I replied. "Sir, I'm coming without a fight. Not gonna scream or try to escape. No funny business. I don't have any weapons in the purse, but I want it me."

His eyes narrowed while he tried to figure out how I was screwing him over. Since I wasn't, I waited for him to recognize that.

"Boris," he finally said. "Get her bag."

He probably shouldn't have used the other man's name. Didn't they teach that in villain school?

Boris, at least, had the good sense to swing around the back of the gun-toting man so he wouldn't pass though the line of sight. He nearly dropped the bag when he first took hold of it. "Are you sure there's not a tank in here?"

Funny. "As if I'd let you take me if I had a tank stowed away in my purse."

Neither of them laughed, the bastards.

Boris started out the door. I dropped my hands and followed, with the gun man bringing up the rear. He nearly ran into me when I stopped a few steps outside the apartment.

"Keep moving."

I turned toward him. "I just want to lock it up so no one breaks in and ransacks the place. Again." Nothing accusing in my language, but I suspected these two yahoos had something to do with the destruction I'd just finished cleaning.

After another too-long session of the brunette giving me the hard stare, he spoke. "Boris." Brunette jerked his chin toward the door once Boris swung around.

For a heartbeat, I considered exploiting their uneven dynamic. Boris didn't look too happy to traipse back to the door and lock up after us. Less so when I added, "You really have to wedge it to make sure it's closed."

Common sense told me, Boris disliked doing things for me more than he did taking the brunette's orders. They wanted me for something. There was no guarantee they needed me whole and undamaged for that something.

Brunette moved in closer to me than I liked. I held my space without a word. I'd gotten more from these two than any kidnappee could hope for.

He pinned me with another of his hard gazes. He meant serious business. "I'm putting the gun away, but if you try to escape, I will have it out and shoot you before you've made it to the top stair. Make a scene and you will regret it."

I believed him. I nodded my understanding.

Brunette tucked the gun into his waistband nearest me, barely fluffing his shirt over the butt of it. When I looked back up at his face, I found his eyes on me. Making sure I got it. I did.

He grabbed hold just above my elbow before starting us for the stairs again, tighter than expressly necessary. Whatever. The gun was gone. I'd already promised not to scream and carry on if they grabbed my bag, so I did Brunette one better.

Bending the arm and setting my free hand over his won me another one of his stares. This one only half hid his surprise and wariness.

I shrugged. "Best way to kill suspicion, Natasha."

Narrowed eyes. "What did you call me?" His words came out low. Ooo, he no like. Poor widdle gun man.

"He's Boris, so you would be Natasha, right?"

Shock and wordless offense. He probably wasn't expecting that one.

"I guess that would make me the moose and the squirrel." I was tall enough, I guessed.

Boris sneezed behind us. Covering a laugh, I hoped. Laughter bonded people and they might be less inclined to kill me if we shared a laugh or two.

"Shut your mouth until you are instructed otherwise." Natasha barked the words at me, but he kept it to a low volume.

The anger bubbling from him told me poking more at him might not be the best idea. Which was a shame. It kept me from thinking about where they were taking me and if I would survive.

A cherry-red Escalade chirruped at us as we got closer. Such a cliché for a bad guy car, but at least the red was pretty and atypical. Probably not the best thing to commit crime in, but I wouldn't be the one to tell them how to do their jobs. Especially when it meant helping them abscond with me.

Natasha opened the rear driver-side door for me. I thanked him, instead of mentioning he'd probably opened it for me to keep me from marring his shiny vehicle with fingerprints.

The leather stuck to my thighs where my shorts didn't cover, but this side of the car sat in the shade. Natasha grabbed hold of my wrist when I reached for the seatbelt.

"No." He jerked his chin my direction. "Scoot to the other side."

He wanted me in the seat not behind the driver. It made sense, when I thought about it. Messing with the driver would be harder from the passenger side, but I could see heat melting the air above the leather on the sunbaked side of the car.

My top lip curled in a sneer, but I scooched over. To the middle seat and buckled myself in without looking to him for permission. When I finally raised my eyes to him, he'd paused half way to climbing in behind me. Boris brought the red beast to life while the two of us in the back fought a staring contest.

I broke first, kind of. "You said nothing about me burning my thighs off on molten-hot leather." I crossed my arms to emphasize how serious I was.

Perhaps I should have used that kind of stubbornness before I agreed to come with them. Part of me wanted to know what they wanted me for. Part of me wondered if their gun would do anything more than bruise my skin.

Natasha pulled the gun out from his waist before he settled down next to me, wary eyes locked on mine. Ruffling his feathers smoothed mine a bit. He deserved more than a ruffle and I would give it to him. But, later. Head settled back against the seat, I let my eyelids sink shut.

We moved without further ado.

Paying attention to the turns we took and the approximate distances between them might have been a good idea. Opening my eyes and watching would have been a better one. I did neither. Because I couldn't quite find the energy to care or worry enough.

Too many blows to the head and to the heart in too short a time.

Something hard and warmer than it should have been poked into my shoulder. "Wake up, Princess."

I elbowed and whipped my head up in the same motion, eyes squinting at the low light around me, ears open.

Knuckles connected with the side of my face. I used the momentum from the punch to fuel my spring in the other direction. A band around my waist held me firm. I tipped over onto warm, contoured leather. Kicked out. Foot hit something soft with a stiff center.

"Kick me again and I will shoot you," a strained voice said behind me.

Despite the wheezing, I recognized the voice. The increasingly warm leather against my cheek and the tension of the belt around my waist helped remind me where I was.

Escalade.

Kidnapping.

Right.

I retracted my half-primed legs and used them to tilt me back toward vertical.

Natasha's nostrils flared in ready anger, but the gun pointed at me in a steady grip.

I believed he would shoot me. I also believed that smirking at the blood seeping from his lip would push him toward trigger happiness as well.

So, I unbuckled my seatbelt like the last thirty seconds hadn't happened. "You probably shouldn't wake someone with any part of a weapon. People get punchy and kicky."

His frown deepened a moment, before he winced and reset to a less-wide scowl. The lip probably hurt.

The side of my face throbbed more than was healthy.

We'd both gotten our hits in.

He moved back from the car door as I scooted toward him. The interchange between us had broken the low expectations my easy surrender had fostered. I didn't need that kind of complication added to my eventual escape plan. No fixing it now.

The garage I stepped into could have housed at least ten cars. Five spots were taken up. Three colors of Escalade and two less-flashy, sedans of some sort. At least they weren't completely impractical, these criminals.

Natasha ushered me past the cars before I got too good a look at them. Probably, so I wouldn't memorize the license plates. If I'd been so inclined, I would have had the time to get one or two before he shoved me through the set of double doors.

The hallway behind the doors was surprisingly well lit, in a cold kind of blue-white glow. Brushed silver sconces hung on stark white walls above chrome benches on either side of the hall. My eye caught the outline of a door someone wished was better hidden on the right side of the hall, midway between the exit and the elevator. Another door on the left hid half the distance between the first and the elevator.

The elevator opened as we approached it. I flicked my eyes up and found the camera hanging from the sconce above it.

Dark cherry wood lined the walls of the tiny elevator. Even tinier with the three of us pressed too close together. The wood radiated warmth after the visual ice box the hall had been.

We rose when I'd braced for us to drop. Probably the result of too much time spent with the men of the local Gold 4. I stumbled, bumping shoulders with Natasha before straightening. He glared at me. Our honeymoon might just be over.

Sad face.

I didn't know what I'd been expecting. Terror-basement chic certainly did not fit the bill. The narrow bars of windows along the far wall did little to brighten the dank, concrete aesthetic punctuated by pool tables and men smoking cigars. Natasha guided me to the right. A full U-turn from the elevator.

A small, walled room huddled in the farthest corner. Groups of classic, brown leather furniture formed an aisle to the door. Some of the men on the couches spread themselves in obvious ease. Others practically rang from their shaking fear.

One of the seated men, I recognized. Mostly from the shit-eating grin aimed my way. He was every bit as mountain-thick as I remembered from his attempt to keep me out of Lex's art show. He lifted an eyebrow dripping with disdain, "See you in there."

The same thing I'd snared at him. This bouncer-come-body guard was loving this.

Karma. I knew. But that didn't mean I would take it. Not from him.

"Actually, it looks like I'm going inside again while you're left out in the cold." I pouted toward him and batted my eyelashes. "Poor widdle man."

Several low chuckles echoed without apparent source. Not that I needed to know who laughed, precisely, but a smile or two would have made me feel better.

I should have kept my mouth closed, but the overwhelming odds against me had started to work on the apathy that powered me through the initial stages of kidnappery. Snipping at someone insignificant. Decent distraction from the fears growing in me. Much better than putting them on display with this audience.

The frosted glass in the door of the walled room ached for the name of a private eye in bold, black and gold letters. Courier New. Maybe Arial. Nothing too fancy.

The door swung outward before I made my suggestions known.

This side of the room was surprisingly well lit after all the darkness and shadows of the larger room. Almost bright enough to blind a person. The far side, where the man of the hour sat behind a hulking glass-and-chrome desk, had no lights save a low desk lamp. Nothing to highlight the man's face, though I could see him through the room's contrast.

I could also see the back of a head I knew all too well.

"It seems, Ms. Ianto." The man behind the desk splayed his fingers in what had to be a calculated motion, one engineered to set people on edge. "That you owe me some money."

# 30 – PICTURE PERFECT

CHAD—THE LOUSY, lowlife, dogmatic, SOB—sold me out. It was not going down like this.

"The fuck I do." I shook my head and pointed at Chad because it was all I could do to keep from walking over and wringing his pathetic little neck.

"This mother fucker did whatever he did with y'all—nope, I don't need or want to know what it was—and dug his hole without my knowledge. Then, when the water got too hot for him, he abandoned ship. Bailed. Moved out of the apartment and sent me a text to end our relationship on the same day I lost my mentor, my car, my job, and was at the Scientific Art's building the night one of those weird robberies happened." I was panting by the time I finished.

The head honcho's eyebrows lifted somewhere in the midst of my tirade, but he let me finish.

I would have thanked him except for the whole kidnapping thing. I'd said more than enough, so I waited.

He certainly let the silence go on more than long enough. His eyes remained locked on mine, not revealing much more than a keen intelligence lacking in Boris and Natasha. I took the time to look him over in the hopes I could figure something about the man in control of the room.

Despite the light, honey-brown of his eyes, his gaze had a crystalline hardness to it. An emptiness there. The kind slinking in the depths of veterans freshly home from war. He had killed before and wouldn't squirm at doing so again. The scruff on his face softened the square of his jaw more than he probably wanted it to. He'd look more dangerous shaved clean. More like a finely hewn weapon. An assassin of his own employ.

Eventually, Head Honcho shifted the sharp gaze to Chad. The loss of the pressure left my head reeling.

"Is this true?" The rich baritone rolled out, inviting someone to naysay him.

Chad squirmed. I bit my lip to keep the smile contained.

"Not exactly," he finally said.

Anger flared. "You lying sack of—"

Three men grabbed hold of me, lightning quick. The pain on my arms and torso was enough to make me stay my tongue a bit and think through my reaction. Struggling against the men seemed a bad idea. I just let them hold me while I took a moment to breathe. I could do this without getting myself hurt if I breathed through the anger.

My, "You lying sack of shit," came out in sing-song.

The hands gripped me tighter. The barrel of a gun came into my field of vision.

Smart men.

Not that it meant much, but I splayed my hands in surrender. "All I'm saying is that my phone has the text from him. Boris and Natasha—or whoever—came and ransacked my apartment. They can tell you about the empty depressions in the carpet and odd holes from things the bastard took. Clothes stacked where there had been a dresser. Things like that."

Head Honcho's nose twitched? "Boris and Natasha?"

I twisted my head to the man holding me on the right and dipped my chin. "Boris." To the man with his gun on me again, I nodded. "Natasha."

Someone attached to me coughed a little falsely. As the only gun out in the room had its sights on me, I went to diversion. "I didn't get names. Don't really want them. Anyway, he moved and they broke in the same day as the thing at the Scientific Arts building. Mountain-sized bouncer dude remembers me from there."

"Why does that matter to me?" Head Honcho tipped his head to the side, almost like he really cared to hear my answer.

"I figured if I gave you answers you can verify independently of me, you'll realize I'm not the one lying to you here."

He blinked once at me before pressing a button and speaking one word. "Garren."

The tone made me want to ask. I held it back. The door opened behind me. I prepped myself to fight every single person in the room. I didn't need to escape. I just needed to make it to Chad, to ensure he got what he deserved before I died.

Mountain-of-a-Man walked far enough into the room for me to see him.

"Oh look, you made it inside after all. Bully for you." Stupid mouth. Tension eased between my shoulders, but it wouldn't matter once I died.

Mountain twisted a dark, disgusted face toward me, the grey in his eyes swimming with hatred. "Listen here, you bitch—"

Head Honcho's, "Garren," silenced him.

Silenced the whole room, in fact. Couldn't really blame anyone. A chill swept over me at the two syllables.

"You recognize this woman, I gather." The smile that curled on his face reminded me of a snake with a rat.

"Yessir."

"And where did you meet her?"

"She was the—" Mountain cut himself off, but all of us in the room had no illusions the kind of descriptors he yelled in his head. "The night of the botched surveillance on the gallery show opening."

Surveillance. That didn't sound good. Something for later. Now was for shutting it.

Head Honcho nodded to the mountain. "You may go."

He backed away. Rather than turning around to leave. Not necessarily unsettling, but something to mark on. Head Honcho either commanded that level of respect or of fear. Probably both.

"Provided Ms. Ianto can conduct herself like a lady, you may release her, but do not let her leave."

The three men held on to me while I waited for them to get their hands off. It took me longer than it should have to understand that they were still waiting for the actual go ahead from Head Honcho. He, in turn, was waiting for me.

Even without the misogyny in his heavy suggestion that I act like what he thought a lady should act like, I couldn't promise what he asked. I had to word this correctly to not put myself in further danger. "A real lady defends her honor with all the tools at her disposal, and Chad deserves any tool I give him."

Head Honcho's nose twitched again. Me and my big mouth.

"May I see the text?" He held a hand out to me.

Me, still trussed up by the men folk. Refusing would win me more of this. No choice, really. "Sure."

Freedom.

I reached in my left bra cup and stepped toward the desk only to be snatched up again. Two men this time. "What the fuck?"

Natasha jerked his chin toward my left boob. "Concealed weapon?"

"For fucks sake." I pinned the collar of my purple t-shirt down with my chin and used my hands to spread the material thin enough around the phone so there could be no question of me having a gun. "Rounded rectangle. Thin. Phone. Are we good?"

Why they never frisked me, I wouldn't hazard to guess. Except that, perhaps, the women they were sent to retrieve couldn't possibly be a threat to big men like them. No. Surely not. No over-display of machismo happening here. No sirree Bob.

Some sort of head-and-hand signal from the Honcho triggered the men to release me. Like the worlds worse baseball signaling.

The phone vibrated as I pulled it out from under my shirt, followed at close hand by the third movement of the Moonlight Sonata. Someone had impeccable timing. Someone else had quick fingers. Boris plucked the phone from me before I could tap to see who had this kind of luck. It didn't matter too much, except that some important people had my number.

The lawyer, I could call back. "If that's Magus, I should probably answer that." I flipped my hands up and shrugged. I even gave them a winning, if uncomfortable, smile.

Head Honcho laughed and shook his head. He didn't believe me. Who could blame him? It sounded like a ploy, a way to find a lifeline to get me out of there.

I wished he wouldn't laugh over the song. I loved this song.

"You don't know Magus." Chad hissed the last letter a few beats. "You liar."

"You." I pointed at Chad to emphasize and give my fingers something to do that did not involve choking. "You don't know what kind of week I've had."

"Be that as it may." He smirked.

Why was I even paying attention to him?

Blocking him out of my vision helped. I simply needed to focus on the scary guy in charge. No problem. Yes problem, but a worthier one. "The robbery thing complicated my life a bit. I'm a consultant for Magus, on a thing, and that would be the only reason he's calling me. If I don't answer, he'll probably seek me out."

I didn't know that for a fact. But, the People's Fair started tomorrow.

We'd made it to crunch time. Staring nonchalantly at my fingernails would have pushed a little too hard, but this was kind of cool. Someone with that much influence calling me. Being in the know. Head of the Gold 4 asking me for input on a case.

Boris asked, "How do I..." He shook my phone at me.

"Sigma. The Greek letter. Capital. Backward. From the bottom."

We all waited for Boris to give verdict. Instead, he gave me attitude, centering all his disgust and anger on me. "Magically, the person who *needs* to be answered called right now."

Dumb luck, I'd say. I shrugged because I had no control over the universe.

Clearly.

The song cut off. Not much I could do in the situation. I'd warned them. Best I could do. A rescue mission to save me would be lovely.

Honcho flared his fingers at me in a slow wave. I pressed my lips together while my eyes widened almost of their own volition. Since I wasn't a part of his crew, I didn't understand his booga-booga language. Moments wormed their way by with his eyes on me. We both knew who's court the ball was in.

"Call him back," he finally said. "But on speaker phone and if you try anything funny, you will be shot."

Shooting me wouldn't save them from Magus finding me or them. Especially if he witnessed it on the phone. I wasn't one of his people, but I was an asset and involved on this case. To keep myself from mentioning these things, I woke up the phone.

The text icon bounced. Conditioning made my fingers itch to see who had sent me what. I returned the last call. Magus answered after only one ring.

"Greer." He didn't sound excited to hear my voice.

"Sorry about missing your call, Magus. I needed hands clean enough to touch my phone." Plausible reason for me to have missed and called him back in the timeframe. "What's up?"

"She sent more pictures."

He would only call me about one *she*.

"Tomorrow's the anniversary and the first day of the Taste." Not sure why I needed to repeat to him things he already knew. "Is that normal? Her sending things the night before?"

"Yes."

It would have been better if this was an aberration. This fitting her pattern meant she was still moving forward according to her plan. Here was hoping her over confidence gave us enough to defeat her. "Have you had any luck with them?"

"One." Magus said. "I included it in the message I sent you, in the event you see something different than we have. The others, we're still working on and you have those too."

Made sense. "I'll take a quick look at them and tell you if I recognize anything straight away. I should probably also forward them on to Lana." I watched Honcho as I said this, not so much asking permission. Just me letting him know that the texting was an addendum to this call.

His flat expression gave me nothing. So, I dropped my gaze to the desk.

"I can send that to her." Magus pulled me back into the conversation.

"You could, but I think we both know she'll take it better from me than from you."

A couple of beats passed before he confirmed. "Truth."

"Okay. I'll check the photos and let you know."

"Call me back either way. After you've passed the information along. I want to know if she has any insight." Magus had a good point. He'd done this kind of coordination before.

I nodded like he could see it. "Will do."

"I'll be waiting." He hung up without further goodbye.

Trying not to feel the sting from the cursory sign off, I spoke to the dimmed phone. "Of course you'll be waiting." I navigated to the text messages, which were all from him.

"Not so fast," Honcho's baritone crashed into my consciousness.

What did he mean by that? "You heard him. I need to do a few things and call him back."

He shook his head. "You know I cannot allow you to text whatever to whoever. Not until I've decided what to do with you."

Balls.

But I could kind of see his point. He'd brought me here for reasons and I was throwing some serious wrenches in the works. Still, I needed to respond to Magus as soon as possible. All of Honcho's lackeys didn't need to see all the things, though. They already knew more than the public did. I stepped out from under the interrogation lights near the door and headed toward the desk.

Halfway around it, several guns came out to point at me and people yelled at me to stop. I stopped with a sigh.

Answering the three voices yelling at me would win me nothing, so I spoke directly to Honcho. It helped that he hadn't moved, offensively or defensively, except to twist his head to track my movement.

He was quite the cool customer, but he probably also recognized that my movements held no aggression toward him. I'd already shown what I look like when hellbent to maim someone.

"This information, the pictures, is kind of need to know. Since I need to send the info, and you don't trust me not to try something, I thought it would be easier and faster if you just watch over all of the things I'm doing."

Another of those wormy silences where he studied me while I flapped in the wind. Finally, he said, "You could send me the pictures at the same time."

I scoffed. "Not on your life. I'm not willing to cross Magus." Or Lana, but he didn't know about Lana.

His lips twitched on the left side. I couldn't tell if it was the flicker of a smile or that of a frown. I didn't ask. Instead, I went for a conspiratorial moment between us. "And if you could not let anyone in on the information, it would be appreciated by more important people than me."

Flat, lack of amusement or placation in the cast of his jaw. Yep, he saw right through my act. Though, he didn't refuse me. Under the circumstances, I would take the win.

No one yelled at me to stop when I walked the last of the perimeter of the desk to Head Honcho. That was a win as well. Despite their steady aim on me.

I still had the video from Lex's premier on my phone. I could freeze them all and flee. Granted, they'd all unfreeze when I closed the door behind me. Then, there were all the unsavory men on the other side of the door. To handle all of them, I would need to test out the strength of my hypnoboob situation. They were yet another group of people I didn't want to see me exposed, no matter if they remembered.

So, I sucked up my situation, gave up on any immediate escape plans, and set my phone on the desk in front of the man.

The first picture was a close-up of a gold, or gold-like, featureless thing that took up most of screen without much deviation. In the upper left corner, the gold ended in a curve and revealed pale blue.

Then a bronze baby butt sitting astride something also bronze. A statue of some sort, but I didn't recognize it as belonging to the art museum.

The upper right-hand corner of child's red and yellow, plastic television set that had been the rage when I was younger. Turn the knob and it played a song while hidden gears pulled a storybook scene across the "screen" of the television.

Scaffolding or an industrial-like statue in black-and-chrome beams.

A close-up. White on green curves stacked into a tail of a mermaid. The logo of one of the most ubiquitous and familiar coffee shops in the world.

A random assortment if I ever did see one. But knowing the area we were already focused on helped me catch one thing. Siren Coffee had a shop on the north side of Civic Center Park. Not really new info there. The gold looked familiar. The bronze baby butt more so. Gods. It was on the tip of my brain.

I flipped back to the gold. "I *know* I know this."

"The dome of the capitol building?" Head Honcho asked.

I blinked, looked at him, then back at the picture. Damned if he wasn't right. "That's it. Thank you." I lifted a hand for a high five.

One of his eyebrows quirked up at me.

"What?" I retracted my hand in small, jerky increments. Forgetting myself like that, not the best idea.

Honcho steepled his fingers and peered me overtop them. "You're not in a situation people usually thank me for."

"Just because you had me brought here on the word of that..." I jerked my thumb at Chad a couple times before I settled on, "fool, doesn't mean I can't thank you for helping out. Right?"

He gave me a tentative nod, like he wasn't quite certain what to do with me.

Fine with me.

"Right. So, I need to forward these on to a woman, then call her before I call Magus back." I lifted my hands in surrender position and shook them. "I know, I know, speaker phone."

His eyes narrowed at me, flaring in warm honey, but a small smile tugged at his lips. "Who in the hell are you, Greer Ianto, that Magus calls you for input?"

"It's been a hell of a week, Mister." I shrugged. "I'm not sure I know any more."

# 31 – BIG MOUTH

L ANA ANSWERED HALFWAY through the first ring. "You have news?"

"Yes and no." I hated the idea of getting her hopes up. "She sent us more photos, which I just sent to you."

"There are others there with you," she said, before I could ask for help with identifying the pictures. "Not the same as those with you in the crypt. Hostile."

My eyes widened at Head Honcho. I had no way to explain how she could know that. And she was not a person to lie to. "That is true."

Honcho bristled at my admission.

Rock and hard place, USA.

"Do you need me to come for you?"

Rescue would be nice, but it could also lessen her opinion of me. That would not be good for any of us humans in the dance. "Thank you, but no. I ran into my ex-boyfriend and some of his cronies, but I thought this more important to handle before I finish things with them."

No reaction from her. I lifted a shoulder at Honcho. He pressed his lips together in an unreadable expression. Annoying, but he did not appear angry. I would have to take what I could get.

"The pictures have come through," Lana finally said. "Give me a moment to look through them."

She could have all the time she wanted.

"Siren Coffee." Lana's voice sounded rounder and a bit further away. "That is the green and white."

I guessed she'd put me—us—on speaker as well. "I agree. There is a shop on the north side of Civic Center Park."

Her, "Mmm," response sounded half non-committal and half approving my verification.

Silence filled the line again while she took her time. Telling her to call me back later would have been rude. Neither of us would appreciate the results of that.

I wanted to park my butt on Honcho's desk. A long glance at him convinced me not to. He watched me with the attention of a first-time mother, catching every motion I made and reaction I had. That level of attention unnerved me.

What the fuck was he looking for?

"The rest of the pictures are a mystery," Lana's voice pulled me out of the staring contest with Honcho. "Except for the fountain?"

"Fountain?"

"Yes. The bronze statue in the center of the fountain at the Civic park. Did you not recognize it?"

I wouldn't have asked otherwise. To her, I said. "I haven't had occasion to get close enough to the statue to know it in that much detail. Not since I was younger. They fence the area off during festivals now to keep the people out." I'd been an unhappy camper the first year they'd done so. My dad had to buy me ice cream and take me to get my face painted before I stopped weeping.

"And thanks to Gabriel for that. The water was too foul to travel for weeks after just one festival. And now there are so many." Lana trailed off while my mind exploded in several different directions.

Questions about her interactions with Gabe could wait until we weren't on the hunt for the lady the Gold 4 called Anterograde.

"Travel?" I asked as evenly as I could.

"Yes, Greer. You—" She cut herself off a moment. "But you wouldn't know. That statue, among others, resonate with similar structures in my home. They ease the way here and the water absorbs the impact of the energy needed to travel between."

"Like wormholes or quantum entanglement or..."

"More like the second, but we do not have the time to discuss the particulars."

She was right. I stomped down on the tingling in my belly to know more. Mostly. "If you don't use the statues to ease the way here, what would it do to you?" I tapped my thumb with my index finger in my impatience to hear the answer.

"It would take uncommon strength to do so and would leave the traveler weakened. Injured. If they survived. The energy usually dissipated by the water would reverberate in the body, ripping at internal tissues with unchecked ferocity."

Just the kind of thing that would leave a person coughing blood and belligerent to a person who happened upon her.

"Why?" Lana's question broke into my head space again.

"Just trying to put the pieces together about your daughter's condition when I saw her." Also, that her weakened state would have made her a target for any nefarious passerby. It was not the thing to say to a mother worried over her child. Instead, "We'll find her, you know. I can feel it. We're close."

"And I will suck the marrow from the woman who is the cause of all of this."

She disconnected on that cheery note. There was no proper response to that. I didn't doubt her will nor her ability to do so, and I couldn't find it in me to talk her out of it. She had probably saved me some awkward, conversational soft shoe.

"Considerate woman, that Lana," I mumbled over my phone as I scrolled back to Magus' contact information.

A hand settled on mine, halting me from hitting the button to dial. I looked up to meet Honcho's invasive gaze. "I just had the one last phone call to Magus to make."

He gave the barest of head shakes. "What is going on?"

I rolled my lips all the way in. Considering everything he'd overheard, the curiosity was understandable.

The whole of it was bigger than me and what I understood, though. If too many people knew our side if things, word could get back to the woman behind this. She might not change the date, her mother's death and all, but the forewarning would give her the upper hand. She already had one or two of those.

Superheroes jumped in blind like this all the time. The whole thing was mind-bogglingly, fucking brainless. At the very least. Why would anyone choose this?

"Um." I coughed. "I'm not sure I can tell you all of what's up."

His hand tightened on mine. Not enough to pinch my fingers around the phone, but enough. He would hurt me if I pushed him. "I've already heard plenty."

"Exactly. Too many people know too much already."

His hand tightened more. "What can you tell me?"

That was actually a better question. A compromise. Refusing the olive branch could result in the branch jabbing into my chest. "Okay. If you were planning on going to The Taste tomorrow, you should postpone it for another day or two." My lips pulled back into something that was more gnashing of teeth than a smile.

He already knew more than I would have told him. The timing, as far as we knew it, could be released.

Honcho tilted his head to the side a few degrees, before giving a slight dip of his chin and releasing my hand. "Very well. So, about that money."

I pinched my lips to keep the expletives at bay. I realized, even in my anger, that cursing in his face might not be the best idea.

He waited a moment for me to speak. When I didn't he took the floor. "I cannot allow the debt to go unanswered."

I lifted my hands into surrender position again. It seemed the safest. "I get that, but the first I heard about this money was when that fool bushwhacked me leaving my oldest friend's funeral reception. Don't know how much it is. Don't want to know how much it is. Don't want to know what he owes it for. That's between y'all." In the event I hadn't been clear enough, I wagged a finger between them then pointed at me and shook my head.

He tipped his chin toward me. "And you have bigger fish to fry."

If I wasn't mistaken, he smiled a little after he said it. What the hell?

I'd either amused him greatly, or he was circling for the kill and enjoying the hell out of it. If it was time for me to die, I could go out with a shrug and some honesty. "I wasn't going to say it, but I kind of have a lot on my plate."

A low chuckle rolled out of him. It settled me not one bit.

"Make your phone call."

Figuring his motives out could wait for me to get off the phone.

Magus answered with, "Greer?" and nothing else.

Slightly rude, but time saving. I let him have it, marking each one off on a finger as I listed them. "The gold is the capitol dome. The green is a Siren Coffee cup, and there's a shop just outside the northeast corner of the park. The bronze butt is the center of the fountain in the north side of the park. No clue on the metal beams, scaffolding thing. It might be something to check out once they start setting up for the fair." A lot could be checked out at that time, including the faces of the people around.

"And the other picture?"

"It's a toy. An older one, obviously because it's mechanical, not electronic." I clenched the fist of my hand not holding the phone. "I know I recognize it, but that's all I have right now."

"That is..."

I really didn't like his pauses.

"...much better than we had."

My shoulders slumped in relief. I didn't know why I cared so much about how he valued my contribution. But I did.

It was bigger than just him, or revenge on someone who hurt me, because I understood. Staring into the honey-brown eyes of a man who would not hesitate to hurt me to get what he wanted, I understood why men gave their lives for the Gold 4. Despite the threat Honcho posed, I wanted to save him. He deserved justice for every wrong thing he'd ever done, sure. But he didn't deserve whatever Anterograde had planned. No one did. Her threat was a whole different kettle of fish. For whatever reason, I'd been put into a position to reel her in. "I'm happy to help."

"Hopefully, you can come up with the answer for last couple photo clues before you join us this evening."

What? I'd try with the photos, but, "Excuse me, what do you mean by the last bit?"

"Everyone, who is not out actively collecting intel, stays in the same place the night before an operation."

Something that someone should have told me. Or, maybe, asked me. I wasn't a pawn to be shuffled around the board. I pinched the bridge of my nose and forced in a breath. "I'm guessing there's no way for me to get out of this."

"I have someone scheduled to leave in the next ten minutes to pick you up."

Of course he did. "You can't do that because I'm not home right now."

"Text me the address of where you are."

Presumptuous thing. If tomorrow wasn't so important, I would have told him a thing or two about scheduling me like he had. As was, I had to stall him. The melting away of Honcho's good humor only confirmed it.

"I have no supplies with me to spend the night and I'm kind of gross right now. I need some time."

"Half hour?"

I scoffed. "What woman do you know only needs a half hour to get ready? Let alone the commute time back home."

"How long do you need?" Now he sounded annoyed.

He could suck it.

Asking Honcho how long he thought we needed might just be the wrong thing to do. Especially with his lips pressed thin as they were. My decision, then. I checked the clock on my phone. Nearly one. "Four would be ideal."

A long breath of a pause. "Fine."

"Okay. Are we talking car or is someone flying me?"

"Does it matter?"

I frowned at the phone. "It changes how I pack and how I prep."

He half grunted. Probably listing all the ways women were crazy in his head before he answered. "Phoenyx will be along. Flight."

That I could work with. "Okay."

"Okay."

"Hey, Magus." I practically yelled it at the phone in the hopes that he didn't disconnect yet.

"Yes, Greer."

Good. I still had him. "Maybe it would be a good idea to have the scent guy, the one who can smell, go over the area. He smelled the zombies—drones—and they had the same kind of thing in them. The fishy thing. It might narrow down our focus for tomorrow."

"Not a bad idea." He sounded surprised.

As if this were the first time I'd given him something useful. The bastard. "Thank you."

"Anything else?"

I wished. Just to shove it in his face. "That's all for the moment."

"Very good."

And he was gone. Someone really needed to teach him phone etiquette. Considering his prevailing opinion of me, I couldn't be the one.

Since I'd completed the calls I needed to, I set the phone on the desk and threaded my fingers in front of me. Head Honcho got my full attention. The same kind of regard he'd been giving me the whole time.

He narrowed his eyes at me, but I waited for him to ask whatever set his face into motion. "Zombies?"

I sighed. Yet another thing that he should probably not know about. Too late now. Again. "I did mention how crazy my week had been, right?"

"Zombies. You aren't joking?" He seemed really thrown. The confusion on his face held more real estate than any other emotion he'd shown since I'd arrived.

I splayed the fingers of both hands trying to come up with anything. "*Really* weird week."

Good enough.

He leaned back against his chair and steepled his fingers in front of his mouth as he had before. "I don't know what to do with you."

Let me go. Let me live. Let me out of here with nothing but

memories to mark it.

Blurting it out like that seemed too much like begging. Begging endeared a person to no one; it fostered pity. I didn't need the pity of any man in this room. If things turned south, I still had a trick up my...collar. I hoped things wouldn't turn that direction.

Honcho narrowed his eyes at me, warm brown honey. "What was that? What are you thinking?"

Apparently, I needed to work on my poker face in front of bad men. "Is it okay if I just tell you I don't want to tell you?"

He laughed. A loud boisterous laugh that shook his shoulders and tipped his head back. He gestured to me with a flare of fingers, then looked to his men and gestured again. "The balls on this one, I swear."

"Ovaries." I crossed my arms. "Or gonads, if you prefer."

"There it is again." He shook his head, eyes wide in amused wonder. "Men piss at the thought of me, and yet you sit unaffected. Am I losing my touch?"

Such wide boasting was a sign of an insecure man, but the question belied that. Perhaps the first wasn't a lie. Still, he asked a question. "Well, I don't know who you are and I mentioned I've had an odd week."

"Odd doesn't take fear away."

"It numbs a lot." I shrugged. "And I never said I wasn't afraid."

"But more scared of something else."

How did a person soothe the feelings of someone who's sad because they didn't scare you? Pat him on the head? Pinch his cheek? Tell him he's only second to the woman with poison spines growing out of her skin?

I leaned a little toward him without uncrossing my arms. The other people in the room needed to see that I planned no aggressive actions toward him. "You should really stay out of Civic Center Park tomorrow. And if you could, you know, not spread the word about it too far, I'd really appreciate it."

He blinked at me, then nodded. "I will be certain to stay away."

"Good." He could think of it as a warning all he wanted. I didn't need any x-factors mucking about the place when serious business was about to go down.

His eyes slid from mine. "Boris. Samuel. Take her home."

"Boss?" The dark-haired dude who I called Natasha answered. He held his face in a careful blank mask, but his eyes beamed confusion.

"Ms. Ianto has a date with Magus and the rest of his gang. We don't want to be the ones to keep her out of his reach, do we?" The mocking lilt to the question sent shivers over my timbers. In a breath, he'd gone from the edge of warmth to cold-hearted cobra ready to strike.

It reminded me how easily sugar could hide poison.

"Yes, Boss." Samuel's words came out contrite and a little louder than expressly needed.

"Moreover," Honcho continued with his gaze returning to me. "Squeezing Magus' pet for money could end badly for all involved."

"Pet? Hardly." Times when I should have kept my mouth closed. I shook my head at my brain-dead reaction. Who was the drone now?

He smiled like he could hear my inner chiding. "Be that as it may, you are useful enough to him that he is bringing you in. You are simply not worth the risk." He gave the kind of shrug thieves gave to cops with no evidence to hold them.

Galling.

"I'm worth more than a little risk." What the fuck was I doing? Trying to convince him to hold me here and threaten me, maybe torture me, for money? "Strike that. Good decision. I'll just be out of your hair in two shakes."

I scooped up my phone to the tune of his laughter and made it halfway around his desk before I came to a complete stop. Much as I wanted to, I couldn't leave things like this. I swiveled toward him with a rueful sigh. "Hey, Head Honcho Dude?"

"Spencer."

Balls. Now I knew his name. "Spencer. I'm probably shoving myself under the bus with this, but could you not kill Chad?"

Spencer's lips pulled down in the corners.

"I know, I know." Surrender hands again, because why not? "But I've seen faces, and now I have three names, real or not, and if he turns up dead I can't not tell police or whatever. You know?"

"Is that the only reason?" Spencer set his elbows on his desk. "No sentimental memories flicking your twat?"

Wow. Crude. But he probably wanted me to react to the crudeness. In this, at least, I could control myself. "I mean, we had good times, but I can barely remember them right now."

"You stone cold bitch," Chad said from a little behind me. The last word sounded a little strangled.

I nodded to Spencer because I didn't want to look at Chad. "He may be right, but he betrayed me. Several times. Kept secrets that put me in danger. I don't know him like I thought I did. I think you know him better."

"Are you sad at all?" Spencer kept that laser sharp gaze on me.

What was with the seventh degree? If it kept Chad alive and let me leave, though, I would answer. "For the lies and the time lost, sure. But what can you do?"

"You can hit him." Spencer lifted an eyebrow, challenging me.

Warmth surged in my belly. The thought of revenge, even something a small as smacking him silly, again tingled on the tips of my fingers and relaxed my shoulders. My lips even curled. I didn't risk the glance back at him, because his face, no matter the expression, would set me off. I'd seen all of his faces and he still managed to lie to me. Leaving my palm print on his cheek, or the kiss of my knuckles, tasted so very sweet on my tongue.

I shook my head against all of it.

"But you want to." Spencer didn't ask, he spoke a truth we both know.

"Yes." No sense in denying it.

"Why don't you?"

"I don't want him cowed and under the watchful eye of someone who wants something from him. I want him free, on fire, and ready for what I'm going to do to him."

A wide smile peeled Spencer's lips back. "You *are* a stone-cold bitch."

My shoulders rose in an easy shrug. The opportunity and refusal to hit Chad had calmed me considerably. "Like I said. I've had a hard week."

He nodded to me.

I took it as a signal to get the hell out of dodge.

"This will not be the last time we meet." Spencer said, with me half the distance to my goal.

~ 340 ~

Of course not. This was much too simple. I didn't stop my beeline for the door, but rather called to him over my shoulder. "If you want to call, next time, so we can schedule something, that would work better for me."

A man stood half in front of the door. I could have shoved him out of the way. I twisted the upper part of me back to the big man in charge. "Chad should still have my number."

Spencer looked to Chad to verify. The sullen, hopeless nod he gave Spencer might have been his most honest answer in weeks.

At Chad's answer, Spencer nodded to me and the man in my way. "I look forward to it."

For lack of anything better to do, I saluted the man then effected a sharp about-face. The door opened for me, this time. I saluted the man who held the door. I saluted the door. I saluted all the men outside the door.

Sweet, sweet freedom.

# 32 – PROMISES

I NIBBLED AT BACON and worried over the wall of photos taller than me. The red and yellow sang to me. I knew something. If I could just shake it out of my noggin. I'd spent the last hour alone in this room trying to do just that.

"Staring at it won't help you figure it out." Kai's voice, even mumbled, shocked the shit out of me.

"A little warning would be nice," I mumbled to the warm head planted in my lap. The jaguar turned his emerald gaze up at me, letting out a deep, rumbly purr. To Kai, I shook my head. "The answer right on the tip of my brain."

"Do brains have tips?"

Not something that needed a response, mostly because the only responses that came to mind were less than PC. "Did you need something?"

"We're meeting in the lobby."

I didn't know where the lobby was, but I understood meeting. "You're here to gather me for the party, aren't you?"

"Right in one."

Before I uncurled from the chair, I gave the jaguar a good, two-handed scratch at the base of his skull. The deep purr resonated through my body and eased some of the tension that had cropped up at Kai's intrusion. When I got up, the jaguar stayed glued to my side. In just the right place to encourage me to keep scratching with my right hand.

Kai looked back, like I might have trailed off or something. He shook his head as he straightened.

"What?" I asked him because it was better than circling the same five thoughts I had been for an hour.

"He doesn't react that way to anyone but you."

I glanced down at the cat purring away at the end of my fingertips. Powerful, beautiful creature. "I'm sure he's like this with Magus."

"No. There's loyalty and understanding between them, sure." He gave the two of us the side eye before stepping into the bamboo doorway. "But this is love. That is a smitten kitten."

I could neither confirm nor deny if Kai had the right of it. His judgement was usually spot on. One of those skills bartenders developed, even if it wasn't their only job. "I would say that he had good taste, but it probably has more to do with me being the only woman on the premises."

"Or the amount of skin you're flashing."

My lips puckered into a thoughtful bow, hoping against hope that Kai wasn't admonishing me for it. Like one—albeit, fantastic—night gave him leave to govern what I did with my body at any other time. We'd been friends for years. I'd give him the benefit of the doubt.

He must have caught the words I didn't say, though. He turned around to face me and stopped. Part of me wanted to bulldoze through him. I controlled myself.

"Greer. We're supposed to be inconspicuous and you're a walking meal." His eyes flared in that familiar warmth while they danced over me.

Not disapproval, then. Distraction. That, I could work with. "I am an extra set of eyes. If I draw some gazes away from you to me, more's the better. And, anyway. I'm more covered up than I would have been."

Damned shimmering cleavage had to be covered. I could still see the worst of it down the V-neck vest, but most people would not be viewing from my angle. The weather man claimed we'd be peaking at 90 degrees today. It made me want to re-think the patterned, gauzy shirt beneath, but it disguised the glitter on the rest of me. I hoped the crush of people downtown would be enough to keep people from realizing the sparkle came from my skin.

Considering my outfit for the umpteenth time gave Kai the opportunity to step a little closer to me, the heat in his eyes warming.

The musky taste of him flashed through my memory, enhanced by the dark scent of him a breath away.

I forced an exhale out and pushed him back. "We have work to do. People to save."

A snarl trembled on his top lip.

My heartbeat fought against my brain, raising my blood pressure and tightening my neck. I ground out, "Later," then stepped around him because I couldn't bring myself to tell him to move.

The jaguar took the lead. I followed with bones too tight and too loose in the same shaking stride.

Rather than pass through the bamboo into the hallway we popped out into the tree-lined reception area. Lawn chairs had been arranged in front of the curved reception desk in rows of a semi-circle. Lackluster seating for something like this. They should have been able to afford even the metal party chairs or something. Government dollars at work.

Magus stood with his back against the reception desk, but he turned as we passed into the room. His eyes dropped to my new best friend. "If I had known, I would have simply called for you."

The jaguar yawned at him, flashing teeth and tongue. Magus didn't look impressed at the cat's sigh of boredom. I was impressed enough for the both of them.

Two of the chairs sat empty. As comfortable as they looked, I sat on the grass in front of the one nearest the center. The jaguar waited until I had situated myself before sprawling himself all over my lap.

"Oof." I readjusted. By the time I'd gotten comfortable again, Kai had sat in the chair next to the one I'd plopped down in front of. Magus had his eyes on me in an almost patient expression. I didn't know what else to say except. "I apologize."

He shook his head. "If he is not satisfied he will distract us all until he is. I'm glad you're here to appease him."

The cat in question purred for all he was worth. I did as he bade me and scratched.

Having something to busy my hands with calmed me more than I'd realized I needed. Sitting in the middle of this group of people all focused on the same goal. Even if I wasn't really a part of them, I liked this. More than I would ever admit out loud.

Magus straightened and all the extraneous shuffling in the room stopped. The purring even cut down to half. Impressive. I wondered if it was his position that afforded him that kind of respectful attention or if he'd worked a little of his mojo on the room. If I ever asked him, I would make certain that the only other ears in the room were furred, feathered, or scaled.

"You've all been sent the map of the park with the booth assignments for the event labeled. Rather than alphanumeric zones, we'll use streets, directions, and landmarks as marked on the map Attached also, are the general assignments for everyone once we're on site, the best images of the woman we're looking for, and the goggles that Anterograde's hired help wore to mitigate the effect of the light show. Any questions on your information packet?"

No one said a word. Nothing in the info he sent said anything about what I was supposed to do, but he couldn't order me around like the rest. I wasn't a superhero—except for the hypnoboob power I'd acquired— and his power didn't work on me.

Kai's face wasn't well known, though, so I figured sticking to him and blending in would be the best use of my time. Especially, because he had to pull some water samples to test for the starfish chemical.

"Good." Magus finally said. "Stagger your arrivals. Those of you in costume treat those in street clothes as regular citizens. I will have the com in my ear and eyes in the skies. Let me know of anything you see, feel, taste, smell, whatever that is funky. We still don't know exactly what we're up against or what the woman wants."

Somehow, the lack of knowledge rested on my shoulders. And I couldn't shake it, but Magus wasn't finished speaking quite yet.

"As an aside. It is warm and we will be out all day. Tend to your human needs so you can fulfill your superhuman duties." With a nod that somehow encompassed the twelve of us in the room, Magus pushed off from the reception desk and exited the room.

As far as pep talks went, the last of his speech left much to be desired. It was to the point, though. His whole prep conversation had been. He set us all on the same page and it was go time.

Some Oscar-winning anthem pulsed in my blood as I shuffled the jaguar off my lap and stood.

Because I was not alone.

Because Bolt and Phoenyx and several other men I had only met for five minutes stood with me.

Because we were on the side of right.

I had hope that we would prevail.

A mouth slipped over my fingers as I moved toward the elevator. The rough tongue and sharp teeth closed just hard enough on my hand to let me know he would bite me if I pressed him. I looked back down at the animal to see what I'd done wrong.

The jewel-green eyes bore into mine, screaming at me. The intensity scared me more than the teeth did. The danger lies in the eyes, as they say. These had a mission behind the danger. After several frozen seconds, I understood what he wanted. The power of it struck me to the base of my spine.

I took a knee in front of the cat, adjusting so our faces sat at the same level. "I will do my best to keep him safe."

My hand slipped free. Yep. Despite what Kai'd said, this one loved Magus.

"And if I fail, I will take you to deal with who is responsible."

He licked my right cheek before I could think to get out of the way. Not moving gained me the same kind of treatment to the left side. I stood and stomped my way to the elevator hanging open for me.

# 33 – PEOPLE'S FAIR

THE SUN BLAZED down on us while the concrete of Civic Center radiated the heat up from below. Kai had slipped by the metal barriers around the north fountain to pull samples. I trailed him, feeling like a cake baked with a light bulb. Just enough to char the edges and leave the middle warm and molten.

Being apart from the crush of people increased the temperature, somehow. Perhaps I could engineer an "accident" to dunk me in. Only if the water tested clean, though.

Kai straightened from his crouch by the rim of the fountain, shaking a tiny vial and flipping it upside down a couple of times. Holding it up to the light, he frowned. "Hound was right."

I tried to figure what Hound had gotten right, but I missed out on that preliminary conversation. "About what?"

"The fountain water tested positive. He said he smelled the fishiness here and in the air nearby."

"That's good, then, right?" I shifted the metal sawhorse enough out of the way for Kai to slide through. "That you confirmed his nose was spot on in finding these things?"

He shook his head. Kai waited for me to come through before continuing the conversation. "It means that everything else is also true. That it hangs in the air on this side of the park more than it should for a mostly undisturbed water source."

"Makes sense." Disquieting, but not quite the thing to set the alarm bells a-ringing. "But we can deal with that."

I hoped.

"The scent is everywhere. He can't find the source, now, because it comes from so many places. 'Mobile and maddening' were the words he said, I believe."

I could relate to *maddening*. The tiny, obstinate, little toy television set my nerves on fire. The burning hole in the heart of my knowledge pissed me off to no end.

"It's already hotter than it should be for September." Kai cracked his neck to either side, then popped a couple of things in his upper of back.

It couldn't have felt good, but he didn't seem to mind.

"Let's go get you some water." I patted his slightly sticky shoulder.

Kai hadn't thought to bring a bottle. Mine only had a couple more swallows in it and those had grown too warm to refresh. Atlantis water usually had a couple free stands. Oh, they tried to sign people up for their monthly service. I couldn't imagine they got too much more than thirsty customers they never saw until the next festival. Like me.

The handy, cross-referenced map said we weren't too far from the booth on Bannock St.

I did my best to keep my eyes peeled for faces from my video. The heat pressed down on my discipline. When we got to the line for free water, I fantasized about bowing my head under the spigot and letting loose. I would settle for filling my bottle with water lower than human body temperature and wishing ill upon the woman who made the festival a chore rather than a choice.

Watching Kai fill his little wax paper cone, another thought distracted me from my weather woes. All of these people drinking water from a source I didn't know if Magus verified was clean. The woman had been so clear about collecting all the glasses from Lex's gallery opening. To hide the evidence. She could easily have contaminated the water or the cups.

Kai shifted to the side so I could fill my bottle.

I touched his arm before he could bring the cup to his lips. "Maybe we should—"

"Auntie Greer!" The owner of the voice wrapped her arms around my waist. She beamed up at me. "I told Dad it was you."

Balls. Of all the people I didn't want here today. A glance confirmed that the whole crew was here. My brother, his two daughters, his son, and the wife. Shit.

"Hi, Hollyhock." I worked an arm around Holly's back enough that I could hug her and decant some water at the same time. Half of it spilled as I worked. I kept going until the bottle was two thirds full then shifted out of the line so other people could get some. I should have stayed in the way until I was certain, but I didn't want to start a panic. Especially, not with the family here.

Shit.

Kai took the bottle from me with a nod and I could have kissed him. He could deal with the water thing while I dealt with the rest.

"I didn't know you guys were coming here today." Prying Holly off me before she was ready to let go was not worth the fight so I leaned in to hug my brother with her in the middle.

Collin nodded. "I thought about calling you, but you sounded a little harried with everything going on the last time we spoke."

He was right. Things still had not settled. He hulked his shoulders forward and tipped his head down a little, like he used to do before I outgrew him. Same concerned expression too. "How are you doing, Greer?"

"I'm keeping myself busy, right now." I gave his wife a half hug to move partially out of the protective brother radius. His wife had the baby curled up against her chest. "Gods. Penny's practically doubled in size since I last saw her."

Mary smiled, tucking her cheek against the top of Penny's head. "Yeah, they won't let me stop feeding her."

"She wails," Gannon said from behind his parents. "Loudly. Sometimes for no reason."

"Well, she's a baby, Gann. That's what they do. You had quite the pair of lungs on you too."

He leaned far enough to the side to give me sullen teenager face. He didn't turn thirteen until Monday, but it had begun. Of all the problems I had to deal with in that moment, teenage hormones would not be the thing to best me. "Oh, you're too old to say hello to your aunt?"

"Go on and hug her," Mary murmured loud enough for all us to hear.

I shook my head. "He doesn't need to hug me. His body, his choice. But a greeting would be nice. Maybe a high five." I lifted my hand for him to slap it.

He did slap it, then came in for a hug. The top of his head came to my shoulder already. He was getting too big too quickly.

He would stop completely if Anterograde got her way.

"So," Gannon said once he'd straightened. A small flush of a smile clung to him now. "You going to hit the Fair with us?"

If I had freedom to do so, I would do the best thing and usher them all outside the perimeter. "You actually don't know how much I would love to, but I'm helping a friend."

The focus of my relatives shifted from me to the man in question.

My niece's arms lost some of their death grip. She stage-whispered, "He's pretty."

I nodded to her. "He *is* pretty. Holly, this is a good friend of mine, Kai. Kai, meet Holly, my brother Collin and his wife Mary. The boy is Gannon and this little one is Penelope."

Penny wrapped her fist around my thumb. My heart practically fell out of my chest at the dichotomy warring there. The cuteness. I loved seeing them. They gave me hope that last love was possible.

But I needed them to go.

Kai gave appropriate hello nods and murmurings. He didn't have love bursting out of his chest like a Carebear. He needed me to move this along.

I reached out to him with my free hand. "How's the water?"

Widening my eyes to make completely certain he knew what I meant would make my family suspicious. They knew me too well.

Thankfully, he was a new quantity to them. He shook his head in a loose motion as he passed the water toward me. I couldn't quite tell if that was a warning or the all clear. When my fingers touched his, he said, "It's fine. Clean, and all that."

I understood that one. The water had nothing extra in it, which was good. Taking it and not drinking would be hard to pull off in front of my people. I hadn't seen him pull out his testing equipment, but I trusted his judgement. If that proved to be faulty logic, I hoped the weirdness of my skin had other purposes than hypnotizing.

"Clean," Gannon asked. "What do you mean by that?"

Leave it to a teenager. Almost teenager.

"Kai's doing a secret shopper, quality test thing for the fair." The god of lies had danced a happy jig on my tongue for me to come up with that one. I went with it. "Helping him is why I can't join y'all. I kind of need the money. There might be a permanent job in it for me."

Following up the lie with plausible truth was the best way to sell it.

"Then we should probably go and leave you alone." Gannon shook a tiny coffee cup at Kai and me to emphasize.

I could have kissed him for the easy out. But, teenage boy. Teenage boy growing too quickly for me to deal with. "You're drinking coffee now? Should I call you sir? Mister? Master Gannon?" I curtseyed with my ever-present lack of grace.

"Chill, Aunt Greer. Siren Coffee is giving away free samples of something that tastes like cigarette smoke had a baby with ashes."

Chill.

Like I was the most ridiculous—wait.

Alarm bells in my head rang out in choral harmony, echoing something Kai mentioned a few days ago.

Gannon held the cup out toward me and shook it. "Do you want it? It's a little...um...strong for me, but I don't want to waste it."

"Told you," Collin smiled at the back of his son's head.

Almost like he could see his father's expression, Gannon rolled his eyes, but he pressed his lips together.

I relieved him of the cup. "I'll take that off your hands, then. Thank you."

He grinned at me, happy to rid of the cup. A moment where the little boy I remembered shone through the growing disenchanted teen. He wrangled his face back into normal lines before he asked, "You're still coming on Monday?"

"Provided the world doesn't come crashing down, I'll be there."

A conspiring grin ripped across his face. "Good. Dad thinks he can beat us. Says he's been practicing his spike."

"That will make the victory sweeter, won't it?"

He nodded. "Volleyball champs, forever." We bumped fists and exploded fingers outward.

Collin lifted an eyebrow in challenge.

It was on.

More reason to take care of the woman threatening the city as swiftly as possible.

"We'll let you get back to work, then?" Mary said in her diplomatic tone. She eased tensions while forcing everyone to fall in line.

Again.

We all said our goodbyes. I resisted the urge to jab the cup in Kai's face until I'd hotfooted to the shelter of some nearby trees. He didn't even ask about my vehemence in thrusting it at him.

He just took it, sipped, and closed his eyes.

# 34 — BROKEN

I WOULD HAVE PREFERRED a slightly more scientific testing method than Kai tasting for clues. Maybe something I could see. But there was no mistaking the triumphant anger in his eyes when they shot back open. Victory, of sorts.

"How many Siren stands are there?" He started dialing his phone, so I pulled mine out to check for the info.

The map had to be lying.

"M, it's in the coffee. Greer?"

"Five."

I ignored the rest of his call to make my own.

Lana barely let it ring. "Yes?"

"The extracts we isolated before are in the coffee. Siren booths are giving samples away of coffee strong enough to cover the taste." My legs wanted to run somewhere. I had nowhere to run to or from.

"I see." Lana's voice came out calm and collected. Eerie, like she'd gathered the sea to her, a tidal wave recoil before the crash.

Talking to her might fuel the storm, but I would much rather ride in the storm's wake than stand before the fury. "They have five booths. I can't verify right now that all the booths are contaminated. The one near Colfax and Bannock is."

"The nearest location is supplying them, no doubt. I will trace their supply chain while your men handle the civilian casualties."

My men.

Casualties.

"If people have the extracts in them, will you be able to draw them to you like you did the bodies? You know, without them being dead?"

"Hmm." She sounded interested. Something that hadn't occurred to her. "If they have enough in their system and their mind is altered enough to steal their will, perhaps."

Perhaps.

The almost self-satisfied lilt she put on the word rubbed me the wrong way. I hated that I'd given her the idea. At the moment, I didn't have the time to beat myself up about it. "We'll call it an option of last resort, since we don't know the dosage it would take and if it would work."

"I fear we may be making a lot of last resort choices," she said, her tone in the comfortable flatness. Flatness meant her mind had locked back on the job at hand.

That, I could deal with and ask questions of. "Why do you say that?"

"The mother's death. She died at 12:47, five years ago today."

Balls. I checked my watch. 11:35. Little more than an hour before the woman did her thing. "King Rex. Pecker and Pecs."

"What?"

"Nothing. Just thinking out loud." The stress had flipped me into old patterns of holding my tongue. "When you relay the supply information to me, I'd appreciate if you would send it also to Magus. Less steps means quicker dissemination of information."

"True. I will do so when I have learned all I can." She hung up.

When I looked back at Kai, his eyebrows had nearly met in the groove above the bridge of his nose. A nasty frown pulled his face out of whack.

I didn't want to know. "What is it?" I had to ask anyway.

"They're checking, but the other Bannock adjacent booth tested positive. Hound can't smell anything over the scent of the coffee, but he said the in the cooling stations were starting to have a familiar reek." He started up Colfax at a pace that parted the crowd in front of him. Several people looked annoyed at the hulk of him pushing through, but no one seemed up to messing with him.

Not good at all. "And Lana said our time is almost up."

"What?" He stopped so fast I ran into him. Kai caught me as he whipped back around to face me. "How would she know that?"

"The woman's mother died at 12:47 five years ago. I didn't ask Lana how she knew that, but I figure it's—"

"Shit!"

"What?"

He leaned down to me, his face blocking out the rest of the world save the ring of my peripheral vision. "Five booths, a store, and misters all potentially tainted. An hour left. We don't know where the woman is. And you want to know why I'm cursing?"

Kai had a point. His panic set me more on edge than I already had been. The superheroes were supposed to be calm in the face of danger. They faced this kind of thing probably more than lay people were ever made aware. Which was good. We—they—didn't want or need to know their lives and safety were in danger.

I wished I didn't.

But I did. And my family was in danger too. The good guys, the superheroes and me, needed to keep it together.

"We're up the creek, Greer. No paddles and our boat's sprung a leak."

Boat.

Paddles.

Rowing.

Row, row, row your boat.

The song that the toy TV from Anterograde's picture played when it was cranked.

The same song that the sinks on the bottom floor of the Denver Art Museum sang when you used them.

Kai settled a gentle hand on my shoulder. "What is it, Greer?"

"A paddle, I hope."

"What?"

I shook my head. "I've got to check something out. You go check the other booth."

"I can go with you."

Back up sounded lovely, but we were already spread too thin. If I was wrong, I didn't want to be responsible for pulling Kai from his job. "No. You handle yours. I'll call if I need help." Before I changed my mind, I grabbed a hold of the front of his shirt, kissed him hard, and turned the other way.

"What was that for?" He called after me.

I turned my head halfway around. "Luck."

For me. For him. For all of us fighting the good fight.

Naturally, the people didn't part the waters for me like they had for Kai. I had the height and the same objective fueled determination as he did. I also had boobs, which immediately devalued any agency I could possibly have. So, I had to bob, weave, and dance my way through the crowd. The crowd that didn't seem to understand that the center of the street was for moving. If people needed to stop, they could pull over to the side. Not move at a decent clip then freeze in place right in front of me. I bulldozed over a couple of people without remorse.

The trip up Bannock and halfway up 14th to the art museum took more time that I wished it had. The climate-controlled air wrapped around me as I passed through the second set of sliding doors. It should have cooled me down. I was too far gone for something so simple. Panic and determination pulsed in my skin to the beat of my heart leaving no room to cool down.

More people stood in line than normal. Shit. What were the odds? I mean, yes more people were downtown and the museum was air conditioned. It didn't usually matter. Unless it was the first Saturday of the month. Free day for Colorado residents. Which it was.

Shit.

I spent the endless time in line considering my plan of attack.

The special exhibits lived on the opposite side of the building from the park, as did Western and American Indian art. Too many things lived on whole floors and the woman hadn't given any clues as to the type of art. Unless the beams was the art clue, but the modern art would be in the crumpled-paper building and the singings sinks lived in this one.

Maybe it wasn't about the art.

Most of what she sent was location. The capitol building and the huge outdoor pieces gave more location than focus on the art itself. Row, row, row your boat could have simply been a location clue too. The woman could have been holed up in the singing sink restroom.

The pieces didn't quite fit, though. Too many people going in and out for a person plotting some sort of revenge.

When I gave my name to the customer service rep, I decided to start at the top and come down if needed.

The museum had the slowest elevators in creation, but climbing seven flights sounded like death. Five minutes of waiting and the doors finally opened. Several people waddled their way into the elevator after me. I kept my spot near the left panel of buttons. Between the rest of the people, five of the other six buttons were pushed.

Perfect.

I practically vibrated by the time I got to the seventh floor. The pent-up energy sprung me out the elevator and to the glass door which lead to the roof. I welcomed the heat as I climbed the U-turn of a flight of stairs.

People littered the roof. More than I wanted to, but that seemed to be the theme of the day. Shooing the people would give up the goat. Once

I found her, keeping the operation covert might not be the order of the day.

Of the thirty people in the roof, two watered flower beds and most of the rest of them had children with them. One woman, with white-blond hair down to her buttocks, stood on the edge of the building. Her posture. She practically preened over the city.

Yep.

My girl.

Aggression would not win this day. At least not this way. Not with me.

I opened the camera app on my phone and tip-toed a forward to the side of her. Not too close. I just needed to have a conversation first. "Excuse me, miss."

The huge, blade of a nose turned my way. Yep. This was my chickie. I snapped a couple of pictures. The second one, just in case.

"What the hell do you think you're doing?" she half-yelled at me.

It might have been a full yell for her, the way her voice clawed at her throat.

I had to laugh at her audacity as I scrolled to the text list I'd created for this situation. "What am I doing? What the hell do you think you're doing?" I shook my head and hit send.

The woman snatched my phone from my hand and tossed it over the side of the building. I'd hit send. I could only hope the text went through before it hit the ground. "You're going to pay for that."

"You can't take people's pictures without asking and expect them to let it happen. What kind of pervert are you?"

I took the moment to fully take her in. Her slightly over-dilated eyes.

The frown that trembled as much as her hands. All wrapped in a floral dress that would have only been complete with a big hat and her butt in a pew. Her distain for me sat solid on her face and in her shoulders.

"You're poisoning and killing people." I balanced my weight onto both feet. "You don't expect someone to take a picture or two of you?"

She smiled—*smiled*—at me. "Not surprised it took a woman to find me. Bravo."

Ah, she was one of *those* people. Neet. I needed to shake her out of her comfort zone. Gain an edge while stalling her long enough for someone to find us up here and act. "You took a woman too, didn't you? Have her locked up somewhere?"

One blink and anger blazed from her eyes. "That was not a woman. That was a creature. They're all creatures."

"Their mother would disagree."

The naked anger shifted into some cold emotion I couldn't read.

It shivered my timbers, though.

"My mother would understand." Her voice lost some of its tone. but none of the roughness. "The creatures. They're just tools to make them pay."

"Make who pay? And for what?" I didn't really care to know. Nothing she could say would make any of this acceptable.

She jerked a hand out toward the park below us. "Them. All of them. They're all guilty," the hand she left in the air trembled. "They all killed my mother."

I waited for her to add something else. Anything to give the woman some kind of credibility, or make her words sensible. Because that many people being part of killing a woman was difficult enough to coordinate that people would know about it.

A tear escaped from one of her eyes before I realized that was it. The woman's whole motivation. "So, your mother died and now you're going to kill a bunch of innocent people."

"They're not innocent." She yelled it loud enough to draw attention.

Some of the other people on the roof shuffled their way to the glass door into the museum. The rest turned to bear witness. I needed her to be more careful about what she said. And did.

"There are children down there and other people who never even heard of you or your mother." Come on, ma'am. See the logic. Then, the heroes could recognize my predicament and come get me.

"Exactly." She stepped into my personal space. "They could have helped her. But they let the disease take her. She was so close to a cure."

In for a penny. "What disease is that?"

"Huntington's."

That was a bad one. Neurological disease. Degenerative. No cure. Death as soon as early 40s.

Watching a person deteriorate would be hard, especially knowing you would be next, but it did not excuse any of this. Not by a long shot. "Let me get this straight. You're poisoning and killing people because your mother died?"

She sucked in a shaky breath. "She would have lived if they had just funded her research another year. They killed her."

That was about all I could handle. "Oh, boo-fucking-hoo. There are so many worse things. That's how the world is supposed. Parents die before their children. Just because it wasn't at a convenient time for you doesn't mean—"

I went too far with the last. I realized this when chickie had assisted my butt halfway over the guard wall around the building. Even with her muscles trembling, she managed to scoop me up over her head before I could squirm away. Halfway over the wall, I switched to grabbing at her hands to stop her from letting go.

She bent my thumb back until I relented, then she shoved my shoulders hard. I lost contact with the wall.

Stellar way to end the week of shit. One-two punch of being kidnapped and falling to my death because a woman with mommy issues hated the world.

# 35 – W. T. F.

# STARFISH & COFFEE

Veronica R. Calisto

# STARFISH & COFFEE

Veronica R. Calisto

# STARFISH & COFFEE

Veronica R. Calisto

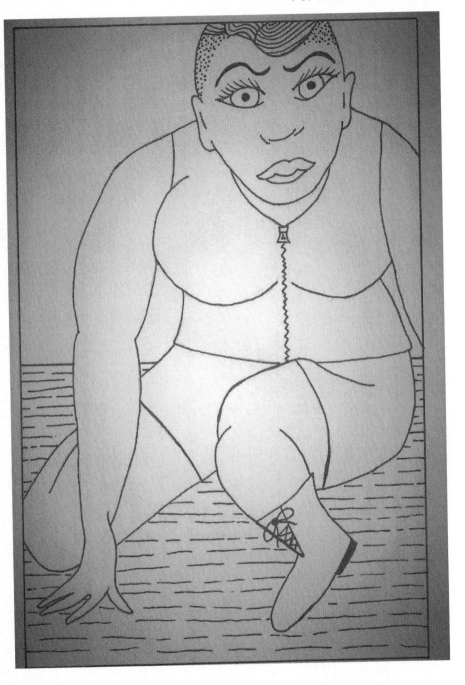

# STARFISH & COFFEE

# 36 – MAJOR FALL, MINOR LIFT

BULLETS HURT. A lot. Not as much as they probably should have, because I was still alive after more hits than I could count. Without uncurling my body, I waved my hands at the guns and the men controlling them. "Stop it. Stop. Stop shooting."

They did. Eventually. Probably because they ran out of bullets. Not from any mercy or in response to my begging them to stop. I looked up to make sure they weren't just reloading.

"Greer?"

I twisted my head as far to the side as I could from that position. The angle only allowed me to see feet and shadows. Carefully, I pushed myself up from my clumped sprawl to somewhat sitting.

Spencer and four of his closest, armed friends stood over me. Thin tendrils of smoke rose from the five barrels. I looked past the guns to Spencer's face. "If I stand up now, will you shoot me again?"

"You should be dead."

The man was righter than he knew. But I gathered that if he was trying to rationalize what happened, none of them would fly off at the handle and shoot me again.

"I should be a lot of things, Spence, ol' buddy, ol' pal." Rolling to all fours granted me the gift of feeling where every bullet that hit me. Several of the bullets in question dropped onto the concrete as I moved. A high-pitched drum solo of spent bullets. More metal than Black Sabbath.

My shirt looked like the love child Swiss cheese and English lace. Very Posh.

"Stop what you're doing right now or we'll shoot again."

I rolled my eyes up to him. "Because it worked so well the first twenty, thirty, fifty times."

His hand trembled around his gun, but it remained pointed vaguely downward as I rose to standing.

Better than I expected.

"Tell me what's going on or I'll get inventive." The panic had slipped out of his voice. All cold precision again. He meant business. Clear-headed was a much more dangerous state to face him in. Too much intelligence radiated off him.

Scrubbing my hands against the sides of my head, I answered. "It's been a weird week."

"Uh-uh." He wagged the gun, aim wavering around my feet. "You're going to do better than that."

How could I? "I don't actually understand most of what's going on."

"Not good enough." It came out colder.

I had about ten seconds before shit hit the fan again. Actions spoke louder than words, and all that. I stepped closer to the wall, which brought me into darker shadow. "I'm going to lift my shirt a little but I don't have a gun."

Once again, Spencer moved his gun rather than his head. A short, sharp nod this time. "Proceed."

I could have pulled the shirt down instead and taken control of the situation. It would have been the easy way out. Like rising to power on a platform of blaming the Jews for dire economic straits or raping an unconscious woman. Last resort, then. Only in defense.

Exposing my glowing belly didn't have the same repercussions, but it got my point across.

"What the hell?" Spencer spoke in a stage whisper.

"Yeah. I know."

"What is it?" One of the other men asked.

I looked to him, Boris, as I stepped away from the wall. He looked more fascinated than scared. The way his eyes tracked my movement made me drop the shirt back down. Nothing said my chest was the only thing that could hypnotize a person. Or that my ability was static. It could be expanding or retracting. Being on the wrong side of several guns was not the time to play with the boundaries of my new power

The shivery feeling as I crossed the edge of the deeper shadow had to be my imagination. "That, I don't know, but it's the same reason the shooting bruised me rather than killed." I did my best to sound definitive about it.

"Well, shit on a stick." Spencer clicked some things on his gun and set it on the desk near him. "I need a drink."

"Is there any way you could take me downtown before you have that drink?" I bore my teeth but it wasn't a smile. We all knew it. We probably all knew why. It was a bold demand, I had no kind of bargaining chip, and asking for the favor stuck in my craw.

But I needed it. Damn it. Oedipus Rex. "I could really use the help."

Spencer lifted an eyebrow and threaded his fingers. "You warned us away from there."

"Yes, and the woman poisoning people tossed me off a building and I ended up here, somehow. Carless."

"And what of that means I have to take you anywhere?"

Gods.

He didn't need to make asking harder than it already was. Or maybe he did. The world, and Spencer, owed me nothing. Trying to stop the bad guy didn't make me special.

I shrugged and let my shoulders jerk back down. I had nothing. "You don't have to do anything. I'm simply asking if you would." Turning away would be the easy route. I maintained our eye contact.

Until he broke it, looking down a moment to pull a keyring out of the center desk drawer. "You will tell me all I ask of you."

Wow. A smile threatened to break out on my face, but I had to complicate things before I agreed to his terms. "Things that are mine to tell, things that pertain only to me, I'll tell you. The rest, I really can't."

Spencer swung his three keys about on the key ring. "Discretion. I approve."

At least someone did. Wait. "That's a yes?"

He inclined his head.

I stepped forward and hugged him hard, with a "Thank you."

Spencer stiffened in my embrace.

I pulled back and patted his shoulders. "Sorry. But, thank you."

He nodded again, without looking offended or taken aback. If I didn't do anything else like that, he might still take me. "We go now?"

"Boss?" Samuel, apparently, didn't learn from the last time to not question his boss.

A long, quiet moment passed between he and Spencer. Even with the time pressure, I kept myself still and quiet. Bunny reflexes. Freeze and let the fox kill the tastier morsel.

"Samuel. When a woman of power askes you a favor, you give it."

Wow, again.

Woman of Power.

I liked that, even in the threatening tones. The rest, though. Not my favorite.

I specifically avoided "favor" for a reason. I hadn't asked for a favor. Favors implied a debt to be repaid. Indebting myself to him, no matter what his flavor of lawbreaking, might be the last thing I needed right then. But I had learned from Samuel, and every movie dealing with bad men.

Never question the man in charge. Especially, not in front of his people or enemies.

Spencer's big red truck shouldn't have surprised me. The size and color didn't, but the thing was old enough to vote and drink. The engine roared with the voice of a well-kept pet. The inside upholstery was nothing special, but clean and like-new. This thing was his baby.

My stomach grumbled as we pulled away from the office building where his operations were centered. I hated to ask. "You wouldn't happen to have a power bar or something."

"No."

Of course not. I had to ask him, though.

"So." He said as he accelerated onto the highway, without a glance my way. "Tell me what you know."

I said I would. "I got hit in the chest with something, not sure what. Now my skin's glowing, shimmery, and tough."

The eyebrow nearest me lifted. "Just *tough*?"

"Yes."

"Understatement."

It really wasn't. "I bruise horribly when I get hit, or shot, apparently, and I've given blood since. So, not impenetrable." I could have kept the last bit to myself and been fine. But I'd given him my word.

"Is that all?"

"Nope." I let the answer ride. The Colfax exit approached fast. We hadn't been as far as I'd feared. I might just make it back in time.

"I don't have to take this exit. I can miss it and take Speer," he threatened in a low sing-song.

Speaking on behalf of the superheroes wouldn't get me anything. He respected the threat that Magus posed, but Spencer made no kind of offer to help them the first time we met. He'd done just enough to not impede Magus. Probably to keep off the superhero radar. Smart move for a criminal. Right then, I needed the criminal to work with me. Shit.

"My chest sparkles in such a way that it hypnotizes people." I forced out a breath, because he'd asked for the whole truth. "And a computer."

Spencer stole a long enough look at me that I felt the weight of his skepticism. But he took the correct exit. Even as he asked, "You're kidding me, right?"

That pissed me off. "Why would I make something like that up?"

"To scare me into leaving you alone."

I rubbed my forehead, hard, in the hopes it would let me understand his nonsense. Nope. Logic prevailed. "Okay. You know I'm working with the superheroes. I showed you that my skin is, in fact, glowing. I haven't flashed you to bend you to my will. And you're fucking questioning me about something I didn't want to tell you in the first place?"

He opened his mouth.

I cut him off before he got started. "Ignoring, of course, that I could make you forget you ever asked the question."

"Why don't you?"

Good question.

"Because you've been fair with me when you didn't need to be and," I sighed. "Even if *you* wouldn't remember what you saw, *I* would remember you'd seen me. And I don't want to remember that."

The thump of wheels on the sectioned road ruled the car until Spencer slowed to a stop at a light. Then, he spoke. "You don't want to use your boobs to get what you want?"

"Not unless what I want is someone naked in my bed."

He laughed at that. The one where he tipped his head back and nearly missed the light turning green. Laughter, I could handle, so long as he wasn't questioning me when I told him facts. Facts I would verify if he pressed me. I leaned against the window and willed him to drive a little faster.

When he stopped laughing I kept my lips sealed.

Spencer had other ideas. "And, what if I wanted you naked in *my* bed?"

What the fuck?

My head jerked back and I blinked in a flutter. He had to be pulling my chain.

He smiled broad and dangerous, like the wild west on the silver screen. I couldn't read it. I couldn't read him. His eyes glowed warm with pleasure when he cast a look at me, but no desire reigned there. None that I could recognize. He still had that analysis glint to his expression. He could have just been poking me to see how I would react.

"Now you're kidding me." I didn't ask it. Stated it. Because he had to be.

"Not in the least."

He had to be kidding me. Either way, my answer didn't change, but I had to know. "What the hell?"

"It isn't often that someone, let alone a woman, holds her own with me in a room filled with my men." He cocked his head to the side. "You may be the only woman who's done so."

How did I dispel this quickly and painlessly? "You can understand why, though, right? With the skin and the sparkle ti..." Damned Lex and his catchy nickname.

Spencer gave me a look. Like he wanted to ask. I glared at him and shook my head.

"There it is again." He chuckled.

"What, you like me because I don't faint at the sight of you?"

He gave me a sidelong glance that went from my face, then south, then back up to my face again before he returned his gaze to the road. "The rack doesn't hurt."

I crossed my arms over the rack in question and turned my head to look out the window. "My inclination is to say no."

"Is it because I—"

He cut himself off.

"Because you what?" I swung around.

Spencer's mouth hung half open and he stared straight forward with none of his characteristic focus I'd come to rely on. I checked my shirt, but the girls were reined in and well covered. The windows were completely up.

He'd frozen.

And the car was moving into a line of stopped cars.

I scooted over and half into his lap. Stomping my foot onto the break slowed the truck and revved the engine. Thanking the gods of the old spacious trucks, I crawled the rest of the way into his lap. I held the brake pedal down with the left foot while easing his foot off the gas.

We jerked to a stop, five feet behind the next car. I let out a breath. The art museum was so close. A block to where the road closed off and another to the right to get to the museum. With a wall of the damned flickering stop lights to surround the park. The drive would be a short one. The walk would take me longer than I wanted to risk.

I could hop out here. I could leave Spencer here in his truck and walk the rest of the way. A glance in the rearview mirror cured me of the thought.

Someone else was on their way this direction. They would freeze and rear-end the truck. If not them, the next person would. Spencer might not get injured, but allowing his car to be hurt was no way to repay him for the ride.

Regardless of his motivations in giving it to me.

I flipped a bitch without looking. Even without the freezing light pattern, the road was closed for the Taste.

The next street, I turned right.

Spencer jerked back to animation under me.

"What...uh..."

I pulled over to a free spot.

He settled his hands on my sides. I wanted to be angry at him, but men tended to think certain things when woman ended up in their laps.

"What just happened?" He didn't sound angry about it.

Moving off him could lead to some unclear feelings between the two of us. But I could give him the low down. "The thing I warned you away from is going on and short-circuited you and I had to keep you from running into a car and another car from running into yours."

"I don't think you're joking."

At this point, he should have been used to me saying things he didn't expect. I didn't have the time to deal with this.

I popped the driver's side door open.

"Wait," he tightened his hands on my sides, though not tight enough to keep me from leaving. "Where are you going?"

"To walk to a fight with the bad lady causing the ruckus." I scooted, trying and failing to refrain from rubbing my butt against his crotch.

"Driving would be faster."

I knew that. "You can't drive. You freeze."

"You don't. Here." He clicked his belt.

Wow. I didn't expect that.

We both worked to get him out from under me and me in the driver's seat. As I buckled in, I gave a warning. "There are fences I might need to skirt by or through."

"Temporary ones aren't as strong. But don't push it."

I whipped the truck around and passed by the way we came. A couple of cars had met with the one we barely avoided. I was glad I'd moved us.

Once I was certain Spencer was out of it again, I rolled the truck up onto the sidewalk. The truck barely fit between the trees and buildings. If time hadn't been of the essence, I would have slowed to navigate with more care. That didn't happen until I turned to 14th street and I needed to maneuver around trees, people, and cars.

Branches and bark scraped against the passenger's side, but I didn't hit the woman carrying a red-faced baby. More people had been passing through the little plaza on the back side of the art museum.

A mist filled the air.

It thickened as I got closer, pulsing with lights flashing somewhere inside it.

Ingenious. Diabolical, but ingenious. Especially because a familiar fishy scent worked its way into the cab of the truck. Poisonous starfish mist to kill everyone.

There would be no weapon to find.

I drove all the way up to the front door of the museum.

The sound of the truck might float all the way up through the mist to the woman on the roof. If she'd stayed on the roof. But she couldn't see down through to the ground. I should still have surprise.

Before I left Spencer, I set the keys in his hand and locked the doors behind me. When people unfroze, he couldn't just drive off without people noticing. I needed to vouch for him with Magus. He should be able to handle any other authorities.

# 37 – ONCE MORE WITH FEELING

SOMETHING SKITTERED ACROSS the concrete as I started for the front door, launched by my big feet. I stooped over without stopping. The mist sat too thick for me to see anything more than a couple feet around me. Whatever it was, I didn't see it on the way to the doors.

The doors didn't open, no matter how I pushed at them. No other choice.

I unbuttoned the first two buttons of my top and tucked them back. The doors opened for me with ease. "Damned sexist doors." Lex would have laughed with me about that. Phoenyx might have as well. But I was alone in a world of wax-figure people.

The elevator wouldn't work. I pressed the button and waited. No sounds indicated that it was coming for me. If I could get to the inner workings of it, I would have been able to make it work. As was...to the stairs I went. Seven flights of them. Eight, including the ones out to the roof.

The first two flights weren't too bad. By the time I crested the top of the fourth flight, words fell out of me that Gabe would have chided me for. I didn't care. My legs burned. My chest hurt. I couldn't stop for too long. And I was hungry. Climbing stairs while hungry made Greer an angry girl. If Anterograde wasn't still at the top of this damned building...

I caught my breath a moment before opening the glass door to the rooftop. Wheezing toward her was not the way to intimidate her into stopping this crazy thing.

I thanked everything good and holy when I glimpsed the top of the last set of stairs. For one, I could stop climbing stairs. For the other, I saw the white-blond head. She stood by the same wall she'd thrown me from.

At the top, I steadied myself and took several deep, breaths. "You bleached-blonde piece of bimbo shit."

She whipped around. Anger, then confusion and shock danced over her face and posture. Her head tilted to the side. "I thought I tossed you over."

Confirming it would fix nothing. Thinking about it pissed me off. I would keep my distance.

"If I'd known you had Huntington's too, I wouldn't have tossed you." She shook a finger at me. "But you really shouldn't have said those things to me."

Ooo, that chiding a misbehaving child kind of tone. She wasn't all there in the head. It didn't change what I needed to do, nor what I needed to say to her.

"Listen, you putrescent pond scum. I don't care what the fuck tragedy happened to your mother. You're not the only one with issues in this world. And if you cared so much about your mother, did you consider what she would think about you killing thousands of innocent people in her name?" I hadn't known her mother, but most didn't have such a vindictive streak.

The woman's confusion left, replaced by twitchy anger. Good. I wanted her off her A-game.

"And what would your mother think about you bullying a grieving woman." She jabbed her finger at me as she spoke, a small device clutched in her hand as she did so. She took two steps toward me.

Bullying? Me. The woman *not* killing a bunch of people?

Cute.

I matched Anterograde's steps, but kept distance between us. "I don't give a fuck what that woman thinks."

That was too much for the woman. She came at me, hands in shaking claws and face lost to rage. I waited. Waited for her to be committed, then dodged to the side and swept her legs out from under her. She rolled into a crouch, rage dimmed to a thinking anger. "How dare you?"

I needed to get that device from her. It controlled something not good for the rest of the world. Pushing her into rage wasn't working for too long. I went with my trump card. Carefully, swiftly, I unsnapped the leather vest and pulled my shirt open, popping buttons neck to navel.

Anterograde dropped her eyes down to my chest, then looked back up to my face. No freezing. No loss of her senses. What the fuck? My one ridiculous power and when I need it, it abandoned me. Balls. I had nothing. So, I let the shirt go. Time to try shocking her with some perspective.

"How dare I?" I stepped back from the woman while keeping her between me and the outer wall. "*That woman,* my mother, beat me. She beat me to within an inch of my life. When I was pregnant. I had an emergency delivery and held my daughter while she fought to live. I only got an hour before her little body gave out."

The woman straightened from her crouch, mouth open. I wasn't done.

"Because of that, I can't have children anymore. My womb is scarred from *that woman's* hate. And she's out of jail. On parole. Living her life free and easy while my child has long sense crumbled to dust."

Anterograde's eyes welled up. "Don't," she said, but had to clear her throat to continue. "Don't you want revenge?"

I halved the distance between us. "I did. For a long time that was the thing that got me out of bed. But what did it get me? Nothing. No happiness. No peace. Just a festering hate and distrust of everyone. Which gives me *nothing.*"

She snarled her top lip. "So, I should just forgive and forget because that's the Christian thing to do?"

"Fuck that. That's preaching to the wrong choir." I couldn't shake my head enough. "Forgiving that woman is like telling her what she did was okay. It wasn't. Forgetting is allowing people to hurt you again and not honoring the memory of what or who was lost."

The woman's smile trembled around the edges. "Exactly. That's what I'm doing."

"No." I closed the distance between us to an arm's length. "What you're doing is putting what's left of my family—my brother, my little nephew, my nieces—in danger."

Her mouth dropped open. Shock. Dismay. An inkling of remorse, perhaps.

It didn't matter.

I jabbed her in the nose with the heel of my hand. Her head rocked back in a satisfying spray of blood. Her hands few to her nose. I jabbed her in the solar plexus. As she fell, I plucked the device from her hands.

Four buttons. That was all there was too it. Two on switches, and two off. I pressed both offs in succession, then simultaneously. Just in case.

I heard a scream. Then more noises. A roar that should have been going on the whole time. The sound of a city and people in the park. I let out a sigh. That was good. If people weren't frozen, they would notice the fishy mist and get the hell out of the area.

I wanted to crush the remote control. Crushing it might trigger something worse. I couldn't risk it, so I tucked it in my bra.

"That's mine, you lying bitch."

"Was yours. And I didn't lie."

She came at me. All fury and nails. I blocked, but the force in her attack pushed me back. I tried. I lost ground. Somehow, she moved me in the direction of the wall again.

I didn't know what happened the last time, with my popping from one place to another before hitting ground. Perhaps some god of mercy decided to grace me with a second chance. My heart didn't trust that it would happen again.

Her hands gripped around my leg. I popped her in the nose again. She dropped to her knees and punched me right in the crotch.

Men always thought they had it the absolute worst when their balls got grazed. The clitoris had more nerve endings. The woman managed to anger all of them.

My knees hit the ground.

Her fist hit my jaw.

My head hit the wall.

Pretty, pretty stars lit my world and she picked me up.

Not again. I wrapped my arms around her as she set my backside up on the wall again. She picked at my hands on her back. I barrel rolled, pulling her up off the ground and onto the wall alongside me.

"Get off." She bit at my forehead.

I butted her with my head. Worked a leg around her too. "If you want to push me off, you're going to have to take the plunge with me, Chickie." Even as I spoke, I tried rolling toward the roof.

The woman made inch-worming my way back to the roof side of the wall more difficult than it could have been. Then, she bucked. One strong, full-body buck and we were airborne. If I'd known she would kill us both, I wouldn't have challenged her like that. I also would have kept a limb free to hold onto the building.

In a last-ditch effort, I tried to roll her under me.

Something caught me mid-air. From behind. Some*one* caught me. The scent of singed fabric wafted to my nostrils. I knew who caught me. "Gods, Phoenyx. Where have you been all my life?"

"Right behind you, SparkleTits."

The woman punched me in my side.

The same side assaulted and peppered with the bullets from Spencer's minions.

My grip loosened in the pulse of unexpected pain.

She slipped away from me.

Phoenyx dropped us down, chasing her. Not fast enough. Maybe, if we had another twenty feet or so to catch her. By the time Phoenyx got us to the ground, the woman had already dropped onto the hood of the big, red truck I'd parked right in front of the art museum.

As soon as Phoenyx set my feet on the ground I ran toward the truck. The passenger side door opened before I made it there. Spencer stepped out smooth and steady. I asked him anyway, "Are you okay?"

He looked at me and stared blankly.

What the—Oh. I buttoned my shirt.

Spencer turned his head to his car and back to me. "You're going to help me fix that."

"I don't really have any money right now, but once the lawyers file all the paperwork, I can—"

"No." He wagged a finger at me. "Not money. Hands in grease and sweat."

"I don't know any more about cars than how to add oil, gas, and coolant." I shrugged.

"Doesn't matter. You'll learn."

This might have been his roundabout way to get me into his bed. It wouldn't work. But I did owe him. For the ride and the damage to his truck. I forced a breath out and nodded. What more could I do?

An oblong shadow in the mist coalesced into Magus. He took in the scene in a cool manner. Eyes flicking between the three living people, the dead one, the truck, and looking up. "On the plus side, the mist hid the drop from view, this time. But who is this." He pointed at Spencer.

I decided me answering was a better idea. "Someone who gave me a ride back here."

"From where and how did you get there?"

"I don't really know."

Magus narrowed his eyes at me.

I flipped my hands up. "Perhaps we can look at that later and focus on the body right now?"

A woman moaned. The body in question. Anterograde wasn't dead. I couldn't believe it.

Almost couldn't believe it. Evil never died as easily as good did.

Magus stepped to her while he poked at his phone. He set his fingers on the side of the woman's trembling neck. "Kai. We need you and your first aid at the art museum."

I wondered, for a moment, what Magus would do to me if I finished the job. Then I wondered what it would do to me if I did.

Another shadow appeared in the mist. Kai was Johnny on the spot. Except I realized it couldn't have been him when two more shadows flanked the first one. Only one person I knew walked in a formation like that.

Lana showing up gladdened me. If I had given in to the darker part of me, she would never learn where her children were.

She brushed past Magus before he noticed she had arrived. "This is the woman?" She asked me and only me.

I nodded. "I'm sorry she's not in better shape. We fought and she fell."

"Good." Lana brushed the back of her hand across the woman's cheek. The gesture looked tender until she pulled away. Bloody grooves adorned her cheek now. Somehow, I'd forgotten about Lana's spikes.

"You need to get away from her," Magus said, pulling himself up to his full height, which wasn't much more than Lana's.

"She is dying. Can you not smell her bowels?"

The fish in the mist had clogged up my nose, but she hadn't asked me. Not in that dismissive tone. When she turned to speak to me, she came with respect. "Her blood already smells of us, but I gave her that which will make her most sensitive to me."

Translation, Anterograde shot herself up with a serum extracted from the starfish and Lana had given the woman her special blend. Got it. "Why?"

"The same reason I came."

To save her daughter.

Kai came through the dissipating mist, but not in time. I hadn't watched Anterograde as she struggled to live. The breaths filled with fluid. The bubbly rasping of her last exhale would never leave my mind. I'd done that. This was the result of me

The superheroes started talking containment and clean up. I didn't care. I tried to figure a way to get home. My ride had a body shaped dent in the hood of it. Spencer needed to get home too. Maybe a taxi or the bus. We would need to walk less for the taxi, but the walk might do us good.

Anterograde moved. Anterograde's body, moved, because the woman was dead. Her dead-eyed stare was that of the zombies I'd seen before, though they hadn't clouded yet.

A dead woman climbing off her place of death was enough to draw the attention of the superheroes. They looked nonplussed. Not the best thing, most of the time, but their surprise soothed me a bit. This was not normal. We could all agree

"Take me to my daughter," Lana told the thing.

It started in a direction.

Magus cleared his throat. "You can't do that."

She could and she had. He meant that she shouldn't, but it didn't sound like the worst plan in the world. Lana ignored him, as we all expected. I tried my hand. "Lana, there were people who helped her on the road to all this. Can you get the information on her network of people and send it to Magus? I would say send it to me, but I lost my phone." Lost it over the side of a building, but whatever.

"Isn't this it?" Kai stooped over and picked up a shiny black piece of plastic that looked familiar.

The weight of it was the same as my phone. This thing was whole, though. Not even scratched. But it opened to my pattern and had all my apps. Inexplicable. I didn't want to take the time to run through the whole thing right then. Instead, "There you go. You can send to me or to Magus."

She nodded. "We will be in touch." She waited for me to nod back at her before dodging into the mist.

The body of the woman followed at the same speed. I didn't want to think of speedy zombies. I didn't want to think of much more than a good meal and a long nap.

"You should not have let her go." Magus. Disapproving. His reaction did not surprise me.

I shrugged. "I figured this was the quickest way to get the body out of here without people seeing it and freaking out. This mist isn't going to last forever."

Magus opened his mouth then closed it. Could it be, he hadn't thought though that part.

Surely not.

He turned from me and went back to incident clean up talk with the superheroes.

Rude.

But I knew when to drop back and punt.

I caught Spencer's eye and jerked my head away from the other three. He frowned at me. Still, when I started moving, he joined. We'd made it ten paces away before Magus called after us. "Stop. You can't leave."

"Actually, I can." I kept going.

Phoenyx landed in front of us, cutting off our escape. "Sorry, SparkleTits." His frown looked genuine as he made himself an effective wall. Just doing his job, then.

Magus spoke from much closer than he had been. He hadn't run to intercept. That would have been undignified. "We're not finished yet."

"You're not finished. Despite everything that just happened, the danger I was in, I got paid for none of it. So, I'm going to go to the apartment and crash. Once everything is swept up, and you want to know what happened on that roof, you know where to find me."

He didn't like it. The desire to argue and order me in line stiffened him, but he knew I was right. Something sparked in his eyes. "I need to adjust his memory of this." He pointed at Spencer.

Damn. Magus had me there. But wait. "Does it need to be you?"

"What?"

"To wipe the memory. Could I do it?"

Now, Spencer stiffened beside me. He kept his mouth shut, though. Smart man.

"Can you?"

I dipped my chin down and pinched my lips. Not a lie either way.

"It's against protocol."

"So's everything else I did today. Just consider it part of the rest."

Magus frowned and narrowed his eyes at me. But he nodded.

I nodded back, waved, "I'll see you later," and dodged around Phoenyx. No one stopped us this time. Spencer and I kept a speedy pace until we came out of the thick of the mist. The sun beat warm down on us like the mist didn't exist. I didn't risk looking back at it.

While we waited for the signal to cross a street, Spencer asked, "What's this business of you wiping my memory?"

"The sparkle ti—hypnobo—chest hypnosis can do it." Probably.

"I thought you said you didn't want to flash me." The smile on his face said he might not dislike it. "SparkleTits."

Gods. This was a problem I could do without. Phoenyx would pay for spreading the nickname. Lex would too. But I couldn't make Spencer pay for their loose lips. Wiping his memory after he helped me didn't seem right either. Still, if we were going to fix his truck, I needed to lay a boundary with him.

I crossed my arms, over the chest so as not to boost them higher. "Don't call me that."

He smiled, mischief written all over his face.

"Don't push me, Spencer. I've had a long week, a long day, and I haven't had lunch."

"I can fix one of those problems," said the spider to the fly. Firefly, in my case.

It sounded like a trap, a way to draw me closer to him. But, what the hell. He couldn't take the sky from SparkleTits. Food was food. And if Spencer tried something, I could always give him his wish.

*Keep abreast of Greer's adventures
in the next SparkleTits Chronical:*

# SINS

## AND

# BARBECUE

## ABOUT THE AUTHOR:

**VERONICA R. CALISTO** is the author of many books, some of which she is willing to let others read. When she isn't writing she is thinking about writing, aka: plugging away at her day jobs whose mundanities make her name plants things like Cleoplantra and force her mind squeak out words like mundanities. Most of the time she can be found in Colorado lavishing on a nest built of her books while she listens and sings (loudly) to music which may or may not be playing outside her own head.

If someone's singing while walking down the hall, it's probably her.

Please visit her at her website:

www.veronicarcalisto.com

Made in the USA
San Bernardino, CA
08 October 2017